No Such Thing as Immortality

Sarah Tranter

W F HOWES LTD

This large print edition published in 2013 by
W F Howes Ltd
Unit 4, Rearsby Business Park, Gaddesby Lane,
Rearsby, Leicester LE7 4YH

1 3 5 7 9 10 8 6 4 2

First published in the United Kingdom in 2013
by Choc Lit Limited

A CIP catalogue record for this book is available
from the British Library

ISBN 978 1 47122 893 3

Typeset by Palimpsest Book Production Limited,
Falkirk, Stirlingshire
Printed and bound in Great Britain
by MPG Books Ltd, Bodmin, Cornwall

For Jamie, Arun and Max
With my eternal love . . . xxx

CHAPTER 1

THE BEND IN THE ROAD

'Yeeeessss!! I just thrashed your anally retentive arse!' James' voice sounded in my head, whilst my ears took in both the roar of his passing car and the snorts of a fast-retreating badger. There were no tail-lights to see, because they weren't on. The potent scent of burning rubber momentarily merged with that of wild honeysuckle as I raced past the hedgerows.

More of James' silent, yet expressive words entered my head. 'How could tonight have *possibly* been more fun had I left you rotting away in that damned tower of yours? Actually, *you* rotting away . . . okey-dokey, but your car, sat barely touched in the garage – now *that's* a travesty!'

My driving provided the comeback. I calmly lowered my right foot, bringing the speedometer reading to 115 mph, fractionally adjusted the steering wheel to avoid the young shrew skittering across the road, and edged past James' flame-red Lamborghini Aventador on the inside of the country bend.

I grinned. Were I more like James, I would no doubt be punching the air and exclaiming, 'Sweet!'

But he did have a point. We had been driving in a similar vein for the past hour, and I would allow there was some amusement in our activity.

'*Shit! Shit! Shit!* I'm glad one of us found that move amusing. Hold that thought though, *sweet my man*, did it zero justice! But . . .'

He was laughing like a hyena as he passed, and punching the air. '*Yes Yes Yes Yes Yes!*' he gleefully gloated. '*Sweet* back to you, mate! And, on the long straight after the next corner, you ain't going to see me for dust.'

I put my foot down in rise to the challenge – just as an extraordinary metallic crushing sound ripped through my senses.

Instinctively, my foot was off the accelerator and smashing the brake pedal to the floor – probably *through* the floor with the force applied.

And then there was . . . eerie silence. I watched the standard-specification airbags inflate as if in slow motion, and found myself absorbed by the thin wisps of smoke that appeared and began their slow, surreal pirouettes through the air before my eyes.

It was my eyes, refocusing on the view through the glass, that brought reality crashing in. On the bend in the road, about one hundred yards before me, a green car, old by the look of its non-metallic paint, was resting on a wooded bank between two trees. Its back end was crumpled, its make indeterminable – but it had clearly been shunted from behind.

Not possible. Absolutely. Not. Possible. There was a moment of unfamiliar confusion . . .

And then I was engulfed.

I made an involuntary, strangled gasp for air, whilst madly hugging my chest and then clutching my head as searing pain stabbed and sliced and tore its way through it. Sensations were consuming me, *alien sensations* that assaulted in a staggering, *overpowering* rush.

My constantly steady heart rate became frenetic.

Shock and anger – *blinding* anger – ricocheted around my now screaming being, along with God knows what else that made up the accumulative, agonising onslaught.

Uncontrolled, unrestrained, all-consuming emotion that had no right being there . . . and it was not my own.

I fought. I fought so damned hard, yet was powerless to expel or control it.

'Make it stop!' I silently screamed, again and again and again.

'Nate? Nate? What's happened? *Talk* to me!'

I had no hope of answering James' words, echoing somewhere in my head. I was wholly consumed by what was spiralling completely out of control inside me.

It was the opening of the passenger door, after I do not know how long, that snapped me from the physical stasis my body had evidently retreated to. And then I had no control over the yelp, or the jumping out of my skin and the resultant hitting of my head on the roof of the car. My growl was instinctual, protective . . . wounded.

James slid into the passenger seat, punctured the airbags with a couple quick stabbing hand movements, and pulled the door shut. There was no relief for me: I had failed to hear his approach.

'Nate?' James' voice was low but audible and undeniably anxious. 'Nate?' he asked again, more forcefully.

I turned slowly to face him, unsure I could complete even this simplest of tasks. He took in my contorted features and, no doubt, the wild, confused agony of my eyes. I saw his momentary shock, before he recovered himself.

'You *crashed*? You bloody well *crashed*? And . . . and – Jesus, Nate, what *the hell* is going on in your head?'

We stared at each other, and he physically squirmed in his seat at what he saw.

A sound, even I couldn't miss, triggered an instinctive response, and we were both whipping our heads around. It had come from the other car . . . and there was movement, too.

I found myself watching a foot, clad in a high-heel, kicking the driver's door open. I was involuntarily taking quick, sharp breaths . . . *surely I couldn't hyperventilate?*

A leg, shrouded in a long black dress or skirt, followed the foot, unwittingly entangling itself in the seat belt that had failed to retract. When the full body of a woman emerged, it was only to then

4

trip and fall into an inelegant heap upon the ground.

Finally making it into an upright position, she instantaneously began to battle through the vegetation separating her from the road. Squealing, yelping and cursing, she tripped over tree roots and wrestled with and through hawthorn and blackberry bushes before sliding down the last half-a-dozen feet of the bank on her backside. Without losing momentum, she jabbed her right foot back into its slipping shoe, picked herself up, blindly brushed herself down, and started marching across the tarmac in our direction.

She was visibly *emanating* pure fury, and I was – *Oh God!* – being consumed by pure fury, being overwhelmed by the emotion I knew, without a doubt, was not my own. My normally highly dependable brain couldn't reach any conclusions in this state, certainly not any conclusions I could remotely trust. But . . .

'Nooooo! Dear God! Noooo!' I whimpered, lowering my head to my hands, vaguely aware of James' horrified glance in my direction.

I made myself raise my head and focus on the girl, who could quite possibly be destroying me. Her ever-approaching march was being regularly broken by stumbles as impractical footwear and inadequate night-vision made her route over the undulations in the country road treacherous. She was accompanying her journey with a fanfare of expletives. I had not heard many of them before;

even from James, who prides himself on adopting the gutter vocabulary of the day.

By the time she drew to a stop, no more than six feet away from the car, I was fast reaching the conclusion: I *could* hyperventilate.

Using her whole body, she began to gesture demonstratively, whilst screaming, 'You complete and utter *moron!*' If the onslaught on my senses was anything to go by, she was on the verge of hysteria.

Pointing dramatically towards her eyes, she continued, 'Eyes see! We *humans* have eyes!'

I managed to draw a sharp intake of breath, an action mirrored by James, but with no doubt less effort.

Squinting, she was clearly struggling to see through the dark. Looking broadly in my direction, 'We generally *use* them – to look where we're *effing* going! Why didn't *YOU* use them?!' Taking a deep breath for more air to fuel her next tirade, she shrieked, 'You *rammed* me off the road!'

Her hysteria was increasing, as was the hysteria racing through me, attempting to destroy my very being. 'Here I am, going about my own miserable life, minding my own sorry business and *you* – you total imbecile – you pitiful excuse for a human being—'

A snarl escaped James.

'—crash straight into me!'

And then she spotted the front of my car. She came closer, running her hands over it to confirm what her eyes were struggling to make out, and then turned to look at what was left of her car, and then back and forth once again. She seemed to be struggling with words, but my whole body was being rocked with what I now innately knew to be *her* ferocious rage – a wrath that continued to grow to monumental proportions.

How could any being survive such volume of emotion?

James unhelpfully added to my panicked thought. 'She should be spontaneously combusting.'

That sent me closer to the precipice. I was in control of nothing and could too easily imagine myself disappearing in a puff of smoke.

'You, you, you . . . there's hardly a scratch . . . but you, you – KILLED my car!' Then making a realisation, her next words were almost whispered, 'You could have killed *me*.'

But hardly sparing a pause for vulnerable reflection, she was back to her maddened state and storming over to my door.

I fought the urge to cringe away.

'Get out of the car, you *coward*!' she screeched, and proceeded to hammer frantically on the window with her clenched fists.

I now surrendered to the urge before watching in horror her hands slide across the outside of the door. Unable to find the handle – *thank the Lord for gull-wings* – she finally took a step back. Putting hands on hips, she spoke ominously.

'Don't make me come in and get you – I will.

I'll come in and haul your despicable arse out of there if I have to!' Not a moment passed before she declared, 'Well – you've asked for it!'

Taking a step back, she took aim – and kicked the car as hard as she probably could. I heard the crack, and it *wasn't* the car door. James and I stared at each other in a state of complete stillness.

A pained, 'Owwwwwww!' was audible as it escaped her lips.

Tentatively moving my eyes to track her movements, I observed her hopping and spinning around a couple of times before she ended up at the back of the car, which she evidently needed for support.

I heard her deep, pained intake of air, followed by deliberately slow exhales. She then squeaked, 'You broke my foot . . . first my car . . . now my foot!'

Oh! The relief! The majority of her torturous emotions were subsiding, assuming a lower ebb, presumably as her extreme physical pain became overriding. I breathed deeply several times, experiencing the unfamiliar need for comfort.

Now, feeling fractionally calmer, my instinctive need for self-preservation took over. I *had* to take advantage of this respite and take stock of the situation. I *had* to be rid of this creature.

What were the options? *Kill her!* She clearly wasn't going away, and I had an overwhelming need to stop the torture inexplicably linked to this girl.

James silently relayed another option. 'Charm her. Then we are out of here, away from whatever . . . whatever *the bloody hell* is happening right now!'

James flinched when I looked him in the eye and responded with a ramble in my head. '*Okaaaay* . . . yeeees – perhaps a *little* optimistic. I accept you aren't yourself, but you can, on odd occasions I grant, be a charming bugger . . .' Breaking off, he continued out loud, 'You know, I have no idea whether I'm getting through to you here. *Bloody hell!* You can't *kill her*, mate!'

Still attempting to absorb his words, I felt a resurgence of her emotions. My torturer was upset, quite possibly feeling sorry for herself, and my guess was, this was only the beginning of things. There wasn't a hope I could deal with what would be coming my way.

I needed to act whilst I still could. Fumbling – *fumbling?!* – I finally found the handle and pushed the door open. I had to move quickly before it was either too late or . . . *I lost my nerve?*

I cautiously unfurled my normally athletic frame, checking all the time my limbs were still working.

James was in my head again. 'Option two, Nate. Option two. Charm the pants off her!'

I grimaced at his crassness, but then any hope of rational thinking and behaviour disappeared: I could smell blood.

Now I was tottering on the edge of a gaping abyss, and this girl was pushing me closer to its crumbling lip. *Option One.* It *was* going to be option one.

'No, Nate. NOT an option!' sounded silently in my head.

I hesitated, fighting to rediscover my restraint, but couldn't begin to think rationally. Yet, if I didn't take care of things, I . . . I . . . simply didn't know what would become of me.

With head down, I took an agonisingly slow step *away* from where I knew the girl to be, fighting all the time the raw need that now coursed through me. I rested my quaking hands on the black, highly polished surface of the car's bonnet. I refused to look through the windscreen to meet James' eyes, or to venture a glance at the source of my torture.

I could hear the girl's rapid breathing and racing heart beat. Her earlier upset emotions were being replaced by something else, something I had no hope of identifying – but I *could* feel her uncertainty and, at its edge, a slow, creeping fear.

And she should fear! She clearly possessed no commonsense at all, no urge for self-preservation. Completely alone in the back of beyond, in the early hours of the morning – I could be *anyone.* Shaking my now pounding head, I thought just how bad her luck was.

Her uneasiness was growing. I couldn't afford to be overwhelmed again. I stepped back from the car, head still down, and began to walk its length. I had no idea what I looked like and was far from sure my eyes were as I needed them to be. The

10

moon was behind the clouds, but I cursed the light coming from the car with its open gull-wing door. I would have closed it . . . had I been psychologically strong enough to be shut outside with this torturous creature.

I concentrated on my movements, stopping . . . not too close to make restraint impossible? I was either hedging my bets or hoping for a miracle, I just didn't know.

Slowly raising my face, I looked at the girl properly for the first time.

She was quite bewitching, which scrambled my mind further. Her strawberry-blonde hair was loose and hung in long waves; her heart-shaped face held a pair of huge green eyes and I could plainly see a splattering of the lightest of freckles across her small pert nose; her lips were full, perhaps slightly too large for her face, but highly pleasing nonetheless; her complexion was pale, probably paler than usual, due to the pain she was in.

I imagined it would normally possess a becoming blood-filled blush.

And then I saw the blood; the scent of which was already bombarding my senses. I was trying not to inhale, but had no control over the periodic gasps for air my body shouldn't, but seemed to, need. The blood was oozing from a wound to the forehead below her hairline . . . and I was transfixed. It was taboo. I had made it taboo. But being taboo made it all the more attractive. A primal compulsion rose within me and its strength was beyond—

'DO NOT do this!' James' soundless yell rang through my head.

But I wasn't myself tonight . . . or perhaps I was? I could justify this. I needed to eliminate the cause of my pain and anguish and her blood would be the most wonderful bonus; it would be the ultimate comfort. I imagined myself relishing in its warmth, its oh so sweet aroma and, what I knew, beyond a shadow of a doubt, would be, its exquisite taste. I would devour every last drop and still want more.

James silently cried, 'You are better than this – think what it would do to Elizabeth!'

He was playing his trump card. The mention of my sister caused a momentary hesitation and my gaze dropped to the girl's eyes. Her look of pained confusion was clear . . . and I could *feel* it.

As our eyes held, she gasped and took a rapid step back. Landing heavily on her damaged foot, she cried out in pain. That terrible sound ricocheted through me. She started to tumble towards the ground.

And I was there.

She gasped again when my hands encircled her waist, stopping her fall. The racing beat of her heart was getting louder and louder as it boomed seductively in my head; it was in perfect time with the pulse that was now so visible under the delectably thin, penetrable skin of her throat. She was mine.

But her eyes . . . They momentarily intruded into my blissful state of anticipation. How would they look in death? I dropped my hands at lightning speed, even before she was quite steady. It still wasn't soon enough to stop the shocking warmth they had felt from channelling up through my arms to course through my body.

The depths of her eyes were fixed on mine. *They would haunt me until the end of time.*

It was I that now took a rapid step back, my whole body trembling. Her eyes refused to release me from their penetrating – was it inquisitive? – gaze. And I refused to release my own, knowing her eyes were the only thing saving her from the basest of my instincts.

Somehow I managed to take another step back.

And then I was at the open door. I wrenched myself away and dived, probably too fast, into the car. For once I was going to take James' advice. He handed me my calling-card and pen. I heard his silent voice again, 'You are doing great. Give her Morley's details. He'll sort it.'

Swallowing hard, I attempted composure, before forcing myself to duck back out of the car. I had no idea whether I could talk, whether my voice would hold steady. There was only one way to find out. Our eyes locked once again.

'I must offer you my sincerest apology.' It didn't sound like me. My voice lacked its normal timbre and seemed strained, but I was talking through a jaw now locked on its own accord, and my whole body was trembling. 'The responsibility for the accident is all mine. These are my particulars . . .'

Ever so tentatively, I moved my eyes away and, using the roof of the car as a rest, wrote on the back of the card the name and number of Richard Morley, the solicitor who handles so much of our day-to-day business. My hand was violently shaking and my normally neat script, a scrawl.

'. . . call and all necessary arrangements to rectify matters will be made.'

I re-met the gaze I knew to still be trained on me. I held the card out at full stretch, positioned between the tips of my two longest fingers. I left it to the girl to hobble forward the necessary paces. She had to use the car for support and her progress was clearly painful. I found myself wincing. But I *had* to remain rooted to the spot.

She cautiously took the card and I snatched my arm back. 'Nathaniel Gray,' she said quietly, reading out loud my name, printed in an elegant typeface upon the front of the card. Her voice was no longer in screaming-mode and sounded soft and melodic, albeit pained. For a bewildered moment, I thought I had handed her someone else's calling-card. But no, that was my name . . . it just didn't sound like my own when said through her lips.

'Again, please accept my sincerest apologies,' I managed to choke out, before turning away to re-enter the car. *I could do this. I could do this.*

Her voice, both indignant and fragile, cried out, 'You can't just *leave* me here!'

I spoke the words that sounded in my head. 'We will organise a car and driver to collect you and take you wherever you need to go.'

'*London?* I'm on my way home to London!' she cried incredulously. 'If you hadn't noticed, this is deepest, darkest, absolutely *never* to be visited again, Derbyshire!'

'The car will take you wherever you need.'

I made it into the driver's seat. I was nearly there but needed to be far away.

With a note of finality, reaching for the key in the ignition, I said, 'You may wish to get your head seen to.'

And then *vrroooom*. It wasn't the car firing up. My body was burning as red-hot fury scorched through me. There wasn't the tiniest part of me that didn't seem to be consumed.

'I should get *my* head seen to! Just who do you think you are, Nathaniel Gray? You nearly kill me, you break my foot, you're preparing to drive off into the night, leaving me alone – and you think I should get *my* head seen to? You—'

Startled, I turned to look at her. She had tried to stamp her foot and forgotten the impracticalities of that action with a fracture and tears now streamed down her face. The feeling of emotional hurt just ploughed in on top of the rage, and this time the physical pain did nothing to lessen it: I was sinking.

Her hands, swiping away the tears, were in the process of revealing blood; it was dark, she couldn't be sure, but a couple more swipes were confirming the discovery. I felt the dawning, and heard in the softest whisper, 'Ah! My head seen to . . . That's why it's hurting . . . Hurting . . . lots.'

And then she was gone.

Her emotions drained from me like plugs had been pulled from the soles of my feet . . . and with them, the savage thirst for her blood.

I watched her legs buckle and she was falling. I was there, under her, breaking her fall before she hit the tarmac.

Her warm, soft, painfully fragile body was still cradled in my arms when James joined me.

'Nate – what *the hell* do you think you're doing?'

I met his bewildered eyes and answered, in a choked, deathly quiet hiss, 'I have absolutely no idea.'

CHAPTER 2

THE AFTERMATH

'We have a situation Freddie and need you to sort the cars . . . You wouldn't believe me . . . You'll see for yourself when you get here.' James snapped his mobile shut and returned his attention to me. 'You have to let me take her, Nate.'

My grip on the girl tightened.

'I agree she needs to go to a hospital, and you don't need to remind me she's bleeding, but you are in no fit state to do this. I mean . . . *Jesus!* You are *so* not yourself! Her torture may have stopped, but your eyes . . . Your eyes look like a wounded puppy dog's!'

There was no wonder. No matter how hard I tried, I couldn't stop the flashback.

Another dark road and I was cradling in my arms another fragile human girl – my beloved sister. Her twenty-three-year-old body had been drained of blood and she was barely breathing. *'Elizabeth? Elizabeth? Wake up – they are gone. You can wake up now, sweetheart.'* The human terror and the pain . . . and I was *feeling* it.

'Nate? Nate – *Bloody hell!* Stop it! Stop it *now!*'

17

James had intruded upon my personal agonies then, too. *'Nathaniel – is that you? Does she live?'* But his voice had sounded very different. Back then it had been . . .

. . . human, groggy, pained . . .

'Nate? *Nate!'*

I was being shaken and finally focused back to the present. James looked at me aghast. I had been too preoccupied to keep him out of my head.

'You couldn't stop or control *that*?' he choked out, before recovering some control of himself.

I slowly shook my head and looked down at the girl now in my arms. The fears for her health— No . . . *my* fears for her health. *My* guilt. *My* shame. Her torture had stopped, but for the first time in nearly two centuries, I had *no* control over what I was feeling. I was completely unable to quash or dampen the terrifying sensations spiralling unchecked through me.

'Jesus . . . Nate . . .!'

There was panic in James' voice. But I couldn't let myself contemplate the full implications of what I was currently experiencing. It had to be temporary . . . a blip . . . it *had* to be . . . because if it wasn't . . .?

'You need to get back to Ridings – NOW! You're right – it's got to be temporary. But you need to be away from this girl. It must be her!'

I clutched her even tighter.

Now crouching down beside me, he spoke gently. I couldn't recall him ever having used that tone with me in this existence. 'Nate, look into my head. I'm no threat to her. I'm in control. You . . . you . . . Too much is going on with you right now and we can't risk— I'm going to take her to the hospital and *you* are going home – *now!*'

I knew he was talking sense; an unusual occurrence in itself. But why was letting her go so hard? She would be safe with James. I could see that in his head, whereas . . . I couldn't make any sense at all out of my own.

Somehow, I let James gently pull the girl from me. As he stood there, holding her in his arms, I had an overwhelming urge to snatch her back – and tear *him* to pieces. But he was gone. She was gone.

I was only vaguely aware of the whoosh of air as Frederick arrived. I was evidently still sat in the road. I was meant to be going home.

'Nate?' I finally looked up, but quickly looked away at the horror so visible on his face.

'I am well,' I said, as calmly as I could. 'Thank you for your assistance in . . . sorting matters.'

'Do you want to talk?' he asked silently.

I shook my head and took to the air.

The sun was rising. Not an issue in itself but only now was I flying over the outer reaches of my estate. I had clearly flown aimlessly throughout the night. My focus had been on purging, *desperate, futile* attempts at purging, because nothing had shifted the emotions – my emotions – now raging so painfully and unchecked through me.

19

As I flew over some of the eleven thousand acres of landscaped parks, lakes, woods and moors, I picked up the anxious voices of Elizabeth and Madeleine a few miles away. They must have cut their shopping trip to London short. And rather than sounding from their own estate properties, they were in the main house. And Frederick was there, too; he had evidently done what needed to be done.

But there was no James.

I pictured him standing there with the bewitching girl in his arms . . . and wanted to tear him to shreds all over again.

He should be back. I ranged out, but he was not at his farmstead to the north. There was nothing. He was evidently too far away for me to get into his head. Retrieving my phone, I pressed speed-dial: voicemail. *Damn it – where was he?*

I immediately lowered a veil over my thoughts. The others had sensed my presence and I couldn't allow them into my head. It was not a good place to be and my little sister was worried enough.

'Nathaniel? Nate? Speak to me, please . . .'

I ignored Elizabeth's desperate, silent plea. I couldn't provide her with the reassurance she needed, not whilst I was incapable of reassuring myself. I blocked her out. I blocked them all out.

The implications had begun to sink in and . . . *terror.* That's what I was now *feeling* for Christ's sake! *My terror.* And I shouldn't be feeling it. I shouldn't *have* to feel a damned thing. Emotion was a struggle enough when human, and now I lacked even the physiology to deal with it.

I frantically tried to dispel the latest of the torturous flashbacks that had plagued me all night. I managed to make it to the main house, entering through the open window at the top of my tower, before crash-landing to the floor.

No, please, not this one . . .

Slumped on the wide elm floorboards, I was again that twelve-year-old mortal boy, discovering his mother on her deathbed.

'Mama? Mama? Wake up, Mama. I beg of you!' I sobbed and frantically shook her. She had to wake up. She had to. I needed her. My baby sister needed her. I was on her bed, trying to pry her eyelids open. My tears falling all over her face. 'Mama? Mama? Please, Mama. Please!'

It felt like hours before I was able to slowly unfurl my arms from around my chest. I was never meant to have to go there again. After my mother's death I had been most commonly described as cold, aloof, detached. Only Elizabeth, and occasionally James, had ever managed to get under my defences. But now, in a form in which I shouldn't have to feel, a form designed to house a more extreme version of my mortal personality, I wanted to weep. But that ability was no longer mine.

I took a deep shaky breath, hoping for comfort. But instead, there was more uncontrolled, non-expellable emotion. In amongst the vying horrors, one was currently screaming louder than the rest.

Worry.

Worry for the girl. Worry . . . for Rowan Locke.

I had gathered her name from James' head after he had taken her from me. He had found her driving licence: Rowan Locke. Born: April 29th, 1977. Address: Flat 3, 212 Barclay Road, Hammersmith, London. A deep growl resonated from my throat. He thought she looked pretty in the photograph. I *should* have shredded him.

And where the hell was he?

I braved tuning in to the others. I knew I would be the topic of conversation, but perhaps James had reported in? They appeared to be in conference in the drawing room. At least they knew better than to disturb me in my tower.

'How *the blazes* can a vampire crash a car?' Frederick was not beating about the bush, as was typical. I would never have matched his brash personality to my genteel little sister's. But the strength of their one-hundred-and-sixty-five-year marriage had proved me wrong.

'That's a *very* good question . . .' Madeleine murmured. 'In four hundred years, I've seen nothing like it . . .' It was the first time I had *ever* heard her worried. 'I would suggest, however, that crashing the car is presently the least of Nate's concerns. If he's feeling again . . .?'

'But he *can't* be!' Frederick roared. 'I know what I saw – but it's a *defining* power, for fuck's sake! It's second only to *immortality!* We CONTROL whatever extent we choose to feel. How else could we remain sane over the years?' It was an argument he regularly used with Elizabeth, who only utilised the power reluctantly – why, I had never understood – but as a result, she remained the most human of us all.

'But out of all of us . . . why Nate?' *Oh, Elizabeth, sweetheart.* She continued in an unsteady voice, 'He's *always* needed to protect himself. He uses the power too much . . . I mean, we all know that. Sometimes I haven't even known if my brother has been behind that cold shell . . . but . . . *Oh, my God! Without it?'*

This was too much. I was barely holding it together as it was. I abruptly tuned out and snatched the phone from my pocket. Calling James' number again, I sank to the Persian rug in the centre of the room. Waiting for connection, I lay back and looked up through my tower's glass roof. This room doubled as an observatory, and in this position I was used to viewing the night sky, spotting planets and constellations invisible to even the most powerful of human-invented telescopes, but today, the sun was overhead. I checked my, now antique, Rolex wrist-watch . . . nearly ten hours had passed since he had taken her from me. And it felt like an eternity. Where *the hell* was he?

Straight to voicemail. What if something had gone wrong? Had her condition worsened? Her heartbeat had been strong but . . . *what if he had lost control?* It was with a roar that I leapt up and hurled my phone across the room. It smashed into

23

the wall above the fireplace, narrowly missing *Starry Night* – or at least *my* version of *Starry Night*. The version Vincent had painted not from memory and as seen through the bars of an asylum window but whilst under the night sky as we discussed religion, death and immortality. The Elizabethan stone wall held, but the phone turned to crumbs and dust.

Focusing for a moment on *Starry Night over Saint-Remy*, I realised I was viewing it differently. I had thought I understood it, had been in receipt of the necessary insight. That I had understood him that night. But now I was seeing new logic to the brush strokes . . . I forced myself to look away. *Was I on the edge of madness?* Such fresh illumination of that which had been viewed pretty much daily over the past one-hundred-and-twenty-three years, provided little reassurance.

There was no question my secret masterpiece had been an obsession of mine. And until last night, I had considered obsessive tendencies to be my kind's only weakness. But nothing was as it was. Until last night, I had not considered myself . . . a monster.

I was pacing like a caged . . . *monster*, when I started picking up James' thoughts. *Why was there nothing in them on Rowan Locke?* I attempted to calm my erratically pounding heart. He was coming straight to me. As he approached the window, I stepped aside to let him enter.

James didn't speak, choosing instead to snap his

sunglasses off and silently observe me. His head remained only full of concern for me, and I was too scared to ask what I wanted to know. *Needed* to know.

'She's going to be fine,' he finally relayed.

I held my head in my hands and calmed myself for a moment, before looking squarely into his eyes. He deliberately thought through everything that had happened at the hospital, and all the conversations he had had both with the doctors, and overheard. After quickly digesting them, I acknowledged I was done with a slight nod, before silently communicating, 'But she remains unconscious!'

She hadn't even woken up yet. How badly had I hurt her head? *What if she never woke up?*

'There's no evidence of permanent damage, Nate. Knowing you'd want her to have the best treatment possible, I flew her straight down to a London hospital and *persuaded* the country's foremost neurologist to fly back from a conference in Belgium to take her case over. All the nurses were charmed by my presence, too, so she couldn't be in better, more attentive hands. She's just not quite ready to wake up. But she *will* get better. She will *not* die from her injuries.'

I reached out and hugged him, an out-of-character action that no doubt worried him. But he hugged me back, and we held each other in silence, until I felt strong enough to move away.

The friendship between James and me had crossed both existences. James had once been my closest of mortal friends. Perhaps my only true mortal friend. It was a friendship inevitably forged by our mothers, for we were chalk and cheese. Yet our mothers' closeness, which saw James as a regular fixture at Ridings throughout our early childhoods, had forged something that would now likely continue into near eternity. Our relationship was volatile – our schooldays being particularly interesting. And it was even more so now with our exaggerated personality traits ensuring the accentuation of our differences. But that also applied to the depth of our relationship and to our understanding of the other.

'Thank you, James.'

'I'm not going to say it was a pleasure . . . *Bloody Hell!* I couldn't risk being spotted flying back in broad daylight and didn't have my car, so opted for the "*high*-speed" train rather than the horror of the car Morley came up with at short notice. You exist and learn. It's been a really shit day, Nate. Oh – did I forget the hour after hour in a human *hospital*!'

Generally, we were all pretty much comfortable around humans. Indeed much of the staff at Ridings were human: Mrs Dawes, the present housekeeper, and her handful of privacy-respecting cleaners, and then there were the tens of ground staff.

Unquestionably, James was the most practised of us all though. He was regularly out partying the night away with mortals and immortals alike. He had always been that way. During our long ago stint at humanity, he had had to drag me kicking and screaming to balls . . .

Come to think of it – it was *he* who had dragged me out last night!

James shifted his feet awkwardly. 'You know, I've really worked up an appetite. I reckon we'd both benefit from some black pudding.'

He was evidently changing the subject. And in my current reflective state, it worked. I found myself thinking of how black pudding had once been my salvation. Or at least our simplified version of it: neat and straight from the pig. We dispensed with the other ingredients such as oats and seasoning traditionally added to pigs' blood to create that particular human recipe.

I had been terrified and painfully vulnerable then, too. Flung from my panicked horse on that dark coach road, I had been unconscious in a sodden ditch whilst Elizabeth and James were attacked. Then, I had found myself in a living nightmare, too. But black pudding, the result of my desperately human quest to find a non-human alternative to Elizabeth and James' new dietary requirements, had saved me . . . saved us.

What could possibly be my salvation now? Two centuries on, no longer meant to be struggling with human weaknesses . . .

Yet, I found myself again desperate, vulnerable, unprotected.

'I still can't believe *you*, the Earl of Ridings, smuggled those walking, snorting pigs up the back staircase in the dead of night so we'd have black pudding on tap. But Nate – giving them a *guest room*? When Mrs Reynolds opened that door . . .'

I stopped hearing him. I dropped to my knees in agony. Confusion, anger, hurt, hatred and God knows what else were consuming me – and they weren't mine. *Oh, God – they were so much worse than mine.* She was back. How could she be back? She wasn't anywhere near me!

James was on his knees by my side. He held my face in his hands and spoke in a calm voice that belied the look in his eyes, 'It'll be easier this time. It will screw with you but you *can* do this. Here or your study?'

He read my answer, and then I was on the chaise on the ground floor of my tower.

It was a long time before I was able to take in my surroundings again.

'Why?' I asked shakily, seven hours, thirty-nine minutes and twenty-two hellish seconds later.

There was a pause whilst James seemed to consider how to answer, or even *whether* to answer. Sighing, he finally spoke. 'I called the hospital. Rowan Locke regained consciousness. It appears you – for the moment at least – experience her *conscious* feelings and emotions. Whilst we thought that part of your torture was at an end, it was simply her unconscious or sleeping. She's obviously sleeping again now. And it clearly has nothing to do with whether or not you are in her presence.' He added quietly, 'I should have let you kill her.'

I was completely and utterly numb and didn't feel able to move my frozen limbs. Her *conscious* feelings? So throughout Rowan Locke's *waking* hours, I would be in hell? My own emotions were bad enough . . . but *hers*? I wasn't strong enough for this.

James let me be for several minutes before coming to sit at my side. 'We are going to sort out a way to best deal with this.'

I shakily moved to my favourite red leather chair by the blazing fire; I felt in need of warmth. Clumsily, I knocked from the reading table my latest acquisition for the library: a first edition of Miguel de Cervantes' *Don Quixote*. Eighteen are known to exist; this was number nineteen. I had been sat reading it before James' hare-brained driving scheme had destroyed my existence.

When my limbs, at least, felt warmed, I asked again, '*Why?*' James looked confused. 'Not why it happened again, but why it happened *at all*. Why *me*? Why not you? Why this particular form of such targeted torture? And why this girl?'

I saw her in my mind's eye again . . . bewitching. I remembered the warmth that had channelled through my whole body as I sat cradling her, and how bereft and cold to the core I had felt when James took her from my arms. And then there were her eyes . . .

'You forget another "why", Nate. With everything

she's doing to you, why are you thinking of her in the way that you are?'

I was taken aback. I was concerned for her well-being . . . It was only right, after I had nearly killed her. I recovered myself in an instant. Leaping from my seat, I roared thunderously and fixed James with a furious glare; he didn't so much as flinch. I provided my response at a decibel level only our kind could achieve. 'That is ridiculous! Completely . . . utterly *RIDICULOUS*! Any excuse! You and your one-track bloody mind! Pathetic James! Pathetic!' I spun around to face the fire, leaning with both hands on the mantle, and attempted to calm myself down.

He chuckled and muttered, at the opposite end of the decibel spectrum to that which I had used, 'I do believe I hit a nerve.'

I was instantaneously before him – and this time I had the satisfaction of seeing him cringe.

'Okay, enough,' he conceded, raising his hands to indicate surrender. 'I was just checking your senses weren't buggered up – your hearing seems well up to par.'

I found myself letting out an exasperated growl, and stalked to the window. He was infuriating when he was like this. Night had fallen again. It hadn't even been twenty-four hours since I had been introduced to my own personal hell . . . and Rowan Locke.

Several minutes passed before I asked, 'Do you have any answers to my *whys*, James?'

30

'If we knew *why*, we wouldn't have let it happen.'

'Does she know what she is doing to me?' I murmured. My instinct was saying no . . . but I wasn't on best form.

James took a moment to respond. 'I honestly don't think she does. But whether conscious or unconscious, the fact remains: this girl is torturing you.'

'Talk!' I growled. 'Advise me of the best way of dealing with this – because I have not the remotest idea. You, no doubt, have had more opportunity for considering things over the last few hours than I.'

I couldn't believe I was in such a desperate state of mind to, yet again, be relying on James. It was such role reversal, and it didn't come easily.

James raised his eyebrows at my thought before plunging straight in at the deep end. 'The most obvious solution is to kill her.'

He saw the look on my face, and held up his hand so I would let him finish. 'You need to tell me why not. It seems to be the only sure-fire way of stopping this. It wouldn't need to be you. Any one of us would do this to end your torment – even Elizabeth. So if it's the irrepressible guilt of doing it yourself, let one of us. You need to seriously think about it, Nate. How can you *possibly* continue like this?'

So that is how they had spent their recent hours: working out how to kill her. And I had thought it was only I who had become a monster.

'That's not fair,' James snarled. 'None of us *want* to do it – but we don't feel we have a choice. And you should take a moment to reflect on what Elizabeth's offering here. It should show you just how worried she is about you. This would affect her more than anyone.'

'Get out of my head!' I snarled back. I knew what they were proposing to do was for me, and I didn't need James to remind me of the significance of Elizabeth's offer. I had bloody well been there when she had made her first and only human kill. And it had been my fault. I was supposed to have been looking after her, but had failed to spot the glaringly obvious. The black pudding solution had come too late to save Elizabeth's conscience. Yet no matter their motivation, it didn't make what they were suggesting any more acceptable. Yes, I needed the torture to end . . . but it *felt* bad enough that I had nearly killed Rowan Locke by accident, and she was lying in a hospital bed, broken because of me.

James cleared his throat and put his finger up as if seeking permission to speak. I raised my right eyebrow.

'The broken foot was *nothing* to do with you – the temper on that girl! That was *her* fault!' He obviously hadn't got out of my head.

'James! She only kicked the car because *I* failed to get out of the damned thing. The answer is NO!'

'You really aren't thinking logically or remotely sensibly at the moment. We all consider it to be the best course of action. It has to be in your best interests.'

'No, it is not!' I squeezed my eyes shut as an image of her eyes – lifeless – flashed before me. Merely the thought of her death caused an excruciating assault of guilt and grief. I knew James had seen it, so added warningly, 'Do *not* read anything into that! After my performance last night, I simply want her safe and well. I would challenge you, in my position, to want anything else.'

'And you think to be tortured by her during her every waking moment is an *option*? In your bloody position, I'd take her out myself! This is all connected to *her*, Nate. All of it. With her out of the picture, you'll get your power back, and will never need to feel anything you don't want to, ever again!'

'I do not know what I think!' I cried. I seemed incapable of making any cool, calculated decision when the waters were so muddied by sentiment. I tried to come up with something that sounded sensible – when sensible was the last description that could be currently applied to me. 'That course of action is premature. If we find her to be doing this to me on purpose, although God knows how and for what reason, then we can revisit the option. But no, not now. And I want a promise that none of you will act against my wishes.'

James sighed and shook his head. 'I told them, you know. I knew you wouldn't bloody well go for it. *But would they listen?* So . . . we move to Plan B.'

The relief flooded through me. *An alternative!*

'Because you refuse to be sensible, and we don't yet know why the hell this has happened, so can't remedy it, we need to look at avoidance . . . Let's go!' James was off the chaise and at the door in a flash.

I was even more confused, and his head gave me no clues. 'James?'

Shaking his head dramatically and clearly annoyed, he groaned. 'The things I do for you! We are going to the other side of the world, to see just how far away you have to be to escape that vicious streak of hers!'

I was pretty lost for words, but had to admit it was a good idea . . . a *very* good idea. I was at his side in less than a blink of an eye.

He gave me a broad smile, which I was beginning to feel like matching. 'Freddie's got the jet on standby, my new games console is on board – so let's get to the airfield. *I'm* driving, though!'

This could be the answer. I even had a property in Australia, which doubled as a highly profitable enterprise; its fifteen-thousand acre vineyard churning out some of the best-selling Australian wines in the human world. Not the ideal choice though . . . I grimaced, recalling the viciousness of the sun and its impact on our sensitive eyes and our pale skin – and the difficulty of blending in with the tanned locals. But then there was the taste of kangaroo blood. I hadn't had that for half a century or so.

But there was one thing I needed to do first.

'*NO!*' James roared. He was obviously still not out of my head. His face was instantly six inches from mine.

'James – you need to bear with me. I have to see her, to reassure myself she is getting better. I feel an inordinate degree of guilt and remorse for hurting her – and for the way I acted.' I shuddered at the recollection. 'I need to apologise . . . and getting some answers would be good, too.'

'But you *know* she's okay!' James spat out. 'Look what she did to you when she woke up. Believe me, now is *not* the time to be honourable! As for answers – leave it to *us* to find them. *You* simply need to get as far away from her as possible, as quickly as possible.'

I shook my head. 'I need to see her, James.'

And therein lay the problem. Yes, I wanted to apologise. Yes, I wanted answers. But no matter how much I attempted to deny it, I felt drawn to this woman. The most sensible reaction was to flee. But I didn't yet feel able to do so.

And there was something else plaguing my mind. I didn't want Rowan Locke to think badly of me. I couldn't fathom the reasons . . . I had never before been bothered by what people thought of me. But I found myself bothered now. I had experienced hatred in her feelings today and I worried it was felt towards me. I didn't want her to hate me. I knew I wasn't acting in my best interests, or hers.

But I needed to see Rowan Locke.

CHAPTER 3

THE HOSPITAL

James was livid and remained that way throughout the car journey to the hospital. 'You're a bloody masochist. Why are you doing this to yourself? You're out of your fucking mind! So what if you didn't behave like a gentleman – you were out of your mind then, too! What choice did you have? She's damned lucky you didn't kill her. *That* should be enough! That's far better than any apology you could ever hope to give.'

He didn't speak to me again for most of the hour-and-three-quarter journey – which was made at, what I considered to be, a reckless speed. He let his acute frustration channel through the accelerator pedal of the car. And tonight, in my post-traumatic form, I was a nervous passenger. No matter how hard I tried, I couldn't reassure myself we were still infallible. If the impossible had happened to me, then technically, it could happen to us all.

My panicked exclamations left James in no doubt as to my concerns: 'James . . . LOOK OUT! *That* car! . . . *Dear God* . . . THAT car! I beg of you – put the lights on so they can see us coming!'

36

And even, 'There is a cat between those cars . . . JAMES! . . . *Jesus!* A rat is poking its head out of that drain . . . if the cat *sees* the rat . . .?'

James' response to each panicked observance was to turn his attention from the road, and to stare at me in absolute disgust; as a result, I only uttered the warnings of most concern. But I could concur with what he was thinking: I had no idea what was becoming of me.

As James drew into the hospital car park, my sentiments were mixed. I couldn't put into words the relief at our having completed the journey without incident. But now we had arrived, I was . . . petrified.

'It's the middle of the night,' James coolly stated, parking and turning the engine off. 'And she's clearly in the land of nod because you aren't acting all freaky on me . . . Well – not *as* freaky. If this had to happen, it should have at least been planned better!'

'You think I have a plan?' I mumbled.

'Well, this wasn't my idea! And do you know what? I've had more than enough of human hospitals. *And* I didn't get to feed.'

I ignored him. I was struggling. Petrified didn't begin to go there and it was a horrid sensation. Yet, at the same time, I was acutely aware of how physically close to Rowan Locke I was. I knew that despite all the corridors I would end up going through, she was less than one-hundred-and-fifty yards away. And I, totally illogically, wanted to be closer.

It was several long moments later that I, alone, made my way to Rowan Locke's bedside. James was giving me space, whilst being on hand in the event of anything else 'fucking freaky' happening. He was not instilling me with confidence.

'I'd wish you luck,' he said as we parted, 'but I think you are going to need more than damned luck!'

Visiting hours were obviously over, but that was not a problem for one such as me. I was soon at Rowan Locke's bedside. And I let the relief flood through me; I wasn't experiencing that thirst for her blood as I had amidst the events of last night. If I had, I wondered, would James have intervened?

However, it hadn't been plain sailing. From the moment I had stepped silently into the hospital building, her intoxicating scent had been clearly discernible above the vile, institutional-chemical stench of the place . . . calling me. But there was a choice tonight. Tonight . . . I was simply being teased. I knew I couldn't be blasé, though. At the first sign of trouble, I would be out of there.

My relief at being in control evaporated the instant I took in Rowan Locke's sleeping form. She was broken, brutalised. Needles were coming out of her hands, connected to various fluid-filled bags hanging on the metal contraption to the side of her bed; her head was taped up, as I knew her right foot would be under the sheets. And I had done this to her. Here I was congratulating myself on not experiencing the urge to suck her dry – yet, I had broken her. I was mortified and ashamed.

I might feel vulnerable, I realised, but she was the epitome of vulnerability. But even broken and so unquestionably fragile, she was still bewitchingly beautiful.

I recalled appreciating her physical charm, even in the midst of our previous encounter. Looking at her now, I concluded she was, without doubt, the most pleasing woman I had ever seen.

I seemed unable to control the direction of my thoughts. As I stared at her, transfixed, I caught myself wondering, had I met Rowan Locke as the human Nathaniel Gray, would I have rested until she was my wife? Would I have said, to hell with the list of prerequisites I had so carefully prepared? I had had a lot of them. So many so, Elizabeth had considered them to be quite impossible to meet, thus a fail-safe method of ensuring I *never* became exposed to the vulnerability that opening up my heart would entail. But I found myself thinking, had Rowan Locke been the housemaid, I would have still wanted her. Whoever she was, I would have attended countless balls, undertaken no end of small-talk, and would have laid my heart wide open. I would have done *anything* to secure her.

I dragged my eyes away. Clearly coming tonight had *not* been a good idea. *Damn James for being right!* And yet . . . I didn't want to leave.

There was no logic whatsoever to my thoughts.

I had met this woman less than twenty-four hours ago, and she was the cause of the most painful and traumatic moments of my immortality. It was nonsensical I should *feel* this way. I shook my head. It was nonsensical I was feeling at all.

Nevertheless, I found myself thinking how it could have been. Had I met Rowan Locke as a human, our first meeting would have been so very different. And without the devastating side-effects to us both. I even imagined a little heart-faced, freckle-nosed girl, with strawberry-blonde ringlets and my mother's soft brown eyes, and a boy, with dark unruly hair like my own, and Rowan Locke's incredible green eyes and fair complexion. I imagined them running noisily and happily from room to room at Ridings, and their splashing in the lake as I, and Rowan *Gray*, looked proudly upon our exquisite children.

Enough! This could absolutely not be happening – how could I have possibly thought things could get no worse?

I was a vampire for Christ's sake! And she was so clearly human. And I had already nearly killed her – twice! She almost certainly hated me – and I still didn't know if she was *knowingly* torturing me.

God, I prayed James hadn't been tuned in. I doubted it. Had he been, he would have stormed in by now and physically dragged me away, as I would have done him.

My mind was a rambling mess. Logic was my

forte, yet it had deserted me. I reminded myself why I was here: to apologise before closing the chapter and escaping to the other side of the world; and to establish whether she was an innocent. If she was *knowingly* doing this to me, then . . . I wasn't going there.

I was thankful she was sleeping. I had no idea what I was going to say to her. I had always been a creature of few words – one-to-one always being easier for me – but how was I going to be able to express my mortification? How could any words express how badly I felt about hurting her? How could I ensure she neither hated nor feared me?

And then there was the not insignificant complication of my being tongue-tied in her conscious presence; our torturous connection was hardly going to ease my already limited conversational skills. I wasn't quite sure how I was going to manage things.

I wrenched my eyes away, and moved to the end of the bed to look at her medical chart; they had doubled her painkillers tonight. The thought of her in pain stabbed me to the core. It had hurt last night too, even in the midst of everything that had happened. I took in the flowers around the room. I had forgotten that's what humans did. I would get some of the early flowering roses from Ridings. I realised I had never, either as man or vampire, given a woman flowers . . . not even Elizabeth, despite my knowing her love of them. Sending this woman flowers didn't mean anything,

I reassured myself: it was the very least I could do in the circumstances.

I moved silently to pick up one of the half-a-dozen cards standing on the mobile hospital table. The card in my hand was made from a piece of standard white A4 printer-paper. Folded only approximately in half, it had obviously been made by a child. On its front, a stick-figure with a skirt and long red hair had been drawn in coloured pen; two smaller stick-figures with spiky hair were either side. They were all holding stick-hands; some with six fingers, some with two, and some with three and four. I was . . . touched at the innocence, and the fact that, by chance, not one of the hands had the requisite five digits.

All three figures had impossibly large smiles lighting up their faces. In the sky was a bright yellow sun; under their feet, what I could only assume to be, blue grass. I read the words within the card: *get Well Aunty rowAn and come and play witH Us Soon. LOVE Nathan and Tom*. Every bit of available space was covered in kisses. Ninety-seven of them, I instantaneously processed.

I continued to inspect each of the cards around the room. As I put the last card back, my eyes were drawn to the waste-paper basket under the table. It contained a discarded bunch of fresh flowers, still in their wrapping, and a piece of, what must have been, the small card that accompanied it. I retrieved the piece and quickly found three others, slotting them back together. Their

42

scent was repulsive, but they had come from the bin.

On the front of the card was a nondescript picture of a pink gerbera flower, and inside, in a tiny swirling script, the words: *'My Dearest Rowan, I find myself having to say sorry. I don't know what came over me. It was not yet our time.'* It was signed with an extravagant, flourishing *S*. I was intrigued. Who was 'S'? Why was he sorry? Why were the flowers so clearly discarded? And, most significantly, *Why was he calling her 'My Dearest Rowan'?*

There was so much I didn't know about Rowan Locke, and I found I wanted to know everything; every tiny little detail of her life. It could be argued, it was the sensible thing to do – it might provide a clue as to what had happened, and a solution to my current . . . problems. But it didn't *feel* sensible. It felt borderline obsessive. I could not allow this to happen. Van Gogh's *Starry Night* was one thing; a human woman who tortured me, quite another.

I spent much of the night watching over her, getting progressively angrier with myself for being responsible for her hospitalisation. It was about 4 a.m. when it became obvious she was having a nightmare. Nightmares no longer haunt me, my sleep being deep and dreamless. But I recalled those following my mother's death, and those in the fallout of 1817. I wanted to wake her, to comfort her as I would once have liked to have been comforted myself. But I knew it would terrify her as much, if not more, than the nightmare itself.

I was filled with horror as she started to mumble, 'Get away from me. I'll scream!' Words that were repeated again and again. Was this nightmare about me? Could the events of that night have sparked the sort of terror she was now experiencing? I vehemently prayed not.

The nightmare passed before I was able to put into action any alternative plan for waking her. I had been working through ways of alerting the medical staff to her condition. But despite its passing, I could not bear to helplessly watch her restless sleep further. I saw sunrise from the hospital roof. There I lay within the shadows until official visiting hours, trying to come to terms with my own terror at being face-to-face with a *conscious* Rowan Locke.

I had known when she awoke: 6.49 a.m. From that point, I was party to her deepest, innermost feelings; although how many I understood, I know not. They appeared less extreme than before. I guessed there were fewer stimuli and perhaps the increased painkillers were having an impact? But, nevertheless, they were the reason I lay on the roof, attempting to take deep, calming breaths.

James had checked on me but I needed to be able to do this alone. I was proposing to hold some kind of half-respectable conversation with my torturer that betrayed nothing about me. I had to get things under control.

I missed the start of visiting hours. In fact, I didn't feel able to venture from the roof until early afternoon – fifteen minutes *after* she had been administered another double-dose of painkillers. They definitely had a calming effect.

I walked through the now-busy hospital at human-speed, soundless as a vampire. I, nevertheless, felt clumsy.

I stopped breathing as I experienced that revolting, acrid smell again. My hackles went up. It was no wonder humans contracted God-only-knows-what in hospitals, if they never emptied their bins. The sooner Rowan was out of there, the better.

I walked around a male and female, evidently in argument.

'Your meddling will *not* stop me!' he hissed. 'All these years you hid—'

'You are deluded!' she snapped. 'And call it what you like, but I warn you now, Simeon – you ever come near again, I will consider it an act of war. And you *will* experience my full force!'

Though physically petite, the woman was clearly holding her own. She sounded formidable.

I turned the corner, skirted around a knee-high human child, and found myself at the half-open door to Rowan's room. I fought the urge to walk straight past; I *needed* to do this.

Bracing myself, I tapped on the door, gently nudging it open a little further. I had no idea how this was going to go. Was she terrified of me and about to start screaming the hospital down? Would she even agree to see me? I was nervous as hell.

Looking towards the head of the bed, I connected immediately with those remarkable eyes; the same eyes I had been unable to keep out of my head since first encountering them. My immortal heart produced several extra beats, and I could have sworn I felt light-headed.

I had a distinct sensation that any sense I might still possess was about to go straight out of the window.

'Am I welcome?' A simple question, but not so simple to get the cautious words out in an audible fashion.

She was both surprised and shocked to see me; her expressive eyes communicating what I knew her to be feeling. *But could I also feel . . . irritation?* She blushed becomingly, sending my vampire juices racing. This was going to be difficult.

Breaking eye contact, she awkwardly used her hands to repeatedly smooth her wonderful, sleep-tussled hair and to straighten her bedding and then again back up to her hair. I was pleased to see she was sat up today, propped against pillows, and needles were no longer assaulting her fragile body.

'Nathaniel Gray . . .' she said quietly, in that unique melodic way she had of saying my name.

I felt a warm glow flow through my cold veins.

'. . . it all depends on whether you're going to give killing me another go.'

Not possessing the ability to read human thoughts, it took me too long to take in the mischievous sparkle in her eyes.

And then she grinned at me.

Her face lit up in a way I had never before seen it. Relief flooded through me – unspeakable relief – and I found myself spellbound by her face. A not unpleasant tingling sensation flooded my body.

'It was a joke! I didn't for one moment think you'd take it seriously – unless of course, you *have* come to kill me, and my sister's got it right?'

I had been walking more fully into the room but paused mid-stride at her latest revelation. *What could her sister have got right?* I should be getting seriously panicked. And I was. Yet I couldn't stop thinking that whatever happened, it was worth it to have experienced the pleasure that flooded my being – *my* pleasure – as she smiled and her eyes lit up like that. It *felt* so good. How long had I been without this sensation? Had I ever experienced such a feeling before? I didn't think so. And I had thought it would be *her* emotions that would cause me problems.

She looked abashed but started to laugh; perhaps at me, I knew not – nor cared. It was a wonderful sound to my ears. It was like a harmony of all my favourite sounds: that magical morning bird song that erupts at first light in earliest spring; the sound of a gurgling brook as the first waters start flowing after a big freeze . . . and her own light, melodic voice, when she spoke my name.

And then she winced.

I snapped out of my revelries. My voice raw, I asked, 'Are you in pain?'

She looked at me for a long moment, taking in my face but focusing on my eyes, which I doubted could fully hide my anguish. I was concerned; I knew my unshrouded eyes were far too expressive and intense for human company, and my shroud had never been designed to hide such a depth of feeling.

'No . . . I'm okay,' she replied slowly, before speaking rapidly. 'I'm sorry! I shouldn't have joked like that – it was insensitive and inappropriate and – I don't know why I . . . Around you I – I'll just shut up!' She was red in the face and looking anywhere but at me.

'No!' I cried, slightly too forcefully, almost betraying my desperate desire to hear her voice. I urged more quietly, 'Please do not.'

We held each other's gaze, neither seeming able to look away. Could I be using my charm, unconsciously? I looked at her flushed cheeks and reluctantly turned away. Use of the charm would be unforgivable in these circumstances, but would have explained her feelings, that had, for a moment, been a wonderful complementary symphony to whatever I, myself, was now feeling.

Was I losing control of when my charm was engaged, too? I reached the extraordinary decision: I would worry about that later. For the moment, I wished to focus *entirely* on Rowan Locke.

Released from my gaze, she became fascinated by a bit of fluff on the pink hospital blanket. 'It's really best I do.' She laughed awkwardly, still playing with the fluff.

I inhaled so I had further air in my lungs with which to speak. She smelt delectable. 'I needed to say sorry. I am mortified over what I have done to you.'

'Don't worry about it – it was an accident. Everyone has accidents.'

'Not I,' I confessed, quietly.

'Well – you do now!'

I found myself smiling, despite my nerves and the topic of our conversation. 'Yes, I do now,' I conceded.

Stealing a quick glance at me, she asked, 'You've seriously never had a car accident before?'

'No.'

'How is that possible?'

Disguising my frown, I said, 'I am sorry?'

'You are such a crap driver!'

I stared at her dumbfounded before finding myself laughing. My body and mind were not completely my own; I was being infiltrated, was a bag of nerves. She was asking questions of me I couldn't possibly answer – *and* I was being criticised – yet I was *enjoying* her company. I was finding that when her emotions were placed in context and not a blind onslaught, they were that much more manageable. And then there was, of course, that matter of my being distracted by, what could only be described as, my own pleasure at her company.

But in this particular moment . . . In this particular moment as I laughed and held her eyes, her emotions were as pleasurable to experience as my own.

'It was not a good night,' I mused, after she had looked away. Her blush was so attractive.

'Tell me about it . . . You *are* insured?'

For a moment, I didn't know what to say. I assumed I was, but that sort of thing was handled by Richard Morley. He undertakes our more formal communications with the human world and much of the management of our personal properties and estates, although not the now vast assets of Gray Investments, for which I have my own dedicated team.

But did he organise car insurance?

She looked at me suspiciously, taking my pause as a negative, before again inflicting me with that grin of hers. 'Ha! Ha! Well that was the simplest of the options my sister came up with. But she will be disappointed. Poor Clare! She'd *so* many more exciting explanations.'

'What your sister had right . . .' I murmured.

'You wouldn't believe what she came up with about you, Nathaniel Gray.'

I tentatively met her gaze. *What had she come up with about me?* I didn't think I could feel fear but . . . Hoping I had secured a calm exterior mask, I hedged. 'Please call me Nate.'

She shook her head at me. 'Okay, *Nate* . . .' She paused to grin. 'After your performance at the accident, Clare was all for you being *Mafioso*, or on the run from the police, or a real-life James Bond. Failing that, she thought you might simply be uninsured – but she wasn't particularly enamoured with that one!'

I let out the air I had evidently been holding in my lungs and chuckled, whilst running a hand over my face. We were both smiling broadly now. My smile started as one of relief, but ended up as one of sheer exhilaration at the beauty before me.

She rolled her eyes. 'Honestly, you need to know my sister.' Sounding more serious, she added, 'But you have to admit, it was really bizarre. No police, no ambulance, no insurance companies – being driven to London! That is what happened, isn't it? It just wasn't really *normal*.'

I laughed awkwardly. 'It was all . . . new to me.'

As I watched her gaze now travel over my body I couldn't help but gulp. Everywhere she looked, she left a trail of warmth. I felt aglow . . . and impossibly *alive*. And I was focusing more and more on her soft lips. *Bugger!* I was in so much trouble.

Having completed what appeared to be an assessment, she looked away, clearly embarrassed. I attempted to pull myself together. I couldn't begin to decipher what she was feeling, but her breathing had quickened. She asked nonchalantly, 'And you weren't hurt? Or your passenger?'

51

She thought James had been in the car with me during the crash. 'No.' I grimaced. '*You* came off far the worst physically.'

She returned to that bit of fluff. 'I just wondered . . . bits are hazy . . . but you sat in the car. Later I couldn't see too well . . . but your eyes . . . You are sure you weren't hurt?'

I chose my words carefully. 'I think I was in shock . . . and I was terrified. But that was no excuse for my behaviour. It was abominable.'

'Terrified of what?' She looked at me, surprised.

'Of you,' I replied, meeting her eyes.

'Of . . . *me*?' she stuttered, looking away quickly.

'You were *very* scary.'

'So were you!' she promptly countered.

I groaned inwardly. It was inevitable really, when I remembered how close I had been to surrendering to the creature within. But I couldn't bear to have her scared of me.

She was preoccupying herself with reaching for a glass of water. The manoeuvre wasn't simple for her broken body and I was there, possibly a little too quickly, to assist. There appeared to be a moment of confusion but she seemed to dismiss it. I handed her the beaker of water, careful not to let our hands touch. I hadn't warmed them on the gel hand-warmer in my pocket – standard kit for the modern-day vampire: heat at the touch of a button.

Her hands were visibly trembling. Was I scaring her again? Yet I couldn't feel it – or at least I didn't *think* I could. Surely I would feel her fear? I was so bad at this. As far as I could make out, she was currently experiencing a melee of sensations, unidentifiable singly, yet as a whole . . .? As a whole they didn't *seem* unpleasant . . . quite the contrary. Surely feeling someone's emotions should provide a clue as to what they were thinking? Yet I was presently baffled.

I waited for her to take a couple of sips before taking the beaker from her hand and putting it back on the table. I immediately took a precautionary step back so my proximity couldn't scare her further. I asked gently, 'I scared you?'

'No, *you* didn't . . . I don't think.' She seemed to recall something – *was that a momentary flash of fear . . . or not?* 'The situation . . . not getting out of the car . . . the dark . . . two strange men. I was just a bit exposed.'

Dear God, this was so confusing. Was she scared of me? Wasn't she scared of me? I was confusing myself. I couldn't understand this girl, even with my hotline to her soul. 'You were out late,' I observed, softly.

Almost petulantly, she retorted, 'So were you!'

'True.' I wanted to add: *But I am a vampire and you, a fragile-little-human girl. You were alone, miles away from home, in the early hours of the morning . . . and recklessly screaming at strange 'men'!* But didn't. I settled with, 'But you were miles from home.'

She responded defensively, 'I had a client function thing for work,' before adding more quietly, 'but decided to leave early.'

'In the middle of the *night*?' It came out more forcefully than I had intended.

I was baffled by both the lack of sense she was making, and her feelings that now punched me. Literally. I collapsed into the chair beside the bed. There was no mistaking these. It was that hatred and anger I had experienced yesterday. And they were equally unpleasant today.

'Yes!' was her single-word reply, used to clearly end that topic of conversation. Her anguish was getting worse though. She was clearly recalling something unpleasant. But did it involve me? Or was it something to do with the reason she had left work 'early'?

I was sensible enough to realise now was not the time to satisfy my curiosity. It was becoming increasingly evident those feelings of hers, with the potential to literally cripple, were of the negative variety. The immediate aftermath of the accident being a case in point. The more positive ones, on the other hand, such as amusement and playfulness, and those others that I couldn't readily identify, but which during this encounter seemed to be swimming around her body, rather than torturing me – were wondrous.

A fresh spark of anger stabbed me. Damn. I had not been quite quick enough to divert.

'It shouldn't matter why I was on the road in the middle of the night – it wasn't *me* that rammed someone off it, nearly killing them!'

I needed to calm things down. I had first-hand

experience of the volatility of this girl's temper. If it didn't hurt so much – or debilitate me – I would be fascinated by it. 'Touché,' I replied quietly, unable to get more than one word out. I thankfully felt the anger abate and she furnished me with a smirk. Being conciliatory, and now able to speak more than a single word, I added, 'I of course owe you another apology. It is none of my business why you were out late.' The spoken words didn't betray my wish to *make* it my business, however.

There was a long pause before she spoke. 'That was really rude of me – sorry! I had my reasons for leaving and you just hit a nerve. Can we leave it at that?'

I instantly changed the subject. 'I am getting your car repaired. Although if you would like a different model, something newer and safer in an accident, it would only be right that I provide it.'

Rowan looked at me as if I was insane. 'That *isn't* how it works, Nathaniel – Nate! What world are you in?'

I chose to ignore the question. 'It would only be right. I fail to see the difference between getting the old car appropriately repaired and providing you with a replacement.'

She was feeling really muddled but her response was pretty adamant. 'I like my old car. It is – or *was* – a classic!'

'It would be no trouble at all. There are some exceptionally safe cars . . .'

'No!'

Bugger! Well then, the repair works would have to address safety. I couldn't possibly allow her on the roads otherwise.

'There's no rush though. Fat lot of good the car will do me at the moment.' She pointed to her foot. 'I won't be able to drive for weeks.'

Of course she couldn't. How stupid of me. 'I will arrange a car and chauffeur.'

She fixed me with completely incredulous eyes. 'I'm *sorry?*'

What had I done now? Up to meeting this girl, I had spent nearly two-hundred years devoid of confusion. But it was something I was now feeling near constantly – it was beyond unnerving. Very tentatively, 'I said . . . I can arrange a car and driver . . . to drive you around until you are back on your feet . . . so to speak.'

She started shaking her head in apparent disbelief. Why could I not understand her? 'I thought that's what you said!' She seemed to be finding it hard to choose her words. She was still shaking her head and making exasperated sounds. In the end, she seemed to give up. 'Look, that's really . . . *sweet* of you. But on the rare occasion I need four wheels, I'll use a taxi.'

Had she just called me 'sweet'? 'But it would truly be no trouble – it is the very least I can do.'

'No!'

'But how are you going to get about on a day-to-day basis?' I was beyond confused now.

'How do you think?' she asked impatiently. 'On those!' She nodded towards a pair of crutches, standing in the corner of the room.

Dear God! It frustrated me just *thinking* about the process she was proposing. As a physically invulnerable immortal, I couldn't begin to contemplate it. How could I possibly sit back and let her hobble around the streets of London on those things?

My tone now had a desperate edge to it. 'Rowan – it is not right you should be struggling to get around because of me. It was my fault and, for that reason, you *have* to let me put it right!' I was annoying her; I could see it in her body language as well as feel it. If I wasn't careful, it would become a major issue for me. But this was *not* right. She had to see that.

'I'm an independent woman living in the twenty-first century – in my thirties! I'm perfectly capable of looking after myself.'

I very much doubted that. After all, something had happened before the accident – and look at her irresponsible actions after it.

'I've been on crutches before, and no doubt will be again.'

There you go – I knew it!

'I don't need your excessive degrees of guilt to come up with ludicrous solutions for getting me around. So, *please* – just sort the car out and leave it at that!'

Her annoyance was being added to with a splattering of anger, so I tactically withdrew. But if she honestly thought I could leave her to struggle around on those ridiculous contraptions, she wasn't remotely as intelligent as I suspected her to be.

'Point taken. Are we . . . on amicable terms again?'

She looked at me, shaking her head again in exasperation. 'Of course – just don't get so effing freaky on me!'

I had been called freaky a lot in the past twenty-four hours, I ruefully reflected. But I couldn't help the smile – she really had *no* idea.

I watched Rowan intently as she returned to her piece of fluff, which she had now pulled into a length of fibre. I caught her glance momentarily at me and thought she was going to say something, but she seemed to change her mind. Her emotions were at a more manageable level for me now, although I still couldn't make head nor tail of them. They were as confused as I.

My attention was drawn to a corridor, where I caught her name being spoken. A conversation between two females was taking place, and it was getting closer.

'Are you expecting other visitors?'

Before she had a chance to reply, the door was pushed open. Rowan gave me an odd look. I should have done better than that.

A woman around Rowan's age, and the petite woman I had passed earlier, mid-argument, entered the small room.

I silently moved from my seat and stood at the end of the bed to allow their easy accommodation. The small woman's eyes tracked me, whilst the other started talking.

'Rowan love, sorry we're late! I was all up and ready to go, but Mark refused to *drag* himself out of bed to—' She stopped short on spotting me. 'Oh! Sorry! You've a visitor!' She gushed and blushed. Dropping the bag she held in her right hand, she quickly used both hands to smooth down her hair and non-existent creases from the front of her jeans. Giving me a nervous, self-conscious smile, she then looked pointedly at Rowan, raising her eyebrows.

Rowan sighed and did the necessary introduction. 'Clare, this is Nathaniel Gray – the idiot who ran me off the road. Nate – this is Clare, my little sister – the one who thinks you've something to hide.'

I grimaced. Rowan certainly had a way with words. Clare's blush deepened and she glowered at Rowan, who unashamedly returned the look with a too-innocent smile.

I looked for similarities between the two sisters. Despite my enhanced powers of observation, other than the propensity to blush and smooth down their hair, I couldn't discern any. Clare was taller than Rowan's five foot four by a good three inches, and of a more fragile build. Her blonde hair was cut into a shoulder length bob. Her eyes were blue, to Rowan's emerald green; her nose straight, to

Rowan's impish pert one; and her face round, to Rowan's heart-shape. I really wouldn't have identified them as sisters at all.

Clare held out her hand to shake mine and I took it gently. I had spent the last few moments warming mine, so it would simply feel a little cool. It was no doubt pale, but that's not the sort of thing I find gets noticed with handshakes. On meeting, people normally seem fascinated by my eyes.

I smiled. 'I am pleased to meet you, Clare.'

Clare was giggling like an excitable school girl and I warmed to her instantly. 'Nathaniel? Nate? I've got one of those, too . . . well, a Nathan,' she rambled nervously. 'I've got one, too – haven't I, Rowan?' Rowan shook her head and I heard her sigh. Not waiting for an answer, Clare continued, 'Although he's *much* smaller than you . . . not so . . . tall . . . or dark . . .' She paused as she assessed my eyes and continued more slowly, 'His *eyes* . . . are not so . . . so . . . gorg— umm, brown, either.' She gave a shaky, high-pitched laugh. Her blush had progressively deepened during the course of her last sentence. 'My Nathan . . . his eyes are blue . . . he's six! And Tom is three.'

I checked, and I definitely hadn't been using my charm. I *was* in control of that power.

The petite woman now walked determinedly forward and held out her hand. I tried to place her age, but found it surprisingly difficult. Perhaps late thirties? Standing at five foot, she had short, white-blonde hair. I thought what an unusual hue of grey her eyes were. Much lighter than James' grey eyes.

'Nathaniel Gray – I am Heather, Rowan's aunt. I'm not sure you should be allowed on the roads!' Clearly my 'formidable' first impression had not been wrong.

'*Aunty Hetty!*' Rowan exclaimed. 'It was an *accident.*'

I took the hand that had been raised to me for the handshake. As she held my own, she looked at me with eyebrows raised – perhaps in surprise? I wasn't sure. I looked away. I was disconcerted. I had a distinct sensation this woman knew what I was. Was this paranoia? I could think of nothing which would have given me away. 'It is my pleasure to meet you.' I managed to keep the concern out of my voice.

She proceeded to ask, with a deadpan face, 'I am really *intrigued* – do you have *many* accidents?'

This could be innocent enough, but something definitely didn't feel right. My instinct was on alert. Now *was* the time to use the charm. We tend to limit its use. There is little or no satisfaction to be gained from obtaining a goal through using it. Neither could engaging it be considered honourable. But we did possess it for a reason. I knew my voice would be particularly silky, my eyes particularly attractive and hypnotic to their recipient. 'No, Ms . . .?'

'You may call me Heather.'

I inclined my head. With the charm engaged, I said, 'No, Heather – I am pleased to say I do not. But that does not make what I did to Rowan any better. I am mortified for having caused her injury and pain.' Subliminally, I was reassuring her as to the perfectly normal human event the accident had been, and reiterating my human credentials.

But I didn't quite get the reaction I expected. Instead, she smiled – *could it have been knowingly?* – before moving away towards Rowan.

Rowan's Aunty Hetty was a concern. Some humans do not respond to our charm, but they are few and far between. With everything that had happened, this was beyond coincidence.

I dragged myself away from my disturbing contemplations. I would reflect later. I reached the reluctant conclusion, however, that the arrival of Rowan's family necessitated the end of my own visit; it would be deemed rude to stay longer. I must make my excuses and go.

My eyes met again with Rowan's. 'I will not keep you from your family. Thank you for forgiving me.'

Her eyes were mischievous, imp-like. 'Who said anything about forgiving?'

Rowan Locke was a challenge. It appeared I liked challenges. Continuing to hold her gaze, I smiled wryly. 'I find myself needing to apologise, yet again.' Lost in Rowan's eyes, it was several moments before I was able to continue. 'If you could find it in your heart to forgive, it would be . . .'

The intensity of the moment was broken by Clare's laugh. It brought me more to my senses.

'Don't push your luck!' Clare warned, with humour in her voice. 'There must be something about you . . . not that I can possibly imagine what! Rowan's temper is *notorious*. I'm amazed you're getting out of this room in one piece!'

Heather raised her eyebrows and appeared to give a sardonic smile, unnerving me further. But I said quietly, whilst looking at Rowan, 'I believe I have already experienced her temper.'

She blushed and looked away quickly.

'And you came back for more?' Clare continued. 'Blimey! Thank you, by the way, for making sure she got to the hospital safely. She had quite a night, what with that . . . that . . . *monster!* A corporate get-together, my arse! He should be hung, drawn and quartered! And to think he sent her flowers . . . If I ever get my hands on him . . .!'

I observed Heather blanch. She momentarily met my eyes, before looking away. Rowan shot a warning look at her sister and I could feel her discomfort and anguish. That feeling of hatred was beginning to rise. *It wasn't me!* That feeling had been felt towards *another* monster. The mysterious 'S'? And if I wasn't sorely mistaken, *he* was the cause of Rowan's nightmares.

She didn't hate me! But my inordinate relief was immediately replaced by other sensations. I felt my own anger – no fury – begin to rise. I realised

I would be highly interested in getting my *own* hands on that other monster.

I clutched hold of the window frame within my grasp. I needed the physical support to deal with Rowan's response. And I took a few moments to stop imagining what I wanted to do to 'S'. It would be more appropriate to explore those options when I knew who he was – and where he lived. There was no doubt, however, that my protective instincts towards Rowan Locke were fully engaged. It was definitely time to go.

As soon as I could function, I stated, 'I really must take my leave.' Making myself walk towards the door, I looked fleetingly at Rowan, before saying gently and regretfully, 'Goodbye, Rowan.' It was all I could trust myself to say. I nodded to Clare and Heather.

'Nate!' Rowan called out as I reached the door.

I paused and looked towards her. The expression on her face was as mixed up as her emotions but . . . yes. As she watched me about to leave, I could identify that one; she was sad about something. Which I didn't like one little bit. I never wanted Rowan Locke to be sad.

Finally, she said, '*My* car, Nate. *My* car.'

The edges of my mouth rose slightly and I bowed my head in acknowledgement. And for the moment, I walked away from Rowan Locke. And it hurt like hell.

CHAPTER 4

THE DECLARATION

'I should not be doing this,' I muttered, plucking another white rose, removing its thorns with my fingertips so they couldn't damage their intended recipient, and adding it to the not inconsiderable pile resting in the crook of my left arm. I looked around the rose garden to find another prime specimen. My choice was restricted to the early flowering varieties, but I wanted white.

'I should not have gone to see her,' I continued, this time in my head in case I was overheard, and scooped down to pick my latest selection. 'She is human, for God's sake . . . and is torturing me . . . and her Aunty Hetty is more than disturbing me. I should be settling in Australia. Not . . . not . . .'

I fell to my knees as the latest onslaught of emotions seared through me. *Damn! How the hell was I going to do this?*

All James had been able to do was shake his head at me the whole way back from the hospital. 'Do not dare say "I told you so!"' I had hissed, and he had simply carried on shaking his head.

'I'm out of your head for the rest of the day,' he

had declared, on our arrival back at Ridings an hour ago. 'I can't take it, I really can't. I didn't think it could get worse but all the angst is now mingled with stuff that belongs in one of Elizabeth's God-awful girlie flicks. I tell you, you really should consider a future in writing horror targeted at vampires – you've got the formula spot on! You've actually managed to turn my stomach. If I could vomit, I would.

'But I'll buy you some time. I will keep the others out of both of our heads for the day. It should give you a chance to pull yourself together and come to a sensible decision. That way, they won't even need to get the tiniest whiff of what you're currently thinking. Because, Nate, believe me, hysterics wouldn't even go there!'

'I refuse to think about all the problems,' I muttered, taking myself and the flowers through the French doors into the study. Laying the flowers on my large mahogany Regency desk, I sat in the leather chair and took a piece of heavy, water-marked writing paper from the drawer. I had called the courier. Now all I needed was a note to accompany the flowers that would soon be on their way to the hospital.

'I am definitely not going to think about the tort—' I squealed as the latest sensations, courtesy of Rowan Locke, rocked through me.

Why the bloody hell was she so angry? No, furious! Oh, dear God! What the hell was I thinking? I had no way of coping with this!

I clutched my head in my hands and attempted to ride it out, but on reflection, decided banging my head against the desk was more effective – at least then I had control over something, albeit my repetitive head movements. I thought of wild animals in a zoo, exhibiting repetitive behaviour, stressed due to their confinement; their torture was simply different.

As it ebbed, I realised a rethink was in order. Could this truly be worth it? But then I remembered her eyes and her grin and the wonderful sensations I had earlier felt in her presence. I needed to feel that way again. My head piped up: *there is no way of knowing she will ever agree to see you.* But I had to try.

Taking a deep breath for fortification, I reached out for my fountain pen, whilst trying to discover where the sheet of writing paper had gone. Unclenching my right fist to pick up the pen, I found the missing paper crumpled up into the tiniest ball within.

If only she could learn to control her emotions, it would all be so much easier.

Before talking myself out of it, I retrieved another sheet of paper and wrote:

Dearest Rowan,

I know not whether these are to your taste, so when you are back on your feet, I would be most honoured if you would consider making your own selection from the Rose Garden at Ridings.

   PLEASE find it within your heart to forgive me.

Nate
(Nathaniel Gray – the idiot who ran you off the road)

Putting the pen down, I acknowledged this was not remotely a sensible course of action . . . and there was going to be hell to pay with regards to the others. I frowned at the realisation: I was going to have to tell them my intentions. It was only fair they had a chance to distance themselves from the exposure risks.

   Folding the letter up, placing it in an envelope, and scooping up the flowers, I made my way back out across the extensive gardens to the west of the main house. Even in my current state, I could still appreciate the beauty of Ridings. It was for that reason I had changed little since becoming its master in 1809. As I looked now at the grand Georgian façades, added by my grandfather in the 1760s during his extensive programme of modernisation, and the pinnacled Elizabethan towers, I couldn't help but wonder . . . would Rowan accept my invitation? Turning to take in the classical gardens, the lake and Lancelot 'Capability' Brown parkland as far as the eye could see . . . *Would it meet with her approval?* I utilised some speed, hoping to dispel the disconcerting satisfaction I felt at the thought of Rowan at Ridings.

I passed Elizabeth and Frederick's marital home – one of two dower houses on the estate, the other being occupied by Madeleine. And frowned. Some one-hundred-and-sixty-five years after the event, I still didn't like the fact that Elizabeth had moved out of the main house. What was mine was hers, no matter the traditional laws of succession. Yet she had been adamant – insisting it was time, and that she had always loved the 'dolls' house' appearance of the six-bedroomed Queen Anne property. We all valued our privacy, I more than most . . . but I still didn't have to like her decision.

I was at the gatehouse, at the end of the eight-mile approach to the house, in plenty of time to meet the courier. I could hear him talking through his headpiece, three miles away.

Once the flowers were safely en route, I had time to kill. I wanted to go riding, but couldn't risk it during Rowan Locke's conscious moments. Although I couldn't hurt myself, my constant falling off would no doubt unsettle my mare, Bess. I had not fallen from her for one-hundred-and-ninety-five years.

Neither did I have a hope of concentrating on reading. As for business . . . My current interests: the running of Gray Portfolio, Gray Investments' property arm – or at least its strategic running – and my occasional but highly lucrative trading within the art world, would have to wait until I

69

was feeling less traumatised by events. I would lie down. That's what I would do. It was definitely the best position to be in whilst Rowan's emotions were raging through me.

And then tonight, when she was asleep and I was that bit more in control of myself, I would confess.

Rowan had fallen into a deep, probably drug-aided sleep early, not making it past 8.18 p.m., and I had taken the opportunity to sleep, too. Not that I needed much, only a few hours every three or four days, but I welcomed the oblivion it offered me. As usual, I was ravenous on waking, so had visited the estate farm.

It was now 11.30 p.m., and I realised I couldn't continue sitting in my study's fireside chair, staring into the flames. I was putting off what needed to be done. In any event, whereas the fire could warm my otherwise cold limbs, in much the same way as the intake of fresh blood, it was failing to warm my entire being from the inside out. Nothing had ever warmed me like Rowan Locke. Her touch, her look, her playfulness. Only she made me feel alive.

I sighed and started to make my way to the drawing room. Everyone was gathered there, no doubt talking about me – again. For that reason, I refused to dip into their heads or listen to their voices.

The strange calm I had been experiencing, having

committed myself to a course of action, most likely the wrong one, but a course none the less, was rapidly being replaced with trepidation.

I took a deep breath and pushed open the door. The atmosphere in the room was sombre. The music Elizabeth was playing on the fine grand piano, melancholy. I knew they were worried about me; they were about to get more so. Without as much as making eye contact with any one of them, I addressed the room, before I lost my nerve.

'It is far from easy to keep a secret among us, so I am holding my hands up now. This is difficult for me, so please do not interrupt. Please do not snarl or growl at me. Please do not roar at me.'

I ignored James' hissed, 'Shit!' and frantic rants in my head.

'Having reflected, I have reached the indisputable conclusion, I do not wish to run away from Rowan Locke – but quite the opposite. Indeed, if she is amenable, I wish to spend some time with her.

'In her company today, I felt alive – more alive than I felt even when I was alive. I did not think it was possible to ever feel that way. Do not ask me to explain the logic. There is none. I know it has no future, that I am being irresponsible – but perhaps I have been responsible too long. I have no idea why the accident happened, or why we have this connection, but without it, I would not have had the pleasure of being introduced to Rowan Locke.

'I am being open and honest with you because of the exposure risks, but this is something I need to do. I understand if you wish to distance your-selves from me. Whatever you think, I ask for some privacy, so I have a hope of dealing with this issue in the most appropriate manner. I also require vows from you all, that you will not take matters into your own hands and . . . *eliminate* her.'

I had said it. In fact I had said it to the large eighteenth-century Aubusson rug, upon the floor in front of the fire. But now I let myself look around for the first time. The room contained three stunned vampires – and James. I would deal with him first.

With arms crossed, slowly shaking his head, he was leaning against the window frame with one foot resting against the wall. At an inch shorter than me, he stood at just over six foot. His short blond hair, grey eyes and slight build were as different from my own dark unruly hair, brown eyes and more athletic build, as were our person-alities. Two years shy of my thirty-five mortal years, he had always looked younger. I scrubbed my face with my hand whilst waiting for him to speak. He was as much in need of a shave as I.

He met my look, shook his head and sighed. 'What are we going to do with you? I'm currently resisting the very strong urge to flee, because the moment they un-drop their jaws and start blinking again . . . Believe me, going home to listen to some very loud music, whilst interacting within the far more reassuring world of the Playstation, has never sounded more appealing. But the sick part of me wants to hang around and watch. Because, Nate – you're so for it!'

'*Oh. My. God!*'

I turned to look at Elizabeth, whose whispered utterance had sounded. She was before the piano on a double stool, Frederick at her side.

'You were warned . . .' James muttered.

Elizabeth's soft brown eyes were now focusing on me, staring in incredulous disbelief.

I heard a sigh and spared a glance to her left.

Frederick was shaking his golden-haired head dramatically. 'Just how much more bizarre are things going to get around here?' he demanded. 'And just how the blazes are we meant to deal with this one? Short of chaining him somewhere, that is!' He gave Elizabeth's hand a gentle squeeze before standing up and raising his arms above his head in a full body stretch. Wearing hipster jeans and a designer torn t-shirt, it was hard to imagine him as he had once been – a distinguished twenty-six-year-old cavalry officer who had fought at the Battle of Waterloo.

'Right, I need a drink,' he announced.

'You fed this afternoon. You can't be hungry all ready,' James exclaimed.

'No, a drink, drink. A real drink.'

'We don't drink, drink, Freddie. You know it doesn't work.'

'I know. But I'm struggling to get my head around

all this conventionally. The way ahead always used to be so much clearer after a drink . . . Nothing's as it was, so you never know. Tell me the idea of getting foxed doesn't currently appeal?' James shook his head, conceding the point. Frederick continued, 'It's got to be worth a try. Quantity, I'm thinking . . . Anyway, why continue to waste a cellar full of priceless vintage claret?' Turning to look at me. 'You've no objections?'

I slowly shook my head.

Elizabeth had still to speak further, so my attention turned to Madeleine on the sofa. She was opening and shutting her mouth, seemingly unable to choose the words she wanted to unleash. It was, however, highly evident she wanted to unleash.

'Bring me a glass, too,' she finally choked out.

'A glass? I'm going straight from the bottle, Mads.'

'Bring me a bottle then.'

The moment Freddie had left the room, Madeleine was out of her seat and right before James. The top of her elegant blonde-bobbed head reached his shoulders. She started to prod her index finger in his chest and proceeded to snarl, 'You! This is *your* fault!'

'*Me? Me?* Just how is this, *my* fault? Do you see *me* chasing after a mortal girl who tortures me – and I'd happily drink dry given half a chance?'

I cringed.

'Hey? Do you? No . . . You see muggins here, charged with the bloody impossible, and where's the appreciation?' Emitting a low growl, he continued, 'Stop prodding me, Madeleine. I'm *really* not in the mood for this!'

She hissed, 'You were charged with, at the very least, getting him to the other side of the world. Instead, you take him to her BEDSIDE! All.' Prod. 'Your.' Prod. 'Fault!' Double prod.

It was my turn to now openly gape. I had never before seen Madeleine anything but calm. She had chosen to join us shortly after Frederick – the two of them having formed a close kinship in the decades before. Since her arrival in 1847, she had kept harmony amongst us, always mediating between James and myself, always the voice of reason. Now . . .? I knew it was down to her being worried and because she had no answers as to why our normal existence had been breached. But it wasn't right that their existence should be turned upside down, too . . .

'What did I tell you?' James relayed silently, whilst his audible growl grew louder as Madeleine continued to prod. He continued silently, 'Why am *I* getting the damned prodding? But I know what's going on in your head. Yes, normality has been breached. And yes, it's affecting us all. But we will *not* let you do this alone.'

Madeleine clearly hadn't finished. 'Do you have *any* idea how serious this is? And this afternoon: *Leave him be. Stay out of his head. Give him time.* Look what the result of that is!'

It was time to intervene. I was actually feeling

sorry for James. Things really were so far from normal. 'Madeleine . . .'

'Enough from you!' she snapped, still refusing to lose eye contact with James. 'There is no hope of anything sensible coming out of your mouth at the moment. That is why someone responsible . . .' she continued to prod '. . . was meant to take care of things. I should have known.' Finally turning her round, hazel-eyed, twenty-something face to me, prompting a relieved sigh from James, she spoke gently, 'You are sick. Hence you reaching such a ridiculous decision. You need help. You should have been physically bundled on to that jet before matters got any worse and left us to sort things out.'

My eyes flashed. 'I would have liked to see you try!'

Walking back into the room, with a couple of cases of wine stacked one on top of the other and . . . a *sword* tucked under his arm, Frederick casually reflected, 'Whose to know what normal is any more?'

Depositing the boxes and sword on the Chippendale sideboard nearest the door, he repositioned himself between Madeleine and me. Draping his arms over our shoulders, he said, 'Calm. We need calm. Nate has dropped a bit of a bombshell, but—'

'But he has my support,' Elizabeth interrupted, from her still-sitting position.

'*What?*' Madeleine hissed in disbelief, pivoting around to face her.

I met Elizabeth's eyes. *I love you, sweetheart.*

Smiling meekly back, she continued, 'I'm worried. Very worried. I would prefer another course of action. But I have to respect his decision. Having known him all of my lives, I know he won't have taken it lightly. I've never known him to make a wrong decision. Ever. And if he believes this is the way to get through his current problems, that it's worth going through the pain, for the pleasure of being in this woman's company, then . . . I will do all I can to help him through it. In any event, we haven't a cat in hell's chance of changing his mind!'

Frederick moved back over to Elizabeth, wrapped his hands into her long, wavy brunette hair, and kissed her. He was clearly reluctant to pull away, but finally said, 'Well, the wife's spoken. Seconded. You guys can fight it out amongst yourselves. I'm having a drink!' With that, he gave Elizabeth another quick kiss before moving to the sideboard.

'Has everyone gone stark raving mad around here?' Madeleine shrieked, looking from one to the other of us and waving her hands around in the air. 'Is there something in the blood? Has someone checked the pigs out recently?'

James chuckled. 'Yeah – Mad Pig Disease!'

Madeleine turned to glower at him.

'Is everyone forgetting just how remotely not normal everything is here? And Nathaniel, in his emotionally befuddled, damaged state, is actively seeking out the *culprit*? Is it only me that can see the danger here? I mean – even members of her family are charm-immune! We have to talk some sense into him before—'

'I've tried, Mads,' James interrupted. 'But he really isn't listening. And you know he's never "done" listening.'

A determined look crossed Madeleine's face. 'So how will you feel when you kill her, Nate?' The pain – *my* pain – soared through me. I sank into the nearest chair. I desperately tried to dispel the image of Rowan, lifeless, drained of blood.

'I'm sorry, love,' she quickly added, 'I really am. But can't you see I'm desperate here. You—'

'He resisted it that night, Mads, despite everything that was going on,' James generously interceded. 'There was a moment there when I thought I'd have to enter the fray but he conquered it. In his shoes, I'm not sure I would have had the strength. And at the hospital it wasn't the same. He's pre-warned so—'

'Everyone *has* gone mad! I'm not joking. Seriously not joking! I'm calling the vet tomorrow to get the pigs checked out. I've been on badgers the last few days and—'

'It's *not* the pigs, Mads,' James countered. 'We know you're worried. And we know you're right. But he's made up his mind and there's no reasoning with him. He's going to do this, with or without us. As Freddie said, short of chaining him – and chains wouldn't hold him, anyway – there's nothing we can do to stop him.'

Madeleine now approached and knelt by my side. Putting her hand gently on my knee, she pleaded, 'Please, Nate. You have no idea how painful a journey you're embarking upon. She is mortal and there can never be a happy ending. And all this, when you have *no* emotional protection. I've loved and lost, as you well know. At a time I, too, had no protection. And I would never wish it on anyone.'

I knew why she was doing this. As a seventeenth-century human, Madeleine had had to bury the love of her life, and then her two young children three weeks later, and despite subsequently having the power for four hundred years, she had still to recover from it. But I had made up my mind. I couldn't think about the pain. I couldn't think about the bigger picture. All I knew was an insatiable need to spend time with Rowan Locke, and to keep her safe.

'You can't forgive a girl for trying.' She smiled sorrowfully as she read my thoughts and conceded defeat. I shook my head and put my hand over hers. 'Very well,' she now said, matter-of-factly and evidently fully utilising the power. Standing up, she continued calmly, 'I suppose we'd better get on with business, then. There will be no ditching us. In fact, you are going to let us help you get through this.' She looked at me questioningly, and on seeing my slow nod, declared, 'Good! We'll run through the file I've got on Rowan Locke, then.'

Bugger! I should have known they had been doing

their own investigations into things, but even I hadn't expected them to have been quite so efficient. I wasn't ready for this. 'I need to check on Bess, she—'

'No, you don't!' Madeleine asserted, picking up a brown manila file from the sofa table, before taking it with her to the floor in front of the fire. 'With the concessions being made here and the impact they could have on us all, listening to this is the least you can do.'

I looked anxiously at the file, now laid out before her cross-legged form. She must have put a call into Richard Morley after the accident, and he had no doubt put a private detective on the case. Although I wanted to know everything there was to know about Rowan, I didn't want it to be this way. I wanted to find things out for myself. But whether I liked it or not, nothing was remotely normal about recent happenings and we needed answers.

But . . . *what if there were things I didn't want to hear?*

Elizabeth gave me a quick hug before moving hand-in-hand with Frederick to sit next to Madeleine.

I thought of how this information would have been gained. I didn't like the idea of a private investigator hovering around Rowan. Indeed, I didn't like the idea of anyone but myself hovering around her. I couldn't stop my heart pounding. One beat a minute? I had just counted ten beats in that many seconds.

I thought of what I already knew about Rowan and it comprised pretty much the little snippets I had gained when in the hospital. I *had* noticed she had not been wearing a wedding-band, but that didn't mean much nowadays.

I tried to prepare myself for the fact she may be attached, but the very thought of it made me feel . . . *nauseous?* No matter – he didn't deserve her. I would never have let her drive one-hundred-and-seventy miles alone at 2 a.m.

I found myself out of my seat and nervously pacing up and down. I stopped, aware I was being watched in disbelief by everyone in the room. Such movements were out of character, I conceded.

Madeleine sighed. 'I'll put you out of your anguish straight away, Nate – Rowan Locke is currently single.'

I shut my eyes for a moment and exhaled air I hadn't realised I had been holding in my lungs. I allowed my jaw to relax and quickly ran my hand through my hair.

Madeleine was concerned again. 'But you know there can be no future here? She's mortal . . .'

Had I not made that perfectly clear? 'Madeleine—'

But James interrupted. 'You know humans and vampires aren't *completely* incompatible, Mads?'

The innuendo in his voice left us in no doubt as to what he was referring.

I looked at him aghast. In fact, we all looked at him aghast, although Madeleine's look was mingled with fury.

'Don't look at me like that! You didn't think I'd only feel *blood*lust when I was a vampire, did you? Believe me, we are still *very* compatible!'

We were all speechless.

'Come on! There's a shortage of vampire women around. I still have a man's needs and . . . okay – I wish I hadn't opened my mouth . . . particularly in mixed company.'

James looked shamefaced at the countenances of Elizabeth and Madeleine. He furtively sneaked a glance at my face, set like stone. *How could he have been so irresponsible? So reckless?*

Frederick recovered first. He looked confused and asked in a hushed voice, 'But how can you not damage the human?'

'It's just a matter of control. Look!' James leapt up from the sofa and picked up a marble paper-weight from the nearest table. 'We all know I can crumble this piece of stone into dust – but I'm picking it up and I'm not. Just because I have the strength to break it, doesn't mean I do. Even as a human, I had the strength to hurt a woman – but in the act, even when I may have got a bit overexcited, I never hurt her. It's all about control.'

Elizabeth spoke with feeling, 'But the thirst for blood. Surely in the act you can feel it?'

'You just feed well before. You didn't honestly think my feeding on animals would be enough to satisfy my carnal desires? That's just nourishment. Black pudding or fauna stew simply don't hit the right spots!'

Disgusted sounds emitted from around the room.

'I still have sexual desires towards human women. They're generally separate to the bloodlust. Come on! We all know we are more extreme versions of what we were before.' He shot a rapid glance in my direction. 'Up until a couple of days ago, that is. And I simply have never abstained!'

Madeleine spoke in an ominously quiet voice, 'You have stooped to depths I never thought imaginable. How close have you come to *killing* a human woman?'

There was an awkward silence from James before he sighed. 'There have been moments . . . but I've *never* hurt a woman. There's enough warning to know if things are going to turn . . .' He took a deep breath and continued clinically, whilst inspecting his finger nails, 'The closest it's got is my having to use my charm on one or two occasions after my fangs have accidentally popped out.'

'*Jesus Christ!*' I snarled through clenched teeth.

'Come on! Birds and the bees, Nate! I thought it was an appropriate time to have this chat!'

I didn't trust myself to reply. I was barely in control of a fury I had rarely, if ever, felt. I couldn't believe I had entrusted him to take Rowan to the hospital. And then I remembered he thought she was pretty. That was too much. I was going to tear him limb from limb.

I roared and launched myself at James, only to

be thwarted by Frederick, who had anticipated my move and placed himself between us.

'Move, Frederick – NOW!' I roared, snapping at James over his right shoulder.

James looked horrified as he replied to my thoughts, 'You can't possibly believe I'd have— *Jesus!* As for the *pretty* thought . . . Look, I find Elizabeth and Mads pretty, but I've never acted on it . . .'

Frederick growled now.

'I suggest you shut up, James,' Madeleine warned. 'I'm half-tempted to ask Freddie to stand aside as it is – or let them both at you.'

Elizabeth approached me slowly and gently touched my arm. It would not be appropriate to do this in front of her. And in any event, my 'killer instinct' moment was receding to a 'damage to maim' moment, which wouldn't be remotely as satisfying. 'I am going for a ride,' I growled, before launching myself out of the open French doors to find Bess.

CHAPTER 5

ROWAN LOCKE

Returning to the room four hours later, I fixed James with a look that would have left him in no doubt as to the sincerity of the utterances I then spoke. 'Never talk to me about your carnal activities again. And if I even get a whiff of that *pretty* thought of yours, know that I will personally castrate you.'

James knew it not to be an empty threat. We can tear each other to pieces, whilst being physically invulnerable to everything else. I watched him cross his legs.

'Believe it or not, I just wanted to give you hope and—'

I interrupted him to snarl, 'It can *never* be a possibility.' *How could Rowan ever think of me in those terms – and how could I ever put her safety at such risk?*

'Enough!' Madeleine proclaimed from the sofa, whilst she finished painting the last of her perfectly manicured nails. I couldn't recall her ever having used that particular shade of nail polish before. She put the brush back in the clear bottle, with its blood-red contents, did up its top and popped it back in her handbag, before returning to the paperwork laid out on the rug. 'There have been enough interruptions,' she said, before blowing on her nails and waving her hands around in the air. 'We all need to be prepared here. Particularly as I've just received the latest report.' She looked up to meet my eyes. 'Nathaniel, bless him, has invited Rowan to visit.'

There was silence. *Damn. This private detective was good.*

'Luckily, the investigator picked up on it when he scooted around her hospital room and spotted Nate's note and *flowers.*'

He had been in her hospital room?

'*Flowers?*' Elizabeth exclaimed incredulously, before beaming. 'That's *so sweet,* Nate! And you've *never* invited a woman to Ridings, even before we changed. I can't wait to meet her!'

Frederick, with a bottle of 1794 claret in hand, chuckled. 'I don't think you've really thought this one through, have you, bruv? The estate is overrun by vampires . . . and if *that* isn't bad enough . . . one of them is desperate to welcome her as a sister, and James here will no doubt want to jump her bones!'

'*Shit!*' James muttered.

My furious glare resulted in a more nervous chuckle from Frederick, but his fading smile was wiped off his face completely when Elizabeth provided a hard jab of her elbow to his stomach.

It was true though. *What the hell had I been*

thinking? I just couldn't help but picture Rowan at Ridings.

'Okay . . . I'm continuing whatever here,' Madeleine stated impatiently. 'Rowan Locke: Born April twenty-ninth, 1977.'

'April twenty-ninth? Nate's human birthday!' Elizabeth exclaimed.

'Spoooookyyyyy,' Frederick teased, and promptly got another elbow jab.

'She would appear to have been adopted as a young baby.'

So *that* was why I couldn't identify physical similarities between Rowan and her sister.

'Her adoptive parents were Rosie Fairchild and Seth Locke . . .'

She paused, and I prompted, 'Madeleine?' Now she had started, I was desperate to find out more.

'No, it's just I knew of a Seth Locke . . .'

'There will have been a lot of Seth Lockes in the world, Mads,' Frederick said as they shared a look.

'Yeah, I know,' she said, returning her focus to the pages in front of her. 'Point taken. Anyway, there isn't much on them at the moment but I'll look into things a bit more.' She proceeded quietly, 'Rowan was orphaned at the age of six.'

I shut my eyes against the pain and vulnerability of being mortal.

Elizabeth whispered, 'How?'

Madeleine scanned the file. 'He's going to do some more on that because it looks suspicious.

There was some kind of house fire. One news-paper report stated: Rowan and her adoptive sister Clare, then aged four, were found barricaded in a locked cellar beneath the house by fire-fighters. They had been alerted by Clare's cries for her mummy and daddy. When found, Rowan was apparently desperately trying to keep her sister quiet, because her daddy had said they were playing a game that meant they had to be as quiet as mice.'

'No wonder her emotions are tortuous,' James muttered.

And no wonder they were so overwhelming, I reflected, pinching the top of my nose. This girl had been through so much. She was a tortured soul. Any emotional response to a stimulus in the current day must be determined by her history. And the *grief*?

'Her aunt, Heather Fairchild, aka Aunty Hetty – who there's more on later, for obvious reasons – took in Rowan and Clare and brought them up. The little sister, Clare, is married to Mark Robinson and has . . .'

'Two little boys, Nathan and Tom, aged six and three. I know – I met Clare at the hospital.' I smiled at the memory.

'Rowan went to primary and secondary schools in London, having moved from her first school in Wiltshire after the death of her parents. She looks to have been a straight-A student: A grade A-Levels in English Literature, Art and History. She went on to study English Literature at Cardiff University, where she got a First Class BA honours degree.' I smiled. She must love books, too. 'She's had a number of boyfriends . . .'

'Can we skip this?' I pleaded quickly and silently, my jaw set hard.

Madeleine skim read the information before her, which I deliberately didn't seek to read in her head, before saying, 'You should know about Jonathan Martin. They met at university and lived together. They were originally an item for three years, broke up for a couple of years, before getting back together again. They were engaged with a wedding-date set when they broke up the last time in 2007 . . .'

How could he have ever let her go?

'It would appear he had a fling with her house-mate . . . who was then her best friend, and due to be her bridesmaid.'

Both Elizabeth and I growled in unison, before sharing . . . was it a *comradely grin*? It *felt* good.

'He lives in London and, up until yesterday, worked as an environmental scientist. However, at 3 p.m. yesterday afternoon he abruptly walked out on that job, paying no heed to notice requirements. He announced he was taking up a position in property investment at Frey Investments.'

'Quite a career change,' Frederick observed. 'And in quite a manner. Frey Investments must have made it worth his while.'

Small world despite the number of people within

it, I pondered. I knew of Frey Investments, due to Gray Portfolio.

'The reason I'm telling you all this, is because the investigator says he is still sniffing around. He visited Rowan in hospital late this afternoon and declared his undying love for her.'

Good God!

'Apparently, her close shave with death has made him realise he can't possibly live without her. It's noted here, he seemed to be *quite aggressive in his assertions*, whatever that means.'

I was experiencing a strong urge to do Jonathan Martin harm. He was in no way good enough for her. And what the hell did *'aggressive in his assertions'* mean?

It took me a long time to remove violence from my thoughts and to refocus. I had to ask the question I was terrified of hearing the answer to. 'Does he say what Rowan's response was?' My voice was quieter than a human whisper.

'Sorry, of course he does! I quote, "Said very loudly (bordering on a scream) 'Eff off you pitiful excuse for a human being! If I ever set eyes on you again, I'll not be responsible for my actions!' She threw her full water jug at him before he was escorted from the room by medical personnel."'

Both James and I chuckled. There was no doubt he was investigating the right girl. I found myself beaming with pride in her and experiencing such overwhelming relief, I laughed out loud. I was being stared at again.

'I don't know how this human investigator gets all this stuff,' Frederick said, clearly impressed, whilst slowly removing his astounded gaze from me.

'So this encounter happened this afternoon?' I asked Madeleine.

'A few hours before your flowers arrived.'

That explained the crippling rush of anger and rage I had experienced, when writing her note.

'She's *exactly* what Nate needs!' Elizabeth cried delightedly. I looked at my sister incredulously. 'You may be my brother . . . but sometimes you can be *so* disagreeable. You definitely need to be put in your place. This could actually be fun! *Promise* me, you'll let me meet her?' I shook my head in disbelief. True sadness entered her voice. 'If it wasn't for the fact she causes you pain . . . and she's human, she would be *perfect*!' Smiling, she forced herself to sound more upbeat, 'Oh well, day by day.'

Meeting her eyes now, I smiled gently. 'I am not sure she will even see me.'

'Oh! She will!' she declared confidently, with a huge grin on her face. 'I've seen how human women react to you – how they've *always* reacted to you, actually. Just remember, even with your human cloak on, your pupils go really big and black when you're angry – they always have done – and they used to scare little old mortal me. But when you are content, your eyes are a gorgeous soft brown. I don't think I *ever* remember them sparkling like they did a moment ago when you laughed, though. You should laugh more often. You should prepare, too . . . perhaps practice some small-talk!'

I groaned and she giggled.

'He didn't do too badly at the hospital, Elizabeth. At one stage it sounded pretty flirtatious to me,' James interjected quietly.

Had it? I glanced cautiously at James.

'Yes, Nate – you obviously have hidden depths. And yes – I'd say she was responding.'

'*Yessss!*' Elizabeth squealed in delight. And I had no control over the warm glow that started somewhere around my heart.

So James *had* been listening in at the hospital. *Damn.*

Silently, he relayed, 'I was worried – and still am.'

Looking in his direction, I let him off the hook with a quick nod of my head.

Madeleine looked at me apologetically now, before saying, 'I have to offer, although I think I can guess the answer . . . Do you want me to try and get inside her head?'

I shook my head quickly.

'But I could find out so much. We could then know for sure, if she's an innocent in all this.'

'Thank you, but it would not be right.'

Madeleine, perhaps due to her superior age, could read the thoughts of humans as well as fellow vampires, but the process was painful for both

92

parties. I couldn't have Rowan hurt. 'Besides, I *know* she has no idea what she is doing to me.' I was sure of that.

'Fine – but what about the blessed aunt?'

Now Rowan's Aunty Hetty was another matter. I grinned, and nodded. 'But let us wait to see what we can find out first. What has he managed to come up with?'

'We have an address, not far from Rowan's in London. But he needs to do some more digging. He . . . possibly got a little *confused* here.'

I raised my eyebrows and Madeleine acknowledged my query with a nod. 'Yeah I know. It could be innocent enough, but he's been dropping me emails with information over the last couple of days, including some stuff about her being arrested in the 1980s for her Greenpeace and CND activities. But when it got to the report itself, which was sent through tonight, he stated he'd been unable to find anything on her at all. After James' tip-off regarding your hospital encounter, he was planning on visiting her home this afternoon. I would have expected stuff *on top* of what he'd already provided.'

'Fishy,' Frederick muttered, summing up my thoughts exactly. 'And he doesn't strike me as the sort of character to get confused.'

'We'll get him to give her another go before revisiting things.' Sighing, Madeleine continued, 'Back to Rowan . . . She currently works as an Account Director for a public relations firm in the

City – Dynamic PR. She now lives on her own, has a cat called Tinks, does her grocery shopping in Sainsbury's and regularly visits her sister on a Saturday in Wiltshire. She has near perfect human eyesight, but has some hearing loss and wears in-ear hearing aids.'

I hadn't noticed that at all. Again, I thought how hard it was to be mortal.

Madeleine started giggling as she read further. I read her thoughts and groaned. 'She is *vegetarian*?'

James snorted. 'Only you, Nate!'

Madeleine giggled again. 'She had an official caution from the police in 2007.'

'Go on . . .' I prompted, warily.

'For causing criminal damage to her former best friend's possessions. Apparently, before allowing her to reclaim items from the flat, she'd taken the opportunity to dye all of her clothes – from underwear through to cocktail dresses – scarlet, as it was more, quote, "in keeping with her status as a scarlet woman".'

'Nice one!' chuckled Frederick, discarding his empty wine bottle and reaching for the next. I watched bemused, whilst he picked up from the floor at his side the sword he'd earlier entered the room with. In one swift stroke he had opened the bottle by decapitating it at its neck. 'Although . . . you really aren't going to want to get on the wrong side of her, bruv.' He raised the bottle to his mouth and took a swig of wine.

'Your two temperaments are going to be an issue, Nate,' Elizabeth reflected. 'You are both Taureans.'

'Oh, for God's sake, Elizabeth!' I exclaimed. 'You have been into that ridiculous human mumbo jumbo since the 1960s!'

'Mark my words . . . stubborn, determined, possessive and *ferocious* temperaments. You could be in for some real humdingers!'

'Somehow, I think I have far more important things to worry about than the characteristics supposedly bestowed on us from our human birth dates!'

'Perhaps . . . but with James' latest revelations – the making-up could be fun!'

CHAPTER 6

HOMECOMING

I shut the boot of Elizabeth's Porsche Cayenne on our limited luggage, before holding the driver's door open for her to climb in. 'Thank you, sweetheart. I could not have faced the journey with James driving.'

We were heading to the London town house, kitted out with everything we both needed and liked to have around us, like so many of our properties around the world. I had to be near Rowan.

'Hell will freeze over before James drives me anywhere again,' I muttered, opening the driver's side passenger door, whilst Frederick climbed in next to Elizabeth and lobbed his jacket into the back.

'I heard that – and you think *my* driving's bad!'

I glared at James, now getting into my car, parked up alongside. Madeleine rolled her eyes at me from the passenger seat. It had seemed like much more of a hardship having to listen to James' begging than giving into his pleas to borrow the Mercedes McLaren SLR for a few weeks. I wasn't yet psychologically strong enough to drive any car, let alone that one, which had just come back from the

96

garage. Predictably, my braking foot *had* gone through the floor.

Pulling away, we rounded the corner and I grinned as we passed Rowan's newly repaired Morris Minor, abandoned on the gravel driveway. None of us had been prepared to drive it. Life, even as an immortal, was too short to travel nearly two hundred miles at a top speed of sixty-five miles per hour; I had arranged for one of the groundsmen to take it down later. If Rowan, who had left hospital yesterday, allowed me to return her car in person, then it would be the first time I had seen her since the hospital visit three days ago.

My grin rapidly turned to a grimace and I braced myself for the next onslaught, which I could feel coming my way. I met Frederick's concerned eyes.

'So she's not easing up any, then?'

I shook my head. I had spent the last few days working on my ability – or inability – to function during Rowan's conscious moments. It was getting easier, but not remotely easy enough, and negative emotions could still floor me. But staying away any longer was beyond me.

I couldn't begin to identify what she was currently feeling. It had been easier when I could see her and gather clues as to what was causing particular sensations, and *so much* easier when I had the diversionary pleasure of being captivated by those incredible eyes of hers. When combined with her smile and intoxicating scent . . . it was enough to leave me, a two-hundred-year-old vampire, pretty much gaga. Picturing her now in my mind's eye, the pleasure I felt at the image before me acted as a partial anaesthetic.

'No, Frederick!' I growled, catching an unguarded thought.

'You know, that really isn't a bad idea, Freddie!' Elizabeth exclaimed excitedly.

'I have *no* intention of subversively drugging her to lessen my own difficulties!'

'But you've been saying it's easier when she's on painkillers – and you think she's skipping them—'

My snarled, 'No!' interrupted Elizabeth. 'And both of you swear now, you will not take matters into your own hands!'

I accepted their grumbled assurances, neglecting to admit that the thought had already crossed my own mind when matters had got extreme. But it wasn't going to happen.

When Rowan became less emotive, I pulled myself up into a full sitting position and retrieved what I knew was going to be an issue from my inside pocket. I tentatively asked, 'Can we put this on?'

'What's on it?' Frederick asked, narrowing his eyes at me as he took the CD from my outstretched hand. I grinned. He really wasn't going to like it. It was a compilation I had retrieved from Rowan's car. 'Try it and find out,' I suggested, attempting a casual shrug of the shoulders.

Suspiciously, he inserted the disc into the dash

and Meat Loaf's 'I'd Do Anything For Love' blared out. I cringed, but his reaction was more vocal as he bellowed, 'For fuck's sake! It's not too late to put you in the car with James.' I had to agree. It was a far cry from my usual Beethoven . . . but it made me feel closer to Rowan.

Elizabeth laughed delightedly, and batted Frederick's hands away as he tried to remove it. 'I love this song! I haven't heard it in years.' She proceeded to pump up the volume and start singing along at the top of her voice, bopping her head around manically.

'I really appreciate this, Nathaniel,' Frederick snarled. 'So you've decided to share your torture now, have you? If you think we are having this playing all the way to London, you've another thing coming!'

'What else is on there?' Elizabeth cried.

'You will have to wait and see.' If I gave Frederick, most recently into heavy gothic rock, the heads-up that it included songs by Abba, Cat Stevens, Bonnie Tyler . . . and Take That, it would be out of the dash and through the window instantaneously. James' earlier reaction to those particular entries on the playlist had told me that much.

With each new mile we passed, I concluded Rowan was having a very frustrating day. Or at least I thought it was frustration. It was my best guess, and bearing in mind her mobility issues, it would fit. But I was far from the best person to identify emotion, having avoided it at all costs in

both my mortal and immortal forms. In acknowledgement of the fact, I had spent time in my library
attempting to learn more about the painful subject.
I shuddered as I recalled the re-familiarisation
exercise. It really hadn't provided the clarity and
comfort I had sought.

I had never considered it whilst mortal myself,
but evidently humans rarely feel one emotion
alone – being able to be generally sad, for example,
but then also furious about a particular incident.
It was never going to be simple, but it was discovering more than thirty emotions/feelings that
simply began with the letter A – before, that is, I
had slammed the books shut and fled, panicked,
from the library – that had put paid to the exercise. How could I hope to make any sense out of
them? And how on earth was I going to cope with
feeling them?

Rowan was, therefore, not the only one feeling
frustrated. And I was feeling particularly so today,
because I wasn't there to help her. I hated the
thought of her struggling up the stairs I had discovered on my reconnaissance a couple of nights ago.

We had reached the outskirts of London. Meatloaf
was playing for the fifth time thanks to Elizabeth,
and Frederick had stopped complaining. It hadn't
got him anywhere, and in the end his objections
had been half-hearted; the pleasure he was taking
in Elizabeth's enjoyment was plain to see.

I was lounging in the back of the car, trying to
decipher Rowan's feelings in more detail. A couple

of minutes ago she had become even more frustrated, I thought, and I wondered if it was also impatience that I was feeling? What was she doing to feel this way? Whatever it was, I wished she would stop, because it was causing me significant issues.

During my deliberations, she disappeared. There was no slipping away. She was just gone. My heart began to race. I checked my watch: 1.31 p.m. on a Saturday afternoon. Why would she be sleeping? Normally when she fell asleep, my connection with her gradually waned as she dozed into unconsciousness. Yet she had just gone from acute frustration . . . to nothingness.

'Elizabeth . . . Frederick.' There was undisguised panic in my voice.

Alarmed, they both turned to look at me.

'What time do you make it?' Perhaps she *had* fallen asleep. She had never fallen asleep in the afternoon, even when in hospital. But perhaps it wasn't the afternoon. Perhaps my watch had stopped . . .

'1.31 p.m.,' Frederick replied, tentatively. 'Why?' He fixed me with his piercing blue-eyed gaze.

'Something is wrong. She has gone! I don't think she is asleep, but she has gone!'

'Calm down – tell us what happened,' Elizabeth urged gently, turning the music off.

'She was really frustrated about something and then I just lost her! Something is wrong . . .' I let my panicked mind race through possibilities.

101

'What if she has fallen down the stairs and broken her neck? What if she is dead? Oh, dear God – something is very wrong!'

'Calm down. She's probably fallen asleep. Nothing bad has happened. We know Clare's staying with her . . . remember?'

Despite her words, Elizabeth put her foot down on the accelerator, and I caught her worried glance at Frederick.

'Nate, she'll be fine,' Frederick reassured.

'Elizabeth – pull over – I WILL DRIVE!' I couldn't help that it came out as a pained roar.

'You are in no fit state to drive, and I'm taking it to its limit!'

'Pull over then and let me fly!'

'It's broad daylight. You can't fly now!'

'Elizabeth – pull the damned car over – NOW!' I knew I was at my most intimidating.

Frederick twisted around to look at me again. 'Calm yourself down. If we hit traffic when we're further in – then you can fly.'

I knew this was a big concession. Flying in daylight over London was beyond foolhardy, but it still didn't satisfy me. I looked desperately out of the window to try and gauge where we were.

'We can be there in seven or eight minutes,' Elizabeth insisted. 'There's nothing you can do.'

'I will call her!' I desperately tried to find my new phone. 'I have not got my phone! Where is my phone? Frederick, give me your phone!'

'I'm not giving you my phone. You are in too

much of a state to talk to her. We'll be there in a few minutes and you can see for yourself she's okay.' He was sounding worried.

'FREDERICK – GIVE ME YOUR DAMNED PHONE – NOW!' I was not in control.

He looked at Elizabeth and she gave a slight nod. As soon as I had snatched it from him, I started putting the number in; it wasn't number '1' on Frederick's speed-dial. It took three attempts to get it into the tiny handset due to my shaking hands.

Rowan, pick up, please. Pick up, Rowan – Pick up!

'Christ Almighty! – voicemail!' My mind was racing. What could I do? 'Morley! Morley is based in London. Perhaps he can get someone over there!'

'Number five,' Frederick muttered. When I got through, it went straight to his messaging service.

I roared into the ridiculous piece of technology that was currently doing nothing to help me – or Rowan, 'DAMN IT! Where the hell are you? What the hell do we pay you for? This is an emergency! CALL ME BACK – *NOW!*'

She could be lying dying at the bottom of those stairs – because of me. She had broken her foot – because of me. I had killed her! I was beside myself. I had never known anything like it. *What would I do if she had died?*

I saw Elizabeth and Frederick exchange a more worried look. Neither was letting me access their thoughts, but there was no question they were accessing mine.

'Nate—' Frederick started to say.

'IF YOU TELL ME TO FUCKING CALM DOWN, I WILL BE IN THE FRONT OF THIS CAR BEFORE YOU CAN—!'

'I'm stopping!' Elizabeth interrupted, pulling over into a bus stop.

I was out, and launching myself into the sky simultaneously. I heard Elizabeth in my head say, 'We'll follow on the ground.'

I had no idea whether anyone saw me take off; I had no idea whether anyone saw me in the air. The speed I was moving at was likely to be in my favour – but I didn't care. I had to get to Rowan. So what if I blew the lid on us? Vampires could fend for themselves – Rowan could not!

Images of her broken mortal body filled my mind and I couldn't dispel them.

When I reached her home, a delivery man was at the blue communal door on the ground floor of the Victorian, red-brick terraced property. He was pressing her doorbell, but was now turning away.

Something wasn't right. I had to get in. I could smash the door down, but what if she was lying just behind it? A window was open in the ground-floor flat. I would take my chances. If someone was in, I would move so quickly they wouldn't even see me.

And then I was in the hallway. She wasn't there. She wasn't lying broken and deathly white at the bottom of the stairs. So where was she?

I was at the top of the stairs. Her door was locked. But I could hear water running; it sounded as if it was coming from her bathroom. *Dear God! She had been killed in the shower, like that* Psycho *film, or she had slipped on the bathroom floor and smashed her skull.* I hammered on the door, before getting impatient after half a knock.

I was back outside within the blink of an eye. One of the windows of her flat was open a crack. I took to the air and . . . then I was in her living room.

The bathroom door was in front of me, ajar. Completely and utterly terrified of what I might find, I gently nudged it open with a hand that appeared to be shaking.

I was overwhelmed by a sense of relief so blissful that I would have cried for joy if I was able. She was standing there in the shower and she was moving. There was no blood. She was alive. I didn't know how, but she was alive. I raked my hand through my hair before moving it to hold the bridge of my nose. I shut my eyes and took deep breaths to calm down.

And then realisation hit. She was standing there in the shower . . . and I was standing in her doorway. *Bloody hell!* But it was too late.

In that moment, Rowan Locke partially opened the door of her shower. She twisted awkwardly around because of the cast on her foot, presently encased in some kind of plastic cover, and switched off the jets of running water. And our connection was back. I could feel her frustration again as she attempted to manoeuvre. And, like a *complete* and *utter* idiot, I stayed rooted to the spot, transfixed.

She was beautiful. Stunningly beautiful. She was in profile and water droplets were glistening upon her pale smooth skin. I could see the curve of her hip and the side of her breast and . . .

But then pretty inevitably, as I could see her . . . she could see me. I was interrupted from my inappropriate appreciation by her piercing scream, which in turn led me to jump out of my vampire skin for only the second time in one-hundred-and-ninety-five years. Instantly, I was clutching the door frame for support, to stop from sliding to the floor. Her shock and fear were crippling, and her heart was pounding. And I had bloody well done this to her – and me. *Idiot. Idiot. Idiot.* Her fear ebbed, but then confusion and embarrassment ploughed in, thankfully not remotely as debilitating as the fear. She was frantically trying to find a towel to cover her captivating body.

'*Nate?* Oh *God! Nate?* Oh *Shit! Natha—?* Oh *CRAP!* Nathaniel Gray – *What* are you doing IN MY FLAT?' Her first words sounded as if she were trying not to hyperventilate. By the time she had reached the end of her sentence, it was a scream.

I was looking at the floor now, anywhere but at her enchanting body. Not because I didn't want to, but because I was, at least now, sensible enough to know it wasn't appropriate. And for the moment,

I really didn't want to look into those eyes of hers, either. I knew they would be full of shock and accusation. I wanted to bolt. I had to get out of there. *What had I done?*

She was confused. I could feel it. I was panicked.

And then she squealed as her good foot slipped from under her on the wet bathroom floor, and I was there, catching her, before the back of her head hit the edge of the bath. She was in my arms – again. I heard her gasp and I could feel her racing, skipping heart. Her towel wasn't doing much to cover her and I was on fire. I was aware of her body in a way I had never been aware of a woman's body before. I breathed in her scent – she smelt wonderful – and it *wasn't* the mango-and-passion-fruit shower gel. And it wasn't lust for her blood now consuming me, but a far more human sensation.

I couldn't help but look into her eyes. What could she see in mine? Her confusion increased as we focused on each other. She held my gaze and for a wonderful moment it was as if our sentiments blurred. As if she, too, was feeling that same confusing plethora of emotions that overtook my being in her presence. But she soon put me straight. She shook her head as if to clear it and anger sparked. Thankfully muted due to her state of shock and confusion, but I still felt it. This was Rowan.

'WHAT THE EFFING HELL ARE YOU DOING IN MY FLAT, NATHANIEL GRAY?

How did you get in here?' She was trying to rearrange her towel. 'LET ME GO! You're in my bathroom – and I've NO clothes on!'

I could feel her embarrassment, and see it as her cheeks flamed a deeper red. It was so becoming, so attractive.

'Just get off of me and get out! Don't touch me! Jeez your hands are *not* warm!' She was trying to bat my arms away, but couldn't make them budge.

My voice was strained. I was really struggling to get my words out, but at least the anger had ebbed – for now. 'I am trying not to touch you . . . believe me. It is just where I am holding you. I am . . . so sorry! Just let me . . . get up and I will . . . put you down.'

I stood up with her in my arms. She gasped again. Her racing heart seemed to be working in conjunction with my own.

'Just put me down – put me down now, Nate!' She was pushing at my chest and her legs were flailing. She had no chance of escape. And for that moment: she was mine.

I walked a couple of steps, with difficulty, both due to our emotional connection and the blissful physical sensations that were coursing through my body from where my hands were connecting with her skin. I then set her down on the carpeted floor of the living room. That way, she couldn't give slipping and breaking her neck another go.

She was attempting to manoeuvre herself, so her

back was against the wall and the towel she had picked up – a small hand towel – covered some of her body. I made a point not to look at her, politely shielding my eyes to try and minimise her embarrassment. I retrieved a bath towel from her bathroom and handed it to her, whilst still making myself look away. God, it was difficult.

I could hear her pounding heart. *Alive! She was alive!* And I was, as James would say, in deep shit.

'I am incredibly sorry,' I stuttered. 'I thought something had happened to you – I panicked!'

Rowan was speechless. And at that point in time, it was the preferred option. I really didn't think it would be a good idea to be around when she had got over the shock.

'Do you need help with anything? Can I carry you into your bedroom?' Quickly realising how that might sound . . . 'Or perhaps I should fetch your clothes . . . or a glass of water . . . for the shock?'

She just stood there and shook her head, whether in disbelief or in answer, I didn't know. She was clutching the larger towel tightly and looking at a fixed point on the other side of the room and taking slow deep breaths. I guessed this was the calm before the storm.

'It might be a good idea if . . . I . . . perhaps . . . leave now?' I suggested tentatively.

She ever so slowly nodded her head.

Bugger! I could hardly go out the way I had come in. I took in the locked door . . . but the key was

109

in place! I was through the door without a backward glance.

Frederick and Elizabeth were parked across the road from the flat. I just made it into the backseat before Rowan Locke's shock wore off. And then I paid the full price for seeing her naked.

Frederick and Elizabeth were experiencing hysterical mirth. Neither was in a fit state to drive, and unfortunately, now I was in the midst of the storm, I wasn't remotely capable of taking the wheel or flying. I was deathly quiet.

They were both in my thoughts and I didn't have the strength to keep them out. They knew exactly what had happened; they had probably heard most of it, and the images in my head provided them with the visuals.

'I don't think I've ever had so much fun, Nate!' Elizabeth squealed.

'That was class! True class!' Frederick cried. 'It is probably the funniest thing I've seen in two hundred years— No! It *is* the funniest thing I've seen in two hundred years!'

Rowan's onslaught was relentless. But I was pleased to have it. It not only meant she was alive, but provided distraction from my own grave worries about the ramifications of my idiotic attempt to rescue her, from nothing more serious . . . than a shower.

'Izzy, love – you are laughing so much you're crying!' Frederick exclaimed before wiping away his wife's blood-red tears with both thumbs and tongue. She was the only one of us who could cry.

'I know! Isn't it great? I've never cried with laughter before! Oh, I love this girl!'

A particularly worrying thought intruded into my mind, despite its turmoil. 'Elizabeth . . . Frederick,' I said slowly, struggling to get my words out. 'This is very important. We really need to keep this . . . incident . . . away from James.'

'Sorry – no can do,' Frederick said, with feigned regret. 'We called him when we were all in a panic, and he and Mads parked down the road, just in time for the matinee. Can't you hear their thoughts?'

Dear God! How could this get any worse? Now I focused away from Rowan's turmoil – and my own – I could hear them.

With a great deal of effort, I silently spoke, 'James – bugger off! That is the last time you – no, *any* of us – will ever see her naked!'

'Nate, mate – Congratulations! Who would have thought you'd have progressed matters so quickly? And that wasn't *blood*lust you felt – was it?'

And then I heard his laughter. Not through his thoughts. I could hear it from two hundred yards down the road.

God help me!

CHAPTER 7

THE CHASE

I screwed up another piece of paper and blindly threw it over my shoulder, hearing it ping as it landed plumb in the centre of the metal wastepaper bin in the corner of the room. I was in my bedroom at our Mayfair home.

Built in 1725, the substantial, double-fronted, early Georgian town house had been part of the Gray Estate since being first built. But I was in no mood to appreciate the elegant décor around me.

'This is impossible,' I growled, leaping from my desk and stalking to the attached wet-room, for my sixth cold shower in an hour.

It was the early hours of Sunday morning, Rowan was eventually sleeping, and I was trying to write her yet another letter. But I was having a problem with concentration. My mind seemed reluctant to forget the most beautiful and welcome sight my eyes had ever beheld: Rowan alive in the shower. The benefit of enhanced eyesight and memory ensured that the images repeatedly re-entering my head were of such seductive clarity that focusing on the task in hand was close to impossible.

'What is the point?' I snarled. 'Cold showers do *not* work on the undead.'

Nevertheless, I let the cold water run over my body. I was in serious trouble and wasn't remotely sure I could salvage things. At least with a letter – if I could focus enough to write the damned thing – I could apologise and attempt to explain myself. The aftermath of my earlier ridiculous rescue attempt had demonstrated *verbally* communicating with both a conscious *and* furious Rowan Locke was not an option.

I groaned and violently shook my head under the jets of water, recalling Rowan's voicemail message that had gone undiscovered until I had found my phone half an hour ago.

'Nathaniel Gray! *WHAT* were you doing in my flat? *How* did you get in? I locked that door myself when Clare went out. You can't just invade people's homes and stand gawping at them whilst they're in the shower! Are you some kind of *lock-picking* pervert?'

Clare had clearly been with her, because I could make out Rowan saying, 'NO, Clare! It HAS to be said. You weren't here! NO – I *did* lock the shitting door! NO – I shouldn't have waited for you to help me in the shower!'

She had then continued into the phone, 'You scared me stupid! Is that what you *get off* on? If it wasn't enough that you try and kill me on the road, you then try and give me a heart attack in my own bathroom! – Clare, just butt out! – And then you just left – skedaddled just like you were going to when you tried to kill me *last* time – with no explanation! You'd better have an *outstanding* explanation – or God help me, I'll have to report you! You are dangerous, Nathaniel Gray – really dangerous! Call me as soon as you get this message. Oh! Thank you for my flowers. They were totally beautiful – but *what is it* with you? It's Rowan by the way – Rowan Locke – I'm hanging up on you now.'

Unfortunately, the others were around when I picked up the message, and their highly efficient hearing ensured they overheard it all.

I was not used to being an object of fun, and was finding it far from amusing.

Drying myself off and re-dressing, I decided to give the letter another go. There was no pressure. It was not as if much rested on it. Just everything.

'Go away, Elizabeth,' I growled, before she had a chance to knock on my closed door.

'Forgive me?' she pleaded, cautiously opening the door. 'I'm sorry for earlier. I thought I could help with the letter.'

'Elizabeth!'

'Okay! I'm gone,' she replied quietly, accepting that pestering me in my current frame of mind was not wise.

'No, Elizabeth – I am gone!' I stated petulantly, whilst grabbing my writing implements and exiting the house through one of the room's three large sash windows.

I settled myself on Rowan's roof, with my back against the chimney stack. She was sleeping peacefully. I wrote to the soothing background of Rowan's gentle breathing, so easily distinguishable over Clare's.

London, Sunday, 6 May

Dearest Rowan,

I very much hope you will do me the honour of reading this letter.

I am mortified to have scared, upset and embarrassed you. Please believe it was never my intention to 'gawp' at you in the shower. It is very hard to explain – but I became worried about you. You were not answering your phone or the door, and I feared you may have fallen.

I was even more concerned when I discovered your door to be unlocked.

When I opened your bathroom door, I knew not what I would find. I was simply overwhelmingly relieved you were not lying dead upon the floor or stabbed within the shower.

I beg you to believe I do not make a habit of scaring beautiful women when they are showering.

I seem to be unable to do anything but cause you pain and displeasure – and that could never be my intention. I plead to be given an opportunity to make amends, to be allowed to

*demonstrate that I can behave honourably and,
in many ways, as a gentleman.*

*I seem to be forever putting myself in a
position of having to ask, but* please *find it
within your heart to forgive me. I exist in
hope that you will accept my telephone call
later today.*

*Humbly yours,
Nate*

I had struggled with writing the letter. With its
style I had had to rein in my more traditional
letter-writing tendencies; an issue I have with my
business correspondence, too. But the worst thing
had been lying to her.

I had agonised over how I could get around the
issue of the locked door. But I could see no other
way. I knew if I didn't plant a shadow of doubt
in her head – *had she, hadn't she* locked the door?
– she would want answers I could not give. It was
dishonourable of me.

I wanted to tell Rowan the truth – everything:
the emotional connection, that she made me feel
alive despite my having been dead for one-hundred-
and-ninety-five years, that I had never felt this way
about anyone before, that I had so desperately
wanted to take her lifeblood from her on the night
of the accident but that I had resisted – and hoped
I could continue to resist.

But I knew *that* wouldn't produce the sort of

letter that would result in her agreeing to see me again. There was too much at stake.

I folded up the letter, wrote her name on the outside – reflecting how handwriting had changed much over the years – and silently posted it in the letterbox.

I returned to the roof, not yet ready to leave the enthralling, hypnotic sound of Rowan's breathing.

I could hear her cat – Tinks, I recalled from the private investigator's report. She was meowing from somewhere below and then, shockingly, she was rubbing herself against my legs, and nudging my cold hands for strokes.

Animals are terrified of us unless we use our charm on them, as we do when we feed. In the case of cats, their hackles go up as they momentarily look like a fir tree, before they hiss and flee at top speed. Yet, Rowan's blond tabby cat, with its unusual grey eyes, actually seemed to . . . like me.

I gently rubbed warm, furry feline ears. *Why are you not scared of me, little one?*

On returning home, I was greeted by Elizabeth.

'Did you write the letter? Have you called her back? You're blocking me again. *Tell* me!'

Elizabeth had found me as I made it into my first-floor study. I couldn't recall her ever having disturbed me in the large, well-proportioned room, with its book-lined walls, before. There seemed to be no escape these days.

'Elizabeth!' I uttered impatiently, sitting at my desk.

'Lizzy, we really should give him some space,' Madeleine observed, entering the room too, and taking a seat by the window.

Come to think of it, Madeleine had never before disturbed me here, either.

I looked at Madeleine questioningly. She was the only one not finding mirth in my current predicament and, as a result, I had time for her – even if my space was being seriously invaded.

'It was the shower,' she stated casually.

I looked at her inquisitively and her thoughts applied the context to her words. 'Of course.' I sighed.

'That is *sooo* weird,' Elizabeth muttered.

I hadn't had a chance to work out *why* my connection with Rowan had been temporarily broken yesterday. I had been somewhat preoccupied with trying to deal with the torturous result of my response to that break – and then damage limitation.

Madeleine continued out loud, 'It *is* strange – we've never noticed it having an affect on us before. But it's clear: running water *can* have an impact on vampires. In your case, it either temporarily breaks the connection you have with Rowan, or shields her from you.'

Whichever way, I didn't like it. 'I have read about it, but thought it nonsense – just as with our not being able to go out in the sun, our *inability* to feel emotion, our aversion to silver and the stake to the heart!'

'Lately, it's been suggested we sparkle,' Elizabeth added, with a grin.

Shaking my head incredulously before re-focusing, I said, 'Is it not something about running water being pure, and not being able to hold magic, so it is meant to impede us?'

'Yeah, something like that. We aren't meant to be able to cross streams or rivers, but of course we can. I hadn't thought there was anything in it. You are making some pretty groundbreaking advances in vampire lore, Nate. You really are going to have to watch yourself.' Madeleine looked sympathetically at me.

As I looked at her, her expression changed. 'Yes – if you are *sure* you are happy to do it?' I replied to her silent question. The detective still hadn't come up with anything and Rowan's Aunty Hetty remained a concern. If Madeleine could get inside her head, it might provide us with some answers. Not that I was sure I really wanted any. I currently had enough things to worry about.

'But go careful, Mads,' Elizabeth urged, before James waltzed into the room.

What was it with everyone tonight? And James was in one of his unbearable moods again. I could sense it.

'You know, I am *so* impressed! God knows what talents you have lurking beneath the surface, Nate.

I told you he didn't need any lessons in small-talk, Lizzy.'

My growl was ignored.

'Alright, bruv?' Frederick sent my way as he entered the room to complete our unit. He was chuckling before he had even reached his usual place by Elizabeth's side. 'Sorry – I just can't stop thinking about it. You've made my century!'

My second growl was ignored, too.

Why were they finding amusement in this? I was in one hell of a mess.

James taunted, 'I'm just intrigued to see how you are going to pull off returning her call, when she's off on a rage again. It had better have been one hell of a letter!'

I scowled. I had absolutely no idea how I was going to manage the conversation, and the last thing I needed was to be reminded of the fact. If worst came to worst, I would terminate the conversation – pretend the signal was breaking up – rather than me. I just prayed my letter calmed her down a little.

'Are you sure you don't want me to pop over and lace her morning coffee with painkillers or something?' Frederick asked with a smirk, ignoring Elizabeth's warning look. 'It would be no problem at all . . . I can just use the window like everyone else!'

James high-fived Frederick and they chortled together.

I shook my head and growled, whilst coming to

the unpleasant conclusion: there was no chance I was going to get them to leave me alone tonight. I needed diversion.

'The New Forest or the Kentish countryside, in search of wild boar?'

After sunrise, I lay on my bed waiting for Rowan to wake. Unfortunately, this morning it wasn't until 11.30 a.m. Her late awakening should have been a blessing. It was exactly what she needed, and should have done me some good, too. But it was so much later than usual. I knew with my sensible hat on, she was sleeping – yet I rarely wore that hat much nowadays. I found my brain going down routes not conducive to peace of mind. If it hadn't been broad daylight, I would have visited her roof to check for life-sounds.

In the event, 10 a.m. saw me at the computer googling ways humans could suddenly die in bed. I knew it was highly unlikely she had been bitten by a venomous spider or strangled by a boa constrictor in West London, but I was no longer a rational being: where Rowan Locke was concerned, there was no rationality at all.

When Rowan finally awoke, I was beside myself with relief; not only that she was alive, but she also seemed remarkably calm – compared to her state of mind yesterday, at least. Lying on my bed, I concentrated entirely on what she was feeling, hoping to gauge her reaction to my letter. But hours later, I was still none the wiser. I was sure that thoughts of the day before were never far away though, as I experienced peaks and troughs of various emotions. Even I could identify anger and embarrassment . . . and was that suspicion? But it was impossible for me to gauge whether one of those peaks in anger resulted from her reading my letter or not.

By 2 p.m. I was getting nowhere and knew I could no longer put off making the call. I sneaked out of the house and headed to Richmond Park, far enough away to be out of our hearing range. It was a sensible and no doubt necessary precaution.

There, in an area of dense woodland, I perched in the crown of an old oak tree.

Bracing myself for what was ahead of me, I reminded myself of the pluses of the call. I would hear Rowan's voice again and, if it went well, I would be the happiest being on the planet. It would mean I would be seeing her again, and I was *desperate* for that. Delivery of the car would be the perfect excuse. If it went badly, however, my existence was going to get that much more painful. If it went particularly badly, and she refused to ever see me again, I didn't know how I would deal with it. I couldn't let myself think about that possibility.

I could put it off no longer. Trembling, my finger hit her speed-dial button.

'Nathaniel Gray,' Rowan Locke said archly, picking up after the first ringtone. *My number must be programmed into her phone . . .*

I was shaking so much, I could hardly keep the phone in my hands – and disconcertingly, I had to hold on to the branch to stop myself falling out of the tree.

Retrospectively, the location was all wrong.

She wasn't angry. She was nervous like me. But something else was there, too: anticipation and perhaps excitement – *wishful thinking?*

The way she said my name disarmed me; the way she always said my name disarmed me. It made this vampire's insides turn to jelly. The accompanying warm glow that my body experienced was wondrous. 'Rowan . . .' I could hear her heartbeat down the phone, racing like my own. 'Please forgive me. I promise I am not a pervert!'

I had been called many things before, but never a pervert . . . but I could see how yesterday could have given that impression.

She was silent, bar the sound of her heart that was now racing so fast it worried me.

My voice, raw, said, 'Did you get my letter? I am truly sorry. I was so worried. Can you find it in your heart to forgive me – again? *Please!*'

I heard her shaky intake of breath before she said, 'I still haven't forgiven you for the accident, Nate.' But I could hear humour in her voice. *Was she going to forgive me? Please God!* 'And now this would be something else to add to the list for forgiveness.'

'Let me make it up to you,' I unashamedly begged. I had never before begged to anyone.

I heard her gulp, take a deep breath, before proceeding shakily, 'Just how would you propose to do that?'

I wanted to say: let me into your life; let me cherish you; let me protect you; let me make you happy; let me open up to you in a way I have never before opened up to anyone; let me be totally honest; let me tell you what I am; let us find a way to be together – despite my being a monster.

Instead, I said, 'Let me take you out. Anywhere you like.' I considered that to be the contemporary phraseology.

There was a long pause. That heart of hers was a concern. How fast did it have to go before it gave up the ghost? Her slowly spoken words distracted me. 'I *am* tempted.'

There was hope! I attempted to sound 'normal'. 'How tempted?'

'I don't know anything about you – other than that you're an appalling driver who likes to look at people in the shower.'

I frowned. I needed to put my case; I needed to try and convince her to give me this chance. 'Rowan—'

'No – please, let me finish. I'm sorry for that! I couldn't help myself. Look – I'm trying to say something, but I don't quite know what I'm trying to say, or how to say it. You *really* confuse me! I don't know what you do, what Ridings is – although thank you again for the flowers; they were beautiful, all one-hundred-and-twenty of them! I don't know what you're about. And, because of your track record, I'm associating you with danger. There is something . . . unnerving about you; an intensity about you.'

Bugger! 'Does it scare you?' I asked gently.

'No . . . it did, perhaps . . . I don't know actually! But I've thought about that and I'm not. You are . . . *unnerving* – but no, I'm not afraid of you. But – please don't take offence. I really don't want you to take offence – but . . . *should I be?*'

I felt her momentary fear as she anticipated my answer. She wasn't being truly honest with herself. She didn't *want* to fear me. But she had clearly seen something that night that had more than unnerved her. I *had* scared her. And I had scared her again yesterday. She sensed the danger above and beyond the accident itself and my presence in her bathroom.

I decided to be honest, to a degree. I didn't want her to be scared of me. I couldn't bear that. *But did she need to be?* I would do anything to protect her, but ultimately, even I didn't know if she needed to be. 'I wish I knew for certain, Rowan. That night, and nearly scaring you to death yesterday, would indicate that . . . perhaps you do have cause for concern . . . that perhaps . . . I do represent a danger to you.'

I had added to her confusion. 'That wasn't the answer I wanted.' She laughed, shakily. 'You know, I think I must be suffering post-traumatic stress

from the accident – or losing my marbles – because
. . . I just can't help feeling some kind of . . .
connection. I suppose accidents do that to people.
We were both involved, so it's logical I suppose.
God – I'm sorry! I always say too much. I just
open my mouth and out it comes.' She gave
another shaky laugh.

'I feel it, too.' *Too intense.*

'It could be shock . . . we could both be in
shock!' she said earnestly.

'That is also undoubtedly true.'

'Look! I'm laying my cards on the table here. I
am . . . drawn to you, Nate – despite my near-
death experiences around you. I'd have to be, to
even contemplate saying this . . .' I heard her
inhale deeply. 'I'd very much like to get to know
you better – well at all, actually. And . . . if I haven't
offended you too much . . .'

'Rowan – I would be truly honoured should you
agree to spend some time with me.'

Relief. She felt relief!

'What school did you go to, Nate?'

'I was . . . initially home schooled. Why?'

'It figures. You talk and write letters like no one
I've ever come across . . . except perhaps— You
just seem to be right out of a Jane Austen novel!'

Oh, God! I had been trying to be so careful. 'Are
you making fun of me?' I asked, with mock
seriousness.

'No . . . Yes . . . Perhaps.' She laughed. 'You're
just so . . . different. It adds to this whole feeling

I have that there's something more to you than meets the eye. I must confess: I'm intrigued.'

'Intrigued enough to spend some time with me? I promise to try not to kill you this time.' I had never meant anything more.

'With that proviso . . . yes, Nate . . . I'd very much like to spend some time with you.'

Good God! I leapt to the ground and started pacing up and down excitedly, before weaving around some trees in a few elated aeronautic manoeuvres. 'That is incredible! That is fantastic! That is just so . . . so incredible! Thank you! I am truly honoured!'

I paused to try and take stock and to make some sense out of what was racing through me – but gave up. I just felt better than . . . better than I had *ever* felt. And her feelings were . . . God they were wonderful to experience! Rowan was laughing on the other end of the phone, and I was laughing with her.

'Umm – Where would you like to go?' I continued. 'I would very much like to show you Ridings – my home in Derbyshire by the way – but perhaps we should start with something in London, now we are both here?'

'London would be good. We could catch a show or something . . .' She paused and then laughed again. 'Look, this is a big ask . . . but have you seen *Mama Mia!*? I'd love to see it again – but I'd understand if you didn't want to.'

Mama Mia!. What the hell was Mama Mia!? I

hoped somebody else knew. '*Mama Mia!* it is. When? What about tonight?' I was definitely betraying my desperation to see her.

'I've got Clare this week and I really don't think I could deal with going out – *with you* – with her around. She would be horrendous.'

I knew exactly what she meant. I was having a similar problem at home.

'If you didn't notice, you've got yourself a fan there!'

I laughed. 'I think Clare is charming.'

'You would! She'll love you even more for saying that.'

What the hell? I was having fun. I was going to get more daring. 'Are you not going to ask me, what I think of you?'

She laughed nervously. 'You've seen me in the shower, so I shudder to think. You know, you really are disarming.'

I was incredulous. 'You think seeing you in the shower would . . .?'

But I was interrupted. 'How on earth you felt able to mention the word "beautiful" in your letter, I have no idea! Ummm. Actually . . . do you think we can *stop* talking about the shower? It's *really, really* embarrassing.'

We would stop talking about the shower, but I couldn't let her words pass. 'How could I possibly *not* use the word "beautiful"?' I asked solemnly. 'Beautiful does not begin to even . . . You say I am disarming – you have no idea how disarming you are to me.'

Her confusion increased dramatically. But I was enjoying it. At the moment, it was a good kind of confusion. She laughed nervously and then after a long pause asked, 'What were we talking about?'

'We were fixing a date.' I tried not to sound smug.

'Yes!'

'Why not look at your availability, and let me know? I can change anything to fit around you. I need to return your car, too. I could deliver it to your home . . .' *Was this pushing it?* 'later perhaps – if it is convenient, of course?' I wanted to see her *now*.

'And it is *my* car, Nate?' she asked pointedly.

'But of course.' I didn't like, however, the feeling of guilt that nudged its way into my consciousness as I thought of all the changes I had made – and which I had no intention of revealing. But it quickly passed. It was the right thing to do. 'Is this afternoon convenient?'

'Yes it is – but you know Clare's around.'

'Is it acceptable to you? It would simply be to return the car.'

'Yes – it is *acceptable* to me,' she mimicked, good-humouredly.

YESSS!!! 'Incredible – I will see you in an hour then?'

Rowan laughed and said her farewell, as if she was humouring me – but she was excited, too. I was sure she was. 'Bye, Nate.'

'Goodbye, Rowan.' I was unable to keep the elation from those short words.

Good God! I was courting! I had a date with the most enchanting, most beautiful woman the planet had ever known. I had to calm down. But it was hard.

First things first: the car. I would return it, and at least get a glimpse of her. Then I would try to pin her down on a day of the week for the official date. But I was going to see her again – in less than an hour!

'Well?' Elizabeth asked, finding me in my dressing-room, preparing to shave. I shook my head at her. 'Oh, don't do this to me!' She sounded both exasperated and desperate. 'The fact you are blocking me out means, I'm guessing, you called her. The fact you are preparing to shave and have got a really strange expression on your face . . . that . . . *Oh, my God!* Nate? Are you going to see her? Nate? I'm your sister – I have a right to know!' She now stood with her hands on her hips, glowering at me.

I had to laugh. I couldn't help it. After all, I was happy. I am sure that's what I was.

'You're laughing . . . I love it when you laugh! *Oh, my God! Oh, my God – you're going to see her?* Look – let's make a deal. You need my help. I can help you choose something suitable to wear.' I frowned and looked down at the suit I was wearing. 'Don't think for one moment you are going to see Rowan dressed like that!' My frown deepened. 'Believe me, you need my help.' She smiled broadly now. 'Besides, you are also going to need someone to tell you whether you've a big post-it note stuck to your back, saying, *I'm a red-hot Vampire!*'

No doubt looking horrified, I snarled, 'James?'

'Mmmm,' she said, nodding, 'And Freddie, I'm ashamed to say. They don't for one moment think Rowan will believe it, but are reckoning your reaction would be highly entertaining. *See*, you really *do* need my help! I'll be watching your back, so to speak.'

She was making a very strong case. *And* I didn't know what the hell, *Mama Mia!* was . . . And then there was her concern about my clothes . . . *Bugger, I did need help!*

'All you have to do is keep me in the loop. I'll keep quiet; my lips will be sealed. It will be *our* secret!' She read my thought. 'Yeah – okay. Not quite so easy to keep my mind sealed, but I'll do my best – I promise!'

'And you will be able to keep things from Frederick?' I asked dubiously. I refused to be entertainment for James and Frederick.

She looked momentarily concerned, but rose to the challenge. 'I promise to do my best!'

'Sharing everything would not be fair on Rowan, either. It would be disrespectful.'

'Oh, Nate, you are such a sweetie!' She put her hands on both sides of my face and squeezed my cheeks.

'Deal?' she asked, expectantly.

'Deal,' I said, not believing what I was saying. 'And do not make me regret it!'

'*Yessss!* Okay . . . so what are we facing?'

I let Elizabeth into my head. 'Okay . . . so car now. *Oh, my God! No!* A date? A proper human date, well, you know what I mean!' Elizabeth was squealing now.

Where was my quietly spoken, sedate little sister?

'Keep your voice down!'

'It's alright – they aren't here. In fact they are miles away. Although I think Mads is around somewhere, but she's not the issue. *Oh, God!* How am I going to keep this from Freddie?' she hissed.

She saw my look. 'No – I will! I will! I'll earn your trust. I promise!'

Right, I was going to put her to good use. 'What *the hell* is *Mama Mia!*?'

She looked smug, in an 'I told you so' sort of way. 'I've not been . . . although I've always wanted to . . .' *I wonder if Mads would like to go and see it?*

I read her thought and she saw that I had. 'Okay! Perhaps we *won't* arrange to see it on the same night. It was just a thought . . . a stupid, insensitive thought. *Mama Mia!* is a West End musical, with the music from Abba – that stuff we were listening to in the car and Freddie gagged at. It's meant to be great fun and hugely popular amongst humans.'

She suddenly started to giggle. 'Oh, God, Nate, I'm sorry. I so can't imagine you sitting through an Abba musical!' In fact, she was uncontrollably giggling. 'I *so* need to see you sitting through it – *please*. You can't deprive me of that experience

– I'm begging you. I'll do *anything*. I will *eternally* be in your debt – name the price. Anything! *Anything*, Nate.'

I was getting worried now. Elizabeth's reaction indicated I may well be getting out of my depth. But then I thought it through . . .

It didn't matter where we went, what we did – I would be with Rowan. It wouldn't matter what we were supposed to be seeing . . . The only thing I would be looking at, was her.

I could do this.

'You aren't going to let me, are you?'

I shook my head and ruffled her hair, affectionately.

'But you *will* share it with me afterwards,' she stated. 'Otherwise you're on your own – and the problem is, James and Freddie are *really* getting into this. They now consider themselves to have been starved of quality entertainment for at least a century or so.'

With my nod and sigh, she headed towards the wardrobes lining the room. 'Let's sort you out, then.' Whilst rapidly assessing my clothes, she let out a groan. 'Most of this is way too formal. I need to take you shopping. Do you know, we've *never* been shopping together? Have we got time now?' She read my thought. 'Right! We go shopping before the big date. But for now . . . these jeans – I'm disgusted you've never worn these.' She plucked off the designer label tags. 'I bought them because they suit your build perfectly.

They're cut just right for your slim hips. You're really lucky – you have a pretty perfect shape – you just never show it off! This olive-green jersey top for now . . . it's quite tight – but you can pull it off.'

I was in the new clothes within a flash.

'Stand over there . . . turn around.' I couldn't believe I was doing this. 'Come on – don't be shy! Remember what all this is for. You look gorgeous . . . I love your hair that length, so it's sort of curling on to your shoulders.'

'It has always been this length,' I muttered.

'I know – but it really suits you.'

I was conscious I couldn't recall *ever* having had a conversation like this with Elizabeth. We had never discussed my appearance before.

'That's because there's never been a need before.'

'I must shave,' I said, rubbing my hands over the stubble and heading back over to my shaving equipment.

'No, you don't!' Elizabeth asserted. 'Believe me, that little bit of stubble is attractive. It's modern, and you need to get your act together. Thank God you got rid of those blessed sideburns. We can't have her guessing your age now, can we?'

She read my thought. 'Oooohh. Yeah, you're going to have to work on that one. Jane Austen, though? It could be worse. You ought to be able to pull off Mr Darcy pretty perfectly!'

Was that a smirk on her face? I looked at her, confused.

'*Pride and Prejudice* is hugely popular, Nate – particularly Mr Darcy. Human girls seem to really go for him. Look, just be yourself – but a *tad* more agreeable – and you'll be irresistible.' She smiled to herself, before continuing, 'You're done! Now, as soon as you know when *Mama Mia!* is on, let me know. I'll sort the tickets, and we will set a date to go shopping.'

'Thank you, sweetheart.' I gave her a gentle hug and kissed her head.

This arrangement might just work.

Grabbing the keys to the recently delivered Morris Minor, I headed downstairs on route to the garage. I changed course as I spotted Mrs Neeson, the London housekeeper. She was struggling to open a door whilst overly laden with soft furnishings, which by their scent, were newly laundered. She stared at me – or more precisely, at my smile – astounded, as I opened the door for her. 'Good afternoon, Mrs Neeson.'

She matched my smile. 'It certainly would seem to be, Mr Gray.'

Departing with a quick bow I left the house to the rear . . . my smile now faltering. I had heard her murmur, 'I know only one thing that puts a smile like that on a man's face.' *And* Elizabeth's resultant giggles.

The building now housing our cars had formerly been our stabling and coach house. We had converted it a hundred years or so ago, although

I still kept some stabling to one end, just in case Bess ever needed accommodating.

On entering, I found Madeleine. She was leaning against Rowan's car, with her arms crossed, clearly waiting for me.

'Nate,' she said earnestly, 'promise me, you'll be careful – there are risks to you both here.'

'Of course.'

She still didn't move from her position against the driver's door, so I sighed, raised my eyebrow and said wryly, 'If you want to share what else is on your mind, you might either choose to verbalise, or remove your block.'

'Yeah, I know. I've just been trying to pluck up the courage. It didn't go too well with Heather.' Madeleine lowered her block.

'Ahhhhh,' I said in understanding. 'No, it would appear not.'

'Is that all you can say?' she cried. 'I know you are more focused on Rowan than getting answers, but Nate – I couldn't get into her head at all! And if that isn't bad enough, I was a hundred metres behind her in a darkened doorway, and she turned around and looked straight at me – with those freaky grey eyes of hers. And I *swear* she knew what I'd been trying to do!'

'So it is not only me who doesn't react too well to her.'

'No – I can safely say, she spooked me.'

'It is no consolation to you, I know,' I said, now grinning, 'but personally, I find it rather reassuring

136

that you reacted to her the same way I did. It means something is still working.'

'Thanks!' she said sarcastically. 'Nice clothes by the way. Elizabeth has got to you, then?'

I raised my eyebrows. 'Is it that obvious?'

'Mmmm,' she said, nodding her head and then looking more concerned added, 'She isn't going to stand a chance. Just be careful. But at the same time, anything you can get on Aunty Hetty would be useful. We really are struggling to make any sense out of all this. I'm heading out of town for a couple of days, to do some research of my own.'

Her block was back up. In response to my frown, she said, 'I'm just visiting an old friend – Fergus.'

'Fergus MacArthur?' Before joining us, both she and Frederick had spent a number of years within his group up in Scotland.

'The very one. I'm hoping he can help us get some answers to things because, believe me, we need help! Call me if you find anything out, yeah – or if anything *else* goes wrong?'

With a quick peck on the cheek, she was gone.

CHAPTER 8

THE DELIVERY

I slammed the door of Rowan's Morris Minor and eventually found the right key and turned it in the right manner, to get the damned door to lock. *How the hell could she like this monstrosity?* At least the precarious driving experience had kept me distracted enough to completely forget it was the first time I had driven since the accident – but it had hardly reassured me as to Rowan's safety on the roads.

'Nate?'

I turned to see Clare crossing the tree-lined street, struggling under a mass of shopping bags. I jogged over to meet her, relieved her of her load, and started walking with her towards the house.

She spoke breathlessly. 'Thank you so much! I didn't spare a thought for how I was going to carry them all, until I was packing up at the check-out – by which time it was too late.' Now her hands were free, she rubbed them together to try and get blood flow back into her white fingers. She then used them to repeatedly smooth her hair down. Her heart was beating a little too quickly and she was flushed. 'Rowan never said . . .' she muttered, seemingly annoyed with her sister.

'I am returning the car – a last-minute arrangement.'

I watched Clare put the keys in the door, grateful that Rowan didn't have to tackle the stairs to let me in. As we headed up the first flight of steps, I grinned. I was in a very different state of mind to that of yesterday, when I had last travelled this route.

'Are you sure you can manage all those bags?' Clare asked dubiously, before looking over her left shoulder at me. Her eyes travelled up and down my body. Her flush deepened and she returned her attention to the stairs. She said, more to herself than to me, 'Of course you can.' A couple of steps later, she took a deep shaky breath and asked, 'So . . . how are things? Have you fully recovered from the accident?'

'Good, thank you, Clare.' I chose not to answer the second question. I was never going to fully recover from the accident. And anyway, I was good. Well, no – I was more than good. I was courting Rowan! Smiling, I asked, 'And how are you? I hear you are assisting Rowan in her recovery. Is she happy to be assisted?'

Clare laughed shakily and I heard her heart race a little more. 'What do you think? And she's even more irritable than usual, because she's refusing to take her painkillers!'

I couldn't help the wince, but suppressed the hiss.

'So, how are Mark, little Nathan and Tom

managing to cope without you?' I forced out. I *could* do small-talk, I told myself.

She gave me a huge smile. 'Oh! You remember their names! I'm so impressed! They aren't – coping that is! Mark isn't remotely happy. He's taking them to McDonalds for breakfast, lunch and tea – and is convinced they are playing up especially for him.' She giggled to herself. 'It'll do him good. Believe it or not, babysitting Rowan is a holiday.'

I raised my eyebrows and grinned; her blush deepened.

We had reached the door to Rowan's flat, but Clare was unfortunately continuing the conversation. 'So . . . do *you* have kids, Nate?'

'No.' I didn't like this topic. It hurt. I had never wanted children. Becoming a vampire had represented no sacrifice at all. Yet, for a moment I saw the image I had experienced in the hospital of two children, playing at Ridings.

'It's unlocked!' Rowan called from inside the flat.

My body warmed at the sound of her voice. I had already been listening contentedly to her slightly too fast heartbeat, which I had picked up clearly from the moment I had arrived . . . but her *voice*? I loved to hear her voice.

Clare was, however, standing between me and the door, so I couldn't pass. 'You just haven't found the right girl then,' she observed.

'That is a possibility,' I said quietly, trying to sound casual.

'You'll know when you've found her,' Clare announced.

I *had* found her. But it was never going to be. Did Rowan want children? I hadn't even thought of that. Of course she did, and only a human could give her that. But I knew there was no future for us, I had always known that. But a date – the only date I had ever had – with the only woman I had ever wanted. *What harm could that do?* I needed that more than I had ever needed anything in all my existence.

I extracted myself away from my thoughts as Clare opened the door and made her way into the flat, with the following words: 'Rowan . . . why do you keep leaving the door unlocked?'

A sense of guilt rushed over me – my own. My eyes immediately sought hers. She was standing a few feet away, using the back of the sofa, rather than crutches, for support.

She was as beautiful as ever. She was definitely nervous, like me, and her heart missed a beat before beginning to race. Clare's question, however, had triggered a momentary spark of what I highly suspected to be suspicion. There was an unasked question in her eyes – most likely: 'Was the door *really* unlocked, Nate?'

I looked away quickly. 'Where would you like me to put these?' I asked no one in particular, holding the shopping bags up high.

'Just over here,' Clare said, showing me into the small kitchen. 'Thank you, Nate. You make it look so easy. You aren't remotely out of breath – it would have killed me. I don't know how Rowan does it.'

I tracked Rowan from the corner of my eyes. She was making her way to the kitchen doorway, using furniture for support. It was an excruciating process to watch and it was all my fault! Scanning the number of bags she shook her head. 'How much did you buy, Clare?'

'Yeah . . . I know! But, hey – I'm used to a family shop. At least it will fill your cupboards.'

I looked fully at Rowan now, waiting for her eyes to lift in my direction. When they did, I captured them with my own. I gave her a gentle smile. 'Rowan,' I said. I didn't feel able to say anymore; I was too lost in their depths. They really were, the deepest, most beautifully *pure* hue of green, I had ever seen.

Clare was continuing to natter as she unpacked the shopping, but my focus remained on Rowan. *Fresh uncurling leaves, covered in dew* . . . but no, they were simply green. There was a verdant depth to Rowan's eyes and I couldn't think of any beauty of nature that matched their stunning colour. They appeared to hold flecks of every possible hue of green, with just the right quantity of each, to cumulatively create . . . perfection. Stunning, awe-inspiring . . . gulp-inducing, *perfection*. There was clearly nothing borderline about my obsession now, I conceded, before attempting to pull myself together and replying to Clare's question, 'No, I do not like Marmite.' *What the hell was Marmite?*

Having dragged my attention away from Rowan's eyes, it was with a further twisting stab of guilt I took in the cut at her hairline from the accident. It seemed to be healing well but – *would it scar?* I gritted my teeth. She had been marked by a monster.

I sensed Rowan's confusion increase. Had she seen something in my eyes? I had to snap myself out of this. I turned away and smiled at Clare, 'No, I have never liked Marmite – even as a child.' I made a mental note to find out what Marmite was.

I leaned against the worktop with my arms crossed, in an attempt to look casual. I resisted the temptation to close my eyes and to surrender to the sensation that now started to sweep through my being. That warming glow – and I knew its source. The one source that made me feel alive . . . That made me feel . . . a man.

I looked up to watch Rowan's eyes as they travelled the length of my body. They were leaving their trail of heat wherever they looked. Her breath quickened as did her pulse. Her scent was wonderful, but I was in control. Her eyes met mine, and her cheeks flushed deeper. My heart galloped.

'So I hear you paid Rowan a surprise visit yesterday, Nate?' Clare piped up.

Damn! I took a deep breath. Rowan looked

awkward, and I felt embarrassment and . . . that suspicion again? But she was waiting for my response. I forced myself to smile and laughed awkwardly, 'Yes, it was not one of my better days.'

I heard a meow. *Saved by the cat!*

'Oh! Tinks!' Rowan urgently scanned the room to see where she was. She glanced at me nervously. 'Watch out for her . . . she doesn't like men!' She looked around again. 'I'll put her out as soon as she reveals herself.'

Clare, with a tin of . . . baked beans? in her hands, clarified matters. 'It's not that she doesn't like men. She's absolutely fine with my Mark. What Rowan *really* means, is Tinks has a nasty habit of attacking her boyfriends. She hurt Jonathan quite badly, scratched him really deeply across the face – it scarred, too.'

Clever cat, I thought. I might even develop a soft spot for it. Rowan's cat was the only cat that had never fled from me . . . so perhaps not quite so clever. *I have never tried cat . . .* I quickly dismissed the thought – *too small, not remotely satisfying enough,* and, of course, Tinks was important to Rowan.

Rowan was glaring at her sister. She refocused on me. Tinks had appeared from behind the remaining shopping bags in the middle of the kitchen floor and had started to rub herself against my legs. She was purring audibly and chirping.

'Blimey!' Clare exclaimed. 'Well, there's a first. A seal of approval from Tinks!' Rowan was confused. I was smug.

'This Jonathan character . . . is he still around?' I asked, attempting to sound casual whilst I bent down to stroke Tinks. Her purring increased and when I straightened myself up, she rose on her back legs to nudge my hand with her head.

I hoped I knew the answer to my question. I felt momentary hurt and then a flash of anger as Rowan thought of him; I leant harder against the worktop.

'Huh – that bastard!' Clare spat out, slamming a jar of whatever she was holding on to the worktop. I was far too preoccupied by the current topic of conversation to pursue my earlier curiosity as to the contents of the shopping bags. 'He's started pestering her again. He's already phoned here three times today. I actually think he could be a real issue.' Addressing Rowan now, she continued, 'You should *never* have accepted him back the first time, love. He got drunk and slapped you that time – that should have been enough.'

I was livid. I was beyond livid. I could feel my fury rise. I looked at Rowan, but she avoided meeting my eyes. And the way I was feeling now, it was for the best. I knew the irises of my eyes would be deepest darkest black and if I didn't control myself . . . the black would spread. I shut them for a moment, clenched my fists tightly under the folds of my arms, and took a deep breath to try and calm down.

Rowan was glowering at Clare when I re-opened my eyes. 'That was a *long* time ago Clare – and *private*! Do you think you can learn to hold your tongue?' Almost to justify herself, she added quietly, 'It was a one-off and I was young, a very different person then.'

'I know, love, but you let him back into your life, only for him to cheat on you – and with that woman! They were living under your roof and at it for months. He's set his sights on you again, and it's a case of what he can't have.'

I felt for Rowan. I also felt her pain, and was attempting to repress my own instinctual need to do Jonathan Martin harm. It was difficult to remain standing and I was now clutching the worktop.

'For *pity's sake*, Clare! It's ancient history. It's been over for five years!' Rowan stole a glance at me – my eyes were open again – and she saw something in them, because her eyes opened fractionally wider and her heart missed a beat. She didn't look away. I could feel her uncertainty . . . and curiosity? Her eyes seemed to be silently questioning me again. It was I that looked away. I really didn't have enough confidence in my shroud around her.

Seeming to recover herself, Rowan asked, 'How did the conversation turn to him, anyway?'

Both Clare and I chose to answer silently, by pointing in unison at Tinks, who was now trying to climb my leg. Rowan sighed and I could feel she was over the worst.

'Right! Cup of coffee, Nate?' Clare asked, taking

down three mugs from the cupboard. I noticed their design comprised of words. *Curiously Content*, *Seriously Stupid*, and *Fucking Furious* were now on the counter, and, as *Seriously Stupid* was placed back into the cupboard following my, 'Not for me, thank you,' I caught a glimpse of *Deliciously Drunk*, *Hellishly Horny* and *Snap out of it Sad*. It appeared that the same words were on the back of each mug: *I'm only human.*

'Tea? A cold drink? Wine? Beer . . . although actually, I don't think we've got beer.'

'No, thank you, nothing,' I said, stunned.

As if I needed the reminder – and from a set of mugs!

On pulling myself together, I more calmly reflected. I had most definitely experienced the one now having a spoonful of coffee added to it. But I wasn't sure I had experienced the *Curiously Content*. Was Rowan happy? I so wanted her to be. And what would her *Deliciously Drunk* feel like? I had no hope of calmly reflecting on her *Hellishly Horny*, so dug around in my mind for some small-talk topics, before I got too scarred by all this.

Fortunately Clare expedited matters, although the subject was not so fortunate. 'I still don't get about yesterday, Nate. Why were you so concerned about Rowan?'

Rowan fixed me with those spellbinding eyes of hers again.

'It is really difficult to explain . . . . I just suddenly got worried. Rowan was not answering her phone or the door.'

147

'She doesn't always *hear* the door,' Clare said, in an exaggerated stage whisper, whilst switching on the kettle.

Rowan was furious and I clutched the edge of the worktop, I had only just released. 'Helllooooo? I'm here, Clare! You don't need to talk for me, you know!'

I didn't get the hearing issue. I knew Rowan struggled with her hearing, yet I hadn't once noticed her struggling to hear me. Not once. I thought back: the night of the accident, the hospital, our telephone conversation; even when she came out of the shower, when she surely wouldn't have been wearing her hearing aids?

I wondered if Rowan was thinking along similar lines. She looked at me for a moment, before looking away. The anger was being replaced with that confusion of hers. She was frowning and was definitely going through some kind of process in her head.

'She was in the shower, so could not have possibly heard,' I observed, factually.

It was my turn now. I could resist no longer. I started appraising Rowan with my eyes. I began at her long strawberry-blonde locks that were hanging loose, moved to her face, and the soft pale, vulnerable skin of her neck, pausing *perhaps* slightly too long at the point her pulse was flaunting itself. I took in her tight-fitting khaki-coloured top. She was wearing a delicate chain around her neck and I dragged my thoughts away from where I imagined a hidden pendant might be resting. My eyes travelled lower over her curves.

What was it with my heart though? It had been quite happy with its one beat a minute for one-hundred-and-ninety-five years – but now it was racing. If it was true, that the heart of every creature has a set number of beats within its lifespan – then my immortality, or near immortality, was buggered. *Christ! What about Rowan's lifespan? Her heart beats so rapidly.* I groaned inwardly. Why did I keep thinking these wretched things?

My eyes were at her waist. It was small and led seductively to her voluptuous hips. She had a long denim skirt on today. I remembered the shower yesterday; if I could blush, I would be blushing now. I slowly raised my eyes to her face. She knew what I was doing – and was blushing for me. I immediately stopped breathing. It was a precautionary measure. Her blood-red cheeks did things to me nobody else's did. My smile was guilty, but somewhat satisfied . . . because I had felt her pleasured reaction to the path my eyes had followed.

I didn't intend to let Clare continue with her questions about yesterday and needed distraction, so decided to ask about Aunty Hetty. Madeleine would have been proud of me.

'Oh, she's fine as usual,' Clare answered my enquiry.

To all intents and purposes, I was looking at the tiled floor, but I was aware of Rowan shuffling awkwardly and a momentary grimace. Immediately concerned, I spoke urgently, 'Are you well, Rowan?'

'I'm fine thanks.' She refused to meet my now raised eyes.

'Are you in pain?' My voice was undeniably anxious. I saw Clare glance at me and then Rowan, before returning to me.

'No, I'm fine.' *Was that irritation?*

'Perhaps we should all sit down?' I suggested. How could I have let her stand for so long? I watched as she slowly made her way over to take a seat on the sofa, occasionally putting weight tentatively on her damaged foot. I scanned the room and couldn't see the crutches anywhere. Why did that not surprise me? I didn't dare offer her help, leaving it to my imagination to conjure her into my arms.

'When are you due your next painkillers?' I asked, feigning casual, as I sat down on the sofa next to her, leaving a good foot of space between us.

She looked at me challengingly, before replying, 'I'm not!' I was *definitely* irritating her.

'Clare, have you Rowan's painkillers there?' I called. Clare was still in the kitchen putting the last of the shopping away. I avoided Rowan's eyes because I knew *exactly* what she was feeling.

'Of course!' I heard a kitchen drawer move along its runners and then the sound of tap water filling a glass, before Clare entered the room.

Rowan muttered, 'Thanks,' as she took Clare's

offerings and placed them on the coffee table, making no attempt to take them.

I reached over and picked up the box of tablets. I pulled out the two sheets of pills; one was untouched, the other had a single empty pill pocket. I ignored her indignant gasp. I turned the box over to where a sticky label provided the directions of use: two tablets to be taken four times a day. The date was two days ago. It didn't take a genius, or Clare's tip-off, or the difficulty of our connection, to know that Rowan had not been taking her pills.

I chose now to look intently at Rowan. She looked defiantly back. I could be equally stubborn. I held the pills up, not looking away from her eyes. 'Why?' My voice revealed more anguish than I intended.

The bravado flickered momentarily, before returning firmly to its place. 'What's the big deal? I take them when I need them. Stop looking at me like that! God, you aren't my father . . .' And then she broke off, looking and feeling confused again. She was frowning.

'No, I am not,' I agreed quietly. 'But I *am* the person responsible for your injuries and the pain they cause you. How do you think you being in pain makes *me* feel? You have no idea how much it hurts me.'

There were two elements to that statement, I reflected. But in this instance, I was solely concerned with *Rowan's* physical pain, not my own troubles.

Her bravado was definitely slipping. 'Please take your tablets.' I had vowed never to use my charm on Rowan. But if this didn't work, it would be for her own good.

She gave an exasperated sigh, before saying, 'Give me the effing pills! I don't know what all the fuss is about.'

I handed her the packet and she squeezed out a tablet. I raised my eyebrows. She huffed, and squeezed out the second. Taking the packet, I handed her the glass of water. Her hand touched mine. I knew it would be cold. *Bugger!*

She looked at me momentarily before looking away. She said quietly, perhaps to herself, 'My dad never had warm hands.' That was not the response I had expected, but I was more than happy with it. After she had taken her pills, she dramatically opened her mouth and pointed. 'See – all gone. Happy now?'

'Happier,' I muttered, in response to her sarcastic tone.

I heard Clare chuckle in the kitchen.

'Why do you always refuse help, Rowan? Why do you feel the need to struggle with everything on your own?' I asked gently.

'Don't be ridiculous!' And then I felt a punching surge of anguish and hurt and . . . understanding? *Christ Almighty, what was she thinking?*

She looked at me accusingly, and said ever so quietly, 'You're only here because of guilt, aren't you? You're only here because you feel so *overly* responsible and want to make amends.' Her eyes were full of pain. I had to shut my own for a moment and take a deep breath to deal with her emotion.

When I felt in slightly more control, I opened my eyes and looked at her intently. I heard her gasp. I had lowered my shroud a fraction. I knew what she would be seeing in my eyes: just the tiniest glimpse of the depth of what I felt for her, but no doubt enough to provide some reassurance. Perhaps she could interpret what she saw in my eyes better than I?

I said quietly, my voice raw, 'Rowan . . . I am here because I quite simply cannot stay away.' *Way too intense!*

She was most definitely unnerved, but her pain was gone. She believed me. How could she not? After a moment, she reached out and picked up my hand. I didn't withdraw it. 'Cool, not cold,' she said, as she stroked it with her fingers. 'I don't tend to feel the cold.'

My skin may have felt cool to her, but it no longer felt that way to me. It was ablaze with her touch.

Clare walked back into the room and Rowan quickly removed her hand, much to my disappointment. Placing Rowan's *Fucking Furious* mug of coffee on the table, Clare curled up in the armchair to our right, with *Curiously Content* in her hands.

'Where were we? Oh! I remember – Aunty Hetty. Aunty Hetty's quite a character, isn't she, Rowan?'

153

'She certainly is,' Rowan agreed, affectionately.

'You seem to be close to her,' I observed.

'Well, she's basically been a mum to us,' Clare said. 'We lost our parents young.'

I knew that, but only now I had officially been told, could I express my sympathy. 'I am very sorry,' I said sincerely and looked intently at Rowan. She refused to meet my eyes.

I could feel Rowan's grief and it was still raw. Thankfully, I was seated. I wanted to comfort her, to pull her into my arms and hold her, to make the hurt go away. But would that be possible for me? I had held her in my arms before, but would it always be safe? Could every occasion be safe?

'It was a long time ago. I hardly remember them. They adopted us when we were babies. It affected Rowan more than me. I'd just turned four at the time, but Rowan was six, so can remember them more. Aunty Hetty took us in as her own.'

'Was she your mother or father's sister?' I asked gently, attempting to refocus on the conversation.

'Our mum's,' Clare replied. 'But she was so young. I don't think she'd even hit twenty when she found herself looking after us. She's been wonderful.'

Tinks, who had slinked her way into the living room, now jumped on to Rowan's lap and started purring. Rowan absent-mindedly stroked her.

'She's rather eccentric though, to say the least,' Clare observed.

'Barking, sometimes, I'd say,' Rowan added, fondly.

Tinks meowed loudly and leapt from her lap and stalked off. 'Sorry, Tinks! What did I do?' she called after her.

Clare continued, 'Yeah – Aunty Hetty is really into saving the planet in a *big* way . . . the eco-warrior type. The number of times we must have sat by her side, with her chained to a tree.'

'It was fun though,' Rowan declared, in response to my raised eyebrows. 'We used to get to camp in a tent and climb trees. Now it's evolved more to recycling, and growing vegetables. I shudder to think what she'd say if she saw my pitiful excuse for recycling. I empty all the bins before her visits!'

'Don't worry.' Clare chuckled. 'Her reaction couldn't possibly be as bad as the one to my decision to use disposable nappies with the boys. Blimey, I thought she was going to blow a gasket. But as I said, if you're volunteering to wash and iron shitty nappies all day long . . . come to think of it though – she *did* offer!' Clare laughed. 'But it didn't seem right somehow . . .'

'And there's the talking to her plants,' Rowan smiled. 'No, she seriously *does* talk to them,' she replied to my look. 'She tells them all about her day.'

'When I picked her up, to go and see Rowan in hospital,' Clare interjected, 'I even heard her tell one of them not to worry, that she was on the case and Rowan would be okay!' We all laughed.

'She certainly seems to be quite a character,' I agreed.

We were interrupted as the doorbell went. 'Expecting anyone?' Clare asked, already on the way to the door.

Rowan shook her head.

As soon as Clare was out of the room, I asked the question I so desperately wanted an answer to. 'So have you checked your availability?' I sounded too eager.

'I have.' She nodded and gave me a smile that seemed to seduce me from the inside out. I gulped. 'I could do Saturday night, if that's okay with you? Clare will be gone then.'

Yesss! Yesss! Yesss! 'Fantastic!' *How could she make me feel like this?* 'I will get the tickets booked, and collect you at seven if—?'

I didn't finish my question. I fixed Rowan with a serious, please do as I ask look. 'I will deal with this. Shut the door and lock it behind me.' And I was gone. Perhaps rather too fast before I was out of sight, but I had no intention of letting Jonathan Martin anywhere near Rowan.

He was pounding up the stairs when I blocked his way a couple of steps above the first-floor landing. Clare was running after him. 'Clare, are you hurt?' I asked anxiously. I had heard the air rush out of her lungs as he had pushed her forcefully out of the way on opening the door to him.

'I'm fine. But the bastard won't take no for an answer!' she exclaimed angrily.

'Let me deal with this,' I said quietly. 'Once Rowan lets you in, lock the door behind you.'

So *this* was Jonathan Martin? The same individual who had forced his attentions on Rowan aggressively in the hospital, had cheated on her, and had dared to lift his hand to her. *How fortunate I was here.*

Whilst I waited for the sound of the key re-locking Rowan's door, I took the opportunity to study him, all the time playing with my prey as it naively tried to pass; my movements too quick for him to see, always blocking his route, he had yet to make any contact.

He appeared slightly older than Rowan, despite their having met at university. His dark hair was cut short. He was a little more than three inches shorter than me and of a stockier build. On his face, a line of fine scars across his nose and left cheek were clearly visible. I now *officially* liked cats. I had smelt the alcohol on his breath, the moment I had opened the door . . . and the threat to Rowan. He wasn't just a nuisance; my instincts told me he was a danger.

As soon as the key turned in the lock, I exhaled the remaining air in my lungs, turned my palms upwards, looked skyward, closed my eyes which had yet to be used to meet his, and shed my human cloak. I let the creature I was, seep into my cells. I abandoned myself to the intoxicating sensation of the release and the raw feral energy that surged through my veins, purging that which was human from my physiology. My aura changed to that of the most threatening and powerful of all human predators. Chuckling, a foreboding sound for my quarry, I thought of the range of our personae: how charming we could appear; and how so far beyond terrifying we could reach.

How much had I wanted the opportunity to come face-to-face with Jonathan Martin?

'So, it is just you and me, Jonathan Martin,' I hissed, in an icy whisper that would slice cold and deep into his soul. My eyes were still shut, but I knew he had stilled, ceasing his frustrated attempts to pass. His disquiet hovered in the air, expectant, waiting. His heart skipped a couple of beats before it began pounding uncertainly. The stair creaked as he took an uncertain step back, and I heard his clumsy fall on to the landing a couple of steps below. Some scurrying activity had him standing; I could hear his nervous, shuffling feet. The sound of his gulp, as he struggled to moisten his now dry mouth.

He half choked, 'Who the fuck are you?'

I grinned, widely, sinisterly. No fangs out – this wasn't blood lust for consumption, more for decoration. Or it would have been, were we properly alone. I was very aware of Rowan upstairs; I could hear her, true to form, arguing with Clare about being locked in. She was frustrated, although I no longer felt it; intriguingly, her feelings had been expelled with my human cloaking.

I told myself, this could only be a warning. I had to remain in control.

'*What* am I – is the more pertinent question, Jonathan Martin.'

'Are you sleeping with the bitch? Are . . . you fu—' His voice cracked mid-yell and ceased completely as my powers surged and a prolonged growl reverberated from my chest.

Silly, silly, silly: and he was university-educated? He *really* should not have said that.

My eyes snapped open, instantly fixing on their target. I smiled sadistically, knowing how they would appear: totally black, the whites completely swallowed up in their hellish depths; malevolently glowing as if illuminated from deep within. My snigger at his reaction was pure evil. The colour had drained completely from his face, the whites of his eyes shocked into their bulging, and his mouth gaped open; Edvard Munch's *The Scream* sprang to mind. His body began to tremble, uncontrollably.

Instantaneously, I was right before him, yet he had been observing me through his terror, eight feet away. In contrast, the movement of my head as I leant in was slow, deliberate. I whispered in his ear, 'Try and run.' My taunting movement back was too drawn out to be human. I watched his stumbling and scrambling attempt at flight. And just as he thought he had made it to the door, I was there.

'You can never *run* from me, Jonathan Martin. You can never *hide* from me. I can be in every shadow you see, every breeze you feel across your face, every prickle of your subconscious.'

Taking an angled step closer, so he was pinned

against the wall behind the door, I moved my cocked head closer still. I spoke. My breath skimming across his contorted features, branding my words upon him. My voice could have journeyed directly from hell. 'You *ever* speak about her like that again, I will rip your tongue out and feed it to you. You ever come *near* Rowan again, I will slowly, oh so slowly, tear you to pieces, limb by bloody limb. Your blood-curdling screams will amuse me, whilst your pounding heart pumps your lifeblood out of your agonised, broken body. You will beg for mercy, which I will not give. You will pray for death. And I *will* oblige; but slowly, oh so slowly.'

I hoped that had done the trick. I was actually worried he might have a heart attack, and that would be a particularly difficult one to explain to Rowan. 'Have I made myself clear enough, Jonathan Martin?' A frenzied nod followed. 'Look at me.' His eyes confirmed it. Only then did I reinstate my human cloaking. *Oh, to have had him in an isolated room, all to myself.*

'Then you may go,' I said, stepping aside, my voice having reverted to its more usual human tone.

I watched him struggle frantically with the latch on the door. When he finally got it open, I said politely, 'Please shut the door behind you.' He obliged by closing it gently – not wanting to tempt my wrath with a slam? I heard his stumbling footsteps and his strangled gasps for air as he fled.

★   ★   ★

I knocked gently on Rowan's door and she opened it to let me in, but not before she had looked at me intently, with huge suspicious eyes. I raised my eyebrows questioningly. As I moved into the room, I saw Clare at the window. She turned and looked at me amazed. 'What on earth did you say to him? He's just shot across the road at top speed, narrowly missing a bus. He wouldn't have been able to run any faster if a monster was after him!'

I smiled awkwardly. I looked at Rowan, standing leaning with her back against the now closed door, her arms crossed. I could feel suspicion. 'I simply had a quiet word with him. Man to Man so to speak – or *Monster* to Man if you prefer . . .' I chuckled. I was pleased with myself. There was nothing I could do about that.

'*That* man *is* a monster, Nate. Well done! You've no idea how much he has hurt Rowan in the past. The number of times I've had to come and pick up the pieces with her crying her eyes out. Let's hope that's done the trick.'

'I am very happy to talk to him again, if necessary,' I offered, not for one moment thinking it would be.

Rowan was still eyeing me suspiciously. Yet, amidst her emotions, I could feel relief; relief hopefully that Jonathan Martin had left. Hopefully not relief I had let him leave with his limbs still intact. I looked at Clare. 'Are you sure you aren't hurt? Should I get you a glass of water for the shock?'

Rowan rolled her eyes, but Clare beamed at me.

161

'No, Nate – thank you, though.' Clare started to smooth her hair again. 'He just pushed me out of the way rather too hard. It's so lucky you were here. Our gallant knight in shining armour, hey Rowan?'

An exasperated noise escaped Rowan as she hobbled back to the sofa.

Clare headed back over to the armchair. 'You are such a gentleman. There aren't enough gentlemen in the world today. You could give my Mark a lesson or two.'

Rowan shook her head and I smiled to myself, whilst sitting down in my former position on the sofa next to her.

'In fact, I'd love you to meet him – and the boys, of course!'

I observed Rowan give Clare a warning look and shake her head frantically.

Clare ignored her. 'You really don't have to say yes – in fact, I'd perfectly understand it if you didn't . . . I'm sure you're a very busy man. But Tom's birthday party is next Sunday. It would be *wonderful* if you came along. Rowan's coming, aren't you, love?'

Rowan grunted. I looked at her, but she was fidgeting with her packet of tablets. *A vampire being invited to a human child's birthday party?* This was seriously uncharted territory.

'He'll be four, a great age. It's only a couple of hours. It's a dinosaur theme. I'm hiring a dinosaur fancy-dress costume for Mark to dress up in, not that he knows that yet. I'm going to have to choose my moment for that one! *You* obviously don't have to come in fancy dress,' she added quickly.

What the hell? It was another opportunity to be with Rowan, and I would take any that were offered me. 'Thank you, Clare. It is most kind of you to invite me,' and I flashed a smile that resulted in a sharp intake of breath. 'I would be honoured to accept your invitation . . . but wouldn't dream of doing so, if Rowan is not happy with my attendance.'

Rowan met my enquiring look. She really hadn't expected me to accept the invitation and there was clear surprise and uncertainty there. What was she thinking? Her emotions were shedding no light. She was suspicious of me, no doubt. But how suspicious? How would she respond?

Suddenly she smiled. It was a wonderful, mesmerising smile. I could feel her amusement, and her eyes sparkled. She looked at me mischievously, with a triumphant look in her eyes. 'I'm perfectly happy for Nathaniel to attend Clare, but there's one proviso – he *does* come in fancy dress. I reckon the more dinosaurs the merrier!'

Dear God! How the bloody hell, could a two-hundred-and-thirty-year-old vampire, go to a human child's birthday party – dressed as a bloody dinosaur! If James or Frederick ever got wind of this . . .

But I could tell from the look on her face she thought she had won this one. She thought I would make my excuses. But no, she had underestimated

163

me. I wasn't about to turn down any opportunity to be with her, no matter how humiliating. I did need to gulp before I spoke, but found myself uttering, 'That presents no problem. I would be honoured to come to Tom's birthday party . . . dressed as a dinosaur.'

Rowan stared at me in utter disbelief, and I couldn't quite believe what I had just agreed to. Her mouth was open in an 'O,' to complete the picture. I knew she associated me with danger, probably even more so since Jonathan Martin was seen fleeing from the house after a few quiet words from me. But this would give me a chance to show her I could be safe. But . . . there must be easier ways.

I met Rowan's stare with a broad smile, and a triumphant look of my own. She crossed her arms, shook her head and sighed frustratingly. She was frowning. She looked adorable.

Clare spoke delightedly, 'Brilliant! Are you sure? It would be really wonderful! Mark will *have* to dress up now! Do you want me to get you a costume?'

'No! I'm sure he can sort one out for himself,' Rowan replied on my behalf. She was going to make this as difficult as possible.

'Of course I can.'

I considered a quick retreat to be in order, before matters deteriorated further. Rising rapidly from the sofa, I reached into my pocket, retrieved my sunglasses and pulled out Rowan's car keys. 'I really should take my leave . . .'

'Hold up!' Rowan interrupted. 'You are *not* going to leave the car, without my having inspected it.'

'Rowan, that really is rude!' Clare exclaimed, giving me an apologetic look.

Why did Rowan's response not surprise me? 'I can understand Rowan's concerns. Shall we?' I held my hand out to Rowan, in order to help her up. She shuffled around a bit to see if she could get up quickly and easily by herself, sighed, and reluctantly put her hand in mine. The heat that channelled through my body from our physical connection was pure bliss. Pulling her gently to her feet, I said my farewells to Clare and promised I would remember the address for the damned party.

As soon as the flat's door closed behind us, I turned to Rowan. I was not going to let her struggle down the stairs, I just couldn't do it. And I knew if she was given a choice, she would refuse my assistance. I took a deep breath. No, I took *two* deep breaths. 'Rowan . . . I know you aren't going to like this . . . and I am sorry – truly I am sorry. But it really is by far the best way for you to get down the stairs safely.'

I carefully swept her feet up from under her and, cradling her gently in my arms, took a moment to gauge her feelings: they were in turmoil, but there was, much to my surprise – and relief, as I really needed to do this – no anger or fear there. I was not at all sure what was there. But I could function! I proceeded to carry Rowan down the stairs. She was speechless, probably because her breathing was so rapid.

I spoke gently, amazed my voice remained even and didn't betray my body's delirium at our physical contact. 'I have no intention of watching you struggle down the stairs, not when you do not have to, and this way is quicker, too. I think I need to get home, before you get me to agree to something else that—'

Rowan broke her silence with a giggle.

'I am glad *you* find the situation amusing. You have just got me agreeing to dress up as a dinosaur! Do you have *any* idea how humiliating that is?' The full extent of what I had agreed to was only just beginning to sink in.

'I'm sorry! I really didn't expect you to do it. It's not very Jane Austen, is it?'

No, it wasn't actually, but neither was that a bad thing. *Was there a way of viewing this wretched dinosaur business positively?* Not answering her question, I gently asked the one that was on my mind, 'Do you really not want me to be there? If you do not, I can make my excuses.'

She paused for a moment, looked up at me, before playfully saying, 'No – it's fine. I really wouldn't miss it for the world now.'

I was going to get a complex. I was currently proving to be the object of fun for everyone.

'You can put me down now,' Rowan said, once we had reached the bottom of the stairs. I ignored her and effortlessly opened the front door. 'You're

166

not going to walk down the road, carrying me in your arms,' she warned.

'Am I not?'

'No! Please . . . *for pity's sake!* I live here! I'm likely to know people!'

But what harm could it do? I was in control, and this way she need not hobble.

Rowan half-heartedly struggled for a few moments, but knew she had no chance. She was now trying to undertake damage limitation. I liked what that entailed. She snuggled ever closer to me, hiding her face from anyone we saw. My body was rejoicing – and God she smelt wonderful. Too wonderful, I reflected, and took the precaution of holding my breath.

Rowan's attempts at anonymity didn't work. The car was only one hundred yards down the road, but we encountered three different people in that short distance, all of whom knew Rowan. There was a casual, never-bat-an-eyelid, 'Hi, Rowan,' that continued to saunter on his way, listening to one of those musical gadget things that James has; the curious, intrigued friend, '*Rowan?* That *is* you, isn't it? Um, I'll call you tonight!' that then walked backwards down the street, seemingly unable to remove her eyes from me, following my, 'Good day to you,' and the, 'Wow! Rowan – way to go!' that smirked and continued on his own way. To each greeting, Rowan kept her face hidden, and simply waved her arm. She was acutely embarrassed, but it appeared I could function with embarrassment.

I, on the other hand, was feeling pretty damned happy with myself. Rowan felt so good in my arms. I refused to put her down, until I had opened the car door, and could place her gently on the seat. I stayed down at her level for a moment. I knew she wasn't happy with me, but at least she wasn't angry; I wasn't sure what she was. 'Sorry – I couldn't help myself,' I said gently. But I was not sorry at all.

'That was so humiliating!' she gasped. Her face was flushed and her breathing erratic.

I continued to speak gently, 'What is the point of hobbling, when I am around?' Sensing a retort coming, I quickly changed the subject. 'So – what do you think of the car?'

Rowan recovered herself and inspected it, suspiciously. She noticed the new seatbelts, steering wheel and door panels – the last two had had to be fitted to accommodate some of the countless air bags, but I indicated they *might* be simple replacements. But there was nothing else for her to really see. I thought I had got away with it, at least until she drove it, which wouldn't be for a while yet.

'See – nothing to worry about!' I proclaimed, ensuring my relief didn't sound in my voice, and pleased my glasses were now on, as I doubted the guilt in my eyes was fully hidden.

She was still uncertain, but failed to find anything to justify her suspicions, so she beamed at me. 'Thank you! You know, I had this crazy idea you'd do something above and beyond with the car. Thank you for respecting my wishes – it means so much to me!'

Bugger! Bugger! Bugger! Well, I was going to stop feeling guilty. It was to keep her safe, and I had a few weeks' grace.

'My pleasure, Rowan.'

CHAPTER 9

MOVIE NIGHT

It was 9.30 a.m., Monday morning, and I was sat on the edge of my four-poster bed, psychologically preparing myself for the shopping expedition Elizabeth had scheduled for the day. The shutters were open and the sun was already casting shafts of light through the large sash windows, spotlighting pieces of gleaming mahogany antique furniture around the room.

I didn't like shopping. I had *never* liked shopping – but I knew it had to be better than what I had agreed to do on Sunday. I trembled again at the thought, but reflected if the trembling stopped within eight minutes, I was improving.

My mind and body had begun to react badly to the invitation acceptance at 5 a.m. I considered I had probably either been in denial, or delayed shock, up to that point. But since then, my mind had somehow identified the 'dinosaur crisis' as something not at home in my head; it didn't have anywhere remotely suitable to file it. Homeless, with nowhere to go, it kept flashing before me in crystal clarity. I kept, therefore, seeing my acceptance play before me again and again and again

170

– and in a cruel twist, I was never able to see or hear Rowan in the playback; only myself uttering the immortal words, 'I would be honoured to come to Tom's birthday party . . . dressed as a dinosaur.'

My body had not taken kindly to the situation either. It was now breaking out into periods of uncontrollable trembling, whenever my mind involuntarily flashed the memories up. It was as if it was attempting to purge itself of such alien matter – 'a vampire detox' was how Elizabeth had chosen to describe it.

I still didn't know how I had ended up committing to something so completely and utterly alien to my character-traits, as well as to my vampire alter ego. I recalled Elizabeth's words, when I had finally let her into my head – and it had taken until we had reached the Isle of Wight. Only then had I felt confident we were far enough away from James and Frederick, to lower my guard on this one: '*You* are going to do this? You – Nathaniel Gray, Earl of Ridings, who has always been too proud and disagreeable to practise the art of small-talk – *you* are going to do this?' She had then promptly fallen off the roof of Carisbrooke Castle in shock.

'Sweetheart, are you improving?' Elizabeth asked, now appearing at my side.

Did I detect an undertone of humour in her voice? I weighed up the evidence. After she had got over her initial shock last night, she had moved on to

171

hysteria. She had laughed so hard and so long that she was unable to fly under her own steam and I had had to carry her all the way home. Indeed, I had had to fly at a higher altitude than usual, to prevent the eerie supernatural sound of her unrestrained laughter causing untold terror amongst the human populace below. Yes – there was definitely humour in her voice, I deduced.

I was going to reply silently as the quaking made it difficult to verbally speak, but it stopped. *Yesss!* I exhaled deeply. Checking my watch, I advised her dryly, 'Down from forty-six minutes at the start, to two minutes and three seconds now. And you know this really is not remotely amusing . . . I have no idea what is becoming of me.'

I sensed Elizabeth's mood change and gave her a questioning look.

She spoke quietly, 'I do . . . it came to me this morning. You are *in love* with this girl – and will do absolutely anything to spend time with her.'

Love? Obsession yes, but . . . 'Elizabeth, I will grant you obsessed. You know what we are like but there is not—'

'You wouldn't do what you are proposing, for anything short of love, Nate,' she said, shaking her head. 'I was worried about the future before . . .' she looked at me with such concern. 'But now – I'm scared stupid!'

This wouldn't do. Any thinking about the future or the bigger picture would not do. 'I have to take this day by day, Elizabeth.' I tucked a stray strand of her hair behind her ear. 'Just know that right now, I *need* to see her. I need this much.'

'I know . . . it's just sometimes . . .' She shook her head rapidly and attempted a smile. 'Forgive me . . . I'm meant to be making this easier for you, not harder!' With determination, she continued, 'And if you can do this, so can I. Day by day it is.' Teasingly, she continued, 'But I still think it's love!'

'Elizabeth, I am obsessive . . .'

'Obsessively in love, Nate. You'll see. But for now, are we going shopping or what? I'm going to make the most of the here and now, too!'

We were on the human escalators in Selfridges, when I sought reassurance from Elizabeth that the Rowan situation wasn't causing problems between her and Frederick. I knew I was asking so much of her, excluding him from events.

She was swinging her bags enthusiastically. 'No, honestly – our marriage is great! In fact, it's spiced things up. You wouldn't *believe* the things he'll do to try and get information out of me . . .'

Dear God! No! 'Elizabeth, I really do not think . . .'

We stepped off the end, and I was herded towards the shoes. She grinned. 'Okay, point taken . . . *But* I do have a great idea for protecting my thoughts from him *and* enhancing my marriage! I've bought a new book from Amazon. I'm going to read it and then simply think of it when he's around. It's going to drive him nuts, completely preoccupy him, and then hopefully *unite* us!'

A book? 'What book have you bought? I know the library here is not up to the standards of Ridings, but there are still more than 40,000 volumes.'

'You haven't got this book. I checked both the town house and the inventory for Ridings. Don't worry – I'll be pleased to donate it to your collection once I've got it in my head.' There was definitely a mischievous play to her mouth.

I was intrigued, and she knew it. Chuckling, 'Go on then . . . put me out of my misery . . . And no! I am *definitely* not wearing those shoes.' Elizabeth had held up a pair, too modern and too casual.

Pausing from the shopping for a moment, she beamed at me. 'Ha Ha! It's so clever – *The Complete Illustrated Kama Sutra.* It's a bit tame; obviously designed with human limitations in mind, but it will get his imagination going on how a vampire might improve on the positions. Now how clever is that?'

'Good God, Elizabeth!' I muttered. I was beginning to wonder if it wasn't women full stop, rather than just human women, who were unpredictable and disturbing.

'Don't be so prim and proper, Nate – it's only sex – although I'm being insensitive, bearing in mind how long big brother's been without! But don't you think it's a good idea?'

Once my initial shock ebbed, I *could* see its merits. My sister was proving to be more cunning than I had ever considered she could be. It was strange; I wasn't seeing her two dimensionally anymore, but most definitely three. Previously she had simply been my little sister, whom I had always felt the need to protect.

I shook my head. 'Actually, Elizabeth, I think it is genius – and I am most proud of you. I am beginning to feel sorry for Frederick though!'

'Oh, don't feel sorry for him – he so deserves it! I'm finding this whole experience liberating. I really appreciate you letting me be involved.'

'Just make sure you do *not* think about that book when James is around. James needs no such encouragement.'

'No, I have a different book for him,' she confessed smugly. 'Well, a series actually – which I *did* find in your library: ancient Latin journals, written by some celibate monks. I thought he'd like those!'

I laughed. 'I love you so very much, Elizabeth!'

'Ditto, big brother! And you have no idea how much I love hearing you laugh!' Snapping herself back to the task in hand, she continued, 'Okay, let's make do with the other shoes – now, on to the next stage!'

I couldn't believe how surreal life now was, nor that Hamleys, one of the world's largest toy shops, was being visited by two vampires, one more intent than the other on shopping for a birthday present for a four-year-old mortal boy. I had been reluctant; in fact I had been *very* reluctant. But Elizabeth had convincingly argued, if I was going to be around a group of human children on Sunday, I should at least get some practice in.

The experience was enlightening in more ways than I could have imagined. As I wandered around the seven floors of the shop, much more than a fish out of water, I realised for the first time what Elizabeth had lost when she had become immortal. I had become a vampire primarily to help her deal with the change, to ensure we could still be together, but it was painful to realise how I had missed the glaringly obvious.

Elizabeth shielded her thoughts from me for much of the time in this particular shop, but all I had to do was look into her eyes, to know why. Elizabeth could never become a mother and have children of her own, as I could never become a father. She had found the love of her life in 1847, in the form of Frederick. They had been together all this time – and would be for eternity, of that I was sure. But they could never have a family of their own. As I watched Elizabeth crouch down, with a look of such tender love on her face, to return a toy thrown from a pushchair to a tiny grasping hand, I felt my heart breaking. A life for an immortal was not without its sacrifices. *How had I been blind for so long?* As she returned to her feet, she met my eyes. She knew I knew, and she gave me a sad smile.

'Don't tell Freddie,' she whispered. We hugged, surrounded by giant cuddly toys and helicopters buzzing around our heads. We left with some kind of soft robotic ride-on dinosaur.

'You seem to be getting more of a hold on Rowan's emotions,' Elizabeth mused, as we flew over Trafalgar Square. It was 10 p.m. and Elizabeth and I were heading out to find supper. 'In the main, you've been able to function today.'

I recalled finding myself slumped against walls on a number of occasions and on others, clutching desperately at Elizabeth. 'You mean, I managed to stay on my *feet*?'

'Well that *is* an improvement, love!'

I reflected. 'Indeed it is,' I concluded, whilst grinning. Perhaps my attempts at compartmentalising those problematic stronger, negative feelings of Rowan's, were working? I had been putting concerted effort into trying to segregate them, trying to find a place for them within me that allowed for physical function.

'Are you still sceptical about being in love?' she teased.

I sighed. She had shocked me with mention of that word. I couldn't analyse what I felt for Rowan. But I knew it couldn't be love. 'Everyone says love is selfless,' I declared. 'Having any contact with Rowan, whilst I am a threat to her, is selfish – not selfless.'

'I'm not sure it's anywhere near as simple as

that. And in any event, I don't think you're a threat to her. Not any more. Deep down, I believe you know that, too. Otherwise you wouldn't be spending time with her.'

'Thank you, Elizabeth, but I do not know that for sure!' *How could I ever know that?* 'And anyway, there is the trust issue, too. I am not being honest with her.'

'But you want to be . . .'

Too much, I thought. I hated deceiving her. *But if she knew . . .*

'The fact you are feeling that, should tell you something. I just can't help but think— I just don't know why we're all ruling out a future with her. It's so obvious to me, that you've *finally* found someone you can love. Perhaps if you told her—'

'She would quite rightly run away screaming! You are being a hopeless romantic. Just say, I no longer considered myself a threat – which is NOT the case – and she didn't run, when she discovered my monstrous secret – which she WOULD. She is a *human* woman. She needs a normal physical relationship and to have a family, children. There can be NO future, Elizabeth, which is why I cannot think about it, and why I pleaded with you not to talk of it! Do not ruin this for me!'

'We know a physical relationship is possible, because of James.'

Jesus! 'No, we do not!' As far as I was concerned, that simply was NOT possible.

'Yes, we do – you're just in denial. So it's about children.'

'No, it is not just about children,' I snapped. This was a topic I *really* didn't want to discuss with Elizabeth.

'I would have liked to have children, as you gathered today, so I know why you're thinking like this. But what if she chose to be with you, rather than to have children?'

'Elizabeth, she should not have to make the choice!'

'But if she did?'

'It is not an option!'

'You are so pig-headed, you know! It's pointless having such a discussion with you, because your mind's made up.' She paused before proceeding, 'But I'll put the cat amongst the pigeons . . . You could adopt.'

'I am sorry?' I must have misunderstood. Not a usual occurrence, but what was now usual?

'You could adopt children.'

'We could adopt *human* children?'

'Why not? *I've* been thinking about it and with Rowan being adopted . . .'

I snapped my head around to look at her. *She couldn't be serious. She really couldn't.* '*You* have been thinking about what? *Adopting?*' My voice was half way between snarl and roar.

'I haven't spoken to Freddie about it.' *Dear God. She was.*

'Good God, Elizabeth! No wonder you have not. It is insane!' That was a roar.

'But why? We could give them a loving home.' Elizabeth spoke shakily.

I instantly regretted roaring. 'Elizabeth . . .' I said gently. Then sighed, 'Elizabeth . . . Rowan was not adopted by vampires.'

'Agreed, but that's beside the point. Look, I can love deeply and—'

'I know you can. So how could you bear to love your children – *human* children – and watch them grow old and die? Even if you used the power, so as not to feel the pain, the gap in your existence would be—'

'Who says I'd need to?'

'You are not *seriously* thinking what I think you are thinking?'

'They would know what we are, and if as adults they wanted to join us, then it would be their choice.'

'I cannot believe you could even consider—'

Clearly not wishing to continue the subject, Elizabeth interrupted me quickly with something guaranteed to distract. 'Enough about me – would you consider changing Rowan?'

'NE—' I couldn't finish my furious response. My whole body was overwhelmed by the most agonising sensation. It felt like grief! Elizabeth grabbed my left arm as I went into free fall, and dragged me to the nearest high-rise rooftop.

I was crippled. It couldn't get worse than grief.

What had happened? What was making Rowan feel this way? I had to help her, to be with her, but I was completely incapable of functioning. 'Rowan . . .' was all I was able to choke out, and Elizabeth immediately took control of things.

I was writhing around in agony when she deposited me in the park around the corner from Rowan's flat. 'It'll by okay, I promise,' she whispered, before fleeing to investigate. When Elizabeth returned a few minutes later, laughing, I thought she had gone mad.

'It's going to be okay,' she reassured quickly.

I looked at her wildly. She smiled and stroked my face, asking gently, 'What have you got yourself into, sweetheart? Rowan is absolutely fine! I've seen her, she's fine. I reckon you've only a few more minutes of this, before the film reaches a more acceptable point.'

She must have seen some kind of reaction in my feral, panicked eyes, because she grinned and nodded slowly. 'Yes, *a film*, Nate. She's simply watching a devastatingly sad film. She's currently sat in her living room with Clare, and they are both bawling their eyes out at a film, I gather is called *Truly Madly Deeply*. I understand it's about a human couple desperately in love. He dies, comes back as a ghost to help her through her grief, and I think they are at the point where he leaves her. She'll perk up soon, I promise! Believe it or not – they appear to have watched it before and *know* what it does to them!'

Why would she willingly do this to herself? And how could she deal with such emotional onslaught?

Would it all get easier for me the longer I experienced emotion – or would it always be this hard?

By the time I could pull myself up into a sitting position to rest my back against the nearest tree trunk, I realised I was both bewildered and terrified. What terrified me the most was how incapacitated I could still become. What would I do if Rowan got into serious trouble and really needed me? My attempts at compartmentalising were obviously not working after all. I was going to have to work even harder at it. There had to be a way.

The inevitable culmination of the Monday-night movie was my sitting on Rowan's roof regularly. Now, more than ever, I needed context. It was the only way I would be able to gauge whether Rowan's emotions merited a full-blown rescue mission, or were simply the result of a human woman's bewildering pastimes.

I would be there most nights, and as much as possible during the day. I knew it was risky, but the tree on the other side of the chimney was in leaf now and pretty much disguised me, as long as I kept a low profile.

It felt wonderful being closer to her. It was liberating not worrying whether she was still alive if she wasn't awake by 7.30 a.m., or whether my losing her again ten minutes later was, indeed, because she was only taking a shower; I could now check on her breathing and hear the sound of the water.

Listening into Rowan's days was fascinating, bewildering, awe-inspiring, humbling, but whatever the occasion – sustaining. The invasion of privacy I suppose was unforgivable, but as far as I was concerned, it was justified. I was there for her if needed, and context being applied to her emotions, made the whole connection that much easier for me.

And it had been in the nick of time, I reflected on Saturday morning, clambering back on to the roof, totally traumatised. *How the hell could a woman get herself into such a state – about a 'freakily long' facial hair she swore appeared overnight?* I had been half way through the window, desperately fighting against the physical restrictions her feelings placed on me, before I had discovered what her horror and terror related to. *Jesus!*

And there was the obsession with her weight, for Christ's sake! Who cared if she was in size 12 or size 14 clothes? She was beautiful. And how surreal had my existence become? I now found myself either depressed or joyous – depending on the result of Rowan's ritual weigh-in each morning! Today's had not been good. The muttering and wittering had prepared me for that one. But nothing had prepared me, in my usual rooftop perch, for her outraged declaration as the scales provided their reading: 'Someone up there is taking the effing piss!'

The day could only get better, I reflected, and grinned broadly to myself – it was the official date tonight. But then I spotted Aunty Hetty approaching Rowan's door, and immediately lost my good humour. I inched myself even tighter to the chimney stack before hearing, 'Nathaniel. I very much doubt Rowan would approve of your choice of campsite . . . but for the present, your secret is safe with me.'

There was no way she should have been able to see me! And how did she know I would be able to hear her so quiet words? 'What are you?' I gasped, as much to myself as to her.

'A concerned mother-figure, Nathaniel. DO NOT break her heart.'

I was too shocked to respond, but when my heart rate had returned to normal, I focused intently on the conversation now taking place in the flat below. I should have known it would provide no enlightenment. It was all about the birthday party – which did nothing to make me feel better.

Her timing could not have been better, I thought, angrily. Why did she have to act even more damned abnormally on today of all days? I was struggling with keeping the 'bigger picture' issues out of my head as it was. Rowan was human and I was . . . And I was deceiving her . . . There could be no future and . . .

And Madeleine's call hadn't damned well helped matters. She was on her way back and *insisting* I meet with her urgently. Well, she was going to have to wait. Nothing was going to ruin my stepping-out with Rowan. *Nothing.*

CHAPTER 10

MAMA MIA!

Elizabeth found me in my dressing room. The theatre tickets were in the pocket of my new coat, along with my hand warmers. My wallet was in the inside pocket. The taxi was booked to pick us both up from Rowan's, but I knew I was looking perplexed. *Had I remembered everything?*

'No, you haven't,' Elizabeth silently replied to my thought, coming over to reposition my jacket collar. 'I, however, have! I believe these days *flowers* are required on a first date?' She smiled smugly.

I looked at her horrified.

'You weren't to know, so are excused. In keeping with your previous floral gift – so *very* impressive, Nate – I arranged for more flowers from Ridings to be sent down. They are a mixture of red and white this time. Ben, the head gardener, thinks the *rabbits* are the reason for the shortage in white . . . *Aaaaanyway*, my florist has made them into what you will hopefully find to be an acceptable bouquet.'

Red for blood, I thought. *And white for innocence.* They would no doubt smell sweetly fragrant.

'Stop it, Nate!' Elizabeth snapped. 'Give yourself

a break! That sort of thinking is hardly going to help. They are ready to go on the table by the door. The boys are out of the way.' The sounds of clashing swords confirmed James and Frederick to not be as out of the way as I would have liked. They were evidently fencing in the cellar. 'But if you don't want the roses, then . . .'

'Elizabeth, thank you – of course I do!' I said, shaking myself out of the momentary gloom. I put it down to worry, and the guilt at deceiving Rowan, which was now forever rearing its head. I should be walking away, not . . .

'Now, off you go – and enjoy. And you *will* tell me all about it when you get back!'

I was at Rowan's early. I hadn't flown, or driven, but had arrived by foot, effortlessly weaving between tourists and resident Londoners as they went about their Saturday evening human lives. No doubt there were many, not quite like me, but who, *like* me, were on their way to greet their cherished ones.

I stood across the road from Rowan's home. Was it impolite to arrive five minutes early? I hadn't a clue. I had never done this before. Not as human; not as vampire. I paced around for a few moments, before giving up. I needed to be with her. What was four minutes and thirty-nine seconds?

As I rang the buzzer for Flat 3, I felt her nerves and anticipated excitement – so in tandem with my own. I smiled contentedly.

But I was snapped out of the good place I was

at by the horror that dawned. Now Clare had returned home, Rowan was going to have to struggle down the two flights of stairs on her own to answer the door. I could so easily prevent that treacherous and dangerous journey by arriving through the window, but how could I? I could think of no way to prevent what was about to happen.

I felt Rowan's frustration as she slowly made her way down the stairs, but it wasn't a patch on my own. I was in agony. *What if she fell? What if she broke her neck and died?* I ended up gently (only because I didn't want to draw attention to myself), but repeatedly, banging my forehead on the door as I tracked her progress – ready to smash it down should she come anywhere close to missing her footing. I could hear each step she made, and her occasional accompanying curses. It was excruciating. When she had safely navigated the last step, I was beside myself with relief. When she opened the door . . . I was simply beside myself – *Rowan.*

Those eyes of hers looked shyly at me, and her smile would have taken my breath away – had I, at that point, any air in my lungs to take away. I could hear her heart beating erratically, most probably due to the effort of reaching the door, but I hoped some of it was for me. My heart, previously galloping, was now racing. Her scent was, as ever, intoxicating, and she was pleased to see me – I could feel it. I was elated. This was why I was pursuing Rowan Locke. When I was out of her presence, I worried; in her presence, that was all I ever wanted to be.

I finally pulled myself together. 'Rowan,' I said, just loving hearing the sound of her name.

'Nate, hi,' she said, giving me a smile that turned into a laugh. Even though it was a nervous laugh, it was a magical sound. I laughed, too; whether it sounded as nervous as I felt, I wasn't sure.

'You look *breathtaking*!' I observed, as I was finally able to drag my eyes from her face to take in the full picture. She was wearing a dress, the colour of which allowed the subtle copper tints within her hair to shine and made her sparkling eyes look like emeralds of such clarity, that no amount of money could ever afford them. No, I corrected myself. Such priceless perfection could *never* exist other than within the exquisite face before me.

'Thank you.' She smiled, clearly pleased with my spoken words. 'You don't look too bad yourself!' Her eyes had swept quickly over my body, and now started the more leisurely journey I so loved. But she stopped. She seemed to be making herself deliberately stop, and she shook her head, laughing nervously, and raised her eyes to mine; she knew they would be watching.

Remembering myself, I handed her the flowers with a slight bow of the head, 'For you, Rowan.'

'They are gorgeous – thank you!' She took a moment to look at them, letting her finger tips run and . . . linger over selected petals . . . *Lucky petals . . .*

Swallowing hard, I forced myself to refocus: *She liked the flowers!* Yes, she *liked the flowers*! *Thank you, Elizabeth.* 'Come on up, then,' she piped, shuffling aside to allow me in.

When she had closed the door, I looked at her with pleading eyes. 'May I?' She looked confused and clearly needed clarification. My arms swept towards the staircase and then to her. 'May I *please* assist?' She had categorically refused such assistance after the car inspection last weekend. Indeed she had appeared to get distressed at the prospect of me carrying her up the stairs. I had therefore had to reluctantly put her down at their foot, and go through the excruciating process of watching her tackle the two perilous flights by herself. That had then been *my* turn to be distressed.

Today, she looked taken aback at my suggestion, and I could feel her uncertainty; her heart was now racing and she was biting her lower lip. She shook her head, blushing deeply. After taking a deep breath, she said, 'I don't think that's a good idea. I *very* much doubt you'd make it up there with me, I'm *way* too heavy.'

It was about her *weight*? This was such an unhealthy obsession! 'It will be effortless,' I insisted. Waiting for her to meet my eyes, I looked at her intently. I gently asked, 'Is that your only concern?'

She nodded whilst again looking at the floor. 'That and the fact you might hurt yourself. Last

189

time you were coming *down* the stairs, going up them – you wouldn't have a hope!'

I smiled reassuringly. 'Not a chance, Rowan.' My smile turned to a grin. '*Not. A. Chance.* And on that basis . . .' I gently scooped her into my arms. 'I thank you for letting me do the honours.' Experiencing surprise from Rowan, rather than distress, I proceeded to carry her – with no physical effort at all – up the stairs. The effort was more in putting her down again, when we had reached her living room.

She smelt beautiful and my body was blazing where it touched hers. Although I could hear her quickened heart rate, and knew what it would be doing to the pulse on her neck, it was her lips and the delicate little freckles on her nose that I was fixating on. I wondered how it would feel to kiss them. No – I *needed* to know how it would feel. But how could I take the risk with something so precious and fragile? How did I know I was strong enough to shield her from the monster within? It was pure, unadulterated agony. When I refocused on Rowan's eyes, she was looking worriedly at me and I could feel her hurt and anxiety.

'You're in pain! I can see it in your eyes. I've hurt you, haven't I? I *told* you I was too heavy. I am so sorry! Put me down quickly – is it your back?'

I shook my head and chuckled, 'Rowan, you were as light as a feather.' *She was concerned about me!*

She huffed and shook her head in disbelief. 'You're simply being a gentleman. If I am as *light as a feather*, why are you hurting?'

I was determined to be as honest as I could be. 'Because . . . I never want to put you down.' *Bugger! Why was I always so intense around her?*

The atmosphere between us deepened, as did the seductiveness of her gaze. I noticed her lips part fractionally. *Bloody hell – I could* not *handle this! I had* to put her down – and quickly. I very gently lowered her to her feet. She was standing there, with the flowers in her hand, biting her lip again. I wondered what it would feel like to gently nibble that lip. *Christ!* And feeling her disappointment at being put down wasn't helping matters one little bit. I had to recover myself. I had always taken pride in my self-control, so why was this so damned difficult? 'Shall I get a vase for the flowers?' I asked, attempting to sound casual.

She was distracted, blinked a couple of times and said, with a slight tremor, 'Oh! Of course . . . thanks – in the corner, by the sink.' She started to hobble to the kitchen, but I intercepted her and retrieved the flowers.

'Let me do this. You sit down.'

She seemed amused. I noted she didn't sit, but continued to stand and watch. I could feel what her eyes were doing to my back. Her feelings had lost their amusement; they had reverted to what they had been when she had been in my arms.

Dammit! How was I supposed to do this? How was I

supposed to resist? I tried to concentrate on what I was doing, but that really didn't help because I had just realised something . . . how the hell was I supposed to arrange flowers? I started to laugh nervously.

'You don't have the foggiest idea what you're doing, do you?' Rowan giggled as she hobbled to my side. I shook my head as she began to run water into the sink. 'Somehow that doesn't surprise me. We'll leave them in the sink.' She took the blooms from my hands and stood them within the bowl. 'I'll sort them in the morning. They are gorgeous, Nate. Thank you again.'

Rowan's proximity was causing me some significant issues, and I sighed with relief as the doorbell rang. I knew it was the taxi; I could hear the meter ticking in the cab, which was sat with its engine running on the street – it was early. But that really wasn't a bad thing. The chemistry in the room was *far* too dangerous.

I took a deep breath, reached out and tentatively took Rowan's hand. I asked gently, 'Are you sure you want to do this?' I think my subconscious was giving her a get-out clause.

Rowan grinned. 'I should be asking that of you! I can't picture you at *Mama Mia!*.'

I asked quietly, 'Where *do* you picture me?'

She blushed scarlet. I immediately held my breath. There were those feelings again . . . *God, this was punishment*. Thankfully, the impatient cab driver beeped his horn, snapping me to my senses.

'Perhaps we should go?' I said quickly, before Rowan had a chance to answer my very reckless question.

'Have you been here before?' Rowan asked casually, at odds with her racing heart. We were walking into the lobby of The Prince of Wales Theatre. My arm was around her waist, providing her with some support. She denied the need for crutches and insisted she was supposed to walk on her foot whenever she could. In this moment, where I could act in their place, I wasn't going to argue.

I wished she hadn't asked that question though. My mind was recalling my attendance in 1884, or, at least to the previous theatre that had once sat on this site. It had been the opening night of, what was then, The Princes Theatre. I was remembering the performance I had seen with Elizabeth – a comedy about faeries called *The Palace of Truth*. The memory was particularly disturbing to me tonight. The play had been about an enchanted palace, where every visitor had been bound to speak the truth: it was impossible to keep a secret in The Palace of Truth. My recollection seemed to be twisting the knife in, ramming home to me how wrong I was, being with Rowan with the catastrophic secret that I held. Of all the venues in London, it had to be this one, and tonight, of all nights.

Shoving both memory and thought roughly aside, my reply was strained, but as light as I could make it, 'Yes, but not to see *Mama Mia!*.'

She giggled. 'I'm sorry – if you'd rather not . . .'

I stopped, and looked meaningfully into her eyes. 'Rowan, it would not have been my first choice . . . but it is not the performance I am here to enjoy.'

Rowan's heart was pounding again and her feelings were all over the place, but in an *incredibly* pleasant way. Mine, I simply could not describe in detail. All I knew was I felt whole when I was with Rowan and empty when I was not.

Reluctantly dragging my eyes away from hers, I attempted to diffuse some of the intensity. 'We should find our seats.' We were in public, but I still intended to carry her up the stairs. As we approached the first step, I took her into my arms.

She gasped. I said, 'You know no one here, so you cannot even plead embarrassment.' My teeth were gritted as my body reacted too pleasurably to the sensation of her fully in my arms again.

When we'd reached our destination, I slowly lowered her to her feet and waited for her to gain her balance, before stepping back. She looked around and exclaimed, breathlessly, 'Wow – a box? For *us*?'

I nodded, smiling at her excited reaction.

'Thank you *so* much. You really didn't need to go to this . . .'

'I wanted to have you all to myself,' I admitted, grinning.

She blushed becomingly, before exclaiming, '*God though, this must have cost a fortune!*' She frowned and continued quietly, 'I was going to insist on going Dutch, but I'm not sure—'

'I would not dream of it!' I interrupted, astounded. 'You would offend my sensibilities!'

'What about *mine*?' she responded defiantly.

I would *never* understand women.

'How about we, "Go Dutch" next time?' I offered, nevertheless feeling appalled by the suggestion, but sensing it was what she needed to hear.

'You promise?' she urged.

'I promise.'

She smiled happily, whilst I hid my scowl by busying myself with rearranging the chairs to ensure she would have the best vantage point to see the stage from, and with room enough to comfortably position her foot.

As the performance started, I both watched and felt her excitement. It was captivating. I had positioned my chair close, but not too close; I didn't think I could take it. She was to my left and my chair was positioned just perfectly to allow me to watch her whilst, I hoped, not alerting her to the fact I was paying no attention to the stage.

I sat there and reflected: if only. If only things were different; if only I were mortal; if only we could grow old together – then everything would be perfect.

'You aren't watching this, are you?' she asked suspiciously, a few moments later.

'Why do you ask?'

'Because I can feel your eyes on me.'

I wondered if my eyes on her body could elicit the same reaction as hers, on mine. It was probably very different for a human. 'I apologise. I am just finding it hard to look at anything else. Is it making you uncomfortable? I will stop.'

'No – don't, please – it would offend my sensibilities!' She turned to grin at me. 'I know you were home schooled, but your use of language is extraordinary!'

'As you have said before,' I observed wryly, but feeling concerned.

'I just find it . . .'

I interrupted sadly. 'Disconcerting? Unsettling? Unnerving?'

'No.' She thought for a moment. 'Intriguing!'

That was an improvement on unnerving. 'In what way?' I was intrigued myself.

'So many, Nate, so many,' she said, shaking her head.

'Would you care to expand?'

Another dangerous question, but at this point, the honourable Nathaniel Gray was struggling desperately with his guilt, and wanted any opportunity to offload it. I was fighting an internal battle between the part of me that wanted her to know everything, and the other part – the selfish part – that was frantically resisting anything that would destroy things.

She repositioned herself in her seat to look at me attentively. 'Yes, I would – *very much*. But . . .' she frowned and looked almost desperate '. . . not tonight?'

I nodded and shut my eyes, more relieved than disappointed. 'I will try to stop looking at you, so you can enjoy the performance.' I wasn't being fair.

'No, don't, please. To be honest, I find myself too easily distracted with you here to pay attention . . .' She was blushing. 'I like it when you look at me in *that* way that you do, although I can't for one moment understand *why* you choose to!'

I leaned forward in my seat, resting my elbows on my knees and steepling my hands. I looked at her closely. The lights were down, but I could see her perfectly. I spoke softly, but couldn't keep the surprise entirely from my voice, 'But you know the answer to that, you must.'

She shook her head and refused to look me in the eye. Her blush was deeper. 'I know you are going to say something really charming now. But I simply don't understand it. You have an incredible presence about you – people react to you. There wasn't a single female we passed on the way in, that didn't ogle you – *unashamedly* ogle you – and that was just the women! So I just wonder, why me?' She quietly added, 'I'm still concerned it's misplaced guilt.'

I sighed and said gently, 'I thought we had addressed that one.' I waited for her to look at me again, before continuing, 'I do not deny I feel guilty about the accident. Of course I do . . .' More urgently, 'I could have killed you, for Christ's sake! But from the moment I saw you in the hospital . . .'

I shook my head – I couldn't believe she needed me to explain it. It should be self-evident. I said, softly again now, 'I have never felt this way about anyone before. I know it is quick. I know it is intense – and I apologise for that. I just do not seem able to help myself. I *miss you* when I am not with you; I think about you all the time. But . . .' I laughed self-deprecatingly. 'I am going to stop saying any more – because I really do not want to scare you!'

Rowan sat forward in her seat, bringing herself closer to me. Meeting my eyes, she said forcefully, 'It doesn't scare me.' Then, looking down at her hands, and speaking more quietly, 'I feel the same way.'

But how could she? 'But I unsettle you.'

'You do.' She paused, taking a deep breath. 'And Nate – I know there's something you aren't telling me, and I get a feeling you want to . . .'

My body froze to its core. I felt my heart seize and doubted it would ever beat again.

'. . . and I can't believe I'm saying this.' She took another deep breath. 'But for the moment, I'd rather not know. Just don't lie to me, Nate – that's all I ask.' She looked imploringly at me.

It took me longer than it should have done to absorb what she was saying. And when I had, it felt wrong. So wrong. She had no idea what she was dealing with or the risk I represented. Yes, it was a stay of execution, but in that moment, I realised I couldn't continue deceiving her.

My voice was choked. 'Rowan—'

But she interrupted me, urgently. 'Nate – *please!* There *will* be a time when I need to know. Tell me then – not now!'

There was pure anguish in my voice when I spoke. 'I am not *safe.*'

She shook her head vigorously. 'You don't scare me – and I don't want to know yet. Can't we enjoy what we have, for now? We *do* have something, don't we? This isn't just me?'

'How can you ask that?' I put my head in my hands for a brief moment, before raking a hand through my hair. I made it into a fist that I rested against my mouth. I fixed Rowan intently with my eyes, lowered my fist and said with agonised conviction, 'I do not *ever* want to be without you . . . but do not know how we can *ever* be together.'

I could feel her pain . . . and her denial. 'We are together now, aren't we? Can't we take it day by day?'

Day by day? Just as I was attempting to deal with things so as not to lose my mind. *Oh, Rowan.* I shut my eyes, knowing that I couldn't make the right choice whilst looking at her pleading eyes. And I *needed* to find the strength, to make the right choice.

It was all wrong. I needed to walk away – now.

But if I was honest with her and told her whatever she wanted to know? If I spoke openly, but stopped short of telling her what I was? She would be in the

199

driver's seat. I wouldn't be deceiving her – it was what she had asked for.

No – it was still wrong. So very wrong. I had to walk away.

But it would be a chance to be with her that little bit longer.

'*Please,*' she urged again.

I couldn't do it. It didn't matter how many times I told myself I was doing the wrong thing, I simply wasn't strong enough. I opened my eyes to meet Rowan's gaze. I could not give her up . . . not quite yet. I was a caitiff. A monstrous, selfish caitiff. I spoke gently, 'Day by day, Rowan . . . day by day.'

'Thank you!' Her overwhelming relief rushed through me. She beamed at me and her eyes lit up. 'So tell me!' she said, leaning closer, a wicked grin on her face, 'Have you got your costume for tomorrow?' and promptly burst into giggles.

Denial – but her eyes, and her smile and the musical lilt of her giggles . . . Hell, I could do denial, too. I would make the most of every second we had. And I *would* be honourable, just not tonight. I had to have tonight.

I shook my head and spoke with mock disapproval, 'It was not nice, pimping me out as a dinosaur.'

'*Pimping?* Now there's a word I didn't expect to hear you use,' she smirked.

I smiled. 'Am I unsettling you again?'

She started to laugh softly. It was a wonderful sound, and then shaking her head, she said 'I just can't gauge you. I think I can and then you do something totally unexpected – like agree to dress up.' She glanced at the stage and smiled. There was amusement in her voice. 'So, does your costume have big feet?'

I raised my eyebrows, 'You think I am going to tell you and ruin the impact?'

'It's just . . .' she started giggling as she looked at the stage again. I followed her eyes. On stage, members of the cast had flippers on their feet and the dance sequence was causing much laughter amongst the audience. She finished her sentence, 'I was just thinking, big feet, flippers . . . same sort of thing. It could be entertaining.' I couldn't repress a shudder, but at least tonight, I managed to keep it momentary.

'You think I am going to look silly, do you not?' There was humour in my voice, although I didn't feel it on this particular subject. I *knew* I was going to look silly. I mean, Barney *the bloody* Dinosaur, for crying out loud! Elizabeth was still insisting it was the only costume she could get.

'Now, did I say that?' she asked, with mock innocence.

I sighed. 'You really have no idea how completely out of character all this is for me, remotely no idea. Elizabeth, my sister, was in shock when she found out.' That was a bit of an understatement, I realised.

'Do you have any other brothers or sisters?' she asked.

I shook my head. 'Just Elizabeth.' I thought how close we had become again recently. 'I am twelve years her senior, so for a while I was more a father-figure to her. Our mother died shortly after Elizabeth was born.'

Rowan reached out. She seemed to want to touch my face, but had second thoughts. 'I'm so sorry.'

'It hurts, does it not?' I asked huskily. I was only beginning to come to terms with the pain of grief again. She nodded. I saw her eyes were sparkling with unshed tears. This was not what we should be talking about. 'I inherited Ridings at the age of twenty-seven, following the death of my father . . .' I felt her stab of pain again and quickly added, 'We were not close.'

'And Ridings is your home in Derbyshire?' she prompted.

'Mmmm. I am currently dividing my time between Derbyshire and London. I share Ridings with Elizabeth and her husband Frederick, and James and Madeleine.'

'Oh, my God – you house share?' Rowan shook her head dramatically. 'I flat-shared for a while. I don't know how you put up with it! Doesn't it drive you nuts, going to the cupboard and finding your emergency chocolate gone?'

I had to chuckle and shake my head, I couldn't help it.

'No, I'm serious! It used to completely do my head in. It *must* try your patience . . . it can't just be me!'

I smiled. 'Yes, they do try my patience. I have found them particularly trying of late . . .' And never a truer sentence had been spoken. 'We are in separate properties which you would *think* would help – but nevertheless . . .' raising my eyebrow, 'we have at least never squabbled over . . . chocolate.'

'You must have more patience than I do,' Rowan muttered, through clenched teeth.

I shook my head. 'I very much doubt that.' I started to laugh. *Why not?* I said disparagingly, 'Elizabeth thinks we could be in trouble, because we are both Taurus star signs.'

'How do you know I'm a Taurean?' she asked, with evident surprise – and perhaps a little suspicion.

'Would you believe me, if I said it was a lucky guess?' I was chuckling. She didn't for one moment believe it. I sighed. 'Your driving licence at the accident.'

'Oh . . .' She nodded, and then her eyes narrowed, 'Are you saying I demonstrate Taurus tendencies?'

'I didn't say *I did* . . . I do not even believe in it. My sister believes me to be rather temperamental and . . . well; I am not going into it. But she seemed to think we were capable of having some pretty explosive rows,' and added wryly, 'but that the making up would be fun.'

What the hell was I saying?

She smiled broadly, and said in a manner so

unconsciously seductive that my heart raced erratically, 'I like the idea of that – not the rows of course, but the making up.' She was blushing now and biting that lower lip of hers.

Damn. There was no escaping the chemistry. 'So do I,' I muttered quietly.

'Do you?' she asked keenly.

Had she just heard me? I looked at Rowan, confused.

'Do I what, Rowan?'

'Do you like the idea of making up?' She was blushing again and feeling embarrassed.

How on earth could she have heard me? I had spoken at a level and pitch a human should NOT have been able to hear. In fact, come to think of it, how was she managing so easily with our quiet conversation, with all the music going on in the background? Her hearing aids would, I knew, amplify all sounds, not just the voice she was trying to hear. She struggled with her hearing – yet I'd noticed before how she never seemed to struggle with hearing me. I would test intermittently as the night went on . . . but could she be *attuned* in some way to my voice? I could think of no other explanation.

But it made no sense whatsoever. But then again, neither did the emotional connection. It felt like everything seemed to be binding us together.

I realised she was waiting for a response to her question. I fixed my eyes on hers and spoke honestly, although the answer was a painful one,

'I do very much. But it would not be a good idea.'

I felt her acute disappointment, but she masked it well. After only a slight pause, she continued, 'What do you do work-wise, Nate? I know so little about you.'

'I presently run my property investment company.' This was safer ground.

'Property? Wow – small world – I'm in property PR.'

I nodded and smiled. 'I know – you work for Dynamic.'

'How do you know that?' She narrowed her eyes, *definitely* suspicious this time.

I shrugged my shoulders and said matter-of-factly, 'It was good to know more about you. There was a limit to what could be found out, though. Do you enjoy your job, for example?'

She looked at me for a moment and I knew she was absorbing the fact information had been sought on her. Nevertheless, after a short pause, she continued to say with feeling, 'I *love* my job. I'm back at work on Monday and can't wait.' She sighed, adding, 'Although saying that, come Monday morning I'm bound to have the blues . . .'

I cringed. How could she be going back to work so soon? I had got no hint of that at all whilst sat on her roof. How could she get from A to B with ease and in safety? Surely, she should be resting? And how was I going to cope with her back at work? She would be in the big wide world, where anything could happen to her. More pressingly, she wasn't safe at work. Look what had happened the night of the accident – I guessed that was why I had felt that momentary stab of fear.

I asked with evident concern, but with the depth of my worries disguised, 'Should you really be going back to work so soon? Surely you should be . . .'

Rowan rolled her eyes. 'God! You sound just like Clare and Aunty Hetty. I appreciate your concern, really I do, but I'm fine. In fact, I feel great!'

I couldn't have her going back to work with the still to be identified 'S' in the equation. I simply could not. Something had happened before the accident, and it wasn't safe for her. I was angry with myself. I had lost focus, allowing myself to be distracted too easily by thoughts of the girl before me, and I had failed to consider she would be returning to work so soon. I didn't even know if the private detective had managed to come up with anything on him. All I needed was a name and address. Madeleine could hopefully help when I met her later . . . but perhaps Rowan could shed some light on things?

'What clients do you work for, Rowan?'

She spoke proudly, 'My key accounts include Land Venture Corporation, a couple of the major pension funds . . . and Frey Investments.'

The pause gave her away, but the anxiety invoked by simply saying the name of the company, was

confirmation. So it was someone at Frey Investments
. . . *Frey Investments?* My whole body tensed as I
recalled the investigator's report. Jonathan Martin
had got a job at Frey Investments shortly after
Rowan's encounter with 'S'. *Jesus*, this didn't feel
right. No, this felt bloody wrong – and Jonathan
Martin had felt dangerous. I took a moment to
repress my own growing anxiety. I had to deal
with this logically. What did I know about Frey
Investments? I knew it was run by Simeon Frey
. . . surely it couldn't be that easy?

Simeon . . .? How could I have *missed* it? '. . . I
*warn you now, Simeon – you ever come near again,
I will consider it an act of war.'* He had been there,
right in front of me at the hospital – just yards
away from Rowan! Heather hadn't been having a
domestic – she had been warning Frey off Rowan!
Oh, dear God!

I tried to sound casual. 'Frey Investments – that
is Simeon Frey, is it not?'

I wasn't prepared for quite how much pain Rowan
would feel at my mention of his name. *What the hell
had he done to her?* Her heart was galloping now
and she was deathly white. Struggling to personally
overcome her sensations, I managed to speak as
gently and calmly as I could, 'Rowan?' My voice
was strained. *Damn, I shouldn't have pushed on this.
I deserved to be experiencing this pain, but she did not.*

'Rowan?' Her heart was galloping less. I leaned
forward. She was so fragile and so vulnerable. Her
head was looking down and she was refusing to

look at me. My hand was trembling as I reached out and gently raised her chin. 'Rowan . . . look at me, please.' Her eyes met and held mine and the rhythm of her heart calmed slightly. The pain was subsiding. There were tears on her face which she had attempted to hide from me. I used my thumb tips to gently wipe them away.

'I'm sorry . . . I'm being ridiculous.' She attempted to smile. 'That night . . . I just can't get his eyes and his voice out of my head. But I'm going to try harder!'

Oh, Rowan, Rowan my love.

I stroked the side of her face and then gently cradled it. I fixed her eyes with mine, before saying, 'These eyes before you are the only eyes you need to see. Listen to my voice . . . this is the only voice you ever need to hear. He cannot hurt you again – because I will not let him.'

I felt her fear evaporate. I knew the power of my eyes. It wasn't the charm, but my eyes, with the force of my feelings for Rowan behind them, could not help but reassure.

But what the hell was I doing? I wasn't talking like someone who was going to do the right thing and leave Rowan to get on with her life. I had spoken from my new-found heart – not my head.

'I hope that wasn't too intense?' I asked nervously, after a few silent moments.

She shook her head, still staring at me with huge eyes. 'How do you do that? Why did I *believe* you, the instant you said that?'

'I simply spoke the truth with feeling.' I would never let him hurt her, even if I had done the right thing and walked away. But the bit about the eyes and the voice? I shouldn't be saying such things. But it had felt so right. I paused for a moment before asking gently, 'Can you talk about what happened that night? It might help.'

She shook her head and looked down. She attempted a shrug of her shoulders before saying, 'He just scared me – a lot.'

'Had you been working for them long?' I softly prompted.

She took a deep breath, 'No, that's the thing . . . I'd never met him before that night. It was a new account. If I had, I'd never have been at the bloody hotel! They wanted a corporate event arranged at a country hotel in Castleton. I'd gone up to manage everything on-site beforehand and was meeting him to finalise details.'

She continued in a whisper, 'But he immediately gave me the creeps. He was so intense.' She paused to look at me. 'Not nice intense, like you.' I raised a wry eyebrow. 'With him . . . it was scary, creepy.' She shuddered at the memory and reverted to looking down again. 'And he just seemed to be in my personal space and would stare at me fixedly. He would talk and stare, and there was an edge. It was as if, I don't know . . . I frustrated him or something. I just can't pinpoint it. He scared me. I think he may be unbalanced or something.'

She took a deep breath. 'He would say the most insane things. Do you know the very first thing he asked me?' She looked up at me again. 'This shows you what he was like – the *very* first thing? – *Do I believe in the Fey?* I mean *the Fey* – they are *faeries, right?*'

This man was clearly unbalanced – and dangerous. I would *never* let him near Rowan again. *Ever.*

'Anyway, it was getting really late and I made my excuses and went to my room. But I came out of the bathroom . . . and he was there.' Her heart was racing.

I was attempting to remain calm.

'I asked him to leave, and he wouldn't. He asked me to share a drink with him. I took the glass, but I didn't trust him. I didn't drink anything with him all evening. I don't know, I just sensed it wasn't a good idea. And well . . . it got nasty after that.' She spoke even more quietly. 'He was very insistent. I ended up throwing the drink in his face . . . and then he was all over me.'

I closed my eyes. *I would not – could not – lose it. When I did, it would be with the bastard before me.*

'I don't know how I fought him off. I ended up stopping him with my knee and my nails.'

'I am very proud of you, Rowan,' I choked out, as I attempted to control the fury rising within me. She smiled meekly in response.

'Then I fled like a bat out of hell!' She frowned for a moment, before continuing, 'I can't believe I just told you all that. It *does* kind of help talking about it . . .' She was feeling confused, but the pain and fear were no longer there.

I took a deep shuddery breath. 'Thank you for trusting me enough to tell me.' I stroked the side of her face. 'But you are planning on going back to work *with this mad man on the scene?*'

'No. I'm asking to be removed from the account on Monday, so it's not a problem.' She spoke in a way that saw her determined to end the subject.

But as far as I was concerned, removing herself from the account wasn't good enough. My mind was racing through a plan as she spoke. He might still be around and I couldn't risk anything happening to her.

I had to *know* she was safe at work.

It was so simple, I realised. I would put a call into my MD later tonight to arrange it. First thing Monday morning, I would meet with Dynamic PR. My company was changing public relations firms. I would take responsibility for Gray Portfolio's public relations for the foreseeable future and insist Rowan worked for me – and *only* for me. That way there was no chance she would ever need encounter Frey Investments again. Not only would I have a chance to be near her and keep her safe at work, I would keep that monster away from her, until I had worked out the most painful method of his demise.

'So – is your company any *good* at PR, then?' I asked challengingly, with a smile nudging my lips, and hopefully moving matters on for Rowan.

'It depends on *who* is managing your account,' she quipped. 'I'm good, if I do say so myself . . .' She now smiled broadly. 'I reckon you would be a nightmare client, though!'

I sat back in my chair and could not help but frown.

'Come on, you like to be in control – a lot! You've decided you don't want to see me hobble, so you don't let me hobble. I actually get a feeling you're used to getting your own way *rather a lot* and people don't tend to say no to you.'

I laughed. *Was I that transparent?* James regularly called me a control freak. She seemed to have identified a personality trait, if nothing else. Somehow I didn't think she was being complimentary, however. 'Perhaps . . . I will try to be less controlling,' I found myself saying quietly, before continuing with the broader subject of the conversation. 'We use Shaftsbury Communications at the moment.'

'Shaftsbury? I thought they only had a few accounts, although a couple are big. They have the Gray Portfolio of course . . .' She stopped in her tracks. Her eyes huge, and I felt realisation dawn. Quietly and deliberately, and full of suspicion, she asked, 'Nathaniel Gray – what is your company called?'

I shrugged and smirked.

'How could you keep something that big from me?' Her voice had gone up several octaves.

'I do not recall ever keeping it from you – it just never cropped up in conversation.'

I smiled, relieved at the opportune arrival of liquid refreshments, for one of us, at least, and watched Rowan look around, seemingly bemused as she took in the lights that had just come on and lack of performance. 'The interval? I didn't even notice . . .' before exclaiming, 'Champagne!' with a huge grin on her face. 'I *love* champagne!'

I adeptly opened the bottle and poured a full glass, which I handed to her. I poured myself a token amount, looking away to grimace. I didn't get on with bubbles. For a moment, the thought of warm bubbly blood made my skin crawl.

Rowan raised her eyebrows and said playfully, 'Are you trying to get me drunk, Nathaniel Gray?'

'Do you think I would do that, Rowan?' I asked, equally playfully. I found talking with Rowan so easy and was astounded at how out of character I seemed to be, yet . . . how natural it felt. I felt I had no need of defences around her.

'You know, I'm still reeling about Gray Portfolio.'

'Mmmm,' I said, absorbed by watching her lips drink from the champagne flute. A vampire should *not* have been capable of the thought I was currently having. That old chestnut, blood, hadn't entered into it.

'So, it's obviously a family business?'

'It is.' I realised I could be on a sticky-wicket, so to speak, so dragged myself away from my rather too pleasing human-male thought and clarified. 'Yes, it was founded by a Nathaniel Gray in 1904.' Technically correct. Choosing my following words equally as carefully, I added, 'There has been a Nathaniel Gray in the family for a couple of hundred years.'

'Wow,' she said, sipping more champagne. She sounded rueful when she said, 'It must be lovely to have that sort of blood heritage . . .'

Blood heritage? The terms she used!

'. . . to know where you come from – your roots.' She looked sad.

'Did you ever look into your birth parents?' I asked quietly.

She seemed flustered. 'No . . . Yes.' She attempted a laugh, although amusement was the last thing she was feeling. 'When I was younger, I did try once, but the names on the birth certificate were dead ends. I felt I was being told something, so didn't pursue it.' She looked at me now. 'I'd actually settle for finding out more about my adoptive parents . . . my real parents. Losing them so young means I don't really know much about them. I'd love to know more. Aunty Hetty doesn't like talking about them much. I think it's painful for her. She seemed very close to my mum.

'Do you know, I don't even have a photograph of my dad? But look—' She lifted up the gold chain around her neck to reveal an intricate filigree gold pendant. 'This was my mum's. I wear it all the time.'

I smiled gently, unable to provide words of comfort, her pain acting as a temporary gag. I wondered if I would be able to help in her quest for information.

She continued, 'You know, there's something about you sometimes that reminds me of my dad. I can't say exactly whether it's a mannerism or the way you speak, or your cool hands. I'm not sure. It just . . . I know this sounds silly . . . I find it kind of comforting.'

'I am honoured, Rowan. Thank you.'

'So what do you do in your free time?' she asked, choosing to lighten the subject matter.

I shook my head. 'I want to know more about you.'

'Nate, I know nothing about you! I didn't even know about your company. You know so much about me, have met most of my family . . . and will meet the rest of them tomorrow. May I remind you, you've also had the benefit of the Clare factor!' She wrinkled her nose.

I laughed. That was true. Any conversation with Clare always proved informative. I nodded my head in agreement and chuckled. 'You win.'

'So – go on then . . .' she coaxed.

'Well, I have a new project now . . .' I smiled and looked at her, in a way that could leave her in no shadow of a doubt as to what I was referring. She blushed self-consciously, but nevertheless looked pleased with herself.

'What else? You can't dodge the question. If you aren't careful, I'll push for truth or dare . . .'

I shook my head. 'I don't think either of us would

like that one . . . so, on that note, I will answer your question. I obviously have my business affairs, but . . .' *Why not?* 'I like flying.' I grinned.

'Wow! Did you take lessons?' She seemed really impressed.

'Mmmm.' I nodded. James had shown me a trick or two.

'That's so brave of you. I couldn't possibly do that. I'm *terrified* of heights, nearly as much as I'm terrified of horses. Living on the second floor was *not* out of choice.'

So the only woman I had ever fallen in love with – *had I just thought that?* – was not only mortal, subconsciously torturing me and vegetarian – but also didn't like heights or horses – whilst flying was my preferred method of locomotion, and riding one of my greatest pleasures!

'Why are you terrified of horses?' I asked bemused. 'I have never heard of that before. Heights, I can possibly understand . . . but horses?'

'I don't know. They're just so big . . . and their *teeth* . . .' She shuddered and I couldn't help but laugh. 'All my friends as children dreamt of having a pony. It just never remotely appealed. They scare me. You aren't getting out of my questions by distracting me. Proceed – please. What else do you enjoy?'

I paused and then chuckled. 'I ride!' We laughed together. 'It is something I love and . . .' more intently, '. . . perhaps one day, I can change your mind about horses?'

She shook her head and said emphatically, 'Never.'

Well there was a challenge. If only I got the opportunity to introduce her to Bess. 'I also love books. I have an extensive library and read a lot.'

'Oh, so do I – read a lot, that is! I *don't* have the extensive library!'

I wondered if Rowan would like my library, my favourite room at Ridings. I was aware we could probably talk for days on books, so found myself asking, 'Can we keep the conversation about books, until I have some answers from *you*, please?' She smiled and nodded. I recalled her statement as to what her friends had dreamt of. 'So what did you dream of as a child?'

'That's easy!' she said, although I felt her anguish. 'Firstly, I'd dream that my mum and dad were still alive – don't look so sad, please. And secondly . . . I dreamt of having a Barbie doll!' I must have looked puzzled. 'Did you never have Action Man, Nate?' I was even more puzzled. 'Jeez! What sort of childhood did you have?'

There was no way I was going to answer that one and she was not getting away with an incomplete answer. 'Why a *Barbie doll*?' I asked, fascinated.

'Because I never had one! I had these stupid little Pippa doll things . . .' Her face screwed up into the most wonderful expression and she was using her hands to aid her description of something she was clearly disgusted with. 'Smaller and cheaper versions of the Barbie doll. So it was something I always wanted. Shows how shallow a child can be!'

I smiled. 'So what does Rowan, the woman, dream of?'

She paused and blushed and wouldn't meet my eyes. Her pause continued for a long time. 'I probably dream of the impossible,' she mused, now looking at me meaningfully. *Could she really be dreaming of me?* 'Isn't that what a dream is? Dreams simply don't come true . . . that's what makes it a dream,' she continued quietly.

'But you can *hope!*' I said, with anguish.

'Oh yeah . . . I can hope,' she said, meeting my eyes.

There was a long pause before I felt able to speak. 'I thought you may have dreamt of a cottage, with roses by the door and two point four children.' According to Elizabeth that's what most human women want.

'I used to . . . with a stream at the bottom of the garden and a bluebell wood.' She smiled wryly. 'All that tree-hugging as a kid.'

I smiled. But she was right about dreams. So often they were unachievable, otherwise they wouldn't be dreams. My dream was as impossible as hers.

On cue she asked, 'What do *you* dream of?'

'I do not dream,' I replied honestly.

'Oh, come on – you must dream of *something*,' she insisted.

'Not when I sleep. But when awake . . . I, too, dream the impossible.' I smiled sadly at her.

'We make a right pair, don't we?' She giggled. But the amusement was not there in her eyes, or in her soul.

We then spent the rest of the performance talking about books. And there was the woman I had always sought. Intelligent, well-read, witty, and most certainly with a mind of her own. Yet to be honest, I would not have cared had Rowan been illiterate.

As the curtain came down on the performance, I realised my little sister might be right. *Could I be obsessively in love?* I doubted, however, there were *any* words within any of the human languages of the world that could possibly describe the depths I felt for Rowan Locke . . .

CHAPTER 11

DINNER TIME

Dinner at The Ivy followed the performance; Elizabeth's idea. It was deemed by Rowan to be even more excessive than the box and the champagne – but she was both excited and amazed we had managed to get a table. Elizabeth obviously had her contacts . . . although I had my suspicions that the charm had come into play.

As we were led to our table, Rowan whispered to me, 'I should be people-spotting, but can't believe I've just been to *Mama Mia!*, in probably the best seats in the house, and didn't watch it! I've a feeling I'll be missing things.'

'I am so sorry, Rowan. I will try not to be so intense and let you enjoy the experience.' *How could I have been so selfish?*

'Don't you dare!' she hissed, fixing me with a warning look. 'You're the experience, and you win hands down!'

She quickly looked away, moaned quietly to herself, and I heard her mutter under her breath, 'Just shut up, Rowan.'

I smiled happily to myself.

When we had been shown to our table, I took over from the maître d', leading Rowan towards the seat that allowed her to see the whole room. I was going to *try* to be on my best behaviour and not demand her attention so completely.

'I'm not sure I feel like eating.' Rowan sighed, voicing my sentiments exactly. Her eyes were sparkling, and I suspected the bubbles from the champagne had gone to her head.

'You really should, if only to absorb the champagne from earlier,' I said mischievously.

'*You* encouraged me to drink so much!' She glowered.

I smiled and nodded. *I had, hadn't I?* 'You should eat. You need to keep your strength up.'

'Believe me, the last thing my body needs right now, is *food*!' She immediately blushed a rich, deep, enticing blood-red, and put her hand over her mouth. She looked mortified. 'I can't believe I just said that!' she squeaked. 'I *really* didn't mean to say that. I meant— Oh God, I don't know what I meant. Around you I— Yes, I do! Of course I know what I meant. I shouldn't eat more food because . . . *Oh God!* I'm *so* sorry!'

I started to laugh. I had to rein myself in, because I wanted to laugh freely, which I simply couldn't do; not even alone with Rowan, let alone in a crowded restaurant. It would be like having a flashing beacon over my head, announcing a supernatural, inhuman presence.

Rowan was too honest for her own good, and I

221

knew, at that moment, she wanted me. It felt good; in the safety of the crowded restaurant, it felt good. I wanted her to want me, as I wanted her. It was an amazing sensation.

'Shall I get you more champagne?' I chuckled, reaching for the wine list. This could be particularly enjoyable, and prove a distraction to my not clearing my plate.

'Don't you dare!' she warned, with both her words and the look in her eyes. 'I'm going to order some food before I make an even bigger fool of myself.'

'You are not making a fool of yourself – you are a joy!' I was getting intense again and our eyes met.

I wasn't sure how long the waiter stood by our table before I became aware of his presence. *How could my enhanced senses be so completely, so exclusively, absorbed with this woman?*

Rowan placed her order: the goat's cheese salad with a side portion of mashed potato. Elizabeth had advised I ask about the special of the day. On hearing it was black pudding, I made my selection, too. *I would be having words with Elizabeth.* After playfully checking Rowan didn't want more champagne, I ordered a bottle of mineral water.

'I am sorry about my order,' I muttered, after the waiter had left us.

'Don't worry about it,' she said casually. 'I really don't have an issue about what everyone else eats.' Furnishing me with a grin, she added, 'Although black pudding never quite did it for me.' Widening her grin and her eyes sparkling, she exclaimed, 'Let's play favourites!'

Favourites?

'I'll go first!' she declared, 'What's your favourite smell?' I was confused. 'Come on, Nate. Mine is bacon sandwiches. I know I'm vegetarian, but there you go. What's yours?'

I started to laugh again. She was a complete dichotomy and she thought she couldn't predict me? 'Your favourite smell is *bacon* sandwiches?' I repeated, incredulously.

Laughing, too – such a wondrous sound – she shrugged. 'I can't help it – now your turn!'

Still chuckling, I thought of my favourite smell. It was her . . . the blood racing through her limbs. I took a deep breath and could almost detect the alcohol in her bloodstream. Her life-force was sweet, sensual, intoxicating. Not a good place to go – not good *at* all – but what a question to ask a bloody vampire?

'You.'

She sighed, exasperated. 'Nate – that's such a cop out! You need to play this honestly. I want to find out more about you.'

'We agreed to be honest and I am being honest. My favourite smell is you. Now, how about this one? Your favourite food – evidently it is not bacon sandwiches?'

'Nope. But that's a hard one. I like my food, you see.' She smiled ruefully. I shook my head. 'Um, savoury or sweet?'

'Both.'

'Okay . . . They are both comfort foods. Savoury would have to be mashed potato, which I of course ordered tonight. Sweet would have to be hot chocolate fudge cake with good vanilla ice-cream! See – I truly am a pig!'

I shook my head and leant forward as far as the table allowed. Capturing her eyes with mine, I fixed my gaze. I spoke with a depth I felt unable to contain, 'One day, Rowan, I am determined you will see yourself as you are. You are the most beautiful, enchanting creature I have ever come across . . . and I have had more opportunities than most to encounter people over the years.'

She laughed shakily. 'If you don't stop talking like that, I'm going to have to force myself on you!' She flushed deeply, immediately the words were out of her mouth, and lowered her head to her hands, whilst shaking her head.

'And you think you would need to *force* yourself on me?' I asked in disbelief, before coming rather more to my senses, and saying rapidly and awkwardly, 'But this is a first date and . . . and it is not really . . .' I let my voice trail off and attempted to ignore the smile that had appeared on Rowan's face, although her present unhealthy sentiments were not quite so easy to ignore. *What* the hell *did I just say?*

I was coming fast to the conclusion that this was punishment. That my falling in love with this girl, whom I would never be able to secure, was part of some bigger plan. I didn't believe in a god. Not any more. But if there was heaven and hell, I knew exactly where a monster would go, and exactly where Rowan would go.

'Your favourite period in history,' I clumsily threw into the equation, desperate to move matters on.

Now grinning, Rowan shook her head. 'You are such a cheat, Nate. You don't get to ask a question until you've told me *your* favourite food.'

I didn't like this game. I didn't like this game at all. In fact—

'I can see you're struggling to answer that one, just like me!' she declared.

Not quite. And I refused to *ever* allow myself to consider Rowan as food – not only for the purposes of answering the question. But she still wasn't going to like my answer.

'Black pudding,' I finally said. And it truly was the most palatable answer I could come up with.

'Honestly? Wow . . . then you were really lucky it was on the menu.'

Mmmm. 'Are you going to answer my question now?' It was rather necessary to move matters on.

Our food arrived and I watched Rowan scoop a forkful of mashed potato up and then grin at me. 'My favourite period in history? That so has to be Georgian. I love the elegance of the time. That whole Georgian/Regency period is so appealing. Have you ever been to Bath?'

I inclined my head. Indeed, I had been in Bath regularly during the very period of history that was her favourite, and still kept a town house there on Queen Square.

'It's probably due to Jane Austen, I'm afraid – *Pride and Prejudice* is my favourite book.'

Yes, Elizabeth *had* known what she was talking about. I was going to have to speak to her more on the subject of human women.

'I just feel connected to the period somehow. I love the architecture and when I go to Bath, I just imagine I've gone back in time. I love it!'

I imagined how I would have loved walking through Bath with Rowan on my arm. Perhaps she was of the wrong time, not I? If I had met Rowan in Bath when still human, would we have had the life together that was going to be denied us now? I had my prejudices then, but somehow I failed to see how Rowan would not have smashed them to pieces instantaneously.

'It is my favourite architectural period, too,' I said quietly, thinking of my town house and Ridings – which had been so extensively modernised in the Georgian period. She *would* like it, I was sure. But I couldn't allow myself to dwell on that thought. On *any* of these thoughts. Not if I was going to keep my sanity. 'Your favourite artist?'

'God – you are such a cheat!' Indicating she needed to fully finish what was in her mouth before she could answer properly, I decided to brave my own plate of food. As with anything other than warm, liquid blood, it would be completely tasteless and unpleasantly dry to my palate and not remotely enjoyable, but I would go through the motions. I tentatively placed some black pudding on my fork.

'But that one is so easy, I'll humour you,' she declared, on swallowing her food. 'Vincent van Gogh. It's *Starry Night* that does it I'm afraid.'

I promptly dropped my fork with a loud clatter. *So much for not drawing attention to my efforts at food consumption.* Well, there was no doubt she could see I was shocked.

'I've surprised you? I can't see why. I studied van Gogh for my A-levels and tried to get into his mind for a while, which was a bit scary. But *Starry Night*? It is such an amazing painting! Somehow he manages to express how vast the universe is, how there must be so much more out there we don't know about. And he captures the magic of the night, drawing you into it – listen to me here. You can tell how much I love it, can't you? I love the night, too, so perhaps that's why it appeals to me so much. And the moon. He has a gorgeous crescent moon – but I do love the full moon. You know when it's really low in the sky and almost unbelievably larger than it should be? I remember seeing that first with my dad and it felt so magical. I've loved it ever since.'

I swallowed hard, unable to quite believe what Rowan had proceeded to say. *My Starry Night* featured a full moon. And she loved the night, too? Up until meeting Rowan, nothing compared to the full moon over the lake at Ridings.

'I'm sorry – I don't half harp on sometimes. Especially around you. Talking with you is so easy. Whose yours?'

After a long pause, during which I sat back in

227

my chair, wiped my now food-splattered shirt with my napkin and shook my head a couple of times, I looked up, raised my eyebrows and replied, 'Can you not guess?'

She beamed. 'See . . . I might be scared of heights, hate horses and not eat black pudding – but we *do* have something in common!'

'Have you ever seen . . . any of his night scenes?' I asked, quietly.

'No! Not in the flesh – but I'd love to one day. Have you? I bet you have.'

I nodded slowly.

She leapt straight in with another. 'This is a goodie – favourite *horror* book?'

'I am not a fan of horror and do not tend to read it.' I was still more than a little distracted by her earlier revelation. What I wouldn't give to show her *Starry Night over Saint-Remy*.

'I'm not a fan either, but did love *Interview with a Vampire*.'

Christ Almighty! That brought me right out of my reflections.

'Ah, ha. Scariest film?' Rowan asked, wagging her fork in my direction. 'In my younger years, I stupidly watched a few.'

I could answer that one easily. Whilst *Psycho* a week or so ago would have fit the bill, later developments ensured a clear front-runner. '*Truly, Madly, Deeply*.'

She looked confused. 'That's my *favourite* film, but it isn't scary.'

'Believe me . . . it has its scary moments.' I could

228

see Rowan still wasn't satisfied with my answer, so I elaborated slightly. 'Do you not find the grief and the pain scary?'

'Oh! I *sort* of see what you mean . . .'

I doubted she could. 'Your scariest film?' I prompted, somewhat tentatively.

'*Salem's Lot* – most definitely!' She could tell from my look I didn't know the film. I didn't tend to watch them. I was only aware of *Psycho* because of an Alfred Hitchcock night James had somehow got me to attend back in the 1960s. 'It's Stephen King, about vampires, and scared me *stupid*!'

And if that wasn't bad enough, Rowan chose to expand. 'It's seriously *the* most disturbing thing I've ever watched; it gave me nightmares for months. After I'd watched it – I was probably twelve or thirteen – I couldn't even go to my bedroom window to pull the curtains when it was dark outside. I had to get Aunty Hetty to do it – or make sure I'd already pulled them before sunset. I was absolutely terrified . . .' She paused. 'Are you okay, Nate?'

Far, far from it. My face was obviously revealing more than I would have liked, despite my attempts to make it appear blank. I forced a smile I knew couldn't possibly be reflected in my eyes so looked down at my almost untouched plate of food. There wasn't a hope of stomaching that right now. 'Favourite place in the world?' I murmured.

'I haven't been to as many places as I'd have liked.' She pondered, as I gave myself a good talking to. This was a way to find out more about the woman . . . I loved. But I was beginning to think James was right when he called me a masochist. After finishing another forkful of potato, she continued, 'I'd love to take off around the world, but it's not that easy when you have bills to pay and, to be honest, it's not the same if you aren't sharing it with someone . . .' *How I wished we could.* '. . . Umm. Although the company wasn't great, I did love Prague. And of course I love Bath and London, although I know they probably don't count. And yours?'

'I like Prague, too,' I agreed, although I suspected I had had more of a bird's-eye view of it than Rowan. Forcing focus, I gauged my favourite place in the world would depend on where Rowan was. Currently, it was a table in this restaurant. But if I thought of Rowan in every place I had ever been, that should provide me with the answer. 'Ridings, I think, is my favourite place.' *Would I ever get a chance to show it to her?*

'You haven't been drinking tonight, Nate. So, what's your favourite drink?'

I swallowed hard and focused intently on my cutlery. Under the table, my hands flexed and un-flexed upon my thighs. I couldn't answer this one. There was not a hope.

'Nate?' Rowan prompted.

'What do you think it is?' I asked quietly.

'Well, it couldn't be as controversial as your food choice!' She giggled.

I smiled meekly.

'I know you don't like bubbles . . . I see you as a claret man.'

Claret *had* once been my drink of choice. When, that is, I had been a suitable dinner companion for Rowan. Not that it had been the easiest drink to source due to wars between England and France – but neither had good brandy, my other favoured drink. I inclined my head slightly and forced myself to ask another question. 'What is your—?'

'No! My go, Nate – *please?*' she begged. 'I've got a great one!'

I found myself unable not to smile at her enthusiasm and conceded with a bow of my head.

'What's your bucket list . . . the five things you'd most like to do before you die?' she asked excitedly.

I felt colder than I had ever before felt. *Of all the questions!* I tried to keep the smile on my face, but couldn't prevent it from slipping. I tried to disguise my pain and looked anywhere but at Rowan.

I wanted to be able to die – more than anything else – because it would mean I could have a mortal life with Rowan. If I could die, I wanted to marry her – and I *would not* take no for an answer; to give into my – no, *our* physical needs, and to satisfy her, as Nathaniel Gray the man; to see our children run around Ridings; to grow old together, and I wanted us to fulfil together whatever was on her wish list, which was now my wish list, too.

But I was dead already, despite feeling more *alive* since meeting Rowan, than I had ever felt before.

This was a complete and utter nightmare. This was horror at its best.

'I have not thought about that one before,' I murmured. 'What about you?' My voice somehow managed to sound neutral.

But actually, this was the last question I ever wanted Rowan to answer. Yes, I wanted to know what she wanted to do with her life, but the mere mention of her *death*? I was overwhelmed with a sense of despair so staggeringly great that I felt it was consuming my whole being. Rowan's answer to the question, however, brought me abruptly to a point where functioning was required.

'*I've* actually *thought* about this one! I want to snorkel with turtles, trek the Himalayas, cruise down the Nile; visit a real rainforest and see the whales in South Africa – all holding hands with someone I love more than life itself! Bet you didn't think you'd get an answer that quickly, did you?'

I felt ice cold. It wasn't her list which was the problem, for I would do anything to be able to fulfil that with her, but what she had said to begin with. 'Why have you been thinking about that, Rowan?' I asked slowly. She refused to meet my eyes.

Looking awkward and now fiddling with the cutlery, she replied, 'Well . . . after the accident, I did think a little about my mortality.' *Her and me both.* 'And it just got me thinking. We never know *when* we are going to die – I could get knocked over by a bus tomorrow, so . . .'

I couldn't look at her. The anguish, the pain, the

despair ripped through me. She was mortal: she *would* die. This was why I had created my sanctuary free of emotion.

'Nate?' I could both hear and feel her concern.

'I have to pass on that one,' I finally said.

'Nate?' She was sounding anxious. I looked at her for a moment. And, despite my best efforts, could see from her eyes she had seen something. I felt her momentary stab of fear and pain, before the anxiety returned.

I smiled ruefully. I wondered if she was thinking about why I had been unable to answer that question. *Would she guess what I was?*

I *had* to pull myself together. This wasn't fair on Rowan. I would not have her feeling this way as a result of me. I noted she had finished her food. I glanced around us; most of the other tables were now empty. 'Would you like dessert?' She shook her head, still looking at me worriedly. 'Are you ready to go then?' She nodded.

Out in the fresh air, I felt a little better. But I still realised how impossible all of this was. Our differences were insurmountable.

But Rowan . . . Rowan's company was . . . It was what I now existed for.

In the taxi heading back to her flat, we were more sombre than we had been all night, despite my efforts to nullify Rowan's unease.

'Are we going to do this again?' she asked, attempting to sound cheerful, but unable to keep the fear from her voice.

I knew what the answer should be, what the answer *had* to be. For both Rowan's sake and my own. I would send my apologies with regards to the party tomorrow.

Yet it was relief I felt when I realised I couldn't yet say goodbye to Rowan. I had to sort out 'S'. How could I *not* carry on seeing her with 'S' on the scene?

I smiled. 'Are you asking me out on another date, Rowan Locke?'

I felt her immense relief. 'I do believe I am, Nathaniel Gray.'

I knew Rowan was generally safer with me carrying her up the stairs to her flat. But tonight, I should have reassessed matters. As her arms wrapped themselves around my neck, I was a wreck. When I met her eyes, which echoed my own intense longing, I felt my body ignite. She wriggled in my arms, repositioning herself even closer. I felt her breasts against my chest, her deliriously fast heart beating against my own; her warm breath upon my neck – I was ablaze.

I stood in the living room, holding her in my arms, transfixed as her face moved closer to mine. Our lips touched.

And I, for a moment, was lost.

What started off as a tentative touch became overwhelmingly needy for us both. Her lips parted and I tasted her and I wanted more. My lips were hard and strong and demanding against hers, and she moulded to me perfectly, seeming to anticipate precisely the subtle movement that would ignite me further.

It was Rowan's gasp of pleasure as my tongue flickered along her neck that brought me to my senses.

I all but flung her from my arms – on to the sofa that was behind her. *How did my mouth get to her neck?* My main focus had *not* been her blood, but there I was at a vampire's bull's-eye! My fangs were not in place, I knew that, but I also knew how quickly they could be.

God Almighty! I was gasping for air I shouldn't need and Rowan was dazed. She was breathing heavily, so heavily, so seductively, and her eyes reached a whole new dimension in this state. I shut my own eyes so I didn't need to look at the temptation further, and attempted to stop my gasps, so I need not smell its sweet fragrance. When I felt able to speak in some shape or form, it was to apologise. 'I am so sorry! That should NEVER have happened. That was unforgivable!'

'What did I do wrong?' she gasped. Her breathing was still laboured.

I could feel her hurt. I opened my eyes. 'You did nothing wrong, Rowan – the fault was all mine.'

'But, Nate – what was wrong?' She looked embarrassed, but adopted as authoritative a stance as she could from her sprawled position on the sofa. 'Do you have *any* idea how you just made me feel?'

If it was anything like I had felt before I realised where my mouth was, I could pretty well guess.

Not that I needed to. I had bloody well felt her reaction, too! I didn't answer.

'That was incredible! That was . . . I've *never, ever, ever* experienced anything so mind-blowing. *Where the hell* did you learn to kiss like that?'

I shook my head. 'I am truly sorry. We will not go there again. Please understand. It is *really* important that you understand this.'

'You didn't like it,' she whispered. Her pain was excruciating.

'Rowan . . . I am not coming over to you, because I wouldn't trust myself if I did.' I was now speaking through gritted teeth and my voice was strained.

She looked up at me – beseeching, begging – and I shut my eyes in response.

'Do not *ever* think I didn't enjoy that! *Nobody* has ever made my body feel like that. But you need to trust me. I enjoyed it *too* much and we cannot go there again. Do you understand what I am saying? It is truly *not* safe for you.' I tentatively opened my eyes again.

Rowan was confused. 'How can you say that, Nate? You wouldn't hurt me. I know you wouldn't. I trust you completely and utterly. That's the thing – I really do.'

'Rowan, Rowan, Rowan,' I whispered, shaking my head. 'You have no idea what you are saying. If you trust me, then trust what I now say. We *cannot* do that again.'

She both looked and sounded mortified. 'You

are expecting me to never again seek out how you just made me feel?'

I nodded curtly and closed my eyes again to the excruciating temptation before me.

'Fine!' she declared. 'I can do that!'

I cocked one eye to look at her suspiciously. I could feel her current emotion – and it was one of defiance. She had unconsciously tipped me off, but I should have known this was too easy. Opening my eyes fully, I spotted the crossed fingers she thought were hidden under her crossed arms. '*Rowan* . . .' She knew I had seen, so she smiled sweetly before uncrossing them.

'I promise . . . to be as good a girl as I can possibly be in your presence!' She saw my look. 'What else can I say? I've promised!'

I should have been feeling frustration and nothing else, but she was adorable like this. She was biting that lip of hers again. I could feel my need rising and I really wasn't sure what stable it came from. I needed to go – now! I shook my head and turned to leave. 'I will pick you up tomorrow at noon.'

'I can't wait! And I'll be such a good girl. You just wait and see.'

The way she said that was so tantalising I struggled with myself not to turn around and ravage her there and then, one way or another. One way she *would* die; the other way she *could* die. It was a great choice really, when this woman was essential to my very being.

*   *   *

I chose to feed before returning home. My town house in London was without the on-site food supply of the farms and estate at Ridings and, not at all in the mood for the polluted taste of urban fox, I headed out of town. I was with Rowan again tomorrow. That *damned* party.

But the feeding did nothing to wipe away how she had made my body feel in those moments. It had felt nothing like it did as I fed. Perhaps it *was* possible to separate the two, perhaps James was right? But there again, I was sure James had never had physical relations with a human whom he had previously desperately wanted to suck dry of blood. It was pure lunacy!

There was no sitting on Rowan's roof tonight. I knew I had to get back to meet Madeleine. She had been most adamant about that. For the first time, I viewed the meeting positively. Had I not had to get home I do not think I could have trusted myself not to return to Rowan's, wake her now sleeping form, and finish off that which we had started.

I couldn't face Madeleine straight away, though. I ended up in what used to be the cellars, now the fencing room, ferociously stabbing the target. I was soon joined by James, who allowed me to vent my frustration out on him. My mind was protected, but his was not, and he had correctly guessed what was causing my reaction. We bowed to each other.

'It *is* controllable Nate *and* it gets easier – if you let it.'

CHAPTER 12

UNCLE FERGUS

Madeleine stood before the fireplace of the first-floor sitting room, waiting for me. It was dark outside, but the table lamps remained off, the room lit only by flickers of warm light from the fire that crackled gently in the grate.

She was not alone. Elizabeth sat on one of the two plush olive-green velvet Chesterfield sofas in the room, concentrating hard. Frederick, next to her, looked pained. I guessed what Elizabeth was up to, and grinned, despite my current state of mind.

James had followed me into the room and now sat on the carpeted floor with his back resting against the second sofa. I chose to stand with my hands held behind my back, at one of the floor-to-ceiling sash windows.

'I am assuming from this that what you have found out is of such significance, you feel we should all hear it?'

Madeleine looked awkward. 'If you have no objections – I do think we should all hear it.'

I replied with a shrug. *What the bloody hell had she found out?*

'I suppose the first thing is to reassure Nate that

I haven't discovered anything about Rowan to make anyone think she's anything but innocent. In fact, I have no definitive cause for the accident or the connection.'

I looked at her surprised. *Then what was all this about?*

'I have, however, found out some information that, well, needs to be shared. Perhaps we can collectively make more sense of it than I've been able. It seems to be too much to simply be coincidence, but I . . . I'm really not sure of the best way to say this . . . I . . . It's definitely *too* much to be coincidence. The odds of it happening randomly . . . I'm really struggling to . . .'

'No, Mads – *we're* really struggling! Can you please just spit it out?' James urged.

'Okay.' She sounded flippant now. 'You asked for it! Seth Locke, Rowan Locke's adoptive father – was one of us!' She looked at me as she spoke. There was apology in her eyes. She knew things had just got complicated.

Comprehending immediately what Madeleine was saying, I turned my back on the room. I recalled Rowan's words to me about her father, and it all made the most appalling sense. I knew I had had a bad feeling about this meeting.

Could this be coincidence? No, with everything going on, it was too much for that. *So, what the hell was going on?* I would save reflection however, because things were just about to kick off.

'He was a *vampire*?' Elizabeth hissed. The shock

in her voice summed up the atmosphere in the room pretty well.

I knew what was coming . . . and Madeleine evidently nodded.

'But he can't have been,' Elizabeth shrieked. 'Rowan's father is DEAD!'

Yes. That.

'He died in a house fire! How *could* he have been immortal?' I could feel Elizabeth's terrified eyes on my back.

'Sweetheart, it's alright,' Freddie said gently, before hissing urgently, 'Mads, you said you were going to see Fergus. Please tell me—'

'And I did,' Madeline said, sounding momentarily upset, before recovering herself. 'Rowan's father *was* that Seth Locke, Freddie. He was a member of Fergus' coven. We didn't know him well, but both you and I encountered him in the past. He fell in love and married Rosie Fairchild in 1976, a year before adopting Rowan and then, two years later, Clare. Fergus and his coven accept he was destroyed by some means in 1983. No remains were found, but we all know fire will turn our broken bodies to dust.'

There was stunned silence. James finally spoke. 'Hang on a bit, Mads . . . this *really* doesn't add up. You are saying, he was a vampire . . . yet he was *married* to a *human* . . . and adopted two *human* girls?'

'It's a bit more complicated than that, but, essentially – yes.'

241

'A bit more *complicated*?' he exclaimed. 'Are you absolutely *sure* he was a vampire?'

'Yes!' Both Madeleine and Frederick snapped in unison.

'But . . . but how do we *know* he's dead, and if he's dead – how?'

I turned to face the room. My face was as blank as I could make it and my block was firmly up. All eyes turned to me. I could see Frederick holding Elizabeth's hand tightly.

'There are indisputable facts,' Madeleine continued. 'There was a house fire, we knew that before. Seth and Rosie died at the house, although, obviously, the method of at least Seth's death could not have been solely the fire. There were definitely other parties involved.

'We know he died, because of his last communication with his coven. It was made on the day of the fire and there's been nothing else since. Seth Locke was able to communicate like us, but over greater distances. He made a call for urgent assistance to Fergus. He told him, if he was too late, Rowan and Clare were in the cellar. It wasn't Clare's cries that alerted the human fire services to their presence, but Fergus. Despite responding immediately, they arrived too late to save Seth and Rosie.'

I moved to sit in the armchair by the bookcase, in a darkened corner of the room, and let my head drop into my hands. Rowan wanted to know more about her parents, but any discovery she made would be devastating. Her parents had been murdered. That should be more than enough for anyone to bear. But that wasn't the half of it. She had absolutely no idea – *and why should she?* – what her father, and myself, were. I really wasn't sure how any human could handle that enlightenment.

'But *how* was he killed?' Elizabeth asked, her terror unmasked.

'As we know, there aren't many ways to kill us. The only way we've been aware of is through other vampires severely wounding us and then our bodies being burnt to prevent regeneration. Fergus considers there are other methods, involving dark magic.'

'*Dark magic?*' Elizabeth whimpered.

Frederick snorted in disbelief. 'What is Fergus on?'

'They found a number of strange-scented trails around the house. They attempted to track them, but they led nowhere.'

'Okay, forgetting the method for a moment, which incidentally is giving me the willies – *Why?* Why kill them?' James demanded.

'We don't know. That's where speculation comes in. Nate – are you okay?'

I gave a curt nod. I was currently experiencing the newfound sensation of empathy – and couldn't stop thinking how this would all impact on Rowan. As a result, I was barely holding things together.

'Rowan doesn't know any of this – does she?' It was more statement from Madeleine than question.

I shook my head. I didn't yet feel able to communicate in anything other than small movements of my head.

'Fergus said she'd no idea. He is, incidentally, Rowan's godfather – her Uncle Fergus.'

'You are kidding me!' Frederick cried.

'This just gets better!' James muttered. Both effectively verbalised my sentiments.

'He sends human birthday cards and Christmas cards, but she's never been enlightened as to what he is. The last time he officially saw Rowan was at the funeral when she was six. He volunteered his assistance with bringing the girls up, but was more than a little relieved when Aunty Hetty stepped in.'

'Does Aunty Hetty know what Fergus is?' Elizabeth asked.

'Yes. She also knew about Seth, hence we can assume she senses what we are.'

James exhaled his breath in an amazed whistle, whilst shaking his head. 'So Rowan Locke has been surrounded by vampires and now finds one besotted with her . . .' I could feel James' eyes on me, '. . . and yet she doesn't even know we *exist*!'

'Nate?' Madeleine prompted, obviously checking this was still the case. I nodded again.

'*Why* was he killed though?' Frederick asked quietly. 'Was it . . . because he was involved *with a human*?' I now felt all of their eyes upon me. I refused to read their thoughts.

Madeleine continued, 'No, it wasn't that, but we

don't know the reason yet. And this is where it gets even more difficult, I'm afraid.'

I took a deep breath, pleased my head was already in my hands and my eyes shut. Perhaps Rowan was catching, I reflected. She currently had her head in the sand, not wanting to know what I was. And at this point in time, I relished the idea of doing likewise. I really didn't want to know anything more. I was struggling to resist the urge to get up and leave. All I wanted was Rowan – full stop. I didn't need to know about her history. I just wanted *her* – even though I knew I couldn't have her. I didn't want any more complications; there was no more space inside me for dealing with them.

'He married Rosie Fairchild and they lived a *conventional* human lifestyle for all intents and purposes, even adopting two mortal children, whom they were clearly bringing up as human. As must be obvious with that particular set up, Seth abstained from a human diet, as Fergus and his coven do.

'Fergus assured me all they ever wanted was a human life. Seth and Rosie were desperately in love, and Seth led a human life as much as possible. There was something very compelling about Rosie Fairchild, however.' She sighed, as if she really didn't want to be the harbinger of more bad news.

I braced myself.

'He said she was devoted to Seth and their children, but he sensed something – nothing remotely sinister – but he sensed some kind of innate power from her. He didn't consider her to be . . . defenceless. He considered she may have had some magical abilities, that she may not have been . . . strictly *human*.'

I heard the gasps. I was now staring, in an unfocused manner, at an unidentified point directly in front of me.

'He apparently broached the subject with Seth, but didn't get far. It was clear to him, though, Seth knew more than he was revealing. There is the question, therefore, of whether the target was Seth, or Rosie, or indeed both of them. It's likely, however, some kind of magic was involved in their deaths.'

'Is it just me, or is everyone else getting slightly concerned about this magic crap?' Frederick muttered. 'Because for the record – I don't even believe in magic!'

James laughed derisively. 'Freddie the Vampire, who can fly with no wings, can charm, can live forever; has enhanced senses, can hear our thoughts, is more than two-hundred-years old – oh, and is in all likelihood *dead!* – doesn't believe in *magic!* Freddie, come on! How do you think *we* do it?'

Returning to Madeleine, James asked, 'Could Rosie have been a shape-shifter?'

'Werewolves, James?' Frederick exclaimed, disgustedly.

'Not necessarily,' Madeleine countered. 'Lots of magical entities are meant to have the ability to

246

shape-shift. Werewolves, of course, but the witches and the Fey, too, if they exist. But we don't even know if she was a shifter, so—'

'Oh *please*! I've heard enough,' Frederick snorted.

'Just because *you don't believe*, doesn't mean they don't exist!' Madeleine was clearly exasperated. 'Fergus used to think like you but he's been forced to change his mind. Did you believe in vampires before you became one?' She knew the answer and didn't wait for his response. 'Precisely!'

I spoke for the first time and all eyes were on me. I was currently struggling with a fear that was growing within me and I didn't know how to contain it: the parties involved in the murder of Rowan's parents had neither been identified, nor brought to justice; it didn't sit well with my need to keep Rowan safe. My instinct couldn't be suppressed: I sensed danger.

'Rowan is not safe,' I stated simply, with no feeling; I was trying to contain that within.

'Fuck Rowan . . .' Frederick began his sentence, but I didn't let him finish.

With a roar, I was instantly before him. Elizabeth put herself between us.

'Let me finish, Nate!' Frederick cried, meeting my densely black eyes over the top of Elizabeth's head, with his own frustrated ones. 'I was going to continue with, *what about you*? There's a *dead* vampire in the equation now!'

My eyes remained fixed on Frederick's and growls emanated from my chest.

'You shouldn't get too alarmist,' Madeleine said, calmly. 'This all happened twenty-nine years ago. It's not new news – only to us – and there's nothing to demonstrate that Rowan was ever a target. Nothing untoward has happened to Rowan or to Clare in all that time.'

'Until the night of the accident,' I stated, between tightly clenched teeth. I could see my stance was upsetting Elizabeth, so I let out a last low, guttural growl, before repositioning myself by the window.

'Well, yes . . .' she conceded quietly.

'It might be old news, but there was magic used back then, and it might bloody well explain the impossible things that have happened to Nate,' James exclaimed. 'Come on, not only did he crash, but he ends up crashing into a girl whose parents were vampire and spook, and ends up sharing her soul! That ain't normal!'

'I agree with you about the magic,' Madeleine said. 'It's difficult to see, however, what any *external* party could have hoped to achieve from uniting Rowan and Nate. Is it just me, or can anyone else see what could be gained? *Assuming* Rowan's a target, the result is she now has Nate protecting her. And why would Nate be a target?'

There was silence. Nobody, including myself, could provide any answers. She continued, 'So assuming magic *is* involved, because it certainly wasn't normal, we know it can't be from Rowan because she's human . . . so that just leaves Nate. The magic involved could have been his.'

I looked at Madeleine as if she was insane, but she continued, 'Nate may have developed a new power which targets only Rowan. It can't be ruled out. I actually really like Fergus' view on the matter.'

Fergus' view on the matter?

'I hope you don't mind, Nate, but I told him about your connection with Rowan; he was fascinated.'

Fabulous!

'He thinks it could simply be you were meant to be together, and this was the way of securing it. After all, you were hardly capable of loving before you were reintroduced to emotion, so your magic . . .'

Frederick hissed in disbelief.

'. . . or *power*, whatever you want to call it,' she continued pointedly, 'could have been used subconsciously to target Rowan. This connection could be *completely separate* to what happened twenty-nine years ago . . . and may involve no other parties. It could simply be you two finding each other.'

'The connection is not just one way,' I added quietly. I had remotely no idea whether it added any credence to any of this speculation whatsoever, but it needed to be shared. Everyone looked confused. 'I feel her emotions but there is another link. Despite Rowan's hearing problems, she has never failed to hear me. Tonight she heard me when I was speaking at a level no human, with perfect hearing, could have possibly heard. And no matter how good her hearing aids, they could never have picked up the pitch. Rowan seems to be attuned to my voice. She is connected to me, too.'

Madeleine looked fascinated.

'This is getting fucking weirder by the minute!' Frederick hissed.

'She finds me comforting,' I said quietly.

That was too much for James. '*You – comforting?* Now I've heard it all! Even as a human you were *never* comforting . . . and as a *vampire*? A vampire *comforting*! *Jesus!* You are so losing your knack, Nate!' His face was now contorted with disgust.

'She said she finds me comforting . . . because there is something about me that reminds her of her father.' I was aware of everyone staring at me in amazement. 'She does not remember much of him, but my cold hands – which she, incidentally, considers only to be cool; my mannerisms; the way I speak. I think that is why she refuses to accept I represent a risk.'

Madeleine smiled. 'Then that could be the reason why the connection happened with Rowan. It's what could have made the connection viable and allowed the relationship to develop. Who else would find a vampire *comforting*?'

'You *are* meant to be together,' Elizabeth stated assertively. 'I don't know why all this has happened, or how it happened, but you *are* meant to be together. I know it!'

I didn't know what to think. I believed myself

to be getting a headache for only the second time in one-hundred-and-ninety-five years.

There was a long silence. I remembered Aunty Hetty and everything started to make sense. 'I am assuming . . .'

Madeleine anticipated my question, 'Yes, Aunty Hetty is a Fairchild and Fergus considers her to be of the same ilk as Rosie.' No wonder she unsettled me. She wasn't even human!

'*God in heaven,*' James muttered under his breath, before asking, 'Could she have been involved in the accident?'

I couldn't see why. I had been asking that myself, ever since she had repelled my charm at the hospital. I kept coming up with the same answer: 'It would make no sense. It was putting Rowan at risk.'

Madeleine seconded my view. 'No, it wouldn't make sense. The involvement of *any* outside party makes no sense.'

James shook his head and spoke derisively, 'Yes, I *know!* Nate's magic ensured he crashed into someone, so he could start feeling again, and fall in love with a human who would accept him for what he is. I'm not buying it, I'm afraid – it's nuts! As far as I'm concerned, we are no closer to knowing the cause of the accident – and now we have a dead vampire and spooks on the scene! And as for Rowan . . .'

He leapt up from the floor and started uncharacteristically pacing up and down in front of the fireplace. 'I know we are vampires and should be able to absorb all this information effortlessly, but I'm struggling! Can I just recap on things?' He raised his eyebrows and cried sardonically, 'Shout if I've missed something!

'In summary: Rowan's adoptive dad was a vampire. Her adoptive mum was *spooky* – gifted by magic, or something. Despite this, they lived together as a *human* family, adopting two *human* children. Her adoptive mum and dad were both killed by some, as yet unknown, *spooky* creatures, and Rowan has been brought up by another *spook*, aka Aunty Hetty. Her godfather, Uncle Fergus, is a vampire. Her soul is currently being shared with our very own Nate, another vampire, who has fallen in love with her, to all intents and purposes. But she doesn't know he's a vampire, or that he shares her soul. In fact, she doesn't know *any* of the above . . . but *does* find her relationship with Nate the vampire, somehow *comforting*, despite him ramming her off the road and nearly sucking her dry of blood!'

I grimaced. That appeared to be pretty much as it was.

James shook his head at me and for once, spoke seriously, 'You'd better pray she doesn't find out all this, because she's going to go to pieces.'

There was no question about that, but I couldn't afford to think about it right now. I had to try and get my head around a way forward. There were still people out there involved in the death of

Rowan's parents, and I didn't like it; it made me more than a little uncomfortable. And then there was the issue of Simeon Frey and Jonathan Martin.

'Madeleine, did the private investigator find a home address for "S"?'

'No, I've been meaning to talk to you about that. I'm beginning to give up on the detective. The *exact* same thing is happening in his attempts to find out information on "S", as happened with Aunty Hetty. She must have caused some lasting damage or something.'

'Simeon Frey – Frey Investments,' I growled ominously. 'And he has to be removed.' I let them see Rowan's account of her encounter with him, and their growls and curses reverberated around the room. 'And if that is not enough, he was at the hospital *and* gave Jonathan Martin a job. It could be that he was using him to get to Rowan. Martin, I hope, is already out of the picture.' I didn't mean to, but they saw that encounter in my head, too.

'I take it all back. There's *nooo* way you're losing your knack!' James spoke, admiringly.

'I'd safely say Martin is off the scene,' Frederick added, coming over to clap me on the back.

'Frey is dangerous. I need an address so I can follow this one up personally – I will find it out myself.'

'Look out Frey!' Frederick chuckled.

'Why would the detective struggle with him, though?' I uttered almost inaudibly and more to myself than anyone else. Before I made a connection and the most horrifying thought crossed my mind. *Dear God! No!*

'Madeleine . . .' I hissed so quietly it was close to being inaudible, even to us. I didn't feel capable of speech in this state, so instead opened up my mind.

She looked confused for a moment, after which she looked decidedly uncomfortable. She paused, and glanced at me nervously before speaking, 'I have to admit, it is strange the same pattern is happening there, as with Aunty Hetty . . . more than strange. I hadn't considered that. It's true, if *Frey* isn't human, and of the same ilk as Heather and Rosie, it *would* explain why the investigator has been struggling.'

Everyone in the room was now taking in my horrified expression and reading the frantic things that continued to race through my panicked mind. Something not human had killed Rowan's parents . . . and something *possibly* not human had attacked Rowan.

Madeleine spoke gently, 'Nate, firstly, the problems with the investigator could just be coincidence . . .' I met her eyes and she sighed. 'Yeah, okay, but it's true.'

I remembered the strange scent at the hospital. There had been strange-scented trails at the scene of the fire. It hadn't been bins, it had been Frey! And then there was Aunty Hetty's heated exchange with him, and his words: 'Your meddling will *not* stop me!' And his written words, 'It was not yet our time.' *He would be back!*

Rowan wasn't safe, I could sense it. My instinct was on red alert. We didn't have the facts. But I could sense it. Even if he wasn't connected to events back then, he had Rowan in his sights. And *if* he wasn't human . . . how the hell was I supposed to protect her? To protect her from a creature my strength might not work against, a creature whose powers might extend to killing vampires! I knew neither my charm nor Madeleine's power worked against Aunty Hetty, and she unsettled me big time – was Frey going to be the same?

'What are they?' I snarled, barely in enough control to utter those three little words.

There was a long pause, whilst everyone reflected. Only Madeleine spoke up. Looking nervous, she conjectured, 'The Fey?'

'*Faeries?*' Frederick spat the word out. 'Now I've *officially* had enough!'

I looked at Madeleine. I knew why she had said it. 'Do you believe in the Fey?' he had asked Rowan.

'Do they exist?' I demanded.

'I don't know, Nate – I really don't. There's always been talk of them and Fergus mentioned something about them in passing, but refused to expand or speculate on what he thought Aunty Hetty and Rosie were. All I can say is, it's . . . possible.'

'Faeries! You are seriously talking about faeries

here?' Frederick shook his head, as if we'd lost our minds.

'The Fey – and it's just a suggestion,' Madeleine clarified. 'We don't know for sure they even exist – and certainly not whether that's what Aunty Hetty is . . . or Simeon Frey.'

Elizabeth was in my head. I knew she had been watching me closely. 'Nathaniel – don't panic. We don't know he isn't human, or that he was involved before. *Please*, Nate,' she pleaded.

Frederick tried, too. 'Just because something strange-scented was involved in the death of her parents, and something strange-scented has now turned up to hurt Rowan—' He stopped abruptly, as Elizabeth snarled at him. He said meekly now, 'I'm sorry, that didn't sound quite as reassuring as I wanted it to.'

'Nate . . .' James growled urgently.

But it was too late. None of their words saved Elizabeth's near priceless grand piano, previously owned by Beethoven himself, from my fist – before I disappeared out of the window with a tormented roar.

The instrument's harsh metallic death-cry resounded long after I had made my exit. But the destruction did nothing to suppress the wrath raging through me. Every part of my body was shuddering with its force. Before out of earshot, I heard through the ringing now spiralling out of control in my ears, James' concerned voice, 'I think he took that rather well . . . considering.'

I was letting my rage flare. I couldn't let the blind terror that kept seeping through take hold. If it did, I would be of no use to Rowan at all.

What if there was a greater risk to Rowan than I? Could she be the target of a creature that had managed to kill an immortal? She had my protection, and would forever, but what if my protection wasn't enough?

It was Rowan's rooftop I escaped to. I was in desperate need of hearing her calming, hypnotic night-time breathing. And it worked to a degree. It allowed me to reach a point where I could apply some kind of reason. Nothing was confirmed. This could be a simple overreaction . . . and it wouldn't be the first. But assuming it wasn't, assuming my instinct that Rowan was in great danger, was correct . . . I would NEVER let anything happen to her. I *would* be strong enough to protect her. I had to be. I was a vampire, for Christ's sake . . . a fanatically obsessed, lovesick one at that. I *would* protect Rowan with my very being.

Rowan was returning to work on Monday and I would implement my plans for protecting her from Frey. Then I would dispose of him permanently. I would not have him on the same planet as Rowan: I couldn't take that risk. I would return to the house tonight and finish the meeting, but then, until Frey was out of the picture, I wasn't leaving her side.

★ ★ ★

257

When I flew through the open town-house window just before dawn, they were in pretty much the same positions as I had left them. The evidence of my loss of temper had been cleared away though. Not a single splinter of wood was distinguishable in the plush Wilton carpet, and the fire was roaring strongly; its basket of kindling, overflowing.

I looked at Elizabeth remorsefully. 'I am sorry, sweetheart. I will attempt to replace it.'

She replied to me as silently as I had spoken, 'There are more important things to concentrate on presently. But I will hold you to it when all this gets sorted. And it *will* get sorted. Rowan will be fine.'

Frederick spoke out loud first and was impassioned. 'We don't know it yet, but if Rowan is a target, I'm pledging you my full support – whoever the smelly critters might be! We won't let anything happen to her, Nate.'

Sounds of agreement echoed around the room.

'But I stand by what I've always said . . . of all the girls to bloody well fall for!' James added, with a grin.

I smiled wryly. 'Thank you, but as you said, we do not know yet.' I prayed I had overreacted, because if I hadn't, there was a dead vampire in the equation, and this was my family. How could I put them at risk . . . but how could I not, where Rowan was concerned?

I took a deep shuddery breath and reflected how

my existence was now unrecognisable from what it had been only a matter of weeks earlier. How Rowan's presence in my 'life' . . .

My thoughts were abruptly interrupted.

'NOOOOOOOOO!' James roared, incredulously.

'SHITTTTTT!' Frederick hissed delightedly, jumping to his feet.

'Oh, dear!' Madeleine muttered.

Elizabeth gasped, before she screeched, 'Nate – it wasn't me!' She brought her knees to her chest and covered her face with her hands.

Bugger! Just as I thought things could get no worse, my guard had slipped.

'Barney the *WHAT? – Mama Mia! – Hamleys? – A HORNY KISS!* – You dirty bugger! After everything you said to me . . .'

'I always thought you'd be the weakest link!' Elizabeth cried. 'And it's me now in trouble, thank you very much . . .'

Frederick had stopped in his tracks and was staring at Elizabeth in horror. '*ADOPTION?*' he roared.

My head was in my hands.

CHAPTER 13

LITTLE HUMAN CHILDREN

'Are you sure you're alright?' Rowan asked, for the third time. We were sat on a shaded bench, at the bottom of Clare and Mark's Wiltshire back garden.

'Yes, of course,' I replied, for the third time, before choosing to change my answer. 'Actually, no I am not! They were evil. Evil little demons, disguised as human children.' I was still trying to come to terms with what had just happened. It was beyond humiliating. *How the hell had a group of little human children succeeded in terrifying a two-hundred-year-old vampire, technically in his physical prime?*

'And you can stop laughing Rowan, right now!' I said, in response to her latest bout of mirth. 'They floored me in a rugby tackle, for Christ's sake! All twenty-seven of them! They stamped all over me when I was down and tried to pull my head off. There was no concept of fair play at all. They used everything: teeth, nails, fists, elbows, knees, heads, feet . . . and the girls were the evilest of them all. They actually found a tear in the costume, and they tried to pinch!'

'It was the feet,' she said solemnly. 'I warned you about the feet last night . . .' There was no mistaking the fact her shoulders had started to shake again. But I didn't need to see it. I could *feel* how amused she was by the whole situation. It was resulting in the most bizarre cocktail of sensations for me to deal with: her mirth, mixed with my horror and humiliation . . . and relief. Immense relief. Had I given into the momentary urges to attack or take to the air and flee, the party would have been particularly memorable.

'Barney the Dinosaur's feet aren't the best design for a quick getaway,' she managed to splutter out before exploding into peals of laughter, doubling up and clutching her sides. 'I'm sorry, I'm sorry,' she gasped. 'I'll be okay in a minute.'

'Well, at least one of us will. I have been scarred for eter . . . ever more. And you . . . *you* bursting into hysterical laughter every time you so much as look at me. I am not even in costume now!'

'I know, I know, I'm sorry. I just keep seeing . . . Oh God! – I don't think I've ever laughed so much in my life.'

'And that should make me feel *better*?'

'You should have growled at them earlier,' Rowan managed to choke out.

'You heard that did you?'

'Yep. You were really in character.' She took a moment to gain enough control to get the next words out. 'Why didn't you do what Mark did?'

'You mean run? The feet, Rowan, the feet . . .'

I paused to allow her an opportunity to recover before continuing, 'If you failed to notice, Mark, damn him, was not seven foot and purple, with giant bulbous feet and a deranged grin, but simply had a mask over his face and a tail, if that's what you could call that ridiculous little thing, attached to his bloody waist!' I shook my head. I had lost her again. And by the looks of her, she wasn't going to emerge capable of saying anything for several minutes.

I looked away, taking in the inflatable bouncy castle, balloons and bunting, yet more firsts for me, and chuckled. Yes, it was humiliating. *Bloody humiliating.* But Rowan was happy. And at least it had got my mind off Simeon Frey. I immediately purged him from my head. Now was not the time.

'I'm sorry about Mark,' she finally said. I reached over to wipe away her tears of laughter with my fingers. She beamed. 'Clare called to say he'd put his foot down and—'

'You *knew*?' It was my turn to splutter now.

'I'm sorry! I truly am. Clare may have tipped me off, but . . . you're going to growl again, aren't you?'

'I believe it is my bite you need to look out for, Rowan.'

She raised her eyebrows, suggestively. I looked away and gulped, before replying, 'And we discussed *that* last night.'

'Mmmm, I know. But you never told me where you'd learned to kiss like that!'

'Rowan . . .'

'Oooooo. That was very nearly a growl.'

I turned to look at her again and shook my head, but couldn't help the soft laugh. 'What am I going to do with you?'

'Well, I've a few suggestions that—'

'Rowan . . .' I warned. 'You really are going to be my undoing, you know.'

'Funny you should say that, one of my suggestions included . . .'

I couldn't help it. I bent over and gave her the tiniest peck on the lips, before I moved my head quickly away. 'I did it for you, you know.'

'I know. And thank you. But can you please stop making me feel so guilty?'

'That is your conscience, Rowan. Not me.' I grinned.

'*Possibly* . . . You know, Clare and Mark *really* like you! Mark was prepared to despise you because Clare's not stopped talking about you. But even he likes you. He says he found you quite formidable to begin with – an "aura of power" was the way he put it – but actually, once he got over that, he couldn't help but genuinely warm to you.'

I was relieved. I had been putting a lot of effort into being more agreeable. And small-talk wasn't that bad. All it required was a modicum of effort. I had, surprisingly, found myself enjoying the conversations that had ensued, as they so often involved mention of Rowan.

'They mean a lot to you, do they not?' I reflected aloud.

'Mmmm . . . and of course little Nathan and Tom. Thank you so much for Tom's present. It was so generous, and he adores it!'

I could hear his laughter from inside the house now. He had abandoned the bouncy castle immediately on spotting the Hamleys' purchase, and hadn't voluntarily been off it since. He had even had a tantrum when forced to leave it, to join the table to have his birthday tea.

'Well, I am unable to take the credit for that. I wouldn't have *begun* to know what to buy. It was Elizabeth's choice.'

'You *will* thank her for us, won't you?'

'Of course. She will be delighted it was received so well.'

'Am I ever going to get to meet her?' Rowan asked gingerly, and I could feel her nerves.

I turned to look at her. 'Would you like to?'

'I would *love* to,' she said eagerly, meeting my eyes.

I grinned. 'Then we should see what we can arrange.' *I will do the right thing. I will.* What harm could it do? Elizabeth would be ecstatic. And the idea of them meeting . . . it made me feel . . . God, I knew not; it just seemed right, somehow. They would get on, I knew that. Probably *too* well, I reflected.

'Aunty Rowan, Uncle Nathaniel! Mummy wants to know if you want a plate of food.' Nathan's yell

264

was hard to miss, as he bounded down the garden, leaping over stray balloons, to reach us.

All I could do was observe his interaction with Rowan, when he had finally lifted himself up from the grass he had so dramatically dived upon. The 'Uncle' bit had left me . . . stunned, and I couldn't quite identify how it made me feel. It was a new one for me.

'I thought you told me you were too old for this,' Rowan chuckled, as a giggling and squealing Nathan reacted to her tickles. It was plain to see Rowan was a natural and would make a wonderful mother . . . as would Elizabeth. And the thought caused me so much pain.

'Nathan!' Clare called from the house.

'Tell Mummy not to worry, we'll be in soon,' Rowan said, pivoting him in the direction of the house. He took a step forward, before pausing and slowly turning.

'Uncle Nathaniel?' *Was he talking to me?* From the fact his eyes were now fixed intently on mine, I could only assume so. I raised my eyebrows. 'Uncle Nathaniel?' he asked again.

'Yes . . . Nathan.'

'Mummy told me it was rude to ask . . . but I'm not being rude. And you really don't have to tell Mummy I've asked, if you really don't want to . . .'

'Asked what?' Rowan piped up.

'Uncle Nathaniel . . . can I have a ride in your car? *Please!* It is the coolest car I have *ever* seen.

265

It's better than the Batmobile and Spiderman's and— And when you don't want it anymore, and when I am a man, can I have it?'

I looked at Rowan and we both grinned. My excursion to Hamleys had at least ensured I knew what he was making reference to. I had ventured out in my car for the first time today. It had been quite a traumatic day, all in all. But what was the right answer to give this little human boy? 'Umm. Perhaps you would like to advise your mother . . . I said yes, if it is, of course, acceptable to her.'

He looked puzzled and looked from me to Rowan.

'Acceptable – it means okay,' Rowan added, whilst grinning at me. I shook my head. I had never had to talk to a twenty-first-century mortal boy before and didn't think I had done too badly.

'*Yesssss!!!*' he squealed. 'Thank you, Uncle Nathaniel. You're the best!' After giving me a rapid hug, that caught me completely unawares, he ran back up the garden crying out, 'Mummy, Mummy! He said YES!'

'He's going to be in so much trouble now,' Rowan predicted. 'And you're off the hook. There's no way Clare will let him in your car today, after she specifically told him not to ask . . . Cute though, wouldn't you say?'

I wasn't sure what I called it. It was all pretty overwhelming. And before I knew it, I had asked the question, 'Would you like children of your own?' I immediately regretted it.

Nevertheless, I watched Rowan's reaction closely. She paused before saying, 'Do you know . . . I really don't know. Perhaps when the time's right.' Her eyes deliberately didn't meet mine, but chose to focus on her nails, which she had begun to examine intently.

My thoughts travelled to my own haunting images of our children playing at Ridings. I shut my eyes for a moment, in the inane hope of dispelling them.

'I do enjoy my freedom though, and there's obviously the issue of work, but actually, I rather like the idea of adopting. With both myself and Clare adopted, I don't know, it just might seem appropriate . . . or perhaps a mixture. I'm not sure. I really haven't thought about it a great deal.'

What was it with this current obsession with adopting?

Looking at the ground now, she asked hesitantly, but attempting to sound casual, 'Would you like children one day?'

Why had I asked the damned question? I had promised to be honest with her. *But the repercussions of this . . .? Bloody, Bloody, Bloody Hell!*

But she *should* know. She was mortal, for Christ's sake, and had a right to a normal human life and I simply couldn't give her that. I had no choice.

I shut my eyes, took a deep breath, and prayed I could find the strength to finally do one right thing. I spoke after too long a pause. The distress in my voice evident, 'I am . . .' *I had to do it.* 'I am unable to father children. It has never before been an issue for me, but now I wish with *all my heart*, it was not the case.'

I could feel Rowan's shock and pain and it amplified my own. *Had I just lost her?* It had been the right thing to do . . . *but why did it feel so wrong?* I barely resisted the urge to curl up into a foetal position.

She reached out for my hand and stroked it gently with her thumb. 'Nate, I'm so sorry. That must be so hard for you, so painful. I am so sorry. I really don't know what to say to comfort you . . . Nate, open your eyes and look at me. Why is it something you regret *now*? Nate? Please open your eyes.'

I obliged, but wasn't sure how my shroud could possibly be effective with the degree of emotion currently rushing through me. My voice was raw. 'You know I want to give you everything you could possibly want and deserve, but I simply cannot. I am not able to give you the normal life you are entitled to. I do not think I can give you any life at all!'

Moving closer to me, she gently placed her hands on either side of my cold face and looked intently into my eyes. Her warming breath caressed me. 'I feel pain for you, I really do. But don't for one moment think this changes the way I feel about you. There is nothing, absolutely nothing in this world that could ever change that. I've never felt this way about anyone before. *Ever!*'

'You cannot mean that. You do not even know *what* I am! If you knew—'

She interrupted quickly. 'I know *who* you are. And for the moment that's enough. How could I not love you, for *who* you are?'

Dear God, what had I done? I spoke urgently now. 'Rowan, listen to me. I do not deserve to be loved. This was not meant to happen. This cannot—'

'Well it has. And don't you *ever* talk about not deserving to be loved!'

I was shaking my head, but I simply didn't know what to say. *She loved me?* I had so selfishly ploughed onwards and spared no thought at all for the repercussions on Rowan. All I had worried about was not *physically* hurting her. But now . . . Aunty Hetty had known. 'Don't break her heart,' she had said. And that was exactly what I was going to end up doing. Not because I wanted to, but because it was inevitable. Whichever way I went . . . walking away or, God forbid, telling her what I was. It would be the end.

'Nate,' she cut into my anguished thoughts with a warning, 'we are taking this one day at a time – you *promised*! I can't help but feel we are meant to be together and I won't hear you say otherwise.'

I reached up and put my hands over hers, and gently let my head fall forward until our foreheads touched. *What had I done? How could I possibly let this continue?* I had to . . .

'I come bearing food,' Aunty Hetty's voice rang

out. I quickly put some distance between myself and Rowan and attempted to recover my composure. I hadn't even heard her approach, and she was now standing right over us.

'Are you two kids okay?' she asked.

'Absolutely. Never better,' Rowan squeaked. 'And cheese and pineapple on sticks – *yum!*' She leaned over to grab two from the paper plate Aunty Hetty had put on the little table by the bench, before sitting back in her seat. She was doing a good job of disguising her anxiety.

Why did I get the feeling Aunty Hetty knew exactly what we had just been talking about . . . and had turned up to ensure I didn't do what she had warned me not to?

'A special day, I would say,' she continued. 'Your dinosaur was a hit, Nathaniel; the children have been delightedly imitating your bloodcurdling growl throughout tea.'

I met her eyes and said silently, fully expecting her to hear me, 'We need to talk. What do you know about Simeon Frey?'

She maintained her composure remarkably well, and her eyes revealed nothing, but there was no doubt she had heard me. I observed the draining of some of her cheek colour.

'Well, I'll make myself scarce,' she chirped. Yes, she had *definitely* heard me. 'Ooooo, Rowan, before I forget. I've heard Jonathan Martin's been admitted for psychiatric evaluation. Apparently, he's been blubbering away about some kind of monster. Couldn't have happened to a better person. So very fortuitous. That really made my day. Anyway. Tatty bye.'

Rowan's emotions were all over the place. *She couldn't still care for him? Please no!*

'You are not worried for him, are you?' I ventured, whilst tracking Aunty Hetty's walk back up the garden.

'No, Nate, I'm not. He can rot in hell as far as I'm concerned!'

My heart beat again.

After a moment's pause, she asked, 'What exactly did you say to him that day?'

Ahhhhh. 'You think this has got something to do with me?'

'I didn't say that. I just wondered what you said to him.'

'We just had a little chat. I asked him to stay away. I was actually very restrained.' Rowan was quiet. 'Please tell me I do not scare you?' I said softly. I didn't think I felt fear. It was more like uncertainty.

'You don't scare *me*, Nate, you don't scare my family. If you scare shits like Jonathan Martin, well . . . that's their problem! And back to our earlier conversation. We do this day by day . . . and I DO NOT want to know!'

271

CHAPTER 14

NINE TO FIVE

I let out an immense sigh of relief when Rowan opened her front door. She had made it safely down those damned stairs. I could now unclench my hands from the steering wheel and beep my horn. When she saw me, I felt her surprised pleasure and excitement, at odds with both the roll of the eyes and the irritated look she gave me. I smiled; despite appearances, she was pleased to see me.

I leapt out of the car to greet her. It was 8 a.m., Monday morning. 'Good morning, Ms Locke. I am your chauffeur for the day.' I bowed in a way that was second nature to me, due to the historical period of my formative years.

Rowan was shaking her head disapprovingly, but nevertheless her eyes were travelling over me. And it felt so good; *I* felt good this morning. I was putting into action my plan to keep Rowan safe. Frey, whatever he was, would never get through me.

She spoke distractedly, her eyes continuing to wander, 'I should have known that controlling nature of yours wouldn't let me do this.' She snapped her eyes back to my face and spoke with a little more focus, 'Nate – you *have* to let me do things for myself. I'm getting the bus. I'm a big girl now and, believe it or not, *can* get to work on my own.'

I could feel her irritation, but it wasn't extreme. In fact it was miniscule, as other thoughts created far more pleasing emotions for me to experience. I couldn't help but grin. 'And I will, but all in good time. You are not honestly going to tell me you are going to hobble off now – *with* your crutches, I am pleased to see – but nevertheless, hobble off – when I am here at your service? By the way, it is the first time I have seen you in your business attire . . .'

Rowan was wearing a black skirt suit, with an amber top. I knew about this suit. I had heard her talking to Clare about it. It had been a new acquisition from Jigsaw, an extravagance 'she'd simply had to have'.

'. . . and you look particularly appetising.' I meant it. She both looked and smelt ravishing. But I couldn't dwell on it. I was on a mission this morning. 'I even have a decaffeinated skinny latte in the car ready for you,' I added, as extra impetus.

'How did you know that's how I take my coffee?'

I shrugged and gave her an innocent smile. There were lots of things I had learnt whilst on my clandestine rooftop perch. The suit and coffee, of course, but also that the weigh-in this morning had gone well; I was hoping it would work in my favour and Rowan would be in a reasonably amenable mood.

'Don't look at me with those puppy-dog eyes, Nate.' I shut them for a moment and took a deep breath. *This was going too far.*

'So, does the coffee . . . settle it?' I asked, tentatively re-opening my eyes.

'This morning it does, because you are here, and because the *coffee* is calling me. But this is the first and last time, okay? I really mean it. I'm not some weak, helpless female who needs you running to her assistance all the time. The first and last time!'

I grinned, but there was no chance. My protective instinct was now in overdrive. Besides, I could think of no place else I would rather be than by her side, every moment of every day. I knew we were on borrowed time, so I was going to make the bloody most of it.

'So, any of those Monday-morning blues you were worried about?' I asked, as we weaved in and out of rush-hour traffic.

She turned and grinned at me, shaking her head. Her coffee was in her hands and, although she wasn't intending to let me know, I was totally and utterly off the hook. Her eyes were sparkling and I doubted either of us was oblivious to the chemistry filling the car.

'Are you working today, too? You're all suited and booted.' I wallowed in the sensations her accompanying visual inspection triggered.

'I have a meeting this morning.' I turned and

smiled. She was still assessing me. 'Any meetings for you today?' I was trying to sound casual. She abruptly looked away, and I felt her anxiety. There was no question as to what had caused it. I gripped the steering wheel tightly, but managed to say gently, 'You will be off his account, Rowan, so do not worry. He will *not* be an issue for you again.'

She looked at me suspiciously. I shook my head at myself.

'The first thing I am going to do, before anything else, is go in and demand I'm off that account.' She spoke with deliberate determination. 'I'm not going to let the bastard wreck my career!'

The smile of encouragement I gave vanquished her anxiety, but I was forced to look away and focus on the road. I couldn't get that damned kiss out of my head. I concentrated religiously on my driving until we drew up outside Rowan's offices.

'Don't even think about it,' she warned, when I got out of the car and opened her door. 'There's a lift and you're *not* helping me to my desk!' Her determination was felt loud and clear so I knew there was no point arguing. After helping her out of the car, I therefore had to watch her hobble away. 'Rowan!' I called, unable to let her go quite yet. As she paused and turned, I closed the distance between us, oblivious of all the rushing office workers I no doubt effortlessly passed. Lowering my face, I ever so gently let my lips touch hers. 'For luck,' I said, my voice, husky and desperate.

After Rowan was out of my vampire sight, I

drove around the corner to park. In half an hour I had a meeting with Mike Peters, Rowan's Managing Director. For now, though, I would fret about Rowan's likely reaction to discovering she would be working for me; 'I reckon you would be a nightmare client,' sprang to mind.

I was sat in my car, frowning, when Rowan unconsciously tipped me off to having started her own meeting with Peters. My alarm grew as her fear and anxiety became more intense, and anger began to intrude. In fact, she was becoming incredibly angry and upset, and I soon found myself resting my head on the steering wheel, gripping it with such intensity I was amazed it didn't shatter.

Surely he had let her come off the account? Any reasonable man, for Christ's sake, would have removed her from the account! What kind of way did this man do business?

I tried to hone in my hearing to their meeting, but Rowan's reaction was making it impossible. 'I am not going to be able to sort things out, if she does not calm down,' I wittered away worriedly to myself, whilst banging my head repeatedly on the steering wheel. 'And just how am I supposed to meet with the bastard, when all I want to do is rip his throat out?'

I gave compartmentalising another go, putting into practice all of my recent efforts to sideline Rowan's anger and distress. It wasn't remotely good enough, but my muttering had confirmed my ability to talk.

I pressed speed-dial and Rowan picked up almost immediately. 'Rowan?' I asked as gently as I could muster. She was upset. I knew that already, but I caught a sniffle. 'Have you been *crying*?' I couldn't keep the anguish and outrage out of my voice. I would kill Mike Peters for this! If there was no Dynamic PR, then Rowan was not at risk in the workplace . . . but I knew how much she enjoyed her job. *Christ! This was going to be difficult.*

'He said no!' she stuttered.

'Rowan, this is *really* important; I need you to calm down. Trust me – I *can* make this right.'

'How? I'm going to have to leave my job and I love it!'

I couldn't for one moment imagine why, when it involved working for an imbecile like Mike Peters.

'You have to *trust* me. I *can*, and *will*, sort this out. You will not need to leave. I own Gray Portfolio, for Christ's sake, and will find a way to ensure you are removed from that account. Please believe me.'

She was calming down a little. I could feel some relief entering into her immense emotional cocktail . . . relief, perhaps, that someone was helping her fight this battle?

'Where are you?' I asked gently.

'In the loo.'

'Do you want me to come and get you? I could take you home until this is resolved.'

How I would achieve that, with my current restriction in movement, I didn't know, but I would find a way. Our conversation was helping, though.

'Thanks, but I'll be okay. I promise I'm not normally like this.' I could hear the rustle of the tissue as she wiped her nose. 'I've been working here for eight years and have *never* cried in the toilets before!'

'Rowan, sweetheart – are you sure you do not want me to come and get you? I am fighting an urge at the moment to storm in there and carry you out.'

She wasn't affronted, there was no indignation. *God! She was feeling vulnerable.* Instead, she started giggling. That was better. I could handle this. 'Oh, the girls would *love* that! Perhaps not today though, hey?'

'Not today then – but I am offering my services, whenever required.'

She paused and I felt her feelings go someplace really not good for me, but most definitely put to bed – a bad analogy – the worst aspects of her upset.

'I was going to say something then, but just remembered, I'm meant to be a good girl.'

I moaned. 'Just keep remembering it. I am going now. But trust me.' And hung up.

I had to refocus. Rowan was currently calm enough for me to at least undertake the meeting – that was good. But I knew I needed to calm *myself* down before I saw Peters. I reminded myself how much Rowan loved her job and no Peters meant no job. My own satisfaction could *not* be a consideration here.

Twenty minutes later I was in Peters' office. He was dressed in a charcoal pinstripe suit and lavender shirt, the top button of which was undone; he was wearing no tie. He was, however, wearing eye-catching pink-and-lilac striped socks. His mousy hair was gelled back. I didn't like him, and not because of the socks.

I was *deliberately* making Peters ill at ease. We had started the meeting with him sat behind his large mock-regency, fake-leather-embossed desk, playing nervously with his Montblanc fountain pen and whatever else he could find to keep his fingers active. He had, within the last five minutes, however, retreated as far away from me as possible. He had been subconsciously rolling the wheels of his black imitation-leather executive chair further and further from me. With his last push backwards, he had discovered, to his consternation, that he had hit the wall. He was, therefore, at the limit of his subconscious retreat.

On his lap were a pile of paperclips, spent staples, rubber-bands – even some old herbal teabags, which he had been using as worry-beads.

I realised I was at the edge of what was acceptable behaviour around humans. As far as I was concerned, however, he was lucky I hadn't gone over that edge. I was keeping myself in check, but unashamedly taking pleasure in the beads of sweat

I could see breaking out on his forehead and the sound of his too-fast heart.

But here I was, offering to move my account to his company, an account I knew to be worth at least three times the firm's total annual revenue from all existing accounts combined. I may unnerve him, but he was, nevertheless, a businessman.

'There is one condition to my immediately moving Gray Portfolio's public relations requirements to Dynamic.' He was still unable to meet my eyes; he had made that mistake when I had first walked into the room. 'I expect Rowan Locke to act as Account Director and obviously, with the size of account, I expect her to focus *entirely* on my account and no other. With colleagues already handling Miss Locke's accounts during her absence, I see no reason why she cannot begin working exclusively for me as of this point.'

He both looked and sounded flustered. 'I'm not . . . sure Rowan's the . . . best person for your . . . account.'

'And why is that, Mr Peters?'

'I have another very good Account Director, who would, I'm sure, do as good a job as Rowan. Rowan is needed on her existing accounts.'

'I would like Miss Locke.'

'It's . . . not that simple.'

'Explain,' I uttered ominously.

He stuttered, 'Frey Investments have made it . . . clear they require her on their account too, so . . . she wouldn't be able to work for you exclusively.'

I felt the chill pass through me. Further confirmation Rowan was being targeted by Frey.

I recovered myself before proceeding. 'Mr Peters, Gray Portfolio will move to you today, but *only* on the condition Rowan Locke works exclusively for me.' I stood up to leave. 'On the basis you are unable to give me that assurance then my business will remain at Shaftesbury. I wish you a good day.'

I had only made one step towards the door before Peters caved. 'Alright, then.'

Yessss! I had done it without the charm, although it would most *certainly* have followed, had it been necessary.

But that had not been easy. And I didn't like the fact Peters' heart rate, high throughout our meeting, had got dangerously so as soon as Frey Investments had entered the equation.

But what did it matter? 'It was not yet our time.' I would make damn sure it was *never* his time.

'I am very pleased to hear that, Mr Peters. Perhaps you would like to make the necessary calls to your team – so we can get straight down to business? I was thinking of an introductory meeting in, shall we say, ten minutes? Board Room One, I notice, is empty.'

I had no intention of leaving his office until he had made the calls, determined to see this through, so he did so, whilst I stalked around the room, looking at various newspaper headlines hanging framed on the walls, ignoring the fake leather sofa he had nervously ushered me to.

As Peters terminated his last call on his landline and prepared to address me, his mobile phone rang. Reaching for the phone that was upon his desk, I observed his face turn ashen as he looked at the screen displaying the caller ID.

Simeon Frey.

He glanced nervously in my direction.

I met his look with a self-satisfied grin. And why not? How fortunate was this? 'The sooner he knows, the better. And feel free to tell him *exactly* why Miss Locke will no longer be working with him.'

I wanted Frey to know Rowan was no longer unprotected and if that made me the target, all the better: I neither knew nor cared what I was dealing with. I was going to consign him to history.

Swallowing audibly and with a shaking hand, Peters accepted the call.

'Is she back today?' I heard Frey snap.

And I wanted to snap his neck.

'She is. But I'm afraid Rowan will no longer be able to work on your account.' Peters spoke so quickly, his words stumbled over each other. The nature of his delivery seemed to reflect what his heart was now doing. 'She . . .'

Peters words died away at the sharp intake of breath that sounded on the other end of the phone. Eerily quiet. 'Why? I was under the impression you grasped the nature of the unfortunate misunderstanding between Rowan and me and furthermore assured me it would not be a problem.'

Peters stuttered in response. 'It has been requested she head up the team to work on the Gray Portfolio. I realise it is not ideal but I am very much hoping we can continue with the arrangement we had in her absence? Whilst Rowan is in demand, that Account Director is equally as good and will no doubt do Frey Investments proud.'

Silence.

Prolonged silence.

'Hello?'

The phone went dead.

And I grinned even more broadly. Frey had not taken that well, but I hadn't expected him to. Whatever he had planned, he could un-plan it. Rowan was mine.

Focusing on the still ashen Peters, I said the necessary because his heart rate was far too high. 'Any issue Frey may have, I will ensure he settles it with me personally. I am assuming that would be acceptable?'

I watched the weight visibly lift from Peters' shoulders.

'And whilst we head to the board room, let us take the opportunity to get to know each other better.'

My suggestion resulted in the recovering colour blanching from Peters' face afresh. But he deserved it. *Unfortunate misunderstanding?* I didn't care what Frey may have said to him to convince him otherwise. Or how much he may have intimidated him. This man had been prepared to subject Rowan to that creature after everything she had told him.

And he had made her cry.

Once settled in the board room, there were a few minutes to spare before the scheduled meeting began, so I worked hard – *very* hard – at being civil. All the time I let my hearing range out in search of Rowan. Word seemed to have got around that we were moving our account from Shaftesbury, and my name was being mentioned rather a lot. But Peters had left only a voicemail message for Rowan, and I didn't think she yet knew; she wasn't in conversation and I hadn't felt her reaction. And I was sure there would be one.

In the event, I knew exactly when she became enlightened, for I could both see and hear her through the glass windows going down one side of the board room. I had been listening to her heartbeat, but felt her eyes on me before I saw her. There was no question it was *her* eyes that made me blaze that way. There were a number of other young women standing outside the board room looking at me, but it was only Rowan's eyes that caused that reaction.

I looked up. She was standing with an A4 file clutched to her chest and was feeling confused. It was not confusion in her look, though. When she moved her eyes to meet mine, I tentatively smiled. She questioned me with her look and I shrugged. I had been doing that a lot recently.

'What's going on?' I heard her ask one of the girls stood watching me.

'Oh! There you are, Rowan. We've been looking for you everywhere!'

She must have still been in the ladies' room. I looked at her eyes again. I could see the tell-tale signs of her earlier tears, but doubted a human could; she had used make-up to effectively cover up the redness.

'Haven't you heard? Gray Portfolio is moving its account to us and we're on the team . . . and just *look* who we're working for!' The girl nodded her head in my direction.

Irritation had now been added to Rowan's confusion.

Another girl, also looking at me, piped in, 'I've a friend at Shaftesbury. She says, *he* is the most *seriously* sexy man she has *ever* come across – and he doesn't even know it. Apparently, he's a real gentleman, but there's something else . . . a *promise* of something more, and he's *guaranteed* to get your juices flowing. His eyes, she says, are the deepest, softest, hot-chocolate brown . . . and they melt you. His voice . . . well, she says he's a man of few words, but the way he speaks those words are enough . . . enough to make you come in your panties!'

I shifted awkwardly. Rowan was glowering at me and I quickly looked away. It wasn't my fault! This was all new to me. I tend to zone out human conversations going on around me. And I had only ever met the Shaftesbury PR team once – and even then it had been accidental, their meeting overrunning prior to my own with my MD.

'Apparently all the girls at Shaftesbury lust after him – and now he's ours! This job just got *so* much better! Do you think we will get to see more of him than they did? *Pleeease* let there be a god!'

My eyes returned tentatively to Rowan. She was shaking her head and rolling her eyes at her team, but I also felt something else. She was feeling possessive, and it felt so good.

'So what do *you* think of Nathaniel Gray, Rowan?'

I listened intently. I could feel her eyes on me, but didn't dare look up.

'Oh, I agree with you, the eye candy is pretty incredible . . .' *Eye candy?* '. . . but I wager he might not be the easiest person to work for. This is not going to be plain sailing, girls. *Control* freak probably doesn't even begin to go there!'

I laughed out loud, startling Peters, who now looked at me questioningly. 'Apologies. A personal matter.' I kept my eyes pointedly away from Rowan.

There was no question she was going to have issues with my being her boss. But needs must . . . and I was going to enjoy this!

After they had all settled in their chairs Peters started the meeting. 'I'd like to introduce you all to Nathaniel Gray of Gray Portfolio, our latest new client. The account is substantial and will involve a dedicated approach. Rowan will be heading up the team and will now work on Gray Portfolio *exclusively.*'

I felt that spark of anger of hers but I suspected

286

it couldn't be given fuller vent because of where we were and her need to remain professional. There were evidently benefits to Rowan being in the workplace.

'Mr Gray . . . Nathaniel . . . this is—'

'Rowan Locke,' I interrupted as Peters began the introductions. 'We are acquainted. It is a pleasure to see you again, Miss Locke.' My voice was subtly tinged with amusement, but nevertheless professional.

'The pleasure is all mine, Mr Gray,' she said, with more than a hint of sarcasm.

I spoke quietly and quickly, in a manner normally inaudible to humans, 'No, believe me, Rowan, the pleasure is *most definitely* mine. Do you have *any* idea what your eyes have been doing to me?'

Rowan gasped and exclaimed indignantly, 'Nate!'

Everyone around the table looked at her, shocked. *What had I just done?* Attempting to cover my lunacy, I spoke at a normal volume, 'Indeed, Miss Locke. We will be working together so do feel free to call me Nate.'

Rowan looked around, confused. *Bugger.* Quietly and quickly, for her ears only, I attempted to explain, 'They could not hear me, Rowan. You seem to be particularly attuned to my voice. Forgive me, please. I was unable to resist. I will explain later.'

I was an idiot. A complete and utter idiot. My euphoria at removing Frey from the picture, and being with Rowan, had destroyed any last vestiges of common sense I may have still possessed. And there was going to be hell to pay.

Rowan seemed to recover herself remarkably well – on the surface – but *Christ* was she confused and annoyed – and workplace or not, justice seemed to be at work and I found myself experiencing it all for myself. As for the look that was sent my way, it was harsh to say the least. But I deserved it. I deserved so much more.

I thankfully found I didn't need to speak much during the meeting, which suited me to a tee. Rowan introduced the four other members of the all-female team, rolling her eyes dramatically after each introduction. I thought they had been very sweet, really. She had then taken control of the rest of the proceedings. I was asked for salient information, which I found myself able to provide – although I wasn't involved in the day-to-day running of things, I was still the driving force behind the company – but then matters went back to her. I was impressed, very impressed . . . and proud.

It was about three-quarters of the way through the meeting when Rowan got called out. Somebody was on the phone for her. She had instructed a message be taken but the messenger came back, advising it was the police. I felt her worry as if it were my own.

'If you would please excuse me, Mr Gray . . . Nathaniel . . . Nate,' she said, momentarily meeting my eyes, before leaving the room.

She shouldn't have been worried, however. It was me who should have been worried. My hearing tipped me off to the trouble I was in.

'No, I'm sorry, Officer. I'm just checking you're talking about the right car. Yes, that *sounds* like my car. And yes, that is my car's number plate. But you're telling me . . . an out-of-control double-decker bus has driven into my parked car, and my car is fine, but the bus is a near *write-off*? No, of course I'll get it checked out and get *all* the airbags reset. Oh! I see. Yes, some works were done on it recently. No, Officer, I agree, the sooner the better. Yes of course you can gain entry, um . . . yes, if that's strictly necessary . . . I'm not sure this is really very amusing . . . yes, of course . . . yes, Officer . . . thank you, Officer.'

Bugger! Double bugger! If I wasn't *already* in enough trouble! I had known the time would come, but hadn't expected it to arrive quite so soon, and in quite such a fashion. I was already very aware of Rowan's fury as she re-entered the room. I didn't need to see it emanating from every pore of her body, which it was. Where was her professional hat? I didn't dare meet her eyes. I couldn't even excuse myself from the room, because the fury I had caused was currently rendering my body completely and utterly inca-pable of any form of coherent movement. Although I had discovered, on her return, that it *was* possible to slip a little further down in my chair.

I needed to be pre-emptive here. 'Forgive me,'

I managed to get out, speaking quietly for her ears only. She would have no idea how hard it was for me to get any words out at all.

She pointedly ignored me.

'I do hope everything is okay, Rowan?' Peters asked. He was fishing.

'Oh fine and dandy, Mike. Fine and *bloody* dandy!' She was barely containing her rage. 'An out-of-control bus has just hit my car, and a *laughing* policeman, no less, has suggested he break into it, to deflate the multitude of airbags that inflated on impact. He found great amusement in suggesting the action was necessary . . . in order to prevent it floating away and causing a hazard to air traffic across London!'

Bugger.

Everyone appeared stunned and confused. 'I thought you had a Morris Minor?' the person introduced as Carly bravely ventured.

'Yes, Carly, that's exactly what *I thought* I had. However, it would appear that the *lying, deceitful bastard* who ran me off the road and nearly killed me,' I grimaced, 'undertook some modifications to my car when it went to the garage. Apparently the traffic police have never seen anything like it. They consider the bodywork to now be reinforced with titanium, and when they popped the bonnet – something they simply "*had to do*" – they found a braking system you'd expect to find on a Formula *Bloody* One racing car!'

Snickers erupted around the room. The person

introduced as Jenny took her life in her hands. 'I'm sorry,' and she started to giggle uncontrollably, 'I've just got an image of the Morris Minor taking to the sky. It would be rather Harry Potteresque!'

Rowan glared. But then the whole room, bar me, erupted into uncontrollable giggles and laughter.

'Okay, guys!' Rowan cried, not able to stop smiling herself. 'Enough of my problems; back to business!'

At last. Amusement I could deal with. However, when Rowan looked at me, it was far from amusement in her eyes. She was angry, very angry. We had mercifully passed the fury of earlier, though. I was hopeful.

Smiling sweetly at me, Rowan said, 'I must apologise for the interruption, Mr Gray. It's incredible what deceitful pricks you can meet on the roads these days!'

Ouch.

I wasn't sure how the rest of the meeting went. I was concentrating so intently on trying to isolate Rowan's anger, which had thankfully continued to abate, but which would intermittently resurrect itself every time she looked in my direction, that I just let them talk.

'Mr Gray? Mr Gray?' Ah – an answer was required. The anger was manageable, I should be fine. But I didn't like the anxiety that was beginning to creep in now. I finally looked up into

Rowan's eyes. She was worried about me. My silence had caused her concern. So she should be! I was worried about me. This girl had to learn how to control her temper. And very significantly, I had yet to face her wrath one-on-one. I was unrepentant. I had my reasons for making her car safe. But I very much doubted that would be classed as a reasonable defence. But that was the car. I should have prepared her for the possibility of my working with her. But how could I have risked her vetoing the opportunity I had of removing Simeon Frey from the equation? As for speaking quietly to her . . . I couldn't possibly come up with a defence for that. I was an idiot. It was completely inexcusable. I was worried. Really worried.

'Nate?' She was definitely concerned. I smiled and the worry lessened. 'Are you happy with us proceeding on that basis?'

'Absolutely. Thank you, Rowan, thank you everyone.'

'Mr Gray – Nate – there are a few things we need to finalise. Shall we go to my office?' Peters hovered behind my chair, whilst everybody else started filing out of the room. He seemed a different man to the one who had sat quaking at the thought of speaking to Simeon Frey. And I wasn't remotely happy with *him* calling me Nate. But it was my own damned fault!

'I will be there shortly, if that's acceptable. I would like the room a while longer. Miss Locke, could I talk to you, please?' There was that flare of anger again.

'I've some calls to make,' Rowan muttered, hobbling towards the door.

'I'm sure they can wait,' Peters declared, before shutting the door and leaving us alone in the room.

I spoke urgently and desperately, 'Forgive me. You have every right to be angry with me.'

She was now standing in a *very* angry stance across the table from me, leaning in my direction, with her hands resting palm down on the table top. Trying not to raise her voice because of where we were, but struggling, she hissed, 'So you should be! How could you do this to me? It shows a complete and utter lack of respect! You know, I don't even know where to begin. The car! How about we start there? You even showed me the car, and didn't once come clean. You *must* have known I'd find out!'

'Not quite like this,' I reflected, whilst shaking my head. At least that was one part of my body I had some control over. 'You have to remember, I nearly killed you in that damned car. What did you expect me to do? I was hoping you would never find out about the airbags, because I assumed if you did, it was because you had been in an accident. But if, heaven forbid, that had happened,' I visibly shuddered at the thought, 'the hope was you couldn't be angry with me, because it would have prevented injury to yourself, *and* any passengers you may have had in the car, like

Clare, and Tom, and Nathan.' I was shamelessly using everything I had. 'I failed to account for an out-of-control double-decker bus, or a laughing policeman!'

I was beyond relieved when I felt her anger significantly ebb, and even felt a momentary spark of amusement, although it soon went out.

'You should have *told me*!' she hissed. 'I need to trust you, and something like this doesn't instil trust. You *agreed* to be honest with me . . .'

I leaned closer to Rowan, and looked at her intently, even for me. 'I didn't consider I had a choice . . . I worry about you.' I paused before continuing, 'I was not prepared to give you the option of refusing the additions to the car. Not when they made it easier for me to handle my worry and, at the same time, keep you safe on the road.'

Her anger was controllable, but she was far from happy. 'Why didn't you just *tell* me? Instead, you deliberately misled me!'

'I would now, I promise, but at that point – you *know* how you would have reacted.' She rolled her eyes. '*Please* forgive me. I am trying to adapt, but it is not easy. I respect you more than you can possibly imagine, but there are certain issues I find harder to deal with than . . . other individuals.' She looked away, exasperated, before fixing me with a glare.

I felt the anger flare up again and knew she was moving on to another problematic point. I shut my eyes for a moment. I deserved this. I deserved all of this, but hated Rowan being angry with me. She was upset because of me. She had already had to go through the trauma of her meeting this morning . . . and then me!

'And what about all *this*?' She flung her arms around the room. 'I'm now working for *you*?' Her voice had risen several octaves and could not now be described as a hiss; a screech was probably more accurate. 'Control freak doesn't begin to go there with you, does it, Nathaniel Gray?'

'It is not what it looks like— Are you going to take a seat, or are you going to carry on standing?'

'I'm going to carry on standing, thank you very much!'

I sighed and spoke softly. 'It is not what it looks like. The Gray Portfolio account coming to you is the side-effect. I promised I would help with removing you from Frey Investments, and this is the result. I considered it the only way to both achieve that *and* ensure you could keep the job you enjoy. I will not deny, however, that the idea of spending more time with you appeals – does it not for you?' She looked at me and sighed exasperatedly. 'It is *not* my attempting to control you. I doubt *even I* am strong enough for that.'

Rowan shook her head and muttered, 'You have an answer for *everything*, don't you? Gift of the bloody gab!' She was calming down.

I met her eyes. No one had ever before said that about me. But then I had never before had Rowan as an incentive. 'I do my best . . . but am afraid you challenge me in ways I have never before been challenged.'

'*Finally*, words of comfort!' she cried sardonically, and I had to smile, despite the situation I found myself in, and the fact they were hardly words of comfort.

She quickly looked away from me as confusion became her overriding feeling and she now sat down and rested her arms on the table. I knew what was coming.

She spoke quietly, whilst looking down and fidgeting with her pen, 'So are you going to tell me what happened earlier? Nobody else heard you . . . You've unsettled me . . . no – you've effing freaked me out, Nate! I'm actually not sure I want to know the answer, but . . . *why* did you do it?' She looked at me with pleading eyes and I felt her stab of fear, before it dissipated.

I stretched over to hold her hands, which she instinctively pulled away. She met my eyes for a long moment and then reached out to hold my hands herself. I wanted to hold her in my arms, but I really wasn't sure how this was going to go. I couldn't risk her seeing me debilitated. She had had more than enough to deal with today.

'I failed to think, and it was unforgivable. What that was, was my being an absolute idiot. It was not at all the way for you to find out, and I behaved totally and utterly unprofessionally. I found myself unable to resist, but regretted the situation it put you in straight away. I am more sorry than I can put into words.'

She looked so vulnerable. 'We had an agreement . . . But what you did . . . what happened – is more than I needed, or *wanted*, to know.'

'I realise that . . .' I had no choice but to explain myself, and had absolutely no idea how she was going to react. 'I have an ability to talk very quietly and at a generally inaudible pitch. It is a part of what I am. I was experiencing the most exciting business meeting of my career because of your presence, and I wanted to communicate that to you privately. I discovered at the theatre you can hear me when others cannot and . . .'

She was shaking her head. Her face beyond confusion. 'This makes no sense at all! Why on earth would I hear your *extra quiet* voice, when I struggle to hear everyone else's *normal* voice?'

'I know not – but you *can*,' I whispered, allowing my hand to gently stroke hers.

She frowned and retrieved her hands in order to cross her arms over her chest. 'Did you know I've yet to struggle to hear you at all . . . even . . . I think, with my hearing aids out?' I nodded. '*Of course you did!* It just doesn't make any sense!' She shook her head and then looked even more confused. 'On the one hand it freaks me out,' she looked at my eyes again before continuing quietly, 'but on the other it— You can't begin to under-stand how lovely it is to never miss anything you might say, never needing to ask you to repeat yourself. I can be myself with you completely. It's liberating not to have to struggle, but . . .'

'You find it unsettling,' I added gently.

'Yes, Nate – I find it effing unsettling!' She returned to her pen.

'I would rather look at it as being special, our being attuned to each other. My voice works for you, and your voice works for me.'

'How does *my* voice work for you?' she asked faintly.

'Look at me, Rowan.' I waited for her to meet my eyes. 'Your voice enchants me. It is the most beautiful sound I have ever heard. When I am without the pleasure of hearing it as it is spoken from your lips, it stays with me, keeping me company until I have the joy of being in your presence again.'

She flushed and replied shakily, 'How can one man disconcert, yet comfort . . . and excite, too?'

'Are we still talking about the hearing here?'

She shook her head. Shaking her head harder, she blinked, fixed me with a determined look, and sighed. 'Can it work both ways?'

My confusion must have been apparent.

She explained. 'The talking quietly bit, not just the hearing bit. Is it something that can be taught? Because it *really* isn't right you can get away with saying whatever you want like that – and I can't shitting well respond! You can't imagine what I wanted to say to you in that meeting today, *for your ears only* . . . the car, the working for you, the freaky secret language.'

I *could* imagine. 'Even if I could teach it, do you *honestly* think it would be in my best interests?' I chuckled, whilst shaking my head. Amazingly, she had calmed down, and had accepted my revelation in a way I could not possibly have hoped. She was incredible. 'I am sorry, Rowan . . . for it all. I need your forgiveness.'

'You know, I experience a *lot* of déjà vu around you!'

'I am conscious that I am not the easiest . . . character to be around.'

'Huh, that's putting it mildly! If you aren't running me off the road, you're giving me a heart attack in the bathroom or—'

'But I did dress up as a dinosaur for you.'

She smiled. 'Yes, you did.'

'Am I too much for you?' I asked, trying to stifle my panic at what her answer might be.

She looked at me for a while, appearing to ponder, which did nothing to settle my nerves. What was she thinking? I couldn't make head nor tail of her current confusion of sentiments. Then she grinned. 'Are you saying I can't handle you, Nathaniel Gray?'

I shook my head and looked into her eyes, 'Rowan, if anyone could, you could.'

She met my gaze and said quietly, 'Right answer, Nate.'

'Am I forgiven?' I pleaded, wanting to maximise on my good fortune.

'No, you have a lot of grovelling ahead of you.'

'I can grovel.' I deserved to grovel.

'I don't believe that for a minute!'

I took her hand, which was fidgeting with her pen, and moved my own to gently stroke her lower arm. Her heart rate increased. I immediately stopped as I felt the chemistry between us change. I spoke in a more strained voice now, 'I have never grovelled to anyone . . . but I would for you. I would do anything for you.'

'*Anything?*' she whispered, in a voice that set me ablaze. This was torture.

I shut my eyes and corrected myself. '*Almost* anything.' I sighed, removing my hand quickly. 'I am sorry.'

'Déjà vu again . . .'

I smiled sadly and inclined my head.

I found it to be a strange sensation, feeling Rowan's emotions when she was at work. I had walked her down the corridor to her office fifty-nine minutes ago, before reconvening with Peters.

She appeared to be so much more in control in the workplace. She seemed more ordered, calm, and less confused. I found it fascinating, and highly distracting. I really wasn't focusing on work at all.

I knew there was an issue instantly I felt the surge of terror engulf her.

I knew exactly what it meant, and acted before it could have its inevitable impact upon me. I managed to outrun it. That was a first.

Instantaneously, I was standing between Rowan and the entity causing her to back herself into the corner of her office, between a filing cabinet and a large floor-standing potted plant. The relief she felt at seeing me was overwhelming and dwarfed her fear. *Thank you for having faith in me, my love.* I could function.

I knew from Rowan's reaction the creature before me was Simeon Frey. And it *was* him who I had seen at the hospital. Although built slightly, his six-foot frame emitted a disconcerting sense of power. His hair was straight, ash-blond and held in a small pony tail at the nape of his neck. His eyes were not dissimilar to Heather's, but there was an edge to them; they were harder. And his scent? Now that I was breathing it in, in close proximity, there was a sulphuric harshness to it. Indeed, as I inhaled, it almost felt like it was singeing my nose and throat. He actually smelt of danger. And he was most definitely not human.

'Rowan?' I asked gently, over my shoulder.

'I'm fine, Nate – *now* I'm fine.' I felt her hand reach for mine and I took it, giving a reassuring squeeze.

'Quite an effect you have on women, Mr Frey,' I stated caustically, my voice borderline. My narrowed eyes, fixed upon his and which Rowan couldn't see, had passed borderline.

He didn't flinch. He clearly knew what he was facing.

'Nathaniel Gray, I presume.' His voice was high and acerbic.

I inclined my head, never moving my eyes from his. 'I anticipate *professionally* there are no hard feelings between us?'

He, in turn, inclined his own head. 'Not at all. We are business*men*, after all.'

Talking to my right shoulder in a voice he had clearly attempted to make sound more pleasing, but instead sounded decidedly menacing, he said, 'It's a shame we were interrupted, Rowan. But I can wait.'

I felt Rowan's spasm of terror. I barely suppressed the growl from deep within. It was excruciating having to hold myself in check.

Before I had obtained enough control over my baser instincts, to speak in a manner that would have passed as human, he was gone and the door had closed behind him.

I fought the instinctual urge to pursue, but Rowan was barely holding it together. She needed me. And in any event, her emotional state was having its inevitable impact on my ability to function physically. Taking her gently in my arms, I moved us to the chair at her desk, where I cradled her in my lap, waiting for her emotional release.

She spoke against my chest. 'I don't mind about the car, I don't mind about the freaky stuff, I don't mind working for you. I promise I'll be good.' She then burst into tears.

I held her and gently stroked her back.

Ripping his throat out was too quick. I knew *exactly* what Simeon Frey was: he was my prey.

'What does he mean, he can wait?' she asked, shakily.

'It was just words,' I said, gently brushing her tears away with my fingertips.

But I knew it had been a threat.

'He is gone, and I am here. There is *nothing* to worry about.'

And for the first time, I believed it applied to me, too. My protection applied to anyone and everyone that represented a risk to Rowan. And I *knew*, now, that included me. *How could I ever hurt her?* I could not, and I would not. It would be worse than destroying myself.

I let my lips gently follow the path of her tears and the room electrified. Rowan's emotions were in harmony with my own. 'Nate?' she gasped, and I lifted my head to meet her eyes.

And in that moment, I knew I would do anything for Rowan; anything to relieve her distress, anything to distract her. *But who was I trying to convince?* It was hardly just for her. I found myself uttering the words, 'As for being good, let us work at it, and see if there is any chance . . .

She felt hope, so much hope. 'I can be bad?' she whispered.

I was strained. I had no idea whether I could be strong enough for this. 'There are no promises, but we can work at things.' Frowning, I added quietly, 'But I do not think *you* can ever be bad. Bad is for me.'

'I disagree. You don't know what I'm thinking at the moment.'

I shook my head, forcing myself not to go there. 'Like I said, we can work at it.'

But she would need to know first. She had to know what I was. And there was the problem. I knew what the result of that would be . . . so it was all, in essence, hypothetical.

I saw her look, and quickly interjected, 'But not here and now.' *If only* . . . 'I think we have both had rather too much excitement for one day. It may be the middle of the day, but I am taking you home.'

'I don't want to go home,' she declared, raising her hand to stroke the side of my face. The heat that channelled from her touch soared through my veins.

I attempted to sound in control, 'Well, then, I am taking you . . .' *Where? Where was I taking her?* I knew I had to refocus on the task in hand.

'How about I introduce you to my sister?'

CHAPTER 15

AUNTY HETTY

'I love her, Nate, but you knew I would,' Elizabeth said softly.

It was night-time. Rowan was safely tucked up in her bed and her breathing confirmed she was sleeping peacefully. Elizabeth and I were both sat on her roof, reflecting on our afternoon.

'I can almost forgive her the pain she causes you when her emotions are all over the place. If only she could get a handle on them. But, I suppose she wouldn't be Rowan then, would she?' I smiled fondly and shook my head in response. 'She's sassy! That's the way I'd describe her. And you, big brother, have completely met your match.'

'She likes you too, Elizabeth . . . but I knew she would.' I smiled, echoing her earlier words, whilst affectionately ruffling her hair.

I recalled Rowan's description of my sister, 'She's so beautiful. You both share such beauty . . .' She had paused before proceeding, 'I know she's like you. Are you going to tell me she's not safe, too? Because I don't see it. She's lovely. She's kind and fun and I warmed to her instantly. I don't normally warm to people straight away, I need to get to know them, but I did with Elizabeth. And she loves you deeply, Nate.'

I had looked at Rowan's eyes, unbelievably large and unable to comprehend we could be anything but good and safe. I hadn't known how to answer, because I trusted Elizabeth completely with Rowan, despite my instinctual obsession to protect.

But she was like me; designed to kill. In fact, Elizabeth *had* killed. We might *choose* not to drink the blood of humans, but we were made to do so. The response I had settled on was brief.

'That is not an easy question to answer. As you gathered, she is like me. But I trust her with you . . . in a way I have been struggling to fully trust myself.'

Rowan had looked at me pointedly. 'But you're working on that, right?'

I sighed my response. 'I am, believe me, I am.'

Elizabeth was proceeding with her own appraisal of Rowan. There was a note of sadness in her voice. 'I wouldn't have believed it was possible. In fact, I was shocked. But from what I saw today, I think she feels for you as much as you do her. It's all been so quick . . . so intense. But you two look perfect together. You *must* be able to find a way . . . Rowan's parents did.'

'Mmmm. But we do not believe Rosie was human . . . and that makes quite a difference.'

'Have you felt an urge to suck her blood since that first night?'

I cringed, but answered honestly, 'No, Yes . . . it

would be nice.' I smiled and raised my eyebrows, 'It is always a temptation. You know that. But . . . it has been controllable. It has not been the thirst.'

'Have you felt other urges?'

'Elizabeth . . .'

'Sorry, of course you have. I was just being polite. It's odd seeing thoughts like *that* in your head.'

'Then get out of my head!' I snarled.

She ignored me, choosing instead to insist, 'You'll find a way. You have to.'

Frederick arrived at that point, landing silently on the roof beside us. Elizabeth and he were still experiencing difficulties following my lapse in concentration on Saturday night. And I felt terrible about it. But some kind of truce had been called, following Frey's earlier visit to Rowan's offices.

When Rowan and I had met up with Elizabeth, in an eatery on the ground floor of Selfridges, I had let Elizabeth read my thoughts. Whilst ensuring Rowan ate some lunch, I silently asked for any support on offer to deal with Frey. As soon as Elizabeth had left us, she had brought the others up to date. All had vowed to take whatever action was necessary.

'Time you headed back,' Frederick said in my head. I didn't want to leave Rowan, even for a minute, but needs must, and I absolutely had to be in control of this.

'You can trust me, Nate. I'm armed to the teeth.' He turned to show me the sword strapped to his back, there was a gun poking out of his waistband,

and he wriggled his foot, so I could see the daggers tucked into his boots. 'I knew my combat skills would come in handy again! That's if I need them, of course.' He flashed me a toothy grin. 'I'll range out to listen to everything within our four mile or so hearing range and will call if there's anything remotely out of the ordinary. You can be here within a couple of minutes.'

'Thirty seconds,' I corrected, with Rowan in the equation.

'We need you to promise not to go after Frey on your own, Nate,' Madeleine pressed on my return to the house.

'He is a threat to her!' I hissed.

'No one is disputing that, but we need to bide our time. We are one hundred percent behind you, but we need to be as fully informed as possible and know exactly what we're dealing with. You will have your opportunity, but at the moment, you need to be there for Rowan, not risking your immortal life unnecessarily. Promise us, Nate. What good would that do Rowan?'

I growled. But I knew it made sense. I had pretty much come to the same conclusion already.

'I have spoken to Fergus again. He wasn't aware of Frey, but he's going to use his numerous contacts to find out more. He has not taken at all well the threat that appears to exist towards his goddaughter. That's a major understatement, actually. You would have imagined a vampire of his years had learnt to control his temper by now, but that's another story. He's a cabinet member of the Vampire Council, so his contacts are particularly extensive.'

My sanctuary, in which I had chosen to remain out of politics and the outside world more often than not, seemed to be an existence away.

'Furthermore, he has pledged the full support of each member of his coven. And if Frey is connected to the death of Seth Locke, the Council could be mobilised for support.'

James spoke up from his position, perched on the edge of the table by the window, 'You know? I'd forgotten how much I liked excitement!'

I couldn't meet his beam with any kind of smile of my own. 'I am paying Aunty Hetty a visit,' I announced. 'Enough is enough. She seems to be the key to obtaining the information we need, and she will want to safeguard Rowan, too.'

'We knew you'd say that!' James cried. 'I'm coming with you.'

I paused, but only for a second. His company made sense. Not that I for one moment thought Aunty Hetty represented a risk to me because, surprisingly, I didn't. It made sense simply because, if she was non co-operative, I didn't think I could be held accountable for my actions. Although James wound me up, and had historically been responsible for my worst losses of temper, he conversely knew how to calm me down . . . if he felt that way inclined.

* * *

Heather Fairchild opened the door to us almost immediately, fully dressed, and as if she had been expecting us, despite it being three o'clock in the morning. She smiled faintly and moved aside to let us in.

James immediately started sneezing. I raised my eyebrows in his direction. *'Bloody cats!* She has to have bloody fuck-off cats! These days they don't get close enough to be an issue . . .' He had been speaking silently, but broke off to release a very audible, 'Arrgggghh! *Attisshoooo!!!'*

'Nathaniel,' she said dryly, 'and your friend, James.' She saw our shock, which we failed to disguise quickly enough.

She addressed James. 'Thank you for getting Rowan safety to the hospital, Mr Hartle.'

I was even more shocked now and James was reeling. *How could she possibly know James' human surname? It wasn't even the name he was presently using!*

He tentatively inclined his head to Heather, choosing to silently communicate, 'Shit, Nate! This doesn't bode well, mate.'

I gave him a quick nod in response.

'How are you, Heather?' I asked politely, refusing to let my discomfort sound in my voice. I was actually feeling confused. I was struck by the fact she lacked the distinctive scent of Frey. She smelt human. *How* could *they be of the same kind?*

We were shown into her living room, and true to Rowan and Clare's description, there were potted plants absolutely everywhere. It was like standing in an overgrown garden. The cats, though, must have still been in hiding.

She smiled at me, although it failed to reach her eyes, which appeared guarded. 'We all know you haven't come to enquire after my health, Nathaniel. But I am well enough, thank you. I would like to take this opportunity, if I may, to thank you for your assistance this morning.'

Had Rowan spoken to her? She couldn't have or I would have known about it. She was sleeping now and I had been either with Rowan, or in earshot of her, since the event now referred to.

'And indeed, also with Jonathan Martin. Very efficient of you.'

I was not going to beat around the bush.

'Who or, more precisely, *what* is Simeon Frey?'

She shook her head and I could see genuine regret on her face. Her voice sounded neutral, however. 'I very much wish I could tell you, Nathaniel. But just as the punishments are no doubt harsh for your kind with regards to such revelations, so it is with ours.'

I didn't need to read James' thoughts to know what he was thinking: she knew exactly what we were, yet we did not yet know what she was. We were at a distinct disadvantage, and neither of us was used to that. And I was still confused. *Why had my scenting abilities let me down?*

'I believe, Nathaniel, *danger* has a distinctive smell, does it not? Do not consider yourself to be at risk from me. As long as Rowan requires you in her life, you personally have my support and protection . . . for what it is – whilst it's not at odds with Rowan's, of course.'

'She just read our thoughts, didn't she?'

'I believe that is a fair assumption, James.' And she had just confirmed Frey was dangerous.

'*Shit!*'

'*Double shit!*' I added, finishing that particular silent conversation.

Whilst I observed Heather incline her head and smile, I felt a surge in the room. *Bugger* – James was engaging his charm! Mine hadn't worked, and I knew his wouldn't. I shook my head and couldn't repress a sigh.

James' voice took on a hypnotic quality, and its attractiveness reached a level *humans* find completely irresistible. 'Heather – I can call you Heather, can't I?'

She gave a small smile and nodded.

'Here's the thing, Heather. We *really* need to know what you and Simeon Frey are, and *why* he has this unhealthy interest in Rowan . . . *Attisshoooo!!!* Indeed, whilst you're about it, it would be *really* helpful to know who, or what, was responsible for the death of Seth and Rosie – and anything you know about the cause of the accident involving Nate and Rowan. You are a very kind, helpful being . . . and that haircut by the way, is most becoming!'

I shut my eyes momentarily and cringed.

'You are going to feel you must share your knowledge with us. You will feel unable to refuse answering the questions I am about to ask. So, Heather – what is Simeon Frey?'

Heather looked at me bemused, and I looked at James horrified. He was hovering two feet off the floor, apparently oblivious to the fact.

'What *the hell* have you done to me – *you witch?*' he hissed, on spotting his predicament. He promptly landed back on the floor, much too clumsily for a vampire.

'My apologies, James. It must have been a side-effect of repelling your . . . not *inconsiderable* . . . charm.'

I ignored James' silent rants in my head. He was quite rightly spooked, but we had to get some answers.

'What *can* you tell us?' I was sounding desperate now, and was aware I probably looked it, too: my eyes were shut, my head lowered, and I was holding the bridge of my nose. 'The more we know, the more we can help Rowan.'

'I know how much Rowan means to you, Nathaniel. But you are not alone in your mission to protect her. We are dealing with Simeon Frey. You will not run into him again.'

'*You* are dealing with Frey?' My voice was louder than I had wished it to be. How could they be? If they were, then their methods were sorely lacking. 'Like you did on the night of the accident? Like you did today?' I paused a moment . . . I

313

could find out if they were connected . . . 'Like you did when Rowan's parents were killed?' Heather paled. 'They *are* connected – are they not? Frey was involved then, too?'

Please say no. Please say no. I beg you!

'I cannot comment on your assumption, Nathaniel.' She sighed. 'But neither can I say no.'

NO. NO. NO. NO. This could not possibly be happening. The distress in my voice was unmistakable. 'How can you say you are dealing with it, then? An immortal, and whatever Rosie was, are dead – and now he is after Rowan! Why, Heather? *Why?* She is an innocent!'

'She is an innocent, Nathaniel, and I am determined to keep her so. It was the wish of her parents. We will not allow the same mistakes to be made today, as were made twenty-nine years ago. As for the night of the accident, our radar was down. All those years had passed and our guard – *my* guard – was down. Thankfully, you were on the scene.'

I was roaring now and she didn't even flinch. 'Thankfully, *I was on the scene*? *THANKFULLY – I WAS ON THE SCENE*? Do you know how *close* I came to killing her, Heather? To *killing* Rowan . . . to sucking her life-force clean away?'

'But you didn't, Nathaniel.'

I was lost for words, and violently shaking my head in frustration. James took the opportunity to ask, 'Were you or your kind responsible for the accident? Was magic involved?'

'Magic may well have been involved. It was Beltane, Rowan was distressed and in need of support, and the location – a bend in the road. But I was not involved.'

James snapped back, 'I don't *do brainteasers*! What the hell does that mean when it's at home?'

Heather spoke patiently and calmly, 'It means, I had no part to play and neither, to my knowledge, did my kind. Magic would, however, have been powerful: the date, the location, their paths crossing. I'd say it was a matter of Nathaniel and Rowan finding each other. I can think of no other cause. Sometimes these things are just meant to be.'

I spoke now, exasperated and struggling to keep my calm, 'What about today? Where was your kind then?'

'We were observing. It was not appropriate to step in when you had matters under control. Our involvement may have caused unnecessary alarm to Rowan.'

This was so wrong. *They were observing, but had still let Rowan be exposed to him?* I didn't know how long my attempts to remain calm would hold. 'How could you let him be in the same room as her? You should not have let him within a hundred miles. Do you have *any* idea how terrified she is of him? You had NO right to put her through that!' There was only one way to keep Rowan safe. 'Give me the information I need so *I* can make sure it never happens again.'

'It will not happen again. Matters are in hand. Be alert, of course, as Rowan is precious to us both, but fret not about Simeon Frey.'

'Fret not about Simeon Frey? FRET NOT ABOUT SIMEON FREY?' That was it. I was roaring now, at an inhuman level. The whole room seemed to reverberate as the leaves of the plants shook.

This creature knew everything I needed to know in order to protect Rowan, but wasn't prepared to tell me. She was expecting me to entrust Rowan's protection to those that had failed to stop the deaths of her parents, and had failed to keep that monster away from her. I could *make* her tell me. I could instil such fear she would be begging for the opportunity to tell me. I would do whatever it took.

'She is my very being, Heather. YOU HAVE TO HELP ME!'

I could hear James in my head. He was getting seriously worried. 'Nate, this isn't going to help. Don't lose it, mate – think about Rowan. Heather is like a mother to her!'

'I *am* thinking about Rowan!' I silently roared. 'And I *need* to know!'

Heather looked pained. If she was reading my thoughts, then no wonder. I met her eyes. The look within them changed. They appeared to take on a fluid silver sheen, almost like liquid mercury.

And I was completely unable to look away. I began to feel my anger ebb. *What the hell was happening?* I felt myself become calmer. I wanted to resist. I wanted to feel anger and fury, but I was powerless to prevent the calm from spreading through my body. *What was she?*

James was alarmed. I could see from inside his head that he was looking from her to me, but was unable to help. 'What are you doing to him? STOP IT NOW!' he roared. And then I saw the calm penetrate him, too. This really was not good.

'I am sorry, but do not be distressed,' she said. 'I know you wish to act for love . . . but I act out of love, too. The dangers to your kind are too great, and Rowan need not lose you.' Her voice, for the first time, revealed an emotion . . . and the sadness in it was immense.

'You cannot expect me to leave this to you!' I spluttered, when I found myself able to speak. 'Whether you like it or not, I am involved and—'

She inclined her head. 'You are, Nathaniel. But that was not of our choosing, and we do not intend to have any more deaths on our hands.'

'Nate,' James urged silently, 'we're going, before this gets any more fucking freaky. I want to rip her throat out . . . but can't act on it. She scares the shit out of me – if I had any, to scare out of me, that is. We are out of our depth here.'

We were more than out of our depth here. We were in trouble. Although I was being forced to feel calm, my thoughts were far from those that should instil calm. Sod what she had done to me. What was concerning me was – how I was supposed to protect Rowan from Frey! What use could I possibly be, if he could do what Heather had done tonight? And another question had crossed my mind . . . was Clare at risk?

Heather shook her head. She was at it again. 'Clare and her family do not need the same protection as Rowan. And for your information, Simeon Frey is weakened at present, and his powers are very different to my own. Don't ask me for more information.'

I left the house with her voice in my head, 'The secret is to believe, Nathaniel. Believe in your own strength and believe in your love . . . no matter what. There are challenges before you both, but they can be overcome. Be there for Rowan . . . She will always be as human as they come.'

James had a point. All these cryptic words were clearly designed to . . . But I wasn't even able to feel the damned frustration.

CHAPTER 16

THE SOUTH OF FRANCE

Rowan was excited and her eyes were sparkling, animated, alive. And I was captivated. It didn't matter how many times I saw her face light up in its multitude of ways, it was always like seeing it anew.

'Nice! I can't believe we're going to be in the South of France together. That conference has been the bane of my life for years, but now I'm so excited.'

I smiled from my heart.

'It's our first dirty break away together!' she cried, looking at me mischievously, knowing the effect her words would have on me.

I groaned, whilst raking my hand through my hair, 'Rowan . . .'

She was being playful, and I loved her being playful. But it wreaked havoc on my self-control.

'Oh, come on! A girl can hope! And there is hope. You told me as much. That's what's keeping me going. But, in the meantime, I might just settle for the voice.' I caught a renewed glint in her eye.

Not the voice! I sank further back into her living-room sofa. We had both returned to Rowan's flat after work half an hour earlier. Having adopted a hands-on role where public relations was concerned – much to my MD's utter amazement – I was presently basing myself in Rowan's offices.

She was standing before me now, fixing me with her playful eyes. She spoke seductively, with exaggerated urgency and desperation, 'Talk to me, Nathaniel. Let me hear your voice . . . Oh! I need those few words. Make my juices flow. Say them to me . . . in . . . that . . . way. Oh! . . . Oh! . . . Nate! Oh, they're flowing – they're flowing – *Yesssss!*'

I sighed, 'Rowan, behave,' but nevertheless couldn't resist pulling her on to my lap. If I heard another reference to that ridiculous comment her work colleague had made four weeks ago, I would— Actually I didn't know what I would do. Although Rowan joked about it, I had the feeling I was being blamed, and I had absolutely no idea what I was supposed to do about how my voice sounded . . . and to think, she had never heard it with the charm engaged. Now that really would be interesting . . .

'Make me!' She grinned. I would so love to try.

'You have a one-track mind these days,' I observed wryly.

'And you don't?' she asked smugly. Rowan could be in no doubt as to the effect she had on what was left of my human physiology.

'I am not saying that,' I let the tips of my fingers brush her cheek and trail down her jaw line, 'but

I am going to be certifiable if you continue like this.'

She giggled. 'I'm sorry! But Nice – *with you* – I can't wait!' And with a look that would be enough to turn the most cold-blooded creature, warm blooded, 'I've got a double bed in my room.'

I would humour her, but without her knowing, we couldn't go down this route. 'I know you do – you have advised me of that point before. And I believe there is a king-sized bed in my room? I had to sign-off the expenses, remember?'

'I know! That's why it's one of the best rooms, in one of the best hotels in town – and bang next door to mine! I wonder who sorted out the room bookings?'

'Mind on the job,' I teased. 'It is a conference, remember.'

'It's not any old conference, it's *the* conference, and I can't believe you've never attended before.'

I could. It was the last thing I would ever choose to do. Whilst Gray Portfolio had historically had a presence – never me! 'I still cannot believe you have got me hosting a damned cocktail party,' I muttered. It was truly alarming.

I had discovered Rowan's powers of persuasion were second to none where I was concerned. She could twist me around her little finger on absolutely anything, with one overriding proviso – it did not represent any perceived risk to her.

As to the conference and the party, despite thinking outside the box, I couldn't put it into that dangerous category . . . no matter how hard I had tried. She was in danger wherever she was with Frey still out there, despite Heather's bloody-minded assurances. Her still unidentified kind, currently labelled the spooks and the 'freaking no-way faeries' by our kind, or, in her specific case, 'the fucking witch' by James – were apparently dealing with him in South America. My own attempts to track him with the assistance of members of Fergus' coven seemed to confirm that point.

Chanting the proverb, with a few amendments, 'All work and no play makes Nate a pretty dull . . .' Rowan paused.

I shook my head. 'What to put there? Freak?' She certainly would, if she knew what she should finish her sentence with.

'*Man*, Nate! That's what I'd add there.' She looked at me with such sincerity and trust.

I let my forehead drop to rest against hers. 'Because you refuse to let me tell you what I am.' I spoke sadly, knowing full well the moment she knew . . .

'You are very much a man to me,' she said, suggestively.

'Rowan,' I warned through clenched teeth, but responded fervently as she touched her lips to mine.

I found the strength from somewhere to pull away. My voice was strained, but I tried to keep it jovial. 'You need to pack and then get an early night. Whoever booked the hotel rooms also made a serious mistake by booking us a 6 a.m. flight!'

'Some bosses are so hard to please,' she muttered, with a grin.

I shook my head. Technically she worked for me, but the idea of ever being a boss to Rowan was farcical. She was a complete law unto her own . . . and I loved her for it.

I gently lifted her from my lap and placed her on the sofa beside me. Leaning over to kiss her forehead I said, 'I will see you bright and early tomorrow. I will pick you up at 4.00 a.m. Do not forget to set your alarm. I am taking the spare keys, so there is no need to come down the stairs. I will come straight up.'

'What spare keys?'

'The ones I had cut,' I stated flippantly, already moving towards the door.

'Well – that was a bit of a liberty!' But I could feel she wasn't remotely upset by my actions.

'Call it what you like. I have had enough of you pounding down those stairs. You are still in a cast, yet now it no longer hurts, you have thrown caution to the wind and are even worse.'

It terrified me even more now. This morning, in her reckless haste, she had nearly lost her footing on the first-floor landing, and I didn't think, even as an immortal, I could live through that again. I had had keys cut when she had been in her team briefing. I just wished I had thought of it before.

As I left, I silently said thank you to Elizabeth

and Frederick, who were on patrol on the roof – together again tonight, so things must be improving. I had to feed and pack, but I would take over the night shift as soon as was possible. And then I would sit on Rowan's roof, absorbed in the sound of her nocturnal breathing.

'You have done a fabulous job, Rowan. I am so proud of you!'

We were standing in an elegant nineteenth-century hotel ballroom in the South of France, and my first ever Gray Portfolio cocktail party was in full swing. Large crystal chandeliers hung from the ceiling, lighting the room elegantly, and white flowers in giant stone urns tastefully provided the perfect balance for the event: lavish, yet somehow understated. Waiting staff were inconspicuously distributing canapés from silver salvers and the champagne was flowing. I had to admit, Rowan was bloody good at her job.

'You look ravishing,' I whispered in her ear, with my arm protectively around her waist. In the moment, I was paying no heed to our body language, although I knew questions were being asked. It is quite amazing the gossip you can pick up with enhanced hearing, should you choose to do so.

Rowan was dressed in an elegant full-length black dress. It was sleeveless and simple, but looked like it had been made for her, despite having been a charity-shop purchase. Typically, she had refused to let me buy her one. But it was perfect . . . accentuating her small waist, gently touching the curves of her hips, seductively outlining the shapes of her breasts. She was covered up, but – *dear God!* – it was a dress which allowed your imagination to so easily encapsulate the joys of what lay beneath.

But I was most certainly not happy with the appreciative looks she was receiving from all full-blooded males in the room. Repressing the latest growl beginning to rise in my chest, I sent a look in the direction of the current offender, and watched in muted satisfaction as he took an instinctive step back, and the contents of his champagne glass jumped out to soak his shirt. I could do no more, I reminded myself. My cocktail party was not the venue for plucking out the eyes of my guests.

But removing that from the equation, I was the happiest I had ever been. Heaven was a place on earth, I realised – it was at Rowan Locke's side.

I watched Rowan's hand rise to touch the necklace around her neck, and met her eyes. She loved it. Elizabeth had said she would when I had broached the subject with her. I smiled, recalling Rowan's reaction to the gift I had given her earlier in the evening. 'The rose-gold setting and the diamonds to the sides are Georgian. The central stone I had replaced with a moonstone – in light of your lunar appreciation. It is a family piece.' I hadn't been able to tell her that the necklace had originally been made for my mother, and I had wanted her to have something of the woman I had loved so deeply.

'It's absolutely beautiful! It's the most wonderful present anyone has ever given me,' she had sobbed, as I removed her mother's pendant for the night and placed the new piece around her neck. I had even allowed myself to gently kiss her pulse point. The moment had been magical.

Back in the ballroom, Rowan squeezed my hand. 'Mingle, Nate. You need to mingle,' she whispered in my ear. And all I could think was how her touch and her proximity was making my body feel. Why the bloody hell would I want to mingle?

'You know I do not tend to mingle well, and besides . . . I would rather not leave your side.' I spoke huskily.

She smiled with both her mouth and her eyes. The intensity worked for us both. 'What am I going to do with you?' she asked gently. She raised her hand and I sensed she wanted to stroke my face, but remembered where we were, so lowered it quickly. She took a deep breath. 'I've got to sort out the caterers. Please try and make the most of this event. Everyone is desperate to meet the elusive Nathaniel Gray. I know you don't like these things, but try! And spare a thought for me. It's not easy with my hearing in this sort of set-up, so you aren't the only one struggling tonight. I'll be back before you know it; I'll be here to hold your hand. I promise.'

I sighed as I watched her hobble away, smiling and greeting a number of people en route. Her hearing problems were not obvious, but I knew she just covered it well. I had noticed odd occasions in the office – but she *never* struggled with me.

I watched Rowan shake her head when offered a glass of champagne from a tray. I must get her to drink some tonight, I mused. She insisted she didn't drink on the job, but she was so endearing intoxicated. I would make sure there was a bottle – or two – upstairs for later.

When Rowan was finally out of sight, and I had nowhere else to look but the room, I conceded there were, indeed, rather a lot of people looking in my direction and attempting to catch my attention. My mobile rang. *Saved by the bell!*

My caller display showed it to be Madeleine. Unbeknown to Rowan, we were not the only ones in Nice. I wasn't taking any chances. They had left an hour ago, though. Fergus' team had confirmed Frey was still in South America, so there was no point in their lounging around, attempting to look inconspicuous in the hotel, when they could be heading to the Black Forest to sample some of the regional specialities. It was a couple of hours' flight, at a leisurely vampire pace, so they were going to make a night of it.

'Madeleine,' I said jovially, 'you have just saved me from a fate worse than . . .'

'Nate – you have to listen to me.'

This was not good.

'Fergus' team called. They've lost Frey. One minute he was there, next he wasn't. The hope is Heather's lot have got him, but we're on our way back now. Just be alert.'

My heart was racing and my throat had become dry. Where was Rowan? Why the hell had I let her leave my side? My eyes scanned the room. Thank God! I could see her in the corner of the room, coming out of the door leading to the kitchens. She caught my eye, and I could hear her sigh from across the room. She was waving her arms around and mouthing, 'Mingle, Nate. Mingle!'

'Understood. We will be alert.'

As soon as I hung up, I was at Rowan's side. She jumped. But she was getting used to my strange movements, as she called them. Nobody in the room would have seen me move.

'I wish you wouldn't do that, you scare me half to death every time!' I couldn't help the stomach lurch that resulted from her choice of words.

I spoke close to her ear and felt her tremble, 'Forgive me. But can we mingle together, please?' I had managed to keep my voice calm. It was most probably a false alarm.

'You're useless, you know! Totally useless.' She sighed. 'Come on then!' And we turned to head back into the midst of the party.

But our way was blocked.

I had heard nothing. But before us was Simeon Frey. He was flanked by two more of his kind, both taller and broader. If I hadn't heard them, how had I not smelt them?

Rowan gasped and her heart pounded. Her fear punched me. I put my arm protectively around her shoulders, and spoke in her ear, 'It is fine, my love – leave this to me.' As casually as possible, I changed position, ensuring Rowan was behind me; I was facing Frey head on.

'Rowan . . . It's so lovely to see you again.' Toxic was the way I would have described his voice.

'I do not recall seeing you on the guest list, Frey?' My own voice was strained due to Rowan's anxiety.

'Perhaps not; it was quite an omission. I was hoping to catch up with Rowan.'

'I think you will find Rowan a little preoccupied with helping me host my party. And she will be by my side for the foreseeable future.'

'Yes! A party – with a host the like of which this hotel is unlikely to have seen before,' he proclaimed, with exaggerated wonder.

And in that moment I knew exactly how he was going to play this. He knew what I was, and suspected, quite rightly, that Rowan did not. He was going to play his trump card.

'If you will excuse us?' I couldn't disguise the urgency in my voice.

'I don't think so,' he sneered.

'You *will* move aside!' My body was like a coiled spring. My voice was borderline but my eyes were most definitely not. The two spooks at his flanks took a rapid step back. Frey looked uncomfortable, but held his ground.

'You haven't told her, have you, Gray?'

I felt Rowan tense behind me and her fear increase.

This was my worst nightmare. She could not hear it from him. She couldn't! Our physical location, in the corner of the room, was contained by his party of three. We could escape by going up. I could grab her and fly, if she would calm down a little, but we were in public. We were in a room full of two hundred people, already showing more than a passing interest in proceedings. The charm couldn't be used on them all. I could reveal the monster within and rip Frey's throat out, but Rowan was here. Forget about everyone else. *She* couldn't have a clearer demonstration of what I was. There was nothing I could do.

Rowan spoke shakily, 'I know exactly what he is.'

She wasn't ready for this. She was doing everything she could to avoid the revelation. I squeezed her hand reassuringly. But I knew what was coming next. I spoke rapidly for her ears only. 'I love you, Rowan, more than you will ever know. It was for me to tell you—'

But it wasn't quick enough. As I was speaking, his voice intruded. Both mocking and triumphant. 'You know he's a vampire?'

Her shock consumed me. And then I felt her horror and terror and fear and her heartbreak and then her recoil as she snatched her hand from mine. She was gasping desperately for air. And then denial. She so didn't want to believe it.

'Nate?' Her voice was pleading. I had moved to the wall for physical support, desperately attempting to keep myself between her and Frey as her pain, mingled with my own, took hold.

The cackle of his laugh rang in my ears. 'The worst, of course, is that he used his charm on you.'

'No,' I said as loudly as I could, shaking my head desperately. I used all my strength to reach out my hand to her, but she just stared at me, the horror there in her eyes.

'How else could you fall in love with a bloodsucking monster? He made you love him. But it was never real. It was a spell! You've been under his spell the whole time!'

I watched her wobble and felt her emotions drain from me. My own were still tearing me to pieces, but I could move. I caught her around the waist as it all became too much for her and her legs buckled.

He looked triumphantly at me, his hard metallic eyes glinting. 'All's fair in love and war, hey, Gray? I believe that connection of yours will ensure you're out of action for a while.' And then they were gone.

I scooped Rowan up into my arms, not caring what we looked like, and carried her from the room. It was over. I had lost her. My feelings for the moment were, thankfully, numb. I was acting on automatic pilot. I kept moving. Cradling her unconscious body in one arm, I used my other to find my mobile.

'Madeleine! I need you back NOW! I am about to be out of action – and Frey somehow knows it.'

'Nate! What's happened?'

I hung up.

Once we reached my room, I gently placed Rowan on the bed. The same bed on which, last night, she had fallen asleep in my arms. The smile she had given me when she woke this morning was one of the sweetest, most wondrous sights the universe could offer.

I now looked down upon my beautiful Rowan. So human, so fragile, so vulnerable . . . and devastated because of me. I stroked her face, committing to memory how her skin felt. I inhaled her scent. She was gone from me now. But I would make her safe. I was prepared for the last act of my existence, to be Frey's destruction.

Rowan stirred. I stepped away. I didn't want to scare her any more than she was going to be. I stood by the window. I shouldn't be here. I didn't want her to fear at all. But I couldn't leave her alone with Frey prowling around. And I owed her an explanation. I needed to tell her she was my whole existence, that I had not once deployed my charm on her; that what we had had was the most special, most wonderful thing I had experienced in two-hundred-and-thirty years; that I could never have hurt her. I knew that now.

But I was agonisingly aware that, at any moment, I was going to be crippled by her heartbreak and terror. I doubted I would be able to get any explanation out. If I had had the time, I would have put it all in a letter. The hardest letter I could have ever written.

Her eyes were open now. She lay motionless for a few moments, whilst she experienced confusion. And then it hit – realisation. She sat bolt upright, and as I was spotted, gasped and struggled frantically, clamouring backwards across the bed, to get as far away from me as possible.

My legs had already buckled and I slid to the floor. I used every particle of strength currently at my disposal to stop myself from lying down, wrapped in a foetal position. By resting my back against the wall, with my elbows braced on my raised knees, I managed to maintain a sitting position. My head was clutched in my hands.

Rowan's breathing was on the verge of hyperventilation.

'Rowan,' I managed to gasp.

'Get away from me!' she screamed. It was hysteria on top of horror and terror, heartbreak and grief; she was already grieving for me.

'Do not be scared,' I said as gently as I could, whilst fighting the agony.

'Do not be scared? Do not be scared? You're a fucking vampire!' She choked on the last word before it turned into a sob.

She had made it off the bed and was continuing

to back away from me across the room; not that I was capable of moving any closer. She came to rest with her back against the farthest wall from me. The tears were rolling down her face and her body was convulsed in sobs. More to herself than to me, she stammered, 'You don't exist, you aren't real. You're just in horror films . . . and my nightmares!'

I felt her moment of hope. She was pleading with me, begging me. 'They don't exist, Nate. Tell me they don't exist. You can tell me what you are now . . . tell me what you really are. I'm ready now!'

Her hope disappeared as I slowly shook my head. But she still screamed at me, 'TELL ME!' She slid down the side of the wall and mirrored my position. She had the ability I did not, though, to sob uncontrollably. 'You . . . drink . . . blood?'

'Yes . . . but . . .'

'But you haven't got fangs . . . You're dead . . . You're a monster. Oh God – you kissed me!' Her volume increased so her voice was hoarse with the scream. 'You kissed me, you bastard! You more than kissed me . . . and I enjoyed it! I wanted more. How could you do that?' She twisted around, trying to curl into the wall, and pummelled it with her fists. 'You're a monster . . . Clare . . . the boys. I let you near them. You spent time with them!'

'I wouldn't . . .'

'I loved you, Nate! You let me love you . . . you

made me love you. I loved you more than I thought anyone could love. You tricked me . . . why? Why would you do this to me? I wanted to be with you forever! Forever, Nate! You were everything.'

'I love you!' I desperately managed to get out.

She physically shuddered. 'How can you love me? You're dead! *Dead. Dead. Dead.* Dead people can't love! You kill people and suck their blood.'

'No.'

'You disgust me!' She started laughing hysterically. 'I trusted you with my life. How good must your spell be? I trusted a vampire with my goddamned life! How crazy am I? I didn't want to know what you were – I felt safe with you – but you don't even exist. How could you *ever* have been that?'

She rolled over now on to her knees, and used the console table against the wall, to help her up. Edging her way around the room, with her back as close to the wall as possible, she reached the door. In a voice that could leave me in no doubt of her sincerity, she warned, 'Don't you ever come near me or my family again. If anything ever happens to them, I'll know who it was.' And then so, so quietly, 'And it would be my fault. All my fault.'

'Do not go!' I managed to plead.

Hysterics returned, but I knew they had never gone. 'Do not go? Do *not go?* Well, what the hell? Why don't I choose to stay in a room . . . alone with a *vampire*! I'm obviously stupid enough to do that – aren't I? You stay away from me and my family! Never, ever, ever come near us again! Do you hear? NEVER!!!'

She fumbled blindly through her tears with the door, before wrenching it open and stumbling out, sobbing uncontrollably. And I sat there, unable to move.

My heart had ripped into two.

She had gone. But there was some justice. I was not alone. It was for me to share her tortured soul, to feel for myself the agonies I had caused; the pain that was reeling through Rowan and which there was nothing I could do to stop. And then there was my pain. For Rowan had taught me to feel. I could experience heartbreak for myself now, and guilt . . . and desperate fear.

My own desperate fear, which was reaching terror status.

Simeon Frey was out there. This was his plan. He knew, somehow, what this would do to me. And Rowan was his prey. And I was too weak to save her. *Dear God, help me!* I tried to compartmentalise, but there wasn't a chance.

After I do not know how long I became aware, somewhere in my head, of the phone in the room ringing, and then my mobile. Could it be Rowan? I finally managed to get it out of my pocket, and somehow accepted the call.

'Nathaniel. Where is she?' The concerned voice seemed to be coming through a haze. 'Nathaniel? It's Heather – *where* is Rowan?'

'You must . . . help me!' was all I was able to force out.

'What's happened? Nathaniel? Is it Simeon? We lost him! I can't shield Rowan, she can't have her pendant on. I can't protect her and I can't pinpoint her. You have to find her!' Heather was sounding frantic. Her voice didn't normally sound like this. It was normally non-emotional, flat, almost hypnotic.

'She . . . knows.'

'Knows . . . what?' The fear that managed to creep into those two words was indicative that the answer was dawning.

'I am a . . . monster.'

'Are you hurt? Why are you struggling to talk? Breathe. Do something. I need a connection. I need to hear you.' Heather spoke with an air of authority I didn't feel able to ignore.

I breathed, and then shuddered. My head and body were being shared by someone other than Rowan. There was a sharp intake of breath from the other end of the phone. 'I'm sending support but it will take time. He hasn't got her yet because you'd be feeling her reaction. Why didn't you tell me about the emotional connection? I didn't know – your thoughts didn't . . . but then I wasn't looking for— The connection shouldn't even be *possible!* I don't understand how this has happened. But I can help, Nathaniel! You've experienced what I can do first hand! Why I didn't see it when I was making you calm I don't— She was *sleeping!*

You should have told me, Nathaniel! Why didn't you tell me? I can manipulate feelings so I can bloody well try and segregate them!'

'Do not . . . take . . . her away,' I pleaded desperately.

She sighed, but nevertheless spoke more reassuringly, 'I'm not taking her away. I don't think I could, even if I tried. I'm going to set her apart a bit and talk some sense into you. She was shocked, Nathaniel. She loves you, so don't you dare give up on her! She needs time, which you do not have tonight. So I'm going to help. You have been trying to compartmentalise. I'm going to kick it into touch. You haven't had time to learn to manage emotion yet, and managing Rowan's must be a thing of nightmares!

'But you aren't going to be any help to her, if you don't stop wallowing in guilt and self-pity. If I hadn't seen it with Seth, I'd never have believed an effing vampire could feel like this! There is still hope. Let that guide you. You will sleep. I'm reckoning it should take three days to get over this, but I'm giving you three minutes. I'm counting on your strength, and your love for Rowan, Nathaniel, to pull you through this; to order yourself to help her. If Simeon succeeds, we will both lose her. When you find her, I need you to ensure she puts her pendant back on, and for you to believe in yourself. His body is weak. Yours is strong.'

CHAPTER 17

POISON

I was being shaken. Vigorously shaken and I could hear panic, lots and lots of panic. I felt battered and bruised, which I really shouldn't be feeling. And I hurt. Hurt from deep within.

'What's the matter with him? Wake him up! Wake him up!' It was Elizabeth. She was screaming.

There was an urgent voice in my ear. 'Nate, it's James. It's going to be okay, but we need you here, with us.'

I kept my eyes shut. I was trying to make sense of things. Rowan was still within me. And Christ, it hurt so much. I hurt so much. My heart was still in shreds. But there was a tunnel, a tunnel awash with our combined heartbreak. I was curled up within it, letting myself be submerged by the multitude of sensations that our anguish comprised. But I discovered, if I climbed to my knees and moved forward, I could progress – still touched by those sensations, still feeling them, but I was becoming conscious of some kind of control over them. And then I was at its entrance. And the tunnel disappeared. And she was still there; I was still there. The hurt, Christ the hurt,

339

was still there, but I could see a way through – I had hope.

I gasped. And my heart beat again. I became aware I was on my knees, beside the bed. My forehead was resting on the velvet bed cover.

'Nate?' It was James.

I held my left hand up. I needed more time. I took some deep breaths. I had control of my limbs. God! I physically hurt. It reminded me of when, as humans, James and I had nearly killed each other. We had physically fought over— I remember not. I felt like this for days after. But I had some control over my body.

I rolled over and sat with my back against the bed and opened my eyes. Elizabeth, James, Frederick and Madeleine were before me. Spooked was probably the best way to describe them. That word was a regular in my vocabulary now. As for me? Spooked did not begin to go there. *What, on this earth, was Heather?*

I leapt to my feet. Everything spun for a moment and James steadied me when I wobbled. Alarm reverberated around the room. My guard was down, and I observed their shocked and then incredulous faces for a second as they digested everything that had happened in their absence. And then I was grabbing Rowan's pendant from the dressing table and was by the door.

I refused to give into my grief, or to be swamped by Rowan's. I couldn't afford to – not yet – and Heather had given me a lifeline.

'I have lost her. But I will not let him hurt her. We need to split up. We need to find Rowan before Frey does.' My voice sounded as determined as I felt. I would wallow later – do whatever I needed to do to myself then – but only when I knew Rowan was safe from Frey.

As we started the search, it was evident Rowan had wandered around aimlessly. I had tried her mobile phone but, as I expected, she didn't pick up. I was the last entity she would ever want to talk to again. We were following her scent and picking up trail after trail. The last, and by far the most worrying, led to the taxi rank outside the hotel.

And he had found her. Because as I stood, oblivious to the greetings from party guests that walked by, I felt her fear. I reeled and grabbed hold of a lamp post for support. But instead of surrendering to the sensation, I took a deep breath and found a place for it. It was a bloody big place, and my heart was pounding as my fear combined with hers, but I found I could stand freely. I could more than stand freely. I was going to save her – and I was going to turn Simeon Frey into dog food.

We took to the air in separate directions. Scanning with our eyes, then dropping down to earth at regular intervals, to try and pick up her scent. I could feel something wasn't right, more than not right. Rowan was confused and she was fading in and out. It was like a bad reception and I kept losing her channel. *Rowan, my love – I am coming.*

I was receiving reassurances from the others, but they were cancelled out by their thoughts.

Rowan's confusion was increasing. She was trying to fight whatever it was, but she was struggling. He was hurting her. I knew he was.

'Nate, they're on a boat!' Frederick reported. 'I've picked up her scent and their stench is with it. I'm at the jetty to your north.'

Madeleine perked up. 'They're on a boat. Running water . . . that could be why she's fading in and out.'

I wanted, with all my heart, to believe that's what it was. But I couldn't. Rowan and I had walked on the beach together last night. The waves had been lapping around our bare feet. She had faded slightly, but consistently. Just like turning the volume down a couple of notches – nothing like this.

There were lots of boats on the water tonight and the air was full of the sound of chinking champagne glasses, string quartets and business talk. I had lost count of how many invites I had had to cocktail parties on the yachts below. It was an entirely different world to my own, as was Rowan's. Who had I been kidding?

And then I heard her. It was always going to be me that heard her first. We were so attuned. I honed in on the purpose of my existence. She was faint. She wasn't in this group of boats.

'I don't want any more.' Her voice was weak and shaky.

And then I heard him. 'Don't be scared. It's not poison.'

Poison? Oh, dear God!

'It will help you believe. Don't resist it. You'll find yourself and escape all this pain and heartbreak. You will find a better life.'

'No,' she whispered back.

'Just lie back with me. Relax . . . see, isn't that better? Your skin is so soft . . . so pale . . . so beautiful.'

I will play with my prey, torture him slowly, agonisingly . . .

'There, there. Let me kiss all those tears away, my sweet. You're as beautiful as your mother was. So like her, it's incredible. I can't believe I didn't think to check on you before.'

I will tear out each of his organs in turn, and shred them before his eyes.

'Mum?' Her words were getting fainter and she was fading from me. I was losing her.

'Do you know who you are now, Rowan? Can you feel it? Can you feel the magic . . . Rosie's legacy? Your eyes are the exact same hue as hers.'

'I was . . . somebody else's.' Her voice was so weak.

He tutted. 'They lied to you. They've all lied to you. Your *mummy*, your *daddy*, Heather, Nathaniel Gray. You were theirs. You weren't adopted . . .'

I heard the others' gasps and the disbelief in Frederick's thoughts: 'Psychopathic crackpot!'

'Your mother was like me. You are like me . . .

can't you feel it? Can't you feel what you are? Surrender to it, Rowan.'

She groaned. 'I want Nate.'

Oh, Rowan, my love. What could he be doing to her that she could be driven, for a moment, to want the monster that I am?

He laughed bitterly. There was anger there, I could hear it. 'Have some more. You will see the light and then everything will become clear. You will find the inner truth and embrace our future.'

'No . . . there's something in it.'

'You *will* drink this!'

I could hear her spluttering and coughing, nearly choking. 'I'm sorry.' Her voice was barely audible.

'That's better.'

'I'm sorry, Nate.'

No, Rowan – I am sorry, my love – so sorry! I should have told you. You should never have had to find out like this.

I could see the boat. It was a lone yacht, not currently being powered by its sails, but by its motor. And then I heard the bloodcurdling sound of his fist impacting on her fragile form and she cried out.

I let out an anguished roar.

Our connection intensified. The shock of the physical pain must have brought her to fuller consciousness.

Frey was sounding angry and not remotely in control. 'The monster's spell seems to have been strong – like mother, like daughter!'

Her words were slurring, but she managed a sentence. 'He's more a man than you'll ever be.'

No, Rowan, do not do this. Do not provoke him. Christ Almighty!

'A man, Rowan petal. Is that what you think I am? A mere *man*?' He sounded incredulous.

'No, not just a man – a mad man.'

She was choking. I could hear her gasping for breath.

I am coming for you, my love. I am coming.

Frey hissed furiously, 'You *will* believe and you *will* be at my side! I will NOT be thwarted again!'

I could hear a struggle. There was glass shattering and she cried out.

He taunted angrily, 'There's nowhere to run!'

I was nearing the boat. The door to the cabins below was open and I could see Rowan on hands and knees, crawling up the steps. Her face was bloodied, her dress torn, her flesh exposed. I could see his grotesque finger marks on the skin of her throat. Her arms had reached the deck. The two creatures from the party were in front of her and she was trying to crawl around them.

Frey emerged to stand behind her, watching her painful progress. 'Your mother could have been the most powerful of her kind – the most powerful the Fey has ever seen. There is faerie in your blood, and our destiny is shared.'

I could think of nothing but getting to Rowan.

'Move aside; let her crawl. Let her get that rebellious streak out of her system.'

I aimed for the spot between Frey and Rowan . . . but passed through something in the air that slowed me down. My skin prickled and the hairs on my body reacted as they would to static electricity. I heard the others curse. 'There's something here, I can't get through and . . .!' Elizabeth squealed.

'I've got you!' Frederick gasped, relief evident in his voice.

'Shit, that hurt!' James cried.

Madeleine shouted in my head, 'Nate! It's a force field or something. You're through, but we're stuck!'

I spun around to see the others hovering in mid-air seventy-five yards or so behind me; Elizabeth was fine. Flipping back around, I met the eyes of Frey below me. *So much for the element of surprise . . .*

'Get her back downstairs,' I heard him snap to his two goons, whilst he moved to stand in the middle of the deck. His eyes, still fixed on mine, proffered a silent invitation. No matter what I wanted to do to him, my priority was Rowan. I could hardly feel anything from her now and her heartbeat, distinguishable above the sound of the boat's engine, was slow. My eyes found her. She was curled up on the deck, motionless. As I took in her form one of the two sidekicks reached out and caught hold of her hair.

'Let's get the bitch downstairs.'

I reacted with a monster's roar. Within the blur that was my movement, I was before them, had snapped the wrist of the offending hand and had sent its owner hurtling across the deck with a furious feral swipe. Amidst the roar that was now the inside of my head, I vaguely heard a crack, followed by a thud and then nothing.

The remaining creature backed away, visibly quaking as he took in the full monstrous image before him. My eyes may have appeared like hellish black holes, but it was red I was seeing. I smiled sinisterly, and in less than a step, had my hand around his throat, lifting him off the ground. The sounds resonating from my chest were bloodcurdling; very different to the desperate gurgling sounds coming from his. His arms and legs were flailing aimlessly and his eyes were beginning to bulge.

'Frey's approaching Rowan!' Elizabeth screamed in my head. I cocked my head and with one last squeeze and satisfying snap let my victim drop to the deck, in a lifeless heap.

Spinning around, I took in Frey, who was moving fast, his movements so smooth he could almost be gliding. Nevertheless, I was in front of him before he could get any closer. Rather than stepping back at what appeared before him, he stole closer to sneer, 'I won't be so easy, Gray.'

In one rapid fluid movement, I had both palms flat on his chest and he was flying backwards through the air, his back and head crashing into the boat's wooden mast. I heard the wood fibres creak from deep within. I was at Rowan's side in a flash, wrapping my body around hers, to form a protective cocoon. My head was held low and protective, but watching from raised eyes, I saw the mast splinter and fracture into two. It started its journey down, smashing open the wooden cabin and decking at intermittent points, wherever its metal components made contact. As it neared our position, I rolled us both so it merely brushed past my right shoulder, before embedding itself in the deck where Rowan had been lying. The boat's lighting spluttered before it completely fizzled out.

'Rowan . . .' I whispered, feeling the monster cloak himself. I changed my position so I could prop her against my chest, and gently took her head in my hands. 'It is Nate. I am going to get you out of here. Trust me please.' I tenderly brushed the wisps of hair from her eyes. There was a pool of blood amidst the bruising already appearing around her left eye. It didn't tempt, but rather sickened, me. She was so pale and cold. I removed my dinner jacket and placed it around her shoulders and then, in a blink, was in the air with her in my arms.

'Nate! Watch out!' The silent warning from Frederick came too late as instantaneously something smashed into my back.

The force of the impact sent me tumbling through the air. I must have been momentarily stunned because I snapped back into the horror that was reality as I felt Rowan slipping through my arms. I desperately grasped hold of her. She was securely in my arms again but I was in free-fall and couldn't stop. Looking around, I could see we were still above the boat. I twisted mid-air, ignoring the sharp pain that seared through my back, so that when we hit the deck, I could take the full force of the fall.

I was braced for impact, but nothing prepared me for the pain that shot through me as I absorbed the landing; pain that my body should not be feeling. With no pause, but now gritting my teeth against the pain, I rolled us over so I was lying above Rowan, fully covering her body, whilst supporting my weight on my elbows so as not to crush her.

I could hear light footsteps and focused on the feet of Frey, which I could now see moving towards us. He effortlessly avoided the debris covering what was left of the deck and his fluid steps showed no evidence of damage from my earlier assault. 'His body is weak,' she had said. Well, just what the hell was it like when it was *strong*? Jesus! How was I supposed to protect Rowan as well as destroy the bastard?

I could hear the others' panic. 'I'm diving down to the sea floor to see if I can get through from below,' Frederick was saying.

'Oh, God!' Elizabeth's gasp sounded in my head.

'I'll do it,' James stated.

'I'm the strongest swimmer and by far the best in combat,' Frederick countered. 'Give me your sword, James; Nate has nothing.'

No, I didn't. The plan had been to rip Frey apart with my bare hands.

I suddenly remembered the pendant and used my right hand to root around in the pocket of my jacket, now wrapped around the still unconscious Rowan. Once my fingers felt the chain, I grasped hold of it and, withdrawing my hand, gently, but swiftly, lifted Rowan's head to place the chain and pendant around her neck. When I had carefully lowered her head back to the deck, I kissed her forehead. 'I am not leaving you. I will still be here, my love.' I leapt to my feet, and the monster I was stood directly in the path of Frey.

'So why the interest in Rowan Locke?' Frey asked, glacially, raising his hands before his face and flexing his long spindly fingers and wrists. I heard his joints crack. 'Could you not have just—?'

'Do not ever utter her name . . .'

I stopped my thunderous words with a hiss. Whilst I had been speaking, Frey had stretched his arms out to the side and turned his palms upwards and something was now falling on the deck around us. It looked like golf balls. As one fell from the suddenly densely clouded sky, I caught it in a flash of movement in my right hand. It was cold and seemed to have the consistency of ice. *Giant hail stones?* More and more of them were falling around us; the thuds, as they hit the wooden deck and metal fixtures, like a faster and faster beating drum with intermittent clashes of cymbals. Hissing again, I was forced to raise my own arms to protect my head. I was disconcerted; I was feeling the pain of each impact and any that approached Frey were taking a detour and heading towards me. I cowered lower to the deck.

Rowan . . . If they were hurting me . . .! But, although I could see they were dropping from the sky all around her, it was a fine misty rain that appeared to be falling over her body.

I roared as one of the giant hail stones hit my shoulder hard. As it bounced off me, I took in the size of the stones now falling; they had evolved to the size of tennis balls and their frequency was ever increasing. There was no distinct drum beats now, just a thunderous crescendo of sound. I was going to be battered black and blue.

Throwing caution to the wind, I launched from my crouching position at Frey's approaching form. I landed on top of him and the momentum propelled us both in a rapid skid across the deck. I was aware of wreckage flying around us as we crashed through whatever was in our path. *PLEASE let Rowan be clear of the fallout!* To prevent shooting over the side of the boat, I brought us to a jolting full stop by reaching up and grasping one of the metal railings surrounding the deck's perimeter with my left hand and grabbing Frey's neck with my right. Simultaneously, I lowered my head to tear out his throat with my teeth.

Instead, I whimpered, as a searing pain rushed through me, starting somewhere between my lower ribs.

Momentarily overcome by agony and a rush of light-headedness, I found myself on my back. I reached down with my hand, to where I gauged the source of pain to be. I was wet, I thought. As I raised my hand to my face, I could see it was covered in a red, sticky substance and there was a definite scent of . . . *Blood.* My blood. I hissed. Not possible, Christ Almighty! *Not* possible. I could feel myself slowly mending, or at least that's what I hoped the tingling sensation was, but whatever he had used had penetrated my impenetrable skin and it hurt like I had never physically hurt before.

I blocked out the screams from the others and tried to focus on moving. Frey was now standing over me, holding an intricately carved dagger, its blade covered in my blood.

'Silver,' he mocked.

'Silver does not . . . damage us,' I spat out, through teeth gritted with pain.

'Enchanted silver does. Do you have a preference for where I make my next cut, Gray? Or should I just surprise you? Perhaps I'll go straight for the kill – but I rather think I'm in the mood to play!'

There was no way I could let this happen. I couldn't let this demented being have Rowan. She didn't want me. But he was so far from the happy normal human existence I would have her living.

I heard Elizabeth gasp, 'Freddie's through!'

Frey looked away momentarily, moving his head to the right as if he were listening to something in the water. He raised his hands again and the falling hail stopped. My moment of relief was short-lived. The boat now started rocking unsteadily and the sound of the sea gradually increased. I became aware of waves crashing violently against the side of the boat, and then breaking ever more furiously over the deck. I was covered in a deluge of salt water. *Rowan could be washed overboard!*

With Frey still focusing on whatever he was doing with his hands, I took my opportunity. Bracing myself against the pain, I bent my knees to my chest, and rapidly kicked both legs forward, cracking Frey's sternum on impact. He was sent violently backwards. It was the safety railings surrounding the deck on the opposite side of the boat that stopped his momentum. I had to follow through but, now on my knees, the pain momentarily kept me there. Taking a moment, I focused on Frey – to see Frederick silently appear from behind, and wrap his arms about his neck. *Thank you!* Whilst mercilessly tightening the pressure around his throat, Frederick plunged something through Frey's back, because I heard the squelch and then saw a fast-growing red stain seep through the front of his shirt. Frederick withdrew his weapon after a couple of violent twists, and pulled Frey backwards, letting him plunge into the sea below. I closed my eyes and relief coursed through me at the sound of the splash.

Frederick was before me when I re-opened my eyes. 'The cavalry's arrived!' he cried, flashing me a wide grin.

'Quite an entrance,' I muttered, greeting his outstretched hand with my own. We grasped each other's hands tightly. 'Thank you!'

'Shit! You're . . . Is that blood?' He looked closer. '*You* are bleeding?' he choked out. 'Tell me that's not your blood!'

I attempted to drag myself to my feet. Frederick used our grasped hands to pull me into a standing position and I immediately started to stagger towards Rowan.

'We will get her to a hospital . . . but you. Shit – you! It's *your* blood! You can hardly go to a human hospital, but you need something!'

'I am fine – and am mending.' I hoped. As an immortal, I had never been hurt so couldn't be sure. 'I simply need a moment.' I carefully lowered myself to the deck beside Rowan and gently lifted her head on to my lap. 'No hospitals. We will take her to Castello del Elisabetta,' I muttered.

'That's miles away.'

'If we go straight across the water, we can be there in twenty minutes. The border with Italy is close by. We need a team of doctors there. I am not risking her safety in a public hospital. God knows how many more of those creatures are out there.'

'Ummm . . . I hate to ask this . . . But he is dead, isn't he?' Madeleine asked, silently.

'Why?' Frederick responded.

'It's just the force field is still up.'

No! No! No! I listened intently for a heartbeat

354

but wasn't sure I would hear one from under the ocean.

'If he isn't, he will be any moment,' Frederick reassured. 'If the strangulation didn't get him, then the stab wound through the heart would. And if that didn't do the trick, the water will . . .' He broke off to ask, 'Are you not talking to me, Izzy?'

'Elizabeth is a bit emotional at the moment,' Madeleine said. 'I don't think she's capable of talking, silently or otherwise, quite yet.'

A traumatised-sounding James spoke up. 'I'm thinking we should put Nate under house arrest. Turn his tower into a jail of some kind. He isn't safe, you know.'

'I am ready now,' I said silently, gently scooping Rowan into my arms. 'And heading for home – if I get through the force field, that is. If not, we panic.'

'Only *then* do we panic?' James muttered.

'Are you up to the flight?' Frederick asked. I looked at him and the concern was etched on his face.

I nodded. I had to be. I would have preferred to send Rowan with Frederick, in case I ran out of steam – she would be safer that way – but he could neither get through the force field nor take Rowan underwater with him. She would drown before they got through.

'I'll go under again,' Frederick said. 'We need to stick together, so as soon as we can, we should get into formation. I'll break off later to track down some doctors.'

355

'James, can you call Heather?' I asked silently. I heard his curse but it was immediately followed by an affirmative. 'Tell her what has happened. Find out what it is he has given her and what we need to do. If she thinks we need a hospital, we need extra protection.'

'I'll call ahead and get the property opened up and the caretaking staff out,' Madeleine added quietly.

I held Rowan close for a moment, treasuring the sensation of her in my arms. I knew as soon as she was conscious – and she *would* get better, she *had* to get better – I would never be able to hold her in my arms again. I tentatively took to the air. Christ it hurt – but I could do this.

'I am fine everyone,' I said, in response to their concerned exclamations. 'I plan to pick up speed the other side of the force field, or whatever it is.'

'I'll carry her when you get through,' James said.

'You are *never* getting your grubby hands on her,' I snarled back.

'I thought we'd gone beyond that.'

'You thought wrong.'

'What am I going to have to do, to prove to you that—?'

His voice cut off as Madeleine screamed out. I caught the 'Nate . . .!' before I was engulfed in water. I was in the air but surrounded by water and we were spinning faster and faster and faster. I clutched hold of Rowan desperately, refusing to let my grip loosen. We were being pulled down by the centrifugal force and it didn't matter how hard I tried to fight the pull, I couldn't break us out. *This was Frey! It had to be.*

I couldn't hear them audibly over the deafening roar of whatever we were in, but I could within my head. 'Freddie, if you can hear me, HELP THEM!' Madeleine was screaming. 'There's a giant water funnel pulling them down into a whirlpool below. It's like a giant plug hole. But PLEASE be careful – Frey can't be history!'

I fought all the harder trying to break out of the pull. Rowan needed air and if we went into the whirlpool, she would drown. I was desperate, but nothing I could do would break us through.

'*She is going to drown. She is going to drown,*' I was silently screaming.

'We've got company,' James cried out.

'FRIEND OR FOE?' I screamed in my head. 'Heather said she was sending back-up!'

We were in the whirlpool now; I could sense it because the pressure around us was building and the temperature was nose-diving. There was no let-up to the spinning and we were still being relentlessly sucked down.

And then it stopped. As quickly as it had started – it stopped. I felt something grab my arm, and I spun around instinctively to attack, before realising it was Frederick. I was completely disorientated; no idea which way the surface was, but he was propelling us in one direction, which I could only hope was the right one.

'The force field is down and the whirlpool is gone . . . so we assume . . . *friend?*' James speculated. 'At least I hope they are, because there are five of them and they are approaching us now. Do you need help down there?'

'No! Stay with the girls,' Frederick silently yelled.

As soon as we broke the surface of the water and hit the air, I broke away and headed straight for the boat.

'Nate – we need to go! The fucker's still alive and we have no idea—' Frederick stopped short on seeing the agonised expression my face was no doubt displaying.

'She has stopped breathing . . .'

'They say they are friend, and want to see you, Nate, so if you can . . . *Shit!* . . . NO! *Rowan?*'

I heard Elizabeth's anguished scream and then blocked them out.

I was only vaguely aware of Frederick by my side as I lay Rowan on the deck. Her lips were blue. How the hell was I supposed to do this? I met her lips with mine, blowing gently into her mouth. *Wake up, Rowan. Wake up, my love.*

'Her nose,' I heard Frederick's voice through a haze. 'You need to hold her nose, too. Do you want me to do it?'

I shook my head rapidly.

I held her nose with a shaking hand and breathed into her mouth. *Please. I will believe there is a god again if you can make her live.*

I did it again.

Rowan, my love, wake up.

And again.

Wake up for me now, my love

And again.

I beg of you. Wake up!

Elizabeth's cries were now audible and not just in my head and I didn't have the strength to block them. They joined the roar that was getting louder and louder inside me.

'Rowan,' I choked. 'Rowan, my love, you cannot leave me in this world without you. You cannot.'

Again, although my breath was trembling.

'Nate?' I felt what I assumed to be Frederick's hand on my shoulder and it attempted to pull me back.

I shook my head rapidly and shrugged him off to continue with my desperate actions.

Again.

And again.

And again.

And then she choked and spluttered.

I wanted to collapse on to the deck in a blubbering heap, but instead gently rolled her on to her side to let her empty her lungs of water. My face was inches from hers and her eyes focused on mine with difficulty. I could feel her confusion.

'Nate?' Her voice was barely audible.

I couldn't speak. I was choked with relief, and love . . . and grief – because I had lost her anyway. I wanted to tell her how much I loved her, how I thought I had lost her, but I couldn't. I terrified her. And I had already lost her. I moved my face away, so as not to scare her unnecessarily. I made myself speak. I said soothingly, I hoped, although my voice kept breaking, 'Do not be scared of me. I am not going to hurt you. I am going to get you somewhere safe.'

Her confusion increased, and I felt fear, before I lost her to unconsciousness again. But I could see her pulse. I could hear her heart.

I knelt on the deck with my head lowered, trying to calm my traumatised being. When I slowly looked up, I realised it wasn't only Frederick on board. James, Elizabeth and Madeleine were standing behind him . . . and five creatures were in the air above the deck.

They were hovering in formation before me. They looked otherworldly. All had varying shades of shoulder-length blond hair, ranging from ash to golden, which appeared to glow through the dark night, providing lustre to their almost angelic faces. They were heavily armed, with various metal weapons on their backs, and all were wearing brown leather trousers and jerkins hanging loose over their bare torsos. Their skin was not pale like mine, but golden, sun-kissed . . . and almost appeared to shimmer. On the outer edge of their right biceps each appeared to brandish an identical henna-coloured tattoo. The intricate design seemed to comprise a pair of insect wings either side of what looked to be the alchemical symbol for air: an upward-pointing triangle, bisected by a horizontal line.

The one hovering in the centre was taller than the rest, making him a couple of inches taller than me, with wavy, golden-blond hair. He moved towards me and I met his soft grey eyes. His voice was gentle, calming, yet assured. 'We can handle this now.' He looked at Rowan in my arms. 'You must go.'

Despite being physically shattered, and post-traumatic, I didn't need to be told twice. None of us did. I cradled Rowan and took to the air. The others joined me, taking my flank, just in case.

We arrived in fourteen minutes. The whole flight had been made in stunned silence. The others seemed to have been trying to make sense of what had just happened. Me? All I could think was: She will be fine, she has to be fine . . . And she is lost to me.

I walked through the ancient oak doorway of Castello del Elisabetta, our Italian home just outside Turin, still cradling Rowan in my arms. She was so cold. As I strode into my bedroom, Elizabeth and Madeleine immediately lit the pre-laid fire in the room's large sixteenth-century stone fireplace.

They took control as I lay Rowan's battered, unconscious body gently upon the bed. I noticed they were going at human speed as they started removing her wet, torn clothes . . . scared to use our powers around her fragile, mortal form?

I let myself collapse to the floor, with my knees up and my head in my hands. I rocked myself backwards and forwards.

'She'll be okay.' Elizabeth attempted to reassure me.

'He poisoned her, he battered her, he choked her; he touched her, she drowned – she stopped breathing, she probably has hypothermia.'

'She's strong,' Elizabeth stated. 'But . . . how are you?'

'How the bloody hell do you think I am?' I roared, before stopping myself and choking out, 'I am sorry . . . I am sorry . . . I didn't mean that,' in an anguished whisper.

'She was in shock, Nate. How was she meant to react? Telling her was never going to be easy.'

Madeleine interjected. 'Nate – if you don't intend to let anyone look at your . . . injuries?' I shook my head. 'Make yourself useful, then. She could do with warming up.'

'How? I am dead and cold . . .'

She sighed, 'Like this!' Madeline rubbed her hands quickly up and down Rowan's arm. 'Come on! It's important she warms up, or she could be in trouble.'

At that, I was at Rowan's side instantly and worked desperately. Within minutes, she did seem to be warmer to the touch, and her lips were no longer blue. Was this to be the last time I would ever touch her?

Madeleine and Elizabeth made themselves scarce as I lay by Rowan's side on the bed. I moved her bedraggled hair from her face. The scar from the head wound from our car accident had faded in recent weeks and was now completely overshadowed by the huge, bloodied bruise beneath her eye. I gently wiped away the fresh pool of blood. I so gently touched the vicious bruises on her throat. So fragile, so broken, so human . . . and no longer mine.

When Frederick arrived with the doctors I stood outside the door, listening to every word they said whilst they examined her. They were speaking in Italian, but I understood it clearly. Her heartbeat was sound again. She was warming up. The bruises would heal. The poison was an unknown.

James arrived at my side. I was trying to read his thoughts, to see what Heather had said. He grinned. 'No need. I'm here to tell you. She's going to be okay, mate. And I survived my chat with Heather without one freaky thing happening. Relations have got to be improving! The poison will wear off. She was furious he'd used it on her. She thinks it was . . . wait for it . . . *Water of Enlightenment!*

'It's a hallucinogen to heighten your spiritual awareness. It's meant to help you discover your true course, and some shit about finding your inner self and awakening your innate powers. She wants to speak to you as soon as you're up to it, to find out what Rowan said when she was under it. She appeared anxious about that. Physically it will wear off, but she's going to have the mother of all headaches. She said to say, "Well done." She's going to send something over to ensure your wound doesn't scar – as well as Rowan's pendant?' I frowned. 'Apparently her freaky spooks plucked it from the sea – and it was that, by the way, that let you pass through the force field.' It must have washed off, I hadn't noticed. I was useless at protecting her. 'She's very proud of you; you exceeded what she could have possibly hoped for . . . and the best – you'll love this bit – she would welcome you as a son! Imagine having that in the family!'

As if that would ever happen. But James did have a point.

'She's going to be okay, Nate. She really is. You heard what the doctors said.'

'I know. And I cannot begin to find the words to . . .' The relief was overwhelming – but so too was my grief. My voice broke and I could say no more.

'That girl's a bloody nightmare, but that bloody nightmare loves you. Loves you, as much as you love her – you idiot! Everyone can see it.'

I was choking my words out. 'I have lost her. She is terrified of me. She thinks I am a monster, dead, incapable of feeling . . . that I would hurt her and her family.'

'Hang on a minute! Haven't you been calling yourself a monster and been terrified you would hurt her? And you've known about the vampire bit for nearly two hundred years! I'm assuming you've finally caught up with us all now, with the realisation – you could never hurt her? You've taken your time, mate. She just needs time. And time she hasn't had. How did you think she'd take it?'

I had known all along I would lose her the moment she knew.

'Mate . . . you're forgetting she called for you when—'

'When she was *poisoned*, James. She was making no sense. And her choosing me over Frey is hardly a vote of confidence!' I failed to see how I could go on without Rowan . . .

James' concern increased. 'There's no need to turn into a drama queen. Let's take this one day at a time. She knows. That should be a relief . . . although it presents a few issues for all of us there, mate. But it's up to her now. She's going to get better. You saved her from the desperately freakish clutches of Frey, whatever the fuck he is. He's gravely wounded and—'

'He still lives?' I snapped, immediately alarmed.

'Ummmm . . . *yess* . . . But he's in custody . . . the spooks have him . . . Sorry! I wasn't going to tell you that bit . . .'

Well, at least there was a purpose to my existence now. Frey was going to die.

'Things are looking up! You even have some control over Rowan's more extreme emotions, now. Just as well really, bearing in mind what she's going to be like when she wakes up.

'But I ask you, Nate,' James now spoke in a hushed whisper, 'what the bloody hell happened tonight?'

CHAPTER 18

THE AWAKENING

A s I lay by Rowan's side, praying she would recover as predicted, I listened to everyone speculate. It was a way to escape my own thoughts, which were of the deepest, darkest kind. I was near the edge, and when I no longer needed to hold myself together, I would topple.

And when I did, I would take Frey with me.

It felt dishonourable and selfish lying beside an unconscious Rowan. During a brief telephone conversation with Heather – during which she'd still managed to grill me about all Rowan had said whilst poisoned – I had suggested it may be best Rowan not wake up with her nightmare anywhere near her. 'No! You owe Rowan an explanation. And anyway . . . I'm indisposed,' she had said.

I knew what she was doing. But she hadn't been there. To Rowan I was a thing of terror . . . and dead; both a dead vampire, and dead to her . . .

Not surprisingly, the speculative discussions covered three main topics: What just happened/ what the hell are the freaking spooks? my 'dumping' and its repercussions and, if 'the psychopathic crackpot' could have been trusted to utter a sane syllable, could Rowan be half-vampire, half-faerie/spook?

They weren't really your usual topics of conversation, but what was usual in our existences at present?

As I listened into a conversation on topic one, I realised it was rather like the scary tales that might be told around a campfire.

'So what exactly happened tonight?' James asked quietly.

There was silence. A long silence.

'That's cool,' he finally piped up. 'At least I know you're as freaked out as me – and I'm not the only one feeling bloody vulnerable!'

'I saw it with my own eyes, but still can't believe it,' Madeleine whispered.

'He stabbed Nate,' Elizabeth said in a hushed tone. 'And Nate bled. He could have killed my brother . . .' Her next words were a question. 'Has he let any of you tend his wounds?' They must have been shaking their heads because she continued, 'No . . . nor me. I mean . . . are they healing?'

Silence. I tentatively lifted my still blood-stained shirt – I hadn't even changed my clothes or had a shower – or fed. And my body felt like it desperately needed to feed. Flaking away some of the dried blood, I could clearly see the inch-long puncture wound, but it *was* healing. It had drawn tight, not yet a scar. But the whole of my front torso was black and blue and I could guess that my back would be worse. But the pain was easing up. I was mending.

'What is Frey?' Frederick asked. 'What he did with his hands . . . and – he should be *dead*!'

'And Heather? What she did to Nate . . .' James added. 'That had to be the world's freakiest head-fuck! I mean – *bloody hell* – we aren't just talking reading his thoughts here. She got into his head and . . . and . . . Look what she *did* to him!'

'Just spare me the faerie bullshit,' Frederick muttered.

'It's the best we've got,' Madeleine stated.

'Heather won't confirm one way or the other,' James said. 'And if I'm honest . . . I didn't feel comfortable pursuing the subject.'

'This is all so weird – and scary,' Elizabeth reflected, quietly. 'Let's assume they are the Fey . . .' Frederick tittered, but she ignored him, '. . . they aren't really what I had in mind.'

James laughed nervously. 'No – none of them are very Tinkerbellish, are they?'

'Tinker*hellish* more like!' Frederick corrected, and I found myself grinning, despite myself.

'I like that!' James laughed loudly. 'That fits Heather perfectly! Well done, Freddie!' I heard the sound of a slap to a back.

'And then there were those that Heather sent . . .' Madeleine added musingly. 'They were . . . strangely beautiful. Like wingless angels, but armed to the teeth.' Her voice sounded appreciative.

'For fuck's sake, Mads,' James muttered.

'No, I must agree there,' Elizabeth spoke up. 'They were nothing like Frey. They really were *incredibly* beautiful . . . James, Freddie – don't look at each other that way. They didn't get into our heads. But they were very . . .'

'Hot! Fit? Sex on—?' Madeleine's giggled suggestions were interrupted by James' snarl.

'Mmmmm,' Elizabeth replied. 'If they were faeries – then I want to believe!'

I heard Frederick's hiss.

Madeleine continued, 'I wouldn't mind *having them* in the bushes at the bottom of the garden!'

'Did they charm you?' James roared. 'Freddie – do you think they can charm?'

Madeleine was laughing, 'It wasn't like that. Chill! They just had kerb appeal.' Elizabeth giggled.

I wondered how much Rowan would remember of events. It was going to be difficult enough her waking up to the memory of what I was. I thought of Frey and the poison, and shuddered. I listened to Rowan's heartbeat for reassurance, and lost myself in my own dark thoughts of vengeance.

When I tuned back in a few hours later, I listened masochistically to a snippet of conversation on topic two.

'Nobody could have expected her to act in any other way .. .' Elizabeth was saying.

'But it was bad, Izzy,' Frederick interrupted.

'I know,' she said quietly. 'It couldn't have been worse. He would have most probably told her himself, no matter the repercussions, but they'd reached some kind of agreement and he was just terrified of losing her.'

'Has he lost her?' Madeleine asked.

'Well that's the thing . . . I just don't know. He thinks he has. But she matched his feelings. It was stunning. It was actually almost painful to see them together. I still think it was the shock speaking.'

'But if it wasn't . . . she knows about us now, and—'

Elizabeth interrupted Madeleine's words. 'I really don't think she would reveal our existences.'

'Thinking and knowing are very different things. We may have an issue – and Nate might not like the solution – there's no guarantee the charm would either work or be effective enough. And with their connection . . .'

'Neither would I,' Elizabeth asserted. 'She gave me my brother back . . .' I could hear her anguish and Frederick's comforting, 'Ssshhh, babe.' 'You've seen what he's been like since he met her,' she said in a voice now broken with emotion. There was a pause and I experienced, for a moment, all of their thoughts on the matter. 'You know how he was terrified of feelings. He was a shell. She filled him up in the best possible way. She woke him up. She animated him.

'And without her he's going to . . . He's going to die all over again! Either he'll be a dead empty shell, even more extreme than he was before. Or he'll . . . he will physically . . .' Elizabeth's voice broke off completely before she finally started up again. 'What Rowan was giving him was . . . it was magic, guys. Make of that what you will.'

There was a pause where thoughts momentarily moved to topic number three. I dipped out before returning to the conversation, a few minutes later.

'I don't think it's the end,' James declared. 'And neither does Hea— *Tinkerhell*!' He chortled for a moment before continuing, 'We all heard Rowan call for him. Nate puts it down to the poison, but according to Tinkerhell, it doesn't work that way. She was amazed that in the middle of it all, Rowan was able to call for him.'

'Whatever, it's safe to say Nate won't rest until Frey's dead,' Frederick uttered quietly.

'I don't think any of us will,' James growled, and the others made guttural sounds of agreement.

Frederick continued, 'The spooks have him, but that won't stop him . . . or us. But how we achieve it . . .? That, "his body is weak" stuff, really worries me. Weak? He was indestructible! And look at what he managed to pull on us! I can't help but wonder what else he might have up his fucking freaky sleeve!'

I shuddered and held Rowan close, blocking them out again.

It was dark outside. I had just returned from a quick feed. My self-control had become question-able as my body cried out for blood to replace that which had been lost. Rowan had been unconscious for twenty-four hours now. The doctor had visited again. He was confident all was well. He had even removed the cast from her foot. I had smiled. In other circumstances, Rowan would have been dancing around the room in response to that occurrence. But I would never again be able to share such joy with her.

I escaped such thoughts by listening in again.

'So, just how much of a crackpot is Frey, then?' James asked. I sighed. This one really did require some imagination. 'We know he's psychopathic, but are we giving him any credence at all?'

'By that, are you asking . . . are they all *faeries* – and is Rowan, half-*vampire*, half-*faerie*?' Madeleine spoke in such a disparaging tone, I had to smile.

'Yeah – that's the one! A *Faerpire*, perhaps, or even a *Vamrie*?' James chuckled.

Madeleine giggled and then continued, 'The Fey bit I can accept as a possibility. Heather, Rosie, Frey . . . the angels . . . simply because we don't have anything else yet on the table they can be. With the talk of enchanting and Rowan's pendant, it all sort of fits. But as for Rowan, even if it was possible, and a vampire and faerie could . . . procreate . . .'

'Elizabeth – stop bloody well raising your eyebrows like that – I *will* get angry,' Frederick growled.

Elizabeth teased affectionately, 'You are so easy to wind up, husband of mine.'

'Watch it!' he growled, unable to keep the warmth out of a sound that should have been menacing.

Madeleine continued, 'If they could procreate . . .' There was a long pause before she said, 'Sorry . . . miles away there. Where was I?' Elizabeth was laughing. James and Frederick were snarling in unison. 'Yes!' Madeleine declared. 'I have focus again. A vampire can't father children. Even throwing that out of the window, and say magic was used, half-vampire, half-faerie . . . doesn't make human. And that is what Rowan is. She's fragile, vulnerable, breaks very easily. She is very, very mortal.'

I looked at Rowan. Way too mortal.

'There's the issue of her birth certificate though,' Elizabeth conjectured. 'I saw it in Nate's head. Things didn't seem to add up.'

'There will be an explanation for that. But not this, Izzy, it couldn't be.' Madeleine started giggling. 'There is a Rowan Faerie though . . . if you're going to believe in faeries? I googled it earlier. There's a Heather one, too! I don't for one moment think Rowan is anything but human, but there are people out there who believe in faeries and say—'

'What an absolute load of baloney!' Frederick snarled.

'I know, I know. I just thought it was interesting – and quite, quite nuts!' Madeleine laughed.

I didn't know what to think. Rowan was Rowan

and all this seemed ridiculous. I remembered Heather's cryptic words to me: 'She will always be as human as they come.' Looking down at Rowan's broken body, hearing her heartbeat and feeling her breath on my own dead skin, there was no question on that point. She could be nothing but human.

And as for all the other answers we were still seeking. . .?

They would be forthcoming, of that I was sure. Whether we liked them or not . . . was another matter.

Rowan moaned softly on the bed next to me. She was still unconscious, but her body was writhing. 'Get the doctor – NOW!' I cried to whichever chose to hear my silent communication. I was off the bed and stroking Rowan's face. 'Everything is going to be alright. You are safe now, my love.'

Elizabeth was by my side in a flash. 'He's on his way,' she relayed silently.

The moans were sounding more and more like stifled screams. She was in pain. I knew it, but I couldn't do anything. I was stroking her face, whispering in her ear my useless reassurances . . . before it stopped.

Then I was looking down into her eyes – open, but taking a moment to focus. I moved away. She couldn't see me, or she would be terrified.

And then I felt her fear, overwhelming fear. *I had scared her! I hadn't been quick enough.* I was now as far away from the bed as I could possibly be.

'Nate?' she rasped, shakily. 'Nate?' Her fear was increasing. *Christ Almighty!*

Elizabeth looked at me. 'Speak to her,' she urged silently. I shook my head frantically. I couldn't do this. She was petrified of me. I couldn't do that to her . . . and I couldn't do it to myself. How could I face seeing the terror and horror in her eyes?

I fled. The doctor didn't notice me speed past him as he entered the room. I waited outside, listening.

'A false alarm, I think,' Elizabeth said to him, with relief and in fluent Italian.

'Yes,' he said. His voice sounded like he was smiling. 'It's good to see the patient finally awake.' He continued in English, 'Rowan. How do you feel?'

She didn't seem to be speaking.

'Are you worried about something? It can all be very disconcerting when you wake up after these things.'

I could hear her short rapid intakes of breath and feel her fear. I had done this to her. She shouldn't have been here. I shouldn't have been here.

'Are you in any pain?' he asked.

Rowan had evidently shaken her head because he replied, 'Good. Good.' Now obviously addressing Elizabeth, he said more quietly, 'Try and reassure her. This kind of response is quite common after coming around after something traumatic, but if she doesn't calm down, I would suggest further medication to ease her through the process.'

'We will do what we can,' Elizabeth said. 'But if you could stay close to hand, in case we need you later?'

'Of course,' he said, before leaving the room.

'Elizabeth? Where's Nate?' Rowan gasped, her voice hoarse. There was that fear again!

Elizabeth shouldn't be in there either!

I communicated silently, 'Elizabeth – get out! Can you not see how scared she is? Get out! Send the doctor back in. I will not subject her to this – to *us!*'

Elizabeth's response arrived back in my head, 'Nate – you are wrong. You need to speak to her, not run and lick your wounds. I refuse to leave her with someone she doesn't know. So it is either you, or me.'

I listened to her speak gently to Rowan . . .

And I felt her calm.

She wasn't reacting adversely to Elizabeth – she was saving that reaction for me.

I was out of the window and in the night-time skies. She was terrified of me. I could give her a heart attack and finish the job I had started on the night of the accident. I *had* to stay away.

Rowan deserved the very best a *human* life could offer.

When I returned, Elizabeth was waiting for me. She was not pleased and her arms were crossed. I was alarmed. *Rowan!?*

She spoke angrily, 'She's sleeping and is fine – no thanks to you! She needs to see you, to speak to you. You deserted her. How could you do that?'

'How could I *not*?' I roared and immediately lowered my volume, remembering Rowan's proximity. 'You saw how scared she is of me. I refuse to do that to her. *None* of us should be around her! We must fly her back home and she can stay with Heather. She needs her family around her now, not a bunch of the undead who could give her a heart attack at any moment!'

Elizabeth looked at me pleadingly. 'Nate, you aren't listening to me. If you won't listen to my words, read my thoughts. Look into my head and see—'

I shook my head vigorously. 'I am not going to listen, Elizabeth. Let go! You have to let her go. I know you loved her, too, but it is over. I do not want you anywhere near her, do you understand? I will not have her in fear!'

Elizabeth's eyes narrowed and she spoke incredulously, 'And you think you can stop me? You don't even want to know what she said?'

I spoke quietly, but determinedly. My mind was set. 'No, Elizabeth, I do not.' I couldn't deal with that. 'And yes – I will stop you!'

'Then you aren't the man I thought my brother was,' she huffed.

I spoke angrily now, 'No, and there is a damned good reason for that! Your brother is dead! What is before you is a monster! DO NOT make me lose my temper. You will stay away from her!' I stormed back out of the window up to the skies.

'No, Nate – I won't!' I heard her mutter after me.

'You damned well will!' I replied to her silently.

And as I flew, I relived the events of 1817. The events that had always ensured there could never be a future for Rowan and me. I had known. I had known from day one of encountering Rowan Locke, there could never be a future. That once she knew . . .

But for a little while. A little time, I had 'lived' again. Lived in a way I had never before lived. But at what price to Rowan?

'Elizabeth? Elizabeth? Wake up – they are gone. You can wake up now, sweetheart.'

The human terror and the pain . . .

'Nathaniel – is that you? Does she live?'

If only we had rested for the night at an inn . . . What had happened . . . What was now before me . . . Dear God!

'We need to get back to Ridings now, James. She lives . . . but . . . barely.' I could not let my anguish take hold. 'Where are you?' I called, gently laying Elizabeth upon the seat and clambering out of the carriage that now rested only half upon the road. I unhooked one of the still-burning carriage lanterns from its precarious perch.

Even with the extra light, I tripped over a body in my haste to find James . . .

Garrick, my coachman.

Keep it together. Keep it together.

He had started working in the stables at the age of eleven . . . We had played together before my father had ended such frivolity.

His throat was ripped out and he wore the same horrific, open-eyed death mask that Anne, Elizabeth's maid, now wore.

A twelve-year old could not possibly think they slept.

I emptied my stomach. I thought I had already done so. Finally wiping the vomit from the sides of my mouth with the sleeve of my long overcoat, I forced my leaden feet forward.

'James?' There was no disguising the near hysterical edge to my voice.

'Here.' He sounded weak, groggy . . . pained.

I moved towards his voice, into the copse edging the road. And there he was. He sat with his back against a tree trunk, his face deathly white and scattered with cuts and grazes.

'Everyone else?' he murmured.

I shook my head before crouching down beside him, raising the lantern to see him more fully. His overcoat was shredded and I could make out dark stains over much of his now barely clad torso.

'James?' I urged quietly, not liking at all the look of those stains or the pain so evident in his eyes.

'I think it best you leave me.'

Not a chance.

Feebly, he indicated his body and then held out

his shaking right arm. Turning his wrist, he revealed the underside: ragged torn flesh and still bleeding.

I closed my eyes for a moment and took a slow, calming breath. Elizabeth had similar wounds – one to her neck and another to a wrist – but less . . . violent. And hers no longer bled.

'You saw them?'

I gave a curt nod. The flash of white . . . teeth piercing the black night. The sounds of their inhuman shrieks . . .

I had been riding alongside the carriage, as had James. Bess, my horse had reared . . . and then nothing until I had recovered consciousness in the ditch to find . . .

'Then you know what they were!' He coughed at the effort of his assertive, urgent words. 'They did this with their teeth – their **fangs**, Nate . . . before turning on themselves.'

Enough tales had been seeping into the country from Eastern Europe, but up to this encounter . . .? Up to this encounter I had no reason to believe in vampires, no matter Continental hysteria. I didn't know for sure what we might be facing. But **did** know: I wasn't abandoning my sister and James.

Dismissing his weakening pleas to leave him, I quickly and tightly bound his wrist with a makeshift bandage torn from the hem of my shirt. 'I am getting the damned coach back on the road. We will be at Ridings by daylight.'

Somehow I managed to calm the carriage horses – the terror in the whites of their eyes said it all

– and found both the strength of body and will to return us to Ridings. Fears that Elizabeth and James could become crazed, blood-thirsty savages plagued me. But I could not – would not – let it happen.

If I thought that night was hell . . .

They were unconscious for more than a week. James was feverish and seemed to experience nightmares. Norton, our trusted family doctor's diagnosis was torn between blood poisoning and rabies – due to my tale of us being set upon by wild dogs. Nobody could ever know what had befallen us.

Canine rabies was rife across England and people were discouraged from keeping dogs. And the more I read on the subject, the more I realised the merits of such a diagnosis – should there be complications. Symptoms included wanting to bite others, nighttime insomnia, vomiting of blood and an aversion to light.

Unlike with James, Norton considered Elizabeth to have some wasting disease, unrelated to the attack. He expressed doubts she would recover. Knowing what I did, I refused to let him purge her. Instead, on reading of pioneering research into transfusions of blood, I sent a rider to London with an urgent request for assistance from the researcher in question. The fee offered made refusal impossible.

In the event he transfused some of my blood into Elizabeth. Colour returned to her cheeks almost immediately and her breathing gained in strength. Each successive transfusion saw improvements.

Not once was I asked how her body had become

so wasted of blood; he had a guinea pig – and I would be forever indebted to him. Indeed, I chose to fund his ongoing research.

When Elizabeth woke up, no words could hope to describe my euphoria and relief. It was a rare display of emotion that I now felt all over again. Yet then . . . I could cry.

But why had I not been more vigilant? More prepared. It was all my fault!

She went through a series of convulsions. In a matter of minutes her skin became paler, cooler to the touch. She looked wildly around her with glazed eyes, fearfully focusing on me at her bedside attempting to soothe, and then, less fearfully, at Norton.

From one to the other, one to the other, in rapid, sharp movements.

In the event, it was quick. She sprung from the bed with an inhuman snarl and clamped her mouth to the neck of Norton. He tried to stop her – I tried to stop her. But her arms wrapped around him like a straitjacket.

When Elizabeth released him, his eyes were wide open, his face a—

No twelve-year old could think that he slept.

It was the strange sounds escaping Elizabeth that snapped me from my horrified stupor. She now sat in the farthest corner of the room, knees hugged to her chest, rocking herself back and forth . . . back and forth. As she wiped her eyes, I shared her horror: she was crying tears of blood.

'I am sorry. I am sorry,' she sobbed repeatedly.

I desperately grabbed hold of the ray of hope that I glimpsed. For she still had a conscience – she was still my Elizabeth. There was hope.

After disposing of Norton and providing suitable alibis, it was that hope that I grasped. I had survived the attack for a reason. I had to be able to do something to prevent my beloved sister from becoming a monster that fed on humans. It would destroy her – and most likely me.

When James awoke two days later, I was ready. Despite his confusion, he took the news he would likely become a bloodsucking monster remarkably well. He was, completely, James.

'So, Nathaniel – you are obviously the main course. Are there appetisers?'

'Black pudding?' I tentatively suggested.

Yet despite my black pudding solution, Elizabeth remained terrified of what she had and could become. She had killed and was convinced she would kill again. She imagined herself becoming one of the savages that had attacked her. She imagined herself killing me.

As did I.

So I, through my own history, knew full well the fear a human could experience in the presence of vampires.

But how could I let Elizabeth struggle alone? I, who had been her protector since she was a babe in arms. There was **nothing** I wouldn't do for Elizabeth.

So *I* chose *to become a vampire.*

I chose this course. I chose to become that monster that gave Rowan nightmares, long before she ever met me; that when we did meet – nearly sucked her dry of blood. No matter my efforts, my intentions, my love for her – I *was* that monster. And her terror of me was inevitable. It was . . . sensible.

Until I encountered Rowan Locke, desperate vulnerability and emotional pain were no more. Not that I had ever before experienced the sheer agonising depths of what I now felt.

It had all been consigned to history.

As had regrets . . .

Elizabeth stopped talking and blocked her thoughts as I entered the garden room, twenty-four hours later. She had been deep in conversation with the others, and all had raised their guards.

I spoke only to announce the arrangements I had now made. 'Rowan will fly back to London first thing tomorrow morning on the jet. Morley is arranging a human nurse to accompany her, and she is to be met at the airport by Heather. Our flight is booked, too. We will be back at Ridings noon tomorrow.'

The only response I received was from James, who inclined his head to acknowledge the plans. At least that was something.

Elizabeth had given up on convincing me of my need to speak to Rowan. The more she had tried, the more I had dug in my heels and insisted she, too, keep away.

I had watched Rowan sleep last night. But that hadn't gone to plan. She had woken with a start, somehow sensing my presence – despite the distance I had placed between us. 'Nate?' she had called out wildly, staring disconcertingly through the window to where I stood within the gardens. I had felt both her pain . . . and fear.

I had silently left before I could do any more damage.

Heather had finally given up on her attempts at persuasion, too. Indeed, I was refusing to take any more of her calls after her last threat to 'make me see sense!' A threat like that from Heather could not be taken lightly. I seemed to be the only one with Rowan's best interests at heart. I could feel her fear, her heartbreak, her turmoil – all of which I was the cause of. And with me out of the picture, she had a chance to rebuild a safe and happy life.

As for me? I was going to ensure Simeon Frey was out of the picture permanently. Rowan's well-being was my immediate priority. But then . . .

He should be forever in hell. And when I joined him there, I would destroy him all over again.

CHAPTER 19

THE RETURN

We arrived at Ridings silently. Nobody had spoken to me throughout our journey home and they were all shielding their thoughts. I lacked the patience for it. I knew they would miss the Rowan factor; they had had their fun out of it. But it was high time our existences returned to normal, as much as was possible for a group of vampires, with one heartbroken and on the verge of God knows what.

The sun was shining, the sky was cloudless; it wasn't your usual English summer day. Being back at Ridings should have comforted me, but I felt empty. I still had Rowan's feelings to keep me company, but they were appallingly sad, and all because of me. But they were better than nothing. I was on a mission to see those emotions change, as the impact of my presence in her life was . . . obliterated.

When the others started speaking to me again, they would no doubt insist that the charm be used on Rowan. And . . . I was going to let them. Because I would do anything to stop her hurting and see her happy. My obliteration would stop the hurt. I would give thought and work as to what might make her happy.

I approached my bedroom suite at near human-speed, just taking the stairs three at a time. I was completely mended now. There were no *physical* scars left from recent events. I was going to go riding. I had missed Bess. As I turned at the top of the landing, I painfully reflected how Rowan was so imprinted on my senses. I could almost smell her scent and hear her heartbeat. I resisted the urge to breathe in deeply and allow myself to relish in the sensation. To imagine she was here with me.

Rowan was nervous about something, I could feel it. I wondered what she was doing to make her feel that way. I was concerned. Actually, I was very concerned. I checked my watch. She would be with Heather. I would have to phone just to make sure all was well. The phone was to my ear as I walked into my bedroom, but then it wasn't: it was out of my hand and on the plush-carpeted floor.

I stood motionless, frozen to the spot.

'Hello, Nate,' she said awkwardly, nervously, breathlessly. Her heart was beating frantically, the pulse on her neck mirroring its erratic pace. She was pale, and bruised and fragile . . . but still so beautiful. She bit her lip in that way of hers.

She was standing at one of the large sash windows in my bedroom. Her hand was clutching one of the heavy floor-length ivory drapes. She looked as if she shouldn't be standing, as if her hand on the curtain was holding her up. The sun seeping through the window had turned her hair the colour of copper. Her eyes were the most verdant I had ever seen them. But there was fear there; I could see it and feel it. *They* were behind this. Was this their attempt at removing the issue, of removing the human that knew of our existence? Did they want me to literally scare her to death, to put that problem to bed once and for all?

I was livid, furious. I inhaled. Yes, she really was there. This wasn't one of so many daydreams I had had in which I pictured Rowan at Ridings. No, this was a nightmare. I couldn't deal with this. I turned. I had to leave. I had to leave now. I just needed to get the message to my legs which seemed to be rooted to the spot.

'Nate . . . don't leave me. Please!' Her soft melodic voice sounded haunted. She was begging me.

Christ Almighty, what had they done? How had they got her here? Had they charmed her?

I hesitated and turned to look into her eyes. I would be able to tell if they had used that spell on her; a vampire can always tell the eyes of a charmed human. To our eyes, they appear ever so slightly glazed and, if I was the subject of the charm, then she would be looking at me unblinking.

They blinked right back at me and the only glaze they had was that of a soft sheen of tears.

She had started to walk towards me, tentatively,

shakily. She was holding my confused gaze. I stumbled backwards. Her fear increased again and her heart pounded in my head. Any moment it could utter its last beat.

I looked frantically at her face. There were tears rolling down her cheeks. This wasn't right. *Why had they done this to her?* I resisted the urge to rush to her side and wipe her tears away, soothe her, hold her, cherish her; love her and make all her pain evaporate. But whilst I was the cause of her pain and fear, that plan was pretty much as bad as they got.

I managed to move my leaden legs and turned away. *How could my heart break any more?*

I was at the top of the stairs when I heard her broken sobs and the whispered words, uttered only to herself, 'Don't leave me, Nate. I'm so sorry. Don't hate me. Please forgive me. I love you!'

I froze mid-stride. *NO. NO. NO. She hadn't just said that. She could not have. She was terrified of me. I could feel her fear, for Christ's sake. She couldn't be saying this, I horrified her – I could feel it!*

Just as I had once felt that terror and horror and fear for myself.

She was sobbing uncontrollably now, 'I love you . . . I love you. Forgive me. I know you aren't a monster, I know it. I could make you love me again, I could!'

I was now standing in the doorway, holding the frame for support. 'Rowan?' My voice was choked and my confusion undisguised. As was my anguish on taking in her form. She was on the floor. Her arms were wrapped tightly around her chest in a desperate attempt to comfort and the tears flowed uncontrollably down her face; her body was racked by the most painful of sobs.

'Rowan?' I asked again, in turmoil.

She wouldn't look at me. She was shaking her head. She struggled to get her words out through her wretched tears, 'No . . . I don't want you to see me like this . . . Just go! It's all my fault. I'm sorry. I should have known . . . I wrecked it all . . . It's just Elizabeth . . .'

'Rowan?' *What was she saying? None of this made any sense.*

'*Please, Nate.* I'll get over it. Just go. I'll be gone in a few moments. I just need to find my bag . . . and a tissue . . . and . . . *I'm so sorry!*' The sobs got louder.

I tightened my hold on the door frame to prevent my moving to her side.

'Rowan – I am not coming in there, so do not be scared. But I am confused; I am so confused. Can you try and say something that makes some sense to me? *Please?* Because I am currently fighting the biggest urge to take you into my arms and never let you go. And I cannot do that. I know how much I terrify you. I will *not* do that to you.'

'I LOVE YOU!' she screamed at me through her sobs. 'Yes, I'm terrified – but not of *you* – never again of *you!* I'm terrified of a life *without* you! Because I ruined *everything* and you can't forgive me for what I said, how I reacted . . . And you keep leaving me . . . keep turning your back on me . . . Every time I see you, you turn and walk away . . . it hurts – and I'm scared of hurting and of living without you . . .'

Oh, dear God! Those were the feelings I had felt, but the thoughts behind them were so *very different* to my interpretation of them.

'You are not terrified of me?' I choked out.

'No, Nate – no!'

It was my actions, my avoidance and staying away that had scared her – not me? She wasn't scared of me? She thought I didn't want to be with her? How could she *ever* think that? How could she not know that without her, there was no point to my existence?

I was at her side in a blink and had her wrapped in my arms.

'Forgive me, Nate. Oh, God, please forgive me!' And then she let it all go and she was limp in my arms, sobbing uncontrollably.

I was sat on the floor, gently cradling her, rocking her backwards and forwards, holding her head to my chest, stroking her hair.

'Shhhush, my love. Shussh. I am an idiot, a complete idiot! I thought I terrified you, that you hated me. I never wanted you to fear again. *That* is why I stayed away. Why I avoided you – not because I wanted to. But look what I have done to you! I am so sorry, my love, so very, very sorry. What am I going to do with you? What am I going to do with me? Oh, God, Rowan! Dear God! I thought I had lost you. Please. Shhhhh.'

I carefully repositioned myself so I could look into her eyes. I cradled her face gently between both of my pale cold hands. She looked at me through her tears. There was pain there; so much pain, and I could feel it.

'Rowan . . .' I said, my breath brushing across her face, 'I love you more than you can ever begin to comprehend, with more depth than any human language can hope to put into words. If you really, truly are not scared to death of me, and you really, truly want me in your life, then you have a problem, my love – because you will be stuck – completely and utterly stuck – with a vampire by your side . . . and we are *very* hard to shrug off!'

Her fear evaporated. Just like that. She wasn't scared of me! All that anguish I had caused her and myself. All I had had to do was listen.

'Do not start crying again, my love. Rowan . . . please. I cannot bear to see you cry. *Please!*'

I started to kiss her tears away. Gently first, and then more fervently. And when there were no tears left to kiss away and I was faced with her eyes glowing with an intensity that took my breath away, I started on her mouth. Today, I wondered at what point would I stop? Because I didn't trust myself to stop, not in the here and now.

But this wasn't the time. I knew it couldn't be. I might trust myself not to hurt her – and in this moment, I did – but *she* needed to be sure. I needed to tell her everything; absolutely everything. For Christ's sake, she didn't even know I shared her deepest innermost feelings! *If*, after *that*, she could still trust me, then any brakes going on wouldn't be from me.

But neither of us was ready to stop quite yet. We were hungry, famished, desperate to dissolve ourselves fully into each other's beings, never wanting to let each other go. She was laughing, and I was laughing as I scooped her on to my four-poster bed so she was more comfortable. I was painfully aware of the bruises and damage upon her fragile body. I was gentle now, so gentle.

'Nate,' she gasped, as my lips followed the feathery light touch of my fingers as they slowly moved along the length of her neck. I stopped. *Was she concerned?* Of course she was concerned – she had a vampire at her neck! But I was in control, I was sure I was in control. She met my worried eyes and shook her head.

'No, it isn't that.' She gave a breathless chuckle. 'No – it *really* isn't that,' she said again, rolling her eyes to dispel the look of angst in my eyes, once and for all.

I smiled and repositioned myself so we lay on our sides looking intently at each other, our semi-clothed bodies touching, our faces as close as eye contact would allow.

'What was it?' I asked so gently.

She laughed and became even more flushed.

'You were teasing me, Nate. Driving me to the edge and I was struggling . . .'

I laughed, both relieved and satisfied, and gently stroked the side of her face. 'We need to talk, my love. *Then* if you still feel able to consider . . .' I was unable to stop myself from leaving a trail of kisses along her jaw line, before taking a path downwards '. . . a more physical relationship . . . then I would be honoured . . . so truly, irrevocably . . . unquestionably . . . honoured . . . to oblige.'

Rowan spoke breathlessly and urgently, 'Then talk – fast, Nate!'

I chuckled, returning my face to within a few inches of hers.

'No – I'm *serious!*' she said, with a hint of annoyance and more than a hint of frustration.

'I *know* you are,' I said ruefully, before frowning. 'But what we need to talk about, may take some time . . .'